Helen Rolfe writes contemporary women's fiction and enjoys weaving stories about family, friendship, secrets, and community. Characters often face challenges and must fight to overcome them, but above all, Helen's stories always have a happy ending.

The Little Café at the End of the Pier

HELEN ROLFE

ORION

First published in Great Britain in 2019 by Orion Books,
an imprint of The Orion Publishing Group Ltd,
Carmelite House, 50 Victoria Embankment,
London EC4Y 0DZ

An Hachette UK company

1 3 5 7 9 10 8 6 4 2

A CIP catalogue record for this book is
available from the British Library.

ISBN 978 1 4091 8191 0

Typeset by Input Data Services Ltd, Somerset

Printed and bound in Great Britain by Clays Ltd, Elcograf S.p.A.

www.orionbooks.co.uk

For my husband and my girls

Prologue

The beauty of renting a room in a shared house was that walking away from your life was so much easier to do.

When Jo had received the phone call from her grandmother, suggesting she up sticks and relocate from Edinburgh back to her home town of Salthaven-on-Sea to help out in their café at the end of the pier, Jo hadn't taken much persuasion. She was thirty-one, single, working in a teaching job she lacked real passion for, and her life felt as though it had stagnated for the last year at least. She'd been wanting a change, and one had fallen right into her lap. And so she'd packed up her single room, covered the next two months' rent until her housemates could find someone else, and emailed the school where she worked to tell them of her plans, withdrawing her availability for future teaching jobs now that her position covering maternity leave had come to a close. And rather than feeling daunted, Jo felt more than ready to embrace new possibilities.

Now, with her beaten-up VW Beetle bulging at the seams with her belongings and a few more boxes fixed onto the vintage roof rack using fastening straps and rope, Jo was on her way to a new life on the south coast. She cranked the heating up as she left Edinburgh under the cover of darkness and, with no sign of snow or ice, it was almost as though this change was meant to be. She just had to drive the four hundred miles between her life now and the one waiting for her, and for the first time in years she felt she could see clearly. All through her life her grandparents had been there for her, cheering her on at school sports days, congratulating her on her exam results, talking with her when she was going through tough times at university and stressing over her finals. And now, years later, they were going to be together again. And she couldn't wait.

After hours of obeying the satnav's commands Jo found herself in familiar territory. She turned off the main road and onto a single carriageway. The road narrowed and the sign came into view saying 'Salthaven-on-Sea 10 miles'. The sign was always the marker, the moment she felt as though she was coming home, and today, given the major change afoot, it was all the more powerful. Her heart leapt and she had to quell her enthusiasm so she didn't put her foot down harder on the accelerator and go too fast.

Just before four o'clock Jo drove past the Salthaven Hotel on her left, a couple of guesthouses on her right, went straight on at the mini roundabout, past a restaurant, and followed the road down the hill as the town on one side and the sea on the other came into full view. A huge grin spread across her face and she pulled over on the left to let the person in the car behind her pass. It was a small town and traffic wasn't terrible, but she didn't want to rush. This was the beginning of something special and she wanted to savour the deep pink sunset with the last vestiges of orange hovering below, and the white wispy clouds beginning to fade away across the top of the pier. She could make out a young family braving the blustery new year weather down by the breakwaters, on the sands that would be golden beneath bright sunshine come summer. The two kids were running along the edge of the water, chasing the lapping shoreline in their purple wellies and bright yellow cagoules, and the family had a sense of togetherness that Jo longed for. She wanted an end to the loneliness she felt more often than she'd ever admit to her grandparents.

The pier's supports were black against the sunset, with white lights on Victorian lamp posts dotted at intervals along the wooden structure. In her mind she could smell the wood of the boardwalk under her bare feet as she walked its entire length, looking out at the sea, staying out of the way of any fishermen who were minding their own business, doing what they loved. And most of all she knew the café at the end of the pier, the business she was about to step into in a whole different light.

She put her car back into gear and trundled on, past the pier, and then up the hill on the other side to her grandparents' bungalow situated in an elevated position with an enviable view of the sea. She parked her car in the garage, wrestled on her coat, scarf and gloves and set off for the café. The salty air mixed in a breeze that lifted her dark, wavy hair from her face and carried the promise of a fresh start. The beach was the place where she most felt like herself, where she could think, and where she was most at home.

She made her way down the hill and off the concrete pavement onto the wooden slats of the pier, past the fish and chip shop and the ice-creamery, the shop that sold sunhats and seaside paraphernalia in the warmer months, and as the sun buried itself deep on the horizon she reached the café that was part of the town, part of the pier, and a new part of her life. There were only two customers inside, and when the familiar bell on the door tinkled to announce her arrival Gramps was in the middle of restocking the display shelves and Gran had just set down a teapot in front of another customer.

'Jo!' Molly raced over to her granddaughter, weaving in and out of the three tables that stood between them until she could fling her arms around Jo. 'Oh it's so good to see you!' She pulled back, gripped the tops of Jo's arms and looked at her more closely. 'You look as happy as I am right now.'

'There she is!' Arthur wasn't far behind. He had the same deep silver hair as Molly, but if you didn't know either of them you'd easily put them at a decade younger. 'Let me look at you, my beautiful girl.' He appraised her before giving in and hugging her tight. 'I was so glad when Molly told me you'd agreed to come and help out a couple of old codgers like us.'

Molly swiped him with the tea towel in her hand. 'Speak for yourself, I'm not past it yet.'

His familiar laughter bounced off the walls and flooded into Jo's heart as he pulled out a chair for his granddaughter. 'Sit. We have plenty to talk about.'

'All in good time,' Molly admonished. 'The poor girl has driven hundreds of miles, I don't think she wants to hear all about how to use the coffee machine right now, dear.'

'I can't wait, actually,' Jo admitted.

Arthur whistled through his teeth. 'You know, it's harder than it looks.'

And Jo felt sure that very soon she'd realise how right he was.

I

The next day, Jo was thrown in at the deep end. She put a blue gingham apron around her waist and tied a bow at the back. She slotted a small notepad and pencil into the front pocket and the door opened to announce the first customer of the day.

'You look the part,' Molly admired. 'Off you go. That's Angie. She doesn't bite.'

Feeling like a child all over again, afraid to talk to a stranger, Jo's heart thumped against her chest at the enormity of this new job. And where was Gramps? Surely he should be here to help ease her in on her first day.

She made her way over to the table beside the wall with the blackboard that listed food and beverage choices. Next to it was another board housing postcards from all over the world, from locals getting in touch on their holidays. Jo remembered it from years gone by – she'd always loved reading the postcards, absorbing herself in the excitement they expressed.

'Good morning.' When Jo greeted the customer she tried to sound way more chirpy than she felt. She berated herself. This shouldn't be that hard. She spoke to kids every day in her teaching job, she battled through their chit-chat and fought to be heard. This had to be easier, surely. Ask what the customer wanted, serve it to them, take payment, and make general conversation. How hard could it be?

'Well, hello.' Angie looked up, her interest piqued at the new face around town. An icy breeze had blown Jo along the pavements this morning as she made her way towards the café beneath the cloak of darkness, but this woman's grey hair was curled so tight she didn't look as though the weather had bothered her one bit. 'I don't believe we've met before.' She extended a hand now she'd taken her gloves off and laid them on the chair along with her coat and scarf. 'I'm Angie.'

Jo shook her hand. 'It's lovely to meet you. I'm Jo, Molly's granddaughter.'

Angie leaned past Jo and called over to Molly, 'She's as pretty as you said she was.'

Blushing, Jo asked, 'What can I get you this morning? Would you like to hear the specials?'

She dismissed the suggestion with a wave of her hand. 'No need. I'll have a pot of camomile tea please, and a teacake.'

Jo didn't bother taking her pad and pencil out. And even though she was only remembering one order, it buoyed her confidence. 'Coming right up.'

Molly had been holding back in the kitchen, allowing Jo to take the reins, but she emerged now. 'Well done, handled like a pro.'

'Thanks.'

Jo grabbed a small teapot, a cup and saucer, warmed up the teacake taken from the batch made fresh that morning, and set everything on a tray.

'You're a quick learner,' said Molly as the bell on the door tinkled again. She waved at the man who entered and said, 'That's Mark, your next customer. Let me take the tray to Angie, she likes a good natter in the mornings.'

Jo knew Molly liked to chat just as much. Her grandparents had good business sense but they were also a part of the community and loved to be sociable, and she could see Molly was in her element here in the café. She couldn't imagine either of her grandparents getting old inside that bungalow of theirs, not without other people thrown into the mix. It simply wasn't their way.

Jo introduced herself to Mark, memorised his order, delivered it and took payment, and apart from a cursory glance her way and some minor help with the till, Molly stood back and let Jo run the show. It was exhausting, but exhilarating too, and gave her a buzz she hadn't felt in years. And the feeling kept her going right up until closing time.

After Molly turned the sign on the door to 'Closed' and Jo grabbed a cloth to make a start with wiping down tables, Jo finally had a chance to ask, 'Where was Gramps today? I thought he'd be here with us.'

Her question seemed to unsettle Molly who looked away, then opened the till and began to count through the money inside. 'He thought it would be a good idea to let you handle as much as you could today, give you a feel for the place.'

Jo almost bought the explanation, but dishcloth in hand she joined Molly at the counter. 'Gran, stop for a minute. Is there something going on that I should know about?' Gramps was made up to see her after so long but this morning he'd still been sleeping when they left. She'd expected him to be here by lunchtime at least, marvelling at how she was learning the ropes.

Molly made a note of the money she'd counted and then gestured to the nearest table and pulled out both chairs. 'Sit for a minute, it's been a long day.'

Jo did as she was told and it was only now she noticed how tired her Gran looked. Not just tired from the day, but totally exhausted. She'd put on a good front yesterday and again today but maybe Jo feeling the tiredness herself had finally enabled her to see it in her Gran.

'Gramps is fine,' Molly assured her, patting her hand. 'But we don't only need a bit of help in the café, Jo, we need someone to take it over sooner rather than later.'

'I kind of guessed when you got in touch.' And of course, they weren't going to contact Sasha, their daughter and Jo's mum. As far as Jo knew, none of them had exchanged more than a Christmas card in years.

A look of relief washed over Molly's face. 'We didn't want to worry you, but we're getting older and although part of me can't imagine not being here every day, I know it's what Arthur and I need. What's held us back from retiring so far is thinking of this place changing hands, going to a stranger, and I'm not sure I could've eventually persuaded Arthur to give it all up if you hadn't agreed to come here.'

'It's understandable, Gran. I get it. You made the café what it is. But apart from being tired, is Gramps OK?'

'He had a fall last week.' Jo sat forwards. 'Only a minor stumble, but the doctor said he needed to slow down. You know what he's like. It's like trying to hypnotise a bull who has his sights set on the red flag. Your Gramps doesn't know the meaning of rest. He's only at home today because you're here.'

Jo smiled. 'Your suggestion came at the perfect time. All I needed was a push in the right direction.'

'Well, I'm glad we gave you that push. Now if you could push me home I'd be really grateful.'

'I don't think I have the energy,' she giggled. 'Come on, Gran, let's finish up here and get going. We'll sleep well tonight.'

And when they finally locked up the café and went on their way, even the dark and the cold outside couldn't diminish the euphoria whirling inside of Jo.

Because here she was, by the sea, the place she'd always wanted to be. And this time she was the one who was able to come to the rescue.

The first two weeks of Jo's return to Salthaven-on-Sea moved as fast as that first day and rivalled the crashing waves on the shore that could be seen from the windows of the café. Not that Jo got much of a chance to gaze out of the glass at the town's biggest draw – its sweeping views of the English Channel, the curved coastline that seemed to go on forever. From the minute she stepped into the café until the moment she left, each day passed in a blur, and as she worked Molly shared snippets of information about everyone who came in. The café seemed to be the hub for so many people. Apparently the other two cafés in town had since closed their doors, one replaced by a restaurant and the other turned into a bakery, so this place had become even more in demand.

'Could you please take these to table three,' Molly requested as she set a cappuccino onto a tray next to a plate with two iced biscuits and a glass of fresh orange juice. She lowered her voice and said to Jo, 'The man's name is Ben, the little boy is Charlie.'

Jo sighed. 'I'm never going to remember all these names.'

'You will, in time.'

Jo took the tray over and, as with every customer who came in, was soon on a first name basis with the man and his son. She'd made her introductions so many times she felt as though it would be much quicker and easier to have a label around her neck, but she was enjoying getting to know the people who had been coming to this same café for years.

'Thank you, see you soon,' she said to Peter and Vince, the brothers who had come in for strong cappuccinos this morning after they'd cycled a loop from the pier through Salthaven-on-Sea town centre, onto the next village and up to the pub at the top of the hill, before coming all the way back down to the café again. They'd told her all about their love of cycling, how Vince had taken part in the London to Brighton cycle ride and how Peter's wife described herself as a cycle widow when he disappeared for hours on end at a weekend.

Molly introduced Jo to Melissa, who worked in the local post office, and they were amused when they realised they'd actually gone to school together once upon a time. They talked about former classmates and what they were up to, and even found they had a shared connection to Scotland when Melissa revealed she'd fallen in love with the Isle of Skye after holidaying up there.

'Portobello beach was my nearest view of the sea,' Jo explained. 'It was beautiful there and I'd escape as often as I could to watch the waves and walk along the sand.'

'Well, it's great to see you back here,' said Melissa.

'Hear hear,' said Arthur, passing behind them with cups stacked on a tray.

Jo smiled after him and then back at Melissa. 'Thank you.' She was fast learning that you didn't have to live in Salthaven-on-Sea for very long before people made you feel a part of it. She may have been away for a long time, but it was already feeling like home again.

She took Melissa's order and before Molly could step in, Jo positioned herself in front of the coffee machine. 'Let me do it,' she insisted. 'I need to learn, so the more practice I have the better.'

Molly reluctantly stood back. They'd talked about this a lot over the last few days, how they needed to let Jo have hands-on experience if she was to going to take over completely one day. Jo tried not to panic that she'd likely be running the café on her own, because if she thought about it too much, she might just back out.

She filled the milk jug to the required level. She purged the steam wand on the coffee machine, inserted the milk jug beneath with the tip of the wand just under the surface of the liquid as she'd been shown, and listened to the already familiar sounds of the steam hissing out to warm the milk.

'That's it,' said Molly, anxious to get the drinks right for her customers. 'Now bang on the bench top,' she reminded Jo as the milk reached the desired temperature.

Jo followed the rest of the steps, remembering most of them without a prompt from Molly or Arthur. Watching her grandparents use the machine and go through the motions multiple times a day so expertly was like watching someone execute a perfectly controlled cartwheel – a move Jo could have a go at, but not one she'd ever be able to achieve with such finesse.

'You'll soon be able to use that machine without thinking too hard,' Molly encouraged, as though reading her thoughts.

'Thanks, Gran.'

Arthur joined them after he'd rung up another order on the till, this time for Eddie, a teacher at the local school who had a passion for the job that Jo had never experienced herself. Talking to him had helped her quickly realise she'd made the right choice in walking away and coming back to Salthaven.

'You know,' said Arthur, inspecting Jo's handiwork on the coffee she'd made. 'That looks like the perfect cappuccino to me.' He winked at his wife. 'I think we may have found ourselves the ideal person to carry on this business, don't you?'

Molly gazed across at Arthur and for a moment Jo was under their spell. They'd been married for more than fifty years, together for longer than that, and the way they looked at each other wiped away decades, as though they were still those two teenagers who'd met on this very same pier. Jo longed to one day have something so powerful, so special and everlasting, but she was beginning to think it would never happen for her.

'Come on, Jo,' Molly urged. 'Don't keep Melissa waiting too long.'

Jo gathered herself and delivered the cappuccino. Melissa relaxed and read a magazine, Jo wiped down the table closest to the door, Arthur chatted with Eddie, and Molly chuckled at something another man said. Jo had forgotten his name but she knew it wouldn't be long before she added it to the already long list in her mind. She watched as Ben and Charlie finished up their drinks, the little boy still bundled up in a red coat that he clearly didn't want to part with, and as Jo looked around the café she wondered whether people came in here as much for the cosy atmosphere as they did for food and drink. Twinkly lights lined the windows, looping from one corner to the other to brighten up any dull day, and eight tables filled the room, each with four sturdy chairs. Wooden window seats lined the edges of the café beneath the long windows on either side of the door, and cushions were scattered on top allowing customers to rest and lean up against them, to people-watch or gaze out at the sea.

When Jo went back through to the kitchen and Arthur joined her, he asked, 'Are you tired, love?'

'I should be asking you that.'

When he looked at her she admitted, 'I'm shattered. I'm more than half your age and you two are putting me to shame,' she added with a giggle.

'It's the sea air,' he claimed. His passion was still there for this town, this café, and it ignited Jo's determination to do whatever she could to help. Since Gran had mentioned the doctor's warning to Arthur to slow down, she could see his exhaustion, and what she wanted more than anything else in the world was for Molly and Arthur to have an idyllic retirement and leave any worries behind.

'When we started this place, we had instant coffee,' Arthur remarked. 'It was a whole lot easier.'

'I'll bet it was. It's like learning the intricacies of a space-ship trying to operate that thing.' She gestured to the coffee machine, which looked more friendly now she'd been here a couple of weeks, but was still her nemesis on some days.

'But it makes a great cup of coffee.' Arthur shared a smile with his granddaughter.

She put an arm around his shoulders and hugged him gently. 'I'm glad you asked me to come back to Salthaven.'

It hadn't been that long since she'd left Edinburgh but Jo had had no regrets so far and somehow she didn't think she would. The only thing she was missing was spending time walking beside the sea – she'd been spending every hour at the café, anxious to cram as much information and knowledge into her mind as quickly as possible. But at least she could see the sea now. She knew it was there, waiting for her, every morning, as reliable as the sunrise.

Jo watched Molly chatting with another girl who came into the café, picking up that her name was Jess. Dressed in running gear with a special warming wrap around her neck and ear buds dangling as she took time out, the girl looked like another regular and Jo had a pang of regret that she'd ever left Salthaven, a town that was all encompassing of its residents. She'd made friends up in Scotland, she had a group of people she went out with to the pub after work, but it wasn't like it was here. You couldn't stroll down the smaller streets and be guaranteed of knowing at least half of the people you came across, and Jo missed that.

Jo was slowly getting to know plenty of the faces that frequented the café. Molly and Arthur did their best to introduce her to as many people as they could and Jo had more or less been given a verbal résumé of every customer. But seeing how others her own age were well and truly settled only reminded Jo of the crossroads her life had reached.

Jo's head was swimming with details and by the end of the day she was ready to collapse into her bed. She had already begun to wonder whether she'd ever see a long, lazy evening again. Even after the café shut its doors to the public there was always so much to be done. Money from the till had to be counted and stowed in the safe, leftover food was disposed of, ingredients packed away for another day, counters and tables needed wiping, every inch of the floor had to be swept and the glass surfaces in the café buffed until they shone. Until their phone call to Jo, Molly and Arthur had never once dropped the ball with this business, and Jo couldn't let them down now. She wanted them to be as proud of her as she was of them. The business was flourishing and, like a child they'd nurtured over the years, it was going to be hard for her grandparents to let it go, so Jo would do whatever it took to make the process less painful.

Molly sighed, hands on hips. 'Come on, Jo. Let's sit down, you've earned it. Arthur is finishing in the kitchen, so we'll treat ourselves to a rest before we have to walk up that hill in the freezing cold.'

Jo pointed over to the window seats. 'Let's sit there and watch the sea.'

Molly sat down and settled back against the cushion with red lace trim and a robin on the front. She cupped her hands around her eyes and looked out through the glass. 'We can't see much, it's so dark out there.'

Jo, apron on over a black button-up shirt and jeans, slumped back against a velvet cushion the colour of

17

gingerbread. 'You're right, but I can hear the waves and that's enough.'

'It's a beautiful sound.' Molly closed her eyes. 'Soothing.'

'I never thought I'd be this glad to sit down.'

'You're only young, you'll get used to it.' Molly opened her eyes.

'I thought I was more than prepared.'

'In what way?'

'Teaching is hard work. I had a class of twenty-eight kids, aged eight and nine, and I thought they kept me on my toes, but this is totally different. In a good way,' she added, because she meant it.

They looked out into the darkness, the street lights shining on the curved bay that encompassed the town and led on into the next. Being so busy here Jo hadn't even ventured into the centre of Salthaven-on-Sea with its quaint pubs and cobbled streets leading past the bookshop, the haberdashery she hoped was still there, the sweet shop she'd spent her pocket money in when she was younger.

'So how are you feeling?' Molly asked as Arthur shut the blind on the window next to them but left theirs alone. 'About this place, I mean.'

'Don't worry, I'm not going to back out.' When Molly still didn't look relieved she added, 'I've given my room up, there's no going back. And besides, my trusty old beetle won't ever make it up to Scotland again, I think it'll protest if I so much as suggest it.'

'You need to upgrade that car.'

'Never,' she grinned. 'It's an oldie but a goodie.'

'Exactly the way I describe Molly,' Arthur whispered into Jo's ear as he passed.

Molly looked so offended that Arthur made peace by

stopping, taking her in his arms and kissing her full on the lips, making Molly blush.

'Excuse your gramps.' Molly raised her voice enough for it to be heard behind the counter where Arthur had gone to rummage for something in one of the cupboards. 'He's going to have to learn to behave now we're a trio.'

Jo loved watching them together, she never tired of it. All those tender moments they shared, the unspoken conversations they could have simply because they understood one another so well. 'What's he doing behind there?' she asked when Gramps didn't materialise. Maybe he was finally putting the paperwork for the café in order. Jo had seen papers tucked in drawers, others in a file at the bungalow, more in the kitchen cupboard. The accounts were a total mess and she knew she'd have to get to grips with them during her time here, but it wasn't something she was looking forward to.

'No idea,' Molly shrugged and turned her attention back to Jo's move. 'You came here at the right time, Jo. That's also why we mentioned the idea now rather than at the height of summer.'

Jo gasped. 'No way could I have managed the summer rush. Even thinking about it sends me into a panic.'

'You'd be fine, but at this time of the year we were able to throw you in at the deep end, without it being too much of a shock. In summer we'll get our regulars but also tourists, and it does get a little crazy.'

'Is it always quiet around this time?'

'It is. We have the Christmas Day swim event which always brings people in, followed by the tail end of the school holidays. January can be moderate but eases off until the spring as anyone outside of the town hibernates and wishes the sun would hurry up and shine again. But we like the peaks and troughs. It gives us a chance to recharge our batteries before it's all go, go, go again.'

'What about the theme nights you ran once upon a time?'

'Oh, we never really did too many. We still change the menu for bonfire night when people gather on the pier to watch the fireworks launch from the fields on the edge of town. It's an even better view than you get from being closer up, because they glow over the water.'

'I'll look forward to that later this year,' said Jo.

'We try to do something for May Day, occasionally Easter, introducing a few more chocolate products on the menu.'

Arthur found what he was looking for. 'I knew it was here somewhere.'

Molly put her glasses on as he came over. 'What have you got there?' she looked more closely. 'Is that what I think it is?' A wide smile spread across her face and then her hands covered her mouth in surprise.

Arthur was grinning back at her and Jo wanted to know what was going on. 'Did you get that from a gum-ball machine?'

Arthur nodded. 'I sure did.' In between his index finger and his thumb he held a plastic ring, with a gold flowered edge and a blue bead in the middle.

'Gran, are you OK?' Jo watched as tears welled in her gran's eyes, her gaze fixed firmly on her husband.

'She's getting sentimental,' Arthur explained, although Jo could tell he was feeling the same emotions. 'You see, we thought we'd lost this, her first engagement ring.'

Jo giggled but then stopped abruptly. 'You're serious?' She looked more closely to see whether she'd underestimated the bit of plastic that could've easily been mistaken for a piece of junk.

Arthur squeezed in on the window seat between them, closer to Molly than Jo, their bodies touching as they all looked at the ring. 'I found it when I was clearing out the spare bedroom to make room for Jo,' he told his wife. 'It was tangled up in an old ball of wool, in that knitting bag you pushed to the back of the wardrobe.'

'I remember now.' Molly took the ring. 'I put it in my wool drawer for safe keeping when we lived in the last house and then when we came to move I took all the wool and patterns and needles out but couldn't find the ring. It must've been so tangled no amount of searching would find it.'

'It was buried in the beige wool. I only found it because this morning I managed to drop the bag and everything tumbled out on the floor and I caught the piece of blue in amongst it. I wanted to wait until the café was quiet to tell you.'

Molly squeezed the top of his knee. 'I'm so glad you found it, you wonderful, wonderful man.' She took his face between her hands and kissed him. Jo almost felt like an intruder until Arthur turned to her.

'This ring was the one I used when I proposed to Molly.'

'Why have I never heard this story?' Jo asked, holding her hand out to look at the ring.

'I'm sure I told you it once,' said Molly. 'When you were little, I'm sure of it.'

'No, I'd remember.'

'It must've been your mum I told.' Molly took the ring

back as though she couldn't bear to be parted from it for too long.

'Tell me now, I want to hear.' Jo turned round and sat on the low wooden table opposite the window seat, so she could see them both.

'You tell her,' Molly insisted, eyes twinkling with love.

Arthur held his wife's hand. 'It was Valentine's Day, 1964. Freezing cold it was, the wind howling, making most people see sense and stay tucked inside in front of the fire.'

Molly couldn't help herself as though for too many years they'd helped one another finish off sentences. 'Exactly where I'd wanted to be when Arthur knocked on the front door and insisted we take a walk.'

Arthur took it from there. 'We met for the first time at the ice-creamery on the pier, a year before the night I'm about to tell you about. I saw Molly drop her ice-cream. She looked distraught, so I bought her another, and in return asked to take her to the dance.'

'I decided he was so handsome,' Molly beamed, 'he was worth the risk.'

'Every night after that, we took a walk along the pier,' Arthur continued. 'We'd eat fish and chips sometimes, or enjoy an ice-cream, we'd watch the waves and look out to sea. It was the perfect way to end the day, fill our lungs with the fresh salty air and remember how lucky we were to have found each other.'

'That night, I really wanted to stay by the fire,' said Molly.

Arthur's laughter rumbled from his belly all the way out of his body and around the café. 'You should've seen her pout, Jo, when I wouldn't take no for an answer.'

'He practically put my coat on my shoulders for me before shoving me out of the door.'

'I did,' Arthur agreed, 'but it was worth it.'

Jo didn't miss the look that passed between them. They were older, greyer, but the same love they'd once found burned a sturdy flame between them now. 'So what happened? Come on, don't keep me in suspense.'

'I took your gran out for our usual walk. The rain had started coming down, or should I say coming sideways, and we got soaked, so I took her hand and ran out along the pier all the way up to this very café. She tried to tug me back and tell me the sea was too rough, it might lap up over the pier and it was dangerous. I took her in my arms and told her I'd never let anything happen to her. And then, I made her look at this building.' He looked up at the pitched roof above them as though to remind himself of the night in question. 'Back then this place was dilapidated, neglected. It had once served cups of tea and perhaps hot dogs or some kind of fast food, but I had visions. I'd never been academic, but I knew I wanted to support a family and I dreamed of owning a business. I had planned to talk to Molly about it that very night, but with the storms brewing there was an immediacy I hadn't felt before and all of a sudden I was on one knee.'

Jo gasped and clasped her hands in front of her mouth as he went on.

'I told Molly I had a question for her.'

Molly took over. 'He said, "Will you marry me?" But I realised he didn't have a ring. I told him, you can't ask a girl to marry you without something to seal the deal.'

Enchanted, Jo asked, 'What happened then?'

'He turned to the café, still on one knee and said, "I

can't afford both, but I'm proposing a life together, Molly, and I've put down a deposit on this place. I want to open a café. It's for us, the chance to build a business, me and you", and then he looked as though he might burst waiting for my answer.'

Arthur took back the reins, the perfect partnership between them something Jo hoped to one day find. 'She said that she couldn't put a café on her finger, it was simply too big. So, I dragged her over to the gumball machine that was filled with toy rings instead of candy. I fumbled in my pockets until I found the right money and slotted it in, turned the silver button and into the outlet tray fell this ring.' All three of them looked at it. 'I promised I'd get a real one someday if she'd agree to be by my side for always.'

'And the rest, as they say, is history.' Molly looked fondly down at the real gold flowery ring with a sapphire centre, the delicate jewellery she wore on her wedding finger now.

The wind rattled the windows of the café. 'I can't believe I never knew the story,' said Jo.

'Well your mum isn't much of a romantic, I know, and I think over the years we've been so busy we sometimes forget the little things. It's very easy to do after so long together. And after we thought we'd lost the plastic ring years ago, well I think we both put it out of our minds and carried on with our busy lives. A lot has happened since Valentine's Day 1964.'

'Come on.' Arthur stood and gathered the bunch of keys before turning off the fairy lights at the windows and closing the rest of the blinds. 'Let's get you girls home and have hot chocolates, maybe with marshmallows too.

I think we have some in the cupboard.'

'Fine by me,' said Jo, tugging on her coat from where it hung on a hook in the cupboard at the side of the kitchen. 'As long as I don't have to make it.'

2

Ever since her talk with her grandparents that night at the café when she found out the story of how Arthur and Molly had gone from dating to being engaged and owning a business, Jo had got to thinking. They were into February now and business had slowed, as they'd told her it would, but Jo was beginning to take each day in her stride, no longer the first to fall into bed every night.

As soon as there was a lull in customers, kept away by the grey skies and darkness that blanketed the pier, Jo commandeered her grandparents' attention. She had an idea that had been brewing for the last few days and she wanted to share it with them.

'When you talked about the theme nights the other day, I started thinking,' she began, 'and if it's all right with you, I'd like to give something else a try to drum up some custom.'

'I'm all ears,' said Arthur but was pulled away when another customer came in after a cup of Earl Grey and a slice of flapjack.

'Me too,' Molly agreed, talking more quietly now they had company. 'We don't have many sparks of inspiration between us these days, but you've got enough energy to tackle anything.' She was almost bouncing in her seat. 'Come on, I want to hear all about it.'

With Valentine's Day looming Jo was set to be alone again, and she was done with feeling sorry for herself. She was lucky. She had family, which was more than some, and she had a great relationship with her grandparents plus a new venture to throw her enthusiasm into. But on her loneliest days Jo had often wondered how many other people out there needed company, or needed to inject something new and exciting into their lives, and so what she was proposing was something a lot of people in this town might appreciate.

'What I'm proposing is a Valentine's Day spectacular.'

'That sounds interesting.' Molly was all ears, not that she was ever anything else when it came to her grand-daughter. Jo hoped she would see this as a real business opportunity rather than the chance to indulge a relative.

'I'd like to hold a theme night, a special night of love at The Café at the End of the Pier.' She said the title of the event while drawing her hand through the air like a plane signwriting across the sky. 'And it's for singles or couples, so encompasses love and friendship.'

Molly leaned out to the side and beckoned Arthur before mouthing a request for two cups of coffee which he made and brought them as they discussed the finer details. 'Do you think single people would come too?'

'I'm catering for the possibility, as I think it's important to do so. We don't want to exclude anyone.' Jo's enthusiasm continued. 'We've got fairy lights across the windows, but I can add more. I'll have candles on each table, red and white flowers in the centre, perhaps rose petals on a white table cloth. I'd put together a unique menu – taking our cooking skills into consideration,' she added, before Molly thought she'd totally lost the plot. Jo wanted to get to the end of her suggestion, get it all out in one go, and then ask what her gran thought. 'We could go for canapés or tapas-style foods for the theme of sharing, or we could choose hearty meals like your slow cooked beef bourguignon or the shrimp bisque Gramps makes so well, or the cheese fondue. We could even add starters or the parmesan baked mussels, which I know how to make, or the oysters Kilpatrick you love so much.'

'I'm not sure the café is ready for an aphrodisiac.' When Jo's smile faded, Molly reached over and squeezed her hand. 'But I love this concept.'

'Are you just saying that?'

'I'm too old to be so considerate, and too business minded to let you do something I didn't think was a good idea.'

Arthur had served another two customers – Jerry and Scott, names Jo overheard as Gramps welcomed them – who now occupied the window seat on the opposite side of the café, and when he'd delivered their coffees, he came over to join Molly and Jo.

'Arthur, sit,' Molly commanded. 'I'll take over and you can listen to the brainwave your granddaughter has come up with.' She tapped both of them on the shoulder at the same time. 'I think we could be onto a winner.'

With Molly and Arthur's blessing, Jo went ahead with her plans and over the next few days she raced around town and purchased everything she needed. She drove out to the nearest Dunelm to pick up more accessories, she stopped at the florist to order in the flowers she'd need

28

for the café plus the collection of rose petals, she went to the supermarket and stocked up the fridge and the freezer with everything she could, ordering the rest of the ingredients from the regular fruit and veg delivery guy whose name she one day hoped she'd manage to remember. At the moment it was as though her brain could only hold onto so much information before it registered overload.

When 14 February rolled around, Jo was feeling more excited than she had in a long while. The promotion leaflets they'd had drawn up by a contact of Arthur's had been distributed throughout town, to local businesses, to people venturing on and off the pier, popped through people's letterboxes in the town. They'd put a blackboard outside the café too, Jo colouring in red hearts against the dark background and writing *A Night of Love at The Café at the End of the Pier* in bold letters she went over twice to make them stand out. She'd wound fairy lights around the edges of the blackboard too, as well as adding more around the inside of the café, across the front of the counter and along the wall on the opposite side.

'Too much?' she asked Molly when her gran had finished serving Angie, who was up for an even longer chat than usual today, and come over as Jo pushed the end of the string of lights into a piece of Blu Tac fixed to the wall. 'It's the last one.'

Molly looked around her. 'It's very romantic, I'll give you that.'

When the last customer left for the day Arthur stuck a piece of paper on the outside of the door, fixed with several extra pieces of Sellotape, to say that they would be closed for the next hour in preparation for their big event. Then they locked the doors against the icy winds that felt like something Edinburgh should be experiencing rather than a quiet coastal town down south, shut the blinds and got to work with the rest of the set up.

'Arthur, you make a start on the food prep,' Molly instructed. 'Sorry, Jo, I'm not taking over am I?'

'Go for it. This is my first event, so I need all the help I can get.'

Molly went out to the kitchen to confer with Arthur. They'd decided to go with canapés and tapas items to make preparation and service easy, and because all of them felt that sharing dishes were in perfect keeping with the theme of the evening. Jo retrieved the collection of linen tablecloths from the cupboard. She'd ironed them all last night as she watched Meg Ryan and Tom Hanks fall in love over books and mail, and wished her life was so simple.

Next came the red placemats Jo had found on sale yesterday, followed by the rose petals. She put a few on each table – enough to look classically romantic, not so many it looked like their customers would be sitting in the middle of a makeshift garden. Then it was time to roll the white linen napkins and slot them into silver rings for each place setting, and stand a candle in a glass jar in the centre of each table.

The finishing touches included an enormous arrangement of red roses in a tall vase at the edge of the room and another slightly smaller one by the counter, and once those were in place, Jo dimmed the lights in the café. With another hour left until the event was due to start, there was plenty of time to get busy in the kitchen and by the time Jo joined them, Molly and Arthur were well underway with preparations. Oysters were already prepared and so

Jo chopped bacon to go on top and set the Worcestershire sauce nearby along with a packet of rock salt to make a bed for the shells. She washed small potatoes and popped them into the oven to cook, ready to be stuffed with sour cream and chives before serving. She cut the brownies and the raspberry swirl cheesecakes that she and Molly had made earlier into bite-sized pieces, and as she worked Jo buzzed with the thrill of the evening.

A clap of thunder made Arthur jump. He put a hand against his heart before he carried on rubbing a piece of garlic around the inside of a pan.

Jo peered over his shoulder. 'Is that for the fondue?'

'It is. I'll put in Gruyère, Emmental and Cheddar, plus a generous glug of wine,' he winked.

'You know, if this takes off we could get some proper fondue sets, with flames beneath to display on tables. Customers would love that.'

'I'm sure they would. You know, Hilda Jenkins who works in the toy shop is from Switzerland. She'll know a good fondue when she sees one.' Arthur measured out some wine, generously, just as he'd said. 'You've got a good head on your shoulders, Jo. I'm proud of you for jumping into the business the way you have.'

She kissed him tenderly on his cheek. 'And I'm forever grateful you asked me to. You changed my life.'

A look passed between them before Arthur said, 'Oh, be off with you before I add tears to the fondue as well as wine. I don't think Hilda would approve of the added ingredient.'

Jo left the bread alone for now, wanting it to be nice and fresh when it was served in chunks ready to dunk into the cheesy mixture. She hoped someone would select

fondue from the menu choices. What could be more romantic than sharing something so comforting on a cold
night for Valentine's Day?

When a lightning strike illuminated the entire café and
made the light in the kitchen dim yet again, Jo looked at
her gran. 'I hope we'll have a few customers tonight.'

'Nonsense, they'll be here in droves.' She took out the
spring rolls she'd made earlier and lined them all up on
a tray ready for the oven. 'We've done some great marketing, the town loves this place. Now, where are those
strawberries?'

Jo loved the way they were all pulling together. 'Over
here.' She reached across to the bowl on the shelf down
low and covered over with kitchen towel. 'I've already
washed them so I'll pop them onto skewers, if you could
break up the chocolate in another glass bowl ready for
melting.'

'OK, boss.'

'Am I overstepping?' Jo froze, anxious not to offend.

'Overstep away, that's what you're here for,' said Arthur
without turning round.

As the lightning lit up the café over and over and the
thunder rolled in the skies above making it difficult to
hear one another, they finished their preparation and with
a deep breath Jo drew up the blinds and unlocked the
door. She held onto the door with one hand so the storm
didn't grab hold of it as she leaned around and ripped the
sign from the glass to let customers realise they were ready
for the event she'd planned so carefully.

Half an hour later and Molly, Arthur and Jo were still
leaning against the counter waiting. Jo checked her watch.
'We did tell people seven o'clock, didn't we?'

Molly sighed. 'We did. They'll come.'

Another clap of thunder made Jo jump. She felt a hand on her shoulder and all of a sudden tears welled in her eyes and she thought she would cry. 'It's a good menu – a romantic night at a place the town loves.'

Arthur grunted. 'It's the storm, not you.' He sounded angry at the weather, something none of them had any control over. He went over and stood by the door as though willing people not to upset his granddaughter. 'Just one,' she heard him say.

He was right. If one person showed up it would be so much better than none at all.

Another hour passed and took them well past eight o'clock. Jo slumped against the counter.

When a tear dared to escape from her eye and make its way down her cheek, Jo felt as though each lightning strike was a big fat arrow pointing down to her as if to say: there she is, the lonely girl, trying to live some kind of fantasy dream life that will never come true. But when a second tear joined the first, she decided to turn this evening around.

'Sit down,' she commanded.

'Pardon?' Molly paused from rearranging rose petals on the low table in front of one of the window seats. They didn't need fussing over at all, but there wasn't much else to do.

'Sit down, both of you. Pick a table.' Jo sniffed and took a deep breath.

'What are you up to?' Arthur asked, finally giving up his sentry position at the door and turning to face them both.

'When was the last time you were spoiled on Valentine's Day?' Jo asked.

Molly thought about it. 'We don't need a fuss, we're too old for that.'

'Rubbish, you're never too old. We have all this lovely food, you finally have help in the café you started from scratch, and tonight, Molly and Arthur, you will have a Valentine's Day to remember. Think back to 1964, the day your lives took on another meaning with this place.' There'd be none of the usual feeling sorry for herself; this was a selfless good deed she wanted to savour. 'Now, pick a table.'

Molly giggled coquettishly, already lost in the moment as she went and sat at the table in the far corner of the room, and Jo whispered into Arthur's ear. He whispered back in hers and off Jo went to retrieve his smartphone from his jacket pocket in the kitchen. She scrolled through until she found what she was looking for, then back in the café she set the phone on the docking station.

Molly smiled over at her and Jo saw her mouth the words, 'Thank you, Jo.'

With the piano music playing softly in the background going through *Close to You, She Loves You,* and plenty of other tunes Jo knew to hum along to even though she couldn't identify the artist, Jo went into the kitchen and carried on with the cooking. She melted the cheeses along with the wine for the fondue, she chopped the bread into cubes, she laid everything out on a tray and took it through to her guests. She knew this was Arthur's favourite and she could already imagine them looking at one another as they speared bread and scooped up the melted cheese mixture.

'Join us, Jo.' Molly insisted.

'No, this is your night. I'm here as café worker and chef, nothing else.' She held up a hand. 'And it's no use protesting, I mean it.'

Jo went back into the kitchen but lingered by the open door where she was almost out of sight if she stood back in the shadows enough. She watched this couple, together for decades, at ease with one another in a way Jo could only dream about. All the hard work they'd put into this place and they were willing to share it with her. She might be alone tonight in some ways, but in others she was a real part of something special.

But what if she could do more?

With a flash of inspiration she shut the kitchen door, turned on the light, and grabbed the notepad she knew her grandparents kept in here for jotting down reminders to buy ingredients or stock that was running low. Perched on a stool beside the cooker as the rain pummelled the roof, peeking through the gap in the door every now and then to check on Molly and Arthur, who probably couldn't be distracted even if a bolt of lightning were to hit the café, Jo started to put the wheels in motion.

Because Jo had a plan for this café. Molly and Arthur had given her so much, and Jo wanted to give something back to the town, perhaps even a little bit of magic.

And she knew the perfect way to do it.

Spring

3

It was almost the end of April, and the four months since Jo had arrived back in Salthaven-on-Sea had passed in a whirlwind. She'd scarcely had a moment to think since taking over her grandparents' café full-time and renting her own flat, a stone's throw from the town's quaint little shops and the characterful pub that welcomed locals and tourists alike. Gran and Gramps had never left this town and Jo could understand why. The community had always been a big part of their lives, with people stepping in over the years to help out when times were hard.

Ever since Valentine's Day, her plans to bring something completely different to the café had been bubbling away, and it felt like the time had come to put them into action. She wanted to give something back to these wonderful people who'd always been there for her grandparents, like an extended version of family with its arms wide open. Even when Jo had been living in Edinburgh, she'd heard so much from Molly and Arthur that it was almost as though she knew everyone already. When the café was broken into a couple of years ago, the whole town had rallied round, cleaning up and ensuring Molly and Arthur were safe. There'd been a rota apparently, people taking turns to check up on them at various points of the day. The break-in had made them nervous and it took a while, but eventually, thanks to the community here, they'd got their confidence back. The winter before last, when it snowed more heavily than ever before – which it rarely did on the south coast – Molly and Arthur had had to shut the café because they couldn't even get down the hill. Little Toby Secombe, whose dad ran the local newsagent, had sledged all the way to their bungalow to take them groceries. He'd delivered bread, milk, a homemade cottage pie, and a box of teabags. According to Arthur, Toby had left very happy, rewarded not only with a big hug from Molly, but also a tin of her homemade chocolate brownies.

Jo's trainers tapped their way along the wooden slats of the pier and she paused to take a photo of the scene – the sea in the distance, the café just about visible at the very end – making sure to get a good shot of the boards she'd padded along many a time. She sent the picture to her best friend, Tilly, and her friend didn't take long to reply that she wished she was there too, and that it was summer so they could go for a dip.

Jo continued on down the pier, past the ice-creamery, the fish and chip shop, and the 'bits and bobs' shop that would soon be open all hours selling sunhats, brightly coloured inflatables, goggles for kids to see beneath the murky depths of the English Channel, and spades to dig sandcastles in the golden sands down below.

Living in a shared house in Edinburgh, Jo had rarely had much space – but at times she'd felt surprisingly lonely. When she first arrived in Salthaven she'd begun to wonder how many other people hid their solitude behind a friendly smile in the street, or a chat in the café. She'd started trying to read her customers as they came in: was the woman who ran every morning really happy when she got home at the end of a long day, the tiredness catching up with her? Was Angie, one of their regulars, really as jolly as she seemed? Could it be that the smile the assistant at the ice-creamery gave Jo every time their paths crossed hid the same loneliness that Jo often felt?

Apart from one solitary fisherman at the end of the wooden structure there wasn't another soul in sight, and as she reached the café Jo had begun to think about who she could choose to put her plan into action. She had never thought of herself as a matchmaker, but she supposed that's what she could end up being if her café of love became a success.

There were still a couple of hours before opening time, and Jo was ready to finish off the spring clean she'd started yesterday. She'd done the kitchen, wiping inside every single cupboard and under the cooker. With Steve's help she'd even pulled out the fridge and cleaned up all the dust and debris that had sneaked beneath it over the winter months. Steve had repaired a couple of wobbly tables, while Jo had given the tiny bathroom a good going-over. It came up sparkling, thanks to it being relatively new – the bathroom in the house back in Edinburgh had been years old, and even after a good hour of scrubbing it had never really looked that clean.

As she delved into her bag for her keys to open up, Jo peered up at the frontage. She hadn't given it much thought when she'd arrived back in January beneath the winter darkness and the cold that came with the season, but now they were into spring she'd really begun to notice that the outside of the café was looking very sorry for itself. It hadn't had a facelift in years, so now that she was managing the place – with her grandparents' help on occasion – she'd made a decision and instructed Steve on a new colour scheme.

She turned when she heard another set of footsteps tapping their way up the pier.

'Good morning, Steve!' Her voice was as bright as the shimmering surface of the sea. Since coming to Salthaven it was hard not to feel elated every time she caught a waft of the salty air, or heard the waves tumbling down against the sand.

'Good morning.' He was beaming as usual and Jo doubted the miserable gene ever affected him. 'You do realise your grandparents never made me come here quite this early, don't you?'

'I'm sorry – I'm not a terrible boss, I promise.'

Steve grinned and set down his toolbox and a couple of tins of paint. A builder by trade and son of one of the locals, Steve had come recommended and was Molly and Arthur's go-to person if ever they needed anything done in the café.

'I'm teasing you. This isn't early. I've already been surfing, showered away the sea and I'm ready to go.'

'I was never a morning person before,' Jo said, 'but the sea air certainly does something to you.'

'It sure does. You hear the gulls, the sun creeps above the horizon, and you can't ignore it.'

'Spoken like a true Salthaven local.' She'd always struggled to get up in the mornings when she lived in the city, but she didn't know whether it was the environment or the career choice that had made the difference. Whatever it was, the sea change was already doing her the world of good, and being back in her home town was like being given a new lease of life.

'You should try it sometime.'

'Huh?' She turned the key in the top lock now she'd undone the bottom. 'You mean surfing? No chance of that, I'd swallow most of the sea.'

'You never know until you give it a go.'

'I think I'll stick to dry land.' She gave the door a shove with her shoulder, as she did every morning, and opened it into the café, letting the sunlight filter in across the eight tables inside, each with four chairs. Now the warmer months were approaching she could leave the door open for a while for the air to circulate and really freshen up the place.

'First things first,' said Steve, setting down his toolbox by the door, his floppy blond hair catching every bit of the sun that came his way. 'I'll fix this. You'll give yourself a shoulder injury barging in like that.'

'Shame. I wouldn't be able to surf then.'

'You wait, someday you'll try it. And once you have . . .'

The face she pulled told him she'd do no such thing.

She left Steve tinkering with the door and went to fill a bowl with warm, soapy water. With no time to waste she pulled on a pair of Marigolds. They were slowly getting there. Last week Steve had repainted the interior walls on the brightest day they'd had so far this spring. They'd done the work after closing time, enjoying the mild evening temperature as they flung the door and windows wide open. Now, with no rain forecast for a couple of days, Steve could get on with repainting the outside, including the sign. Jo, meanwhile, cleaned every nook and cranny she could find at floor level, particularly around the wooden window seats that lined the edges of the café beneath long windows. She'd brought a sewing kit in with her today and so repaired a couple of bedraggled cushions that sat on top of the seats on either side of the door. She wiped around the inside of the windows before finishing off with a good clean of the glass, removing finger prints and flecks of dirt before she buffed it to a high shine.

'Door's fixed.' As if to demonstrate, Steve opened and shut the front door which obeyed with ease. 'I've sanded the top where the wood had swollen up, and I've tightened the hinge that was out of alignment.'

Jo wiped the last of the section of window she was on. 'What would I do without you?'

'I'm irreplaceable,' he shrugged, dropping a screwdriver back into his toolbox. He nodded towards the windowsills, went over and ran his hand across the wood, the golden hairs on his arm shining beneath the lights. 'These'll need a fresh coat of paint.'

'They look even worse now the walls look so good.'

'I'll start painting the sign today, finish it tomorrow, then I'll take a look at them.'

The first time Jo had met Steve, she'd noticed how good-looking he was. How could she not? Tall, well-built from the physical nature of his job, tanned from – she now knew – his love of the surf. And he was witty and could hold a decent conversation. She wondered why he hadn't been snapped up a long time ago. Perhaps it was the happy-go-lucky attitude he carried around with him. Maybe it was OK for something casual, but anyone looking for long-term relationship potential wouldn't see it in Steve.

'There are a couple of pieces that need tightening as they've come loose,' he said, and when Jo looked at him quizzically, added, 'The window frames.' He shook his head, amused at her daydreaming, although thankfully he couldn't tell exactly what she'd been thinking about. 'It'll be quick and easy to do, and then with a good lick of paint it'll be good as new.'

As Steve opened a stepladder beneath the front doorway and climbed up with a bucket of soapy water and a scrubbing brush to give the sign a good pre-paint clean, Jo got going with her prep for the day. Since taking over the café Jo had been as stringent as her grandparents when it came to cleaning up at closing time before she was able to go home. And she'd soon learned why. At the end of the day you were exhausted, but in the morning there was so much to do that the absolute last thing you wanted was to scrub crockery, clean the coffee machine or deal with old food that had to be thrown out. It was much easier to start the day afresh like she was doing now.

As she watched Steve go about his work, whistling away, she couldn't help but be reminded of her own single status. Past experience and family circumstances meant she had little faith in her ability to hold down a decent relationship, and no matter how much she wanted it to happen, she'd long ago accepted that maybe it wasn't meant to be. Perhaps she was a lot more like Steve than she'd realised. He seemed to cruise along on his own without being too bothered by it.

Jo dragged her thoughts away from things she couldn't change, and thanked goodness this kitchen was so functional as she made up a batch of buttermilk cookies, followed by chocolate brownies. Apart from a cupboard door that had come off its hinges last week, she couldn't complain. Her friend Eliza up in Edinburgh had worked in a café and was forever lamenting the lack of equipment or the temperamental cooker she had to work with, but this compact little kitchen had everything Jo needed, and it didn't take long to get herself organised.

Using Arthur's recipe, Jo made a loaf of pear and raspberry bread and while it was cooking, laid out a plate of Molly's infamous buttermilk cookies.

'I had breakfast but that smell makes me want a second helping.' Steve had tipped the bucket of dirty water out over the edge of the pier into the sea and was back inside to refill it with fresh soapy suds.

'Pick your poison.' She gestured to the glass-fronted display cabinet that she'd already begun to fill.

'Don't let your regulars hear you say that.'

'We have buttermilk cookies, brownies, and the pear and raspberry loaf is in the oven.'

He patted what looked like a taut stomach through his T-shirt. 'They sound far too wicked. Do you have any fresh fruit?'

When Matt, the café's delivery man, appeared, Jo beamed. 'Just in time.' He had in his arms a colourful collection of fruit and vegetables. 'Steve here is craving something healthy. He's watching his figure.'

Steve whistled. 'The cantaloupe melon looks good.'

With a roll of her eyes, Jo said, 'I'll chop you some.' She took the box from Matt and went out to the kitchen, leaving the men to it. They knew each other well having both been working for Molly and Arthur's pier café for years.

In the kitchen she unloaded the melon and took out some beautiful purple rhubarb she'd make miniature crumbles with tonight or first thing tomorrow morning. One of the features that Jo believed set this café apart from any others in neighbouring towns was the variety in the menu. They had their staples of course – coffees in all varieties, a good selection of teas, shortbread and brownies, and a decent cold drink selection with everything from traditional lemonade and bitter lemon to Diet Cola and Dandelion and Burdock. But Molly and Arthur had explained to Jo how they depended on what fruit and vegetables were in season – or what Matt managed to deliver to them on a daily basis – to dictate what they put on the menu. At first Jo had thought it would be far harder work to try to maintain the variety, but now she loved it. And so did the customers. Over the last couple of weeks Matt had kept the supplies of melon coming, and Jo always had some for morning tea, the fresh orange flesh a delicious boost to her day.

'How's Arthur?' Matt had done the honours of handing Steve the chopped melon and joined Jo in the kitchen, passing her a box of fresh eggs.

She stowed the rhubarb in a straw basket at the back of the kitchen next to the drinks fridge. 'He's doing OK. He's finally listening to Molly and taking it easy. I guess a stint in hospital was enough to scare him.'

Gramps had become dizzy one morning with pounding in his chest, and they'd been terrified it was a heart attack. He'd been rushed in to hospital, given so many tests Jo couldn't remember them all, and left a couple of days later diagnosed with high blood pressure. He'd given Molly and Jo quite a fright, but since then he had accepted the need to rest, avoid stress and perhaps even lose a bit of weight. Jo was surprised her mum hadn't come to

47

see her dad given all the messages and phone calls Jo had made when he'd been at the hospital, but then nothing with their relationship was clear, and asking anyone to fill in the gaps was pointless.

'How's he going with the healthy eating?' Matt wanted to know.

'He found it hard at first. Molly's such a great cook and nothing pleases her more than to make people happy with food, but they both know how important it is to make some changes.'

'I'll take a box of fresh fruit and vegetables to them next.'

'You're very kind.'

'It's my pleasure.' He looked around, hazel eyes roaming the space that had brightened up considerably of late. 'We look out for each other in Salthaven, but it's good that you're here now. There's nothing like having your own family nearby.'

'It's wonderful how close you all are to Molly and Arthur.' Jo took the onions out of the box and put them in the plastic stacker in the corner of the kitchen, along with the garlic at the bottom of the vegetable box.

'We're a tight community,' he admitted. He'd been very shy when Jo met him, and at first she'd thought him serious, but he was starting to mellow as time went on. 'Did I imagine it, or has Arthur taken up lawn bowls? I thought I saw him earlier.'

'You definitely didn't imagine it. He always said he would one day, and now he's finally getting the chance. It's all part of him beginning to manage his stress levels, and I think it helps with Gran's too when he's out from under her feet.'

Matt leant against the counter. 'I bet it's weird for them, not being here so much.'

'Don't worry, he still checks up on me. He came in yesterday and I could tell he wanted to get behind the till and into the kitchen, but I made him sit there with a cup of tea and a buttermilk cookie. I think being here, seeing the place running smoothly, was enough for him.'

'You look like you're enjoying it.'

'I really am.'

Steve stepped inside. 'Matt, I'm going to paint above the door if you want to escape first, otherwise the stepladder will be in the way.'

'That's my cue to get moving.' said Matt. The flecks of gold in his eyes were a match for the sun outside. 'Back to the farm for me. Oh, and before I forget' – he dug a hand into his pocket and took out a business card – 'here's the accountancy firm Molly asked for. Although I'm assuming you put her up to it. I've seen her wrestling with paperwork before now, but she always said she was on top of it.'

Jo took the business card. 'Thank you so much, and Gran has been in denial for far too long.' As part of her spring clean she'd pulled out every single last piece of paperwork to do with the café and organised it all, ready to see an accountant. But after meeting with Molly's regular guy and realising he was a long way off ever joining the digital age, and that he was planning to move up to Northumberland, she decided a long-distance accountancy relationship wasn't what she wanted or needed. Her fresh start meant finding someone new.

'The firm have always been good, as far as we're concerned,' said Matt.

'I really appreciate the recommendation. And thank you for all the beautiful produce this morning. The rhubarb looks especially divine.'

'Pleased to be of service.' He dipped his head. 'Catch you later, Jo.'

As soon as Matt had left and Steve had prised the lid off the first tin of paint using a screwdriver and set to work, the oven timer pinged. Jo took out the loaf of pear and raspberry bread, setting it aside to cool. Next it was on to the quiches – she'd found broccoli in the vegetable box and she had a plentiful supply of eggs. And by the time she'd make two quiches – one with bacon, one a vegetarian option – it was opening time. She sliced the pear and raspberry loaf and arranged it on a plate, before setting it inside the display cabinet. Depending on how quickly that day's food was selling, Jo had to be flexible with her cooking schedule – fitting it in during a lull, multitasking and running on the adrenaline of being in charge.

Steve moved the stepladder away from the entrance and Jo stood back to check out the sign, leaning right up against the white fencing that encased the end of the pier. The main sign was almost finished, painted a warm golden colour to match the sand on the beach opposite, and the outside walls were already scrubbed, with only the windowsills still awaiting repair and a repaint. And tomorrow, when the sign was finished in blue with the words 'The Café at the End of the Pier', it would look like a new place: exactly in keeping with the fresh start Jo had wanted when she came back to Salthaven.

'Good morning, Jo.' As was often the case, the first

customer of the day was Angie, a woman who liked a good gossip. 'Beautiful day today.'

'It's wonderful. Makes such a difference when the sun is shining.'

'Oh you've got the Salthaven attitude all right.' She bustled over to a table and shook off her chunky cardigan that was so long it almost passed her knees. She was well into her retirement – she'd already joked about the joys of a free bus pass – but dressed in clothes that didn't always give away her age.

'I've booked to go see *Kinky Boots*,' she announced proudly.

'Did you get your discount?' Jo knew it'd be the next most important piece of information.

'You bet I did. I'm telling you, Jo, you should join the WI. Oh you're young and free now, but one day you might enjoy it.' Last month Angie had been to see *Wicked* and come back with stars in her eyes, buzzing at the performance and waxing lyrical about the enormous discount they'd secured for a group of them. 'You should definitely see a show this year, Jo. I still can't believe you've never been to a musical.'

'Neither can I.'

'I love going. Reminds me of my youth.'

'Did you see plenty when you were little?'

Steve poked his head around the door. 'You don't know about our Angie, do you?' Grinning, he let the older woman take the floor as he got back to what he was doing.

'I was a professional dancer once upon a time.'

Jo's mouth fell open. 'How did you keep that quiet?'

'I'm not one to blow my own trumpet.'

'What performances were you in?'

'My highlight was being in *42nd Street* in the West End.' She patted the chair beside her and Jo knew she had no choice but to join her. And for the next fifteen minutes, with no other customers to attend to, Jo listened to Angie talk about her life as a dancer – what it was like on stage, the career she'd had before she retired to Salthaven-on-Sea to her terraced house with just enough room in the courtyard garden to dance when it was a beautiful summer's evening.

'Something smells good,' said Angie when she'd fitted in as much of her past as she could in a very short time.

'That'll be the pear and raspberry bread.'

'Delicious. I'll have a slice of that and a cup of peppermint tea, please.' She pulled her cardigan on again, the morning temperature not quite warm enough to be without it, especially with the cooling breeze drifting through the open doors.

'Coming right up.'

Steve leant inside again. 'I'll put the blackboard up today, and the board for those postcards.'

'Thanks Steve.' She was missing the board that usually depicted the choices of the day. It hung on the side wall so that it could be seen the moment a customer entered, or from outside if they were peering through the window, but it had been taken down when the walls were painted, along with the other board that housed postcards from customers on their various trips around the globe. Once both of those were back in place, the café would be as cosy as ever.

Jo hummed as she prepared the tea. Right now, she couldn't be happier.

At least she was, right up until she picked up the phone.

She'd called to request an initial appointment with the accountant and they said they'd get back to her with a time. And now, when the receptionist gave her the name of the person she would be seeing, she had to ask her to repeat it.

Harry Sadler.

Jo put down the phone, her carefree attitude laced with concern as she hovered in the kitchen on her own. It was too much of a coincidence for it not to be the Harry she'd once known so well. And even though he hadn't been in her life for a while, the time he'd spent in it had had a huge effect on her.

Because, once upon a time, he'd been the love of her life. Right up until he'd broken her heart into tiny little pieces.

4

Jo pushed open the door to the café the next morning, almost using her shoulder to barge it again, but remembering at the last moment that it was fixed. Where would she be without the locals who helped out around here and never needed much notice to fit her in? It made her grateful for the reputation and standing her grandparents had built within the community.

She picked up the post from the mat. There wasn't much: a couple of local council pamphlets; an envelope containing the plain postcards she'd ordered to put her plan for the café and this town into action; a flyer for movie times at the local cinema. But Jo smiled when she also saw the loose postcard with a photograph of the passenger ferry in Puerto Pollensa, the small town in northern Majorca where Jo's mum had lived for the past five years. It was a small gesture – not the same as her mum visiting – but it was enough for now.

'You beat me to it.' It was Steve, walking up the pier, surfboard tucked under one arm, wetsuit unzipped to his waist. 'I'll lose my board and then I'm all yours,' he puffed. She wondered if he'd seen her walking along the pier and rushed up here.

She did her best to keep her eyes away from his broad

chest, and the water droplets snaking down his skin. She didn't miss the approving look two girls gave him as they walked past, but he seemed oblivious.

'No hurry,' she said. 'Just the blue words to paint on the sign.'

'I'll give the window frames a lick of paint now they're repaired.'

'Great. It's going to look brilliant.' She looked up at the golden background to admire its gleam in the sunshine.

His breathing evened out as he leant casually against the surfboard propped up on its end. 'How come you're here so early? I thought you'd finished the spring clean.'

'I have, but all those postcards need to go back onto the board you put up for me yesterday. I didn't get a chance last night.' She also hadn't slept well, thinking about her impending appointment with the accountant, when she'd be seeing Harry again after all this time.

He picked up his board. 'I won't be long, then I'll be back to start the painting. The weather is cooperating at least.'

'Yep, long may it last!'

Steve went on his way and Jo closed the café door behind her. The blackboard with the day's menu items was in operation already – she'd put a few selections on last night before she left for the day – but now she wanted to refill the postcard board. She took out the stash of more than forty postcards from all corners of the globe. There was a card from Vince after he'd been to Montreal last year; another from Jess, the local doctor, after she'd been to Miami and Florida last summer; one from Angie after she'd been to Liverpool to see *Les Misérables*; and many more from names Jo didn't recognise. Postcards were supposed to reflect on happy times, good news, adventures and excitement. They weren't vehicles for anything else – at least not anything that brought unhappiness or sadness to the receiver.

Shaking away the thought, Jo read her mum's postcard. It was addressed to Molly, Arthur and Jo, although Jo knew the only reason it had all three names was so that it didn't rock the boat for her now she was back in Salthaven. No matter what had gone on between all three of them, Jo had always been unwilling to get dragged into it and had kept her distance. She hadn't pried because she'd always known she wouldn't get very far.

In the postcard her mum chattered on about a day at the beach with Stuart – Jo's stepfather, and the only dad she'd ever known after her own walked away before she was even born. Jo had two half-brothers, Nicholas and Timothy, and the family had remained in Salthaven until all three children were old enough to fend for themselves. Once upon a time Sasha had been a banking clerk, but now she made jewellery and sold it at local markets.

All three siblings had a good relationship with their mum these days, but Jo wondered if perhaps that was only because she finally seemed happy. Sasha had always seemed like someone at the start of a race, feet in the starting blocks, crouching down and building up energy, ready for the off. But since she'd been living in Spain, even though Jo saw her very little, she finally seemed settled and in a good place emotionally. Maybe Salthaven simply hadn't been for her. It hadn't been for Nicholas or Timothy either. Nicholas had trained as a ski instructor and now travelled all over the world. He could no more anchor himself to one place than his mother could. Jo's younger brother, Timothy, had got married last year at the tender age of twenty-five, and ran his own market gardening business up in Yorkshire, in a sleepy village so far inland Jo doubted he ever got so much as a sniff of the sea.

Jo was the only one of her family, apart from Molly and Arthur, who felt an affinity with Salthaven. And she couldn't imagine it any other way.

When her phone rang Jo snatched it up as soon as she saw the caller ID. 'Mum! I just got your postcard – it looks as beautiful out there as ever.'

'Hello, Jo.' Her mum's voice had always been soft, even when she'd been arguing with Arthur and Molly behind closed doors, so all Jo had ever heard was a muffled row that made no sense at all. 'As a matter of fact I'm right there now, in the exact same place.'

'Near the boats, like in the picture?'

'I sure am. I'm sipping a smoothie, watching the world go by. I might take a dip in the sea later on.'

'That sounds like bliss.'

'You'll have to come and visit again soon.'

Jo hesitated. 'It might be a while.'

'How long do your grandparents need you for?'

This was one of those times when Jo wished her siblings were here so they could bear some of the load. It was hard being the person stuck in the middle, but she'd never been one to run away from a problem. 'It's a long-term plan.'

'How long?'

'They want to retire.'

'Well fair enough, I'm surprised they've lasted this long. You need to put the feelers out, see if anyone else wants to take over the lease.'

Jo sighed. 'They want to keep it in the family.'

'That's all well and good, Jo, but you have your teaching career to think about. You can't throw it all away. If you're out of it too long it won't look good on your CV.'

She wasn't sure she was ready for this conversation. 'I'm not throwing it away, Mum.'

'When are you going back?'

Silence.

'Jo, tell me you *are* going back. Back up to Edinburgh I mean.'

Her second bout of silence confirmed it.

'Oh, Jo. Are you sure you know what you're doing?'

'It's what I want, Mum.'

'Is it? Or did Mum and Dad make you feel so guilty because you're the only one slightly tempted to live in Salthaven all over again?' She made it sound as though it was the worst punishment on earth, rather than anything resembling a positive career change.

'They didn't make me do anything.' She looked around the café as her mum planted the seeds of doubt in her mind. What if she couldn't make this work? What if the café failed under her management? What if she realised she'd made a huge mistake?

'Jo, are you listening to me?'

'Mum, come on. I'm working long hours, I'm tired, there's so much to do.' *And I'm loving it*, she wanted to add, but what was the point when it would only fall on deaf ears? 'I'm going to have to go. Looks like I have a customer.' She didn't, but she had no desire to prolong the conversation. Angie coming in for her morning gossip fix right about now would be more than welcome. 'And please don't go calling Gran and Gramps, berating them for this. It was my decision, there was no pressure.'

Sasha harrumphed. 'I'll phone you again soon. But Jo, make sure this is really what you want.'

After she'd hung up Jo turned to more positive tasks, and as she pushed pins into the board, fixing the post-cards at varying angles, she told herself her mum was wrong. She wasn't here out of a sense of loyalty, or because she'd been coerced. She wanted to be a part of Salthaven again, a proper part, and as she slowly got to know the names of the regulars, some of whom she recognised from years ago, and a bit about their lives here, the happier she was becoming.

By the time she'd almost covered the entire board with postcards, she had a brilliant and varied display of everything from snow, ice and ski slopes, to European cities and tropical beaches.

She turned around to greet the first customer of the day. 'You beat Angie this morning,' she remarked, looking at her watch as Vince came in, dressed in his cycling gear.

'I'll probably be in and out before she gets here.' He tapped his watch. 'Takeaway for me today – got to get to work, unfortunately. Shame, it's a glorious day out there. I saw Steve surfing first thing.'

She thought back to Steve's golden skin and hair still dripping from the ocean. 'I think we're all making the most of spring. Though he told me yesterday he's thinking of braving the Christmas Day swim this year.'

Vince recoiled. 'I usually go into hiding if anyone sug-gests it to me. I think I'll stick with the bike.'

'Good for you. Now what can I get you?' She tied on her apron, a half pinny with chocolate brown and white polka dots. Molly said it brought out the colour of her eyes, but her comment had met with a roll of those very same eyes from Jo. Recently Molly had been obsessing about Jo's single status. At thirty-one she should apparently be at least on her way to settling down.

'I'll have a large skim latte, please, extra hot if you can.'

'Coming right up.'

'How's the flat?' he asked as she set about making the beverage.

'Perfect. And the owner is thinking of selling up.'

'Great news. So you're buying?'

'I hope so.' Because she'd been renting a room in Edinburgh, she'd managed to save quite a bit of money and had enough for the deposit if the owner decided to go ahead with the sale.

'Property prices are on the up, do it soon before it's too late.'

'Well, fingers crossed, I will.' She finished making the latte, fixed on a plastic lid and took payment. 'Enjoy, and have a good day at work.'

'You too, Jo.' He turned and greeted Steve who had arrived, ready to put the finishing touches to the sign above the door.

'Nice,' said Steve as Jo wrote 'Rhubarb Crumble' on the menu board for today.

'Naughty, too.'

He patted his stomach, shook his head and got on with his own task in hand.

Molly had insisted on making the miniature rhubarb crumbles last night and Jo was happy for her to keep helping out. The café had been part of their lives for so long that it had to be hard to completely hand over the reins. She'd stopped off to see them this morning on the way from her flat, which stood further up the hill in a residence that housed five other flats of a similar size, and at her grandparents' bungalow had collected the big plastic box full of the delicious crumbles.

She looked up and waved when the door went again. Jo had come to realise the café was a regular part of local Ben's weekend routine when he would come here with his five-year-old-son, Charlie. Molly had told her all about Ben, and Jo couldn't help thinking how lonely he looked every time he came in, like part of the reason he was here wasn't only to focus on some time with Charlie, but because he needed the company, the conversation and the atmosphere that absorbed you the moment you walked through the door.

'I'm all done.' It was Steve, paint pot and utensils in hand, who stepped through the door next. 'It looks great, even if I do say so myself.'

'Thanks so much. Just a sec.' She nodded to her other customers. 'I'll come and check it out when I've served Ben.'

'I'll have to leave you to it,' Steve explained. 'I've got to get to my next job on the other side of town. Can't be late. I'll do a runner now in case you hate the sign,' he teased.

'Thank you.' She had no doubt she'd love it. She was itching to sneak a peek, having seen it when 'The Café at the End of' had been the only words painted. But the customers came first.

'Hello, Ben. Hello, Charlie.' She went over to their table where the little boy and his dad sat, Charlie still wearing his favourite red coat despite the spring weather. He was racing a miniature toy car up and down the table top. 'What can I get you this morning?'

'I'll take a berry smoothie please,' said Ben. A pleasant

man, an architect by trade, Jo imagined he was one of those people you could never be mad at. Not like Steve, who she reckoned could rile someone enough to make them yell – not that he'd managed it with her yet. But Ben seemed such a softie – someone who would bend over backwards for others whether it suited him or not.

'And for you, Charlie?'

'Berry smoothie too, please,' he answered politely. Whatever job Ben was doing with fatherhood, he was at least teaching his child good manners. And being present as a dad earnt brownie points in Jo's book. Her own dad had done a runner. Her mum had upped and left eventually. Even her siblings had fled far away from here. Somebody who went the distance was to be admired.

'That's very polite,' Jo commended. 'An extra-large scoop of ice-cream for you in your smoothie, I think.'

Charlie's eyes widened. 'Really?'

'If it's OK with your dad.'

'Of course it is,' said Ben. 'And we'll take two of your miniature rhubarb crumbles as well. May as well get the full sugar hit, eh?'

'Good point. Charlie can run it off on the beach later.'

'Can we build a sandcastle?' he asked his dad, eyes lighting up again.

Ben shrugged. 'I don't see why not.'

Jo left them making plans to build a castle with a moat as she went to sort their order. With the crumbles warming, she squirted honey into two glasses, revolving the vessels as she did so to coat the sides. She blended mixed berries, banana, yogurt and ice-cream, poured the mixture into the glasses, and before the crumbles were ready she sneaked out to look at the sign Steve had finished.

She stood right back against the white fence and with the sun behind her, the blue cursive writing that said 'The Café at the End of the Pier' stood out brilliantly. She felt a warm sensation run right through her body, as though this were another step forwards to completely taking over this place. This truly signified a new beginning.

Back inside, she took the crumbles and drinks over to Ben's table.

'Is he OK there?' Ben nodded towards the far corner where Charlie was playing with three toy cars. By the sounds he was making the cars were going pretty fast – and there were a few crashes along the way. 'If it's too annoying, I'll make him sit back down, but it's like he's got ants in his pants most days.'

'He's fine. We're not too busy yet.' Molly and Arthur had prided themselves in making this café a part of the community and Jo intended to keep it that way. She'd kept the decks of playing cards stored on the cubby shelves next to the till, the battered chess board and surprisingly intact set of chess pieces, and a stack of scrap paper with pots of crayons in a rainbow of colours that were popular with some of their youngest customers.

'Thanks. I appreciate it. He'll come running when he eventually sees our food and drinks are here.'

'You look exhausted.' Jo set down a couple of straws for the smoothies. 'If you don't mind me saying.'

'Not at all,' he assured her, 'because I am.'

'It must be full on with a young one to look after.'

'I don't mind, he's pretty good most of the time.'

'Does his mum have him much?' Jo already knew the answer from Molly, although she didn't know the story behind it.

'She's having him more and more lately, which is great, although . . . well, it's hard.'

Jo swished her hands in front of her. 'I'm sorry, I'm being nosy.' She turned to go but he stopped her.

'You're not being too nosy. In fact, it's nice to talk to an adult for a change. I usually have Charlie 24/7 and there are only so many games of cars you can play and silly voices you can use.'

With his dark, messy hair that didn't seem to have any kind of parting, and deep-set eyes that spoke of kindness, Ben was one of her favourite customers and she never minded taking the time to talk to him.

Without prompting Ben seemed to want to share his troubles. 'My wife, Lorna, has had a lot of problems along the way with depression. She didn't cope very well when Charlie was first born, and it gradually got worse and worse until, one day, she upped and left.'

'Oh Ben, I'm so sorry.'

He dismissed her concern. 'It was a few years ago now, and while I'm fine, it's Charlie I feel for.'

Jo didn't sit at the table but leaned against the wood and looked over at Charlie. 'My dad left when I was little, and it was really hard. Mum definitely has her faults, but at least she was there. You say Lorna has started to become more involved?'

'She has him a couple of days a week, which gives me a real break. At first I didn't trust her.' He hesitated. 'She had a breakdown when he was little and it happened when Charlie was with her.'

'Does Charlie remember it?'

'No, he was far too young, but I panic it'll happen again.'

Jo saw his concern in the way his brows knitted together, the way he toyed with his spoon but hadn't even broken the surface of the crumble to let the heat escape. 'It's good she's in his life, I hope it all works out for you.' She hadn't been in Salthaven all that long but already she'd come to care about these people.

'Fingers crossed. It's a lonely old life on my own.'

'Well, for what it's worth, I think you're doing a wonderful job with Charlie. He's a lovely little boy and has very good manners.'

Jo left Ben and Charlie to it. Her customers for the rest of the day were a mixture of people from the adjacent towns to Salthaven and locals she could have a longer chat with. She was getting used to this being a big part of the job, and multi-tasking was becoming even more familiar as she whipped up snacks and made drinks while conversation flowed on, covering weather, surfing, fishing, town events and the upcoming May Day at the café when tourists would descend in droves – a precursor for what to expect in the summer months. Bea and Grant from the fish and chip shop came and admired the new sign for the café, the sign that immediately lifted the whole feel of the place beneath the spring sunshine. Rain was forecast tomorrow, but they'd been lucky and Steve had already painted the insides and outsides of the window frames. Once again The Café at the End of the Pier was a stunning icon, and Jo couldn't be more proud.

After the café closed and Jo finished cleaning up, she dashed home, showered, changed and walked down the hill, then turned left along the cobbled streets that marked the start of the town, at the centre of which was the Salthaven Arms, the local pub that was older than all of Salthaven's inhabitants. Salthaven-on-Sea's biggest draw was the beach and pier, but a close second was the picturesque town centre, with its walkways lacing together shops, some modern, others decades old.

She found Melissa commandeering a table out front. All the others were full, people wanting to make the most of the weather tonight before the downpour arrived tomorrow.

Jo had struck up a good friendship with Melissa, a former classmate who'd never left Salthaven, and they regularly met up for drinks or headed out to see a movie. Melissa was big on going out on a Saturday night given her job at the post office, which thankfully never opened on a Sunday. 'And long may it stay that way,' she'd said the last time they were out on the town.

With Jo guarding the table, Melissa made her way to the bar and returned with two glasses of Prosecco. They chinked glasses.

'Cheers,' said Jo. 'To the end of another hectic week – for you, at least. I'm in tomorrow.'

'How are you coping with working seven days a week?'

'I'm doing five and a half days – Molly and Arthur usually do Sunday mornings for me, as well as Tuesdays. Those are the quietest times and between them they manage well. I think they enjoy it too.'

'Do you think they're checking up on you?'

'Not at all, but it's always been their baby. They joke that I employ them now, rather than the other way round. I think eventually I'd like to get another person in but for now, I'm kind of buzzing with it.'

They chatted about the town, people from school who'd

stayed put, those who'd ventured off to other cities; some to London, others as far afield as Canada. They talked about James, Melissa's boyfriend of two years. When Jo spotted Matt she waved over to him, but Melissa soon had her attention again.

'James has asked me to move in with him.'

'Really? How do you feel?'

'I would've moved in with him after our first date if I'd had my way.'

'You won't be needing my "café of love", that's for sure.' She'd already been busy thinking about who she could set up first, which lonely hearts she could match, and she'd wavered between possibilities until she'd come up with the perfect idea. Out of her daydream she asked, 'Are you moving into his place or yours?'

'His, I think.' Her curly red hair shone beneath the sunshine that crept into the courtyard in front of the pub. 'He has a house; I have a flat. I guess it makes sense. And his house is a cute terraced property this side of town, closer to the post office than I am now, so even in the winter it's easily walkable.'

'That's great, Melissa. I'm so pleased for you.'

'Thanks.' She sipped her drink, her eyes settling on Jo. 'I hear Harry is back in town.'

Jo's drink didn't go down quite as well as it might have done. 'How did you know?'

'Maisy, who I work with, saw him in here last week. She's got a crush on him.' When Jo rolled her eyes she probed some more. 'What happened with you two anyway? You were love's young dream at one point. We were all jealous of you, and then all of a sudden he left town and you went off to Scotland.'

Jo sometimes forgot how small Salthaven-on-Sea was. 'He ended it rather suddenly.' She hadn't shared much with Melissa so far – his name hadn't come up until now, and she'd been glad to avoid the subject.

'Oh come on, you're not getting away with that as an explanation. Out with it, what really happened?'

'It was a long time ago.'

'Doesn't matter. Come on, a problem shared is a problem halved.'

And so, over another glass of Prosecco, Jo told Melissa everything.

Melissa listened quietly until she'd been told the entire story. 'Tilly never said a word, but I'm glad you had her to confide in. And I don't really know Harry very well, but I want to tie him up by the you-know-whats and make him suffer.'

'Thanks, that won't be necessary.'

'You must've been devastated.'

'I was. I got really drunk. On tequila.' She pulled a face. 'Haven't drunk it since.' She remembered it vividly: the tears, the wailing, and her mum finding her stumbling home after she'd sat on the beach on her own with nothing for company but the bottle of alcohol and a shot glass. That had been the night of the biggest row between her mum and her grandparents.

'Are you all right?' Melissa asked.

'Sorry, I was miles away.'

'It sounds as though it was a horrid time for you.'

'It was, but that was then. I'm fine now, don't you worry.' She hooked her hair behind her ear as the breeze whipped around the courtyard and she shivered. 'I'm seeing him on Monday night.'

'You're not! Oh, please tell me you're planning to do something wicked, like spit in his coffee?'

Jo giggled. 'No, he's my accountant.'

She threw her hands up in the air, incredulous. 'You're giving the man work? After what you just told me!'

'I didn't realise he worked for the firm when I made the appointment, but once I had his name I didn't want to change to see someone else. I'd rather control the meeting than bump into him when I least expect it.' And what Jo couldn't bear was people who ran out when the going got tough. She'd always prided herself on not being like that.

'Fair enough. Oh God, you don't want him back do you? Because I'm here to tell you that sometimes it's better to stay single.'

'Don't worry, I have no intention of ever repeating the same mistake.' Although she had to admit, she did wonder whether he still looked as good as he had when they'd been together. She wondered whether being a grown-up and forging a responsible career suited him, whether she'd be attracted to him all over again. Part of her felt excited about seeing him, another part was terrified, and there was a third part that would always be asking – what if things had been different?

'Anyway, enough about loser ex-boyfriends,' Melissa urged, noticing her friend's attention drawn elsewhere. 'Tell me, have you put your other plans for the café into action yet?'

'You mean, since I tried to hold a "night of love" on Valentine's Day and fell spectacularly on my face at the first hurdle when nobody turned up? No.'

Melissa sipped her Prosecco, careful not to let the strawberry piece at the bottom fall into her mouth. 'Hardly your fault. The storm kept people away, or lack of awareness. Whatever. I'm a hopeless romantic, and if I wasn't attached I'd want to be your first recruit.'

'That would be fun.'

'I'm far too happy with James. So tell me, who will be the first victim of Cupid's arrow?'

Jo let the coolness of the Prosecco slip smoothly down her throat. 'I do have someone in mind.' She leant in conspiratorially because the thought had been brewing in her mind for a while now. 'You know Ben, the architect?'

'Oh yes,' Melissa whispered. 'The one whose wife upped and left him and his son. He's cute.'

'He is, and . . . well, I think I might have the perfect match for him.'

Melissa's eyes lit up, and as they called it a night and crossed the cobbled courtyard together, Jo told her everything.

5

First thing Monday morning, before the sun could move round and shine into her bedroom window, Jo double-checked she had all the papers ready for her appointment with the accountant. The only way she could think about Harry was in his official capacity, in the hope it would keep her calm before she saw him.

She wondered if Harry had seen her name yet. She wondered if he was having the same thoughts as her, worried about how they might react to one another after all this time. She wondered if he realised that, on the scale of break-ups, theirs had been one of the worst.

Harry and Jo had dated for four years and they'd been happy for every one of those days – or at least that's what Jo had thought. It had been her twenty-fifth birthday, and as well as flowers from her grandparents, gifts from the Body Shop, and tickets to go and see Robbie Williams playing at Wembley, Jo had received a postcard. But not one of those glorious sunny scenes showing happy holiday makers or a gorgeous snow scene with sleigh rides, but a plain, boring, not even a hundred per cent white, postcard. And on the left hand side, next to her address, was a message from Harry. All it had said was, 'I think we need to break up. I'm sorry. Harry.'

He hadn't had the guts to hand-deliver it. And it had a second class stamp! He hadn't even thought her worthy of being treated to first class.

At first, she'd thought it was a joke, but after trying in vain to contact Harry by phone for the next hour, she realised it was the real deal. She'd kept it from her grandparents. They didn't need the worry. They'd witnessed enough upset in Sasha's life when it came to men. So she phoned Tilly, who came straight over and kept Jo company for the next three days. Tilly went to work, Jo called in sick to the primary school in the next town where she'd worked since graduating, and every evening Tilly brought round a supply of junk food and DVDs, which they watched with Jo intermittently sobbing on her friend's shoulder.

One day Tilly had come over after work and announced she'd been offered a marketing manager's job up in Edinburgh. Jo was heartbroken, until Tilly had suggested Jo come with her. Jo hadn't wanted to run away, so Tilly had struck a deal with her. If Jo could land a job in Edinburgh then she'd come too – it would be an adventure – and if she couldn't, then she'd stick with her job here and deal with the fallout from her break-up. Jo's teaching skills had, of course, been snapped up the second she put the feelers out and almost six years ago Jo had moved up to Scotland. And as for Harry – well, she'd never had to face him again. As well as sending a postcard to break up with her, he'd left town to go backpacking around Europe.

Now, in the café, with a leather document case bulging with papers, Jo knew it was time to put the past out of her mind and get on with work, so she stowed everything in the top cupboard in the kitchen. Geoff, a fisherman dedicated to his hobby, came in for his usual extra-large cup of black tea that Jo knew he took to the end of the pier with him and sipped as he got ready for his morning session and waited for a bite. Next up was Valerie, a woman who'd recently moved to Salthaven, who ordered camomile tea while chattering along with her friend about making the most of the last year of her forties and how she wanted to master something called the 'crow pose' in yoga before she reached the big 5-0.

Jo had only served a handful of other customers when Molly and Arthur came in.

'Your mum has been in touch.' Arthur's eyes didn't meet hers. They rarely did when they were discussing her mum. It was as though he thought distancing himself from the daughter he didn't seem to understand would make the strained relationship easier to bear.

'How is she?' Jo didn't let on that she'd already spoken to her, but she didn't have to.

'You know how she is, she told us she'd spoken with you.'

'Ah.'

'There's no need to keep it from us,' said Molly. 'She's your mum.'

And she's your daughter, she wanted to say.

'She's worried about you giving up your career for us.'

Jo lifted a slice of flapjack onto a plate and then put the glass lid back over the top of the rest of the golden treats. 'I'm doing it for me, not for anyone else. I told her that.'

'But you are doing it for us,' said Arthur.

Jo took the flapjack over to Vince along with a bowl of freshly balled watermelon, as Molly and Arthur settled themselves on the window seat with their coffees – they'd made them themselves even though Jo had tried to suggest they were customers.

When Jo joined them she said, 'If it weren't for you two, I wouldn't have come, no. But I needed a change, and the longer I stay here the more I know it's right. Mum doesn't see it because she's never felt the same way about Salthaven as I do.' She didn't miss the glow of pride from both her grandparents. 'I knew she'd call you as soon as she found out what was going on.'

'She didn't yell at us, that's a start,' said Molly, hiding behind her coffee.

'She isn't capable of yelling,' said Arthur. 'She's got your soft voice.' He smiled at his wife. 'Sometimes I wish she'd visit so we could talk properly.'

It was the first time he'd admitted there was even a problem between the three of them. Usually he tried to sweep it away like the sand that came into the café every summer. Maybe having more time on his hands was making him reflect on their relationship with their only daughter.

'She wasn't overly happy about you taking over the café permanently,' said Molly. 'You'd think she'd be pleased to keep it in the family. When she was little she loved coming here. She'd come in every day, help out, mop up spills on the tabletops, use a dustpan and brush, crouch down and pick up any stray crumbs. Oh, she was funny! Every time the door opened, even if not a speck of dirt came in, she'd still be down there sweeping up.'

Arthur put a hand on Molly's and both of their smiles faded. 'She's moved on.'

Sometimes Jo wanted to jump up and down and stamp

74

her feet at all of them. She wanted to say that just because people moved on it didn't mean they forgot their roots or that they didn't care. Gramps was talking like it was the end of something, as if her mum was never coming back and was no longer a real part of their lives.

'I'm trying to persuade her to come over for a holiday,' said Jo.

'She has the sun and the heat in Puerto Pollensa,' Arthur harrumphed. 'I doubt Salthaven will get much of a look in. When was the last time she bothered to come here?'

Jo couldn't actually remember. Sasha had flown to Edinburgh last year to see Jo and they'd had fun exploring the city together, but her mum hadn't ventured down to the south coast that time – or even the time before that, when Jo had met up with her in London for the day when she'd had a wedding to go to.

'She sent a postcard – to all of us.' Remembering, Jo grabbed the card from the board and took it over to Molly and Arthur as Matt appeared with the delivery of today's box of fruit and vegetables. 'Hey, Matt.'

'Hello, Jo. Molly, Arthur, great to see you.' He handed the box over to Jo and had a chat with her grandparents, who hadn't even picked up the postcard from the table in front of them yet.

Jo took the box out to the kitchen and unpacked. There were small cauliflowers, onions, a nice selection of salad leaves and another sweet-smelling melon.

'They're looking well,' said Matt, following her into the kitchen. He kept his voice low, knowing Molly and Arthur well enough to realise they hated being watched over, even at their age. 'Arthur looks a lot less tired, that's for sure.'

'He does. He had another check-up last week and everything is going really well.' She nodded over to them and Matt looked in the same direction. 'They're almost looking like customers, sitting down. When I first arrived they could barely let me get on with things without wanting to help.'

'Or hinder,' he added.

'Exactly.'

'How did you get on with the accountant?'

Jo had put Harry right to the back of her mind, her mum taking his place at the forefront of her thoughts, but now she was reminded of what lay in store for her after closing. 'The appointment is tonight.'

'Hopefully they'll look after you.'

Once again Jo was tempted to cancel, but she fought the urge. After the way Harry had ended things she hoped this would be as torturous for him as it would be for her. She also wanted him to know that he hadn't completely broken her. She'd picked herself up and got on with her life, and she was doing fine, thank you very much. She might be single, but she was together and a much more confident version of the girl who'd left the beach behind for a time.

After Matt left, Jo went over to her grandparents who had at last read the postcard. Molly set it on the table in front of them both.

'When I spoke to her she was sitting right there,' said Jo, pointing at the photo on the front depicting the idyllic harbour scene: boats bobbing on the water, a tiny strip with cafés and outside tables next to it. 'You two could treat yourselves, go over for a holiday. You haven't seen where she lives yet.'

Gramps shook his head. 'Your gran couldn't get me on a plane to go and see you in Edinburgh, so there's no way Sasha can persuade me to go even further, to another country.'

'The world's your oyster now, Gramps.' Jo tried to make light of it and gloss over the real reason he'd never go, which was that none of them had any idea how the three of them were supposed to exist in the same town, let alone the same four walls. 'You're retired. It's time to start treating yourselves a bit more.'

'We do have some savings,' Molly urged, but looking at her husband, added, 'but I don't think it's a good idea. There's Arthur's health to consider for a start. And travel insurance can be astronomical for people our age.'

Excuses, excuses, thought Jo. They weren't reasons. Gran and Gramps were grasping at anything that would prevent them from going. They were all as stubborn as each other. Or at least two of them were: Sasha and Arthur. They were different in a lot of ways, but far too similar in others.

'Just think about it,' she said.

'Did we put pressure on you?' Molly asked as Jo walked away towards the counter. 'Honestly?'

Jo turned straight back. 'You didn't put any pressure on me that wasn't completely welcome. I mean it.' She looked at both of them in turn. 'I'm a romantic, and sometimes I daydream, but the practical side of me that I got from Mum – and from you, Gramps – went through my decision logically. You know me – I don't walk away when the going gets tough. When I chose to move to Scotland I only did it because there was an opportunity for me there. And it's the same here. I wasn't completely happy teaching. I was content enough for a long time, but a passion was missing and the second you suggested I come here, it's like you took a match and lit the flame. This is where I want to be, and it's where I want to stay.'

Molly squeezed her hand, reassured they'd done the right thing, and when Angie made an appearance Jo left them all to catch up as she served her next customer.

'Hello, what can I get for you?' The man wasn't a regular, and dressed in a suit and tie he looked preoccupied.

'I'll take a black coffee please.'

'Coming right up. Anything else?'

'That'll be all, thank you.' He looked around the café. 'Nice place you have here.'

'Thank you.'

His gaze wasn't on her but still roaming the interior, and Jo felt a surge of pride that even visitors were taking a special interest in the place. She made the black coffee, took payment and watched as he settled himself at the back of the room and tapped away on his iPad, looking up every now and then. But she was too busy with everyone else coming in and chattering as they placed their order that she had no time to wonder what his story was. He was tall, classically dark and kind of handsome, with a chiselled jaw and a well-groomed appearance, and when he left she assumed Salthaven had been a brief respite on a journey to somewhere else.

Molly and Arthur hung around in the café for longer than Jo had expected, but continued to take a backseat. It was rather nice to have them in the wings, watching on as she kept their regulars happy and saw to anyone new who came in. It also gave them a chance to catch up with everyone as they came and went from the café, and she had a sneaking suspicion that was their main motive. The sense of community in Salthaven was like nothing else Jo had ever experienced, and she hoped her mum was finding some kind of home out there in Spain with Stuart. They both seemed happy, at any rate, but Jo knew that if it were she and her mum who were fighting, the tension would be on her mind constantly, marring everything else she did. She hated conflict and preferred to iron it out, rather than let it simmer and worsen.

At the end of the day, as Jo's feet began to hurt and the sun hovered low on the horizon as she turned the sign to 'Closed', her heart began to pound at the enormity of seeing Harry again. She'd come back to Salthaven without giving him more than a passing thought, because she hadn't expected him to be here. Ever since he'd sent that postcard, Jo had assumed Salthaven was too small for Harry Sadler.

She wiped down every table. She replenished napkin dispensers and set the dishwasher onto its final cycle for the day. She wiped down the front of the glass display cabinet where tiny fingerprints had explored the bottom shelf, while adult hands had perused the top. She was about to dunk the mop into a bucket of soapy water and make a start on the floor when a figure at the door told her the wait was over.

It was Harry.

She turned the key and, with a bit of manoeuvring, pulled open the door that had begun to stick yet again.

'Hello, Harry.' She managed a small smile.

'It's good to see you, Jo.'

She stared a moment longer, taking in the short cropped hair, darker than she remembered, the absence of the earring in his left earlobe that he'd had since they started going out all those years ago, the filling out of a twenty-something into this responsible-looking man standing there in a shirt and tie, briefcase clasped in one hand. 'Corporate' and 'Harry' were two words she'd never have put in the same sentence before now.

She stood back. 'Come in.'

When he passed she caught a waft of aftershave, a woody scent that he'd used back when they'd dated and was much more subtle than the Lynx all the boys at school had been wearing. It amused her and, rather than being upset, it helped to lessen her nerves.

'Can I get you a coffee?' They had plenty of paperwork to go through but she needed a distraction first – something to do with her hands. And, more than that, she wanted to be kind. She wanted to rise above what had happened before.

'Black, no sugar. Thanks.' He set his briefcase down on one of the tables. 'Sorry I'm early, I just finished another appointment and it didn't make sense to go back to the office for twenty minutes.'

'Not a problem,' she called from the kitchen, as she made his coffee and a black tea for herself.

'You're looking well, Jo.'

'Thanks,' she said, unsure whether he had heard her or not. She tried to stall on the other side of the door. It was usually open when customers were about, but she hadn't wanted him to see her close her eyes, take a deep breath in and let it out slowly before plastering a smile on her face and going back into the café.

She set the mugs down on the table and pulled out a

chair. He was looking good as well, but there was no way she was going to say it.

'I was surprised to see your name in my appointment schedule.' His briefcase stayed closed. 'I thought you'd left Salthaven for good.'

That's funny. She'd thought he'd done exactly the same thing. But here they both were.

'I'm really pleased to be back.' She offered no further explanation, didn't delve into his own reasons for being in the area. She stood up again, cursing herself for forgetting the paperwork. 'Let me go and get all my information and we'll get started.'

She retrieved the box of papers from the kitchen and prepared to see this appointment through, and for the next hour they went through the last tax return so Harry could explain it in full. Molly and Arthur had done their best, but, to be honest, Jo could tell that they didn't really know half of what they were talking about. They'd let the previous accountant take control, and while that had worked for them and they'd kept the business afloat, it wasn't the way Jo wanted to work. She liked to understand what items were on the statements and exactly what her responsibilities were when it came to the books. Jo made notes along the way as Harry patiently went through all the expenses that had been claimed over recent years, making Jo aware of extras she could and should be claiming, things that Molly and Arthur – or rather, their accountant – had mistakenly overlooked.

'It's not making a huge amount of money,' she admitted, 'but I think it'll begin to do a lot better now I've got my head around some of the expenses.'

When he smiled it showed the dimples in his cheeks

and he looked like the Harry of old. 'It's a lot to take in. From the previous tax returns we have here, and from what I've gone through with you tonight, I don't think Molly and Arthur were claiming for half the things they could've done.'

Jo shook her head. 'I've asked for receipts prior to tonight and either found them floating around somewhere or else Molly and Arthur have lost them.'

'Well, hopefully now you're more aware. And the sooner you get all your information to me in the tax year – as I suggested, once a month is ideal – the more time I'll have to consider your position and ensure additional expenses are claimed.' He sounded so formal. 'If in doubt about whether something is claimable, send it along to me anyway, and I'll look into it.'

'Thanks, I appreciate it.'

'Can I ask, what happened to teaching?'

'You can ask, but I might not tell.' When he shrugged she said, 'I needed a change of pace and I always wanted to come back here to Salthaven. It was a case of an opportunity falling into my lap, and I'm enjoying it. It's a lot of work, but it's worth it.' She didn't admit that, at first, she'd almost been in denial about what was involved in running a café. She'd had the impression of busy days filled with making drinks and snacks, and chatting to locals. She'd factored in the cleaning up, the planning, and the cooking involved, but she'd never really given the paperwork side any thought, much less coming to grips with accountancy terms and practices. When you had a business of your own, the authorities appeared to like nothing more than making you fill in countless forms or going through lengthy official processes. No wonder Molly and Arthur were exhausted.

'You always were organised.' He shut his briefcase with a satisfying clunk. 'You'll do well in this business. If anyone can make it work, it's you.'

Flattery would get him absolutely nowhere. She'd managed to conduct the appointment with confidence, at least outwardly, but the reminder he knew her on a more personal level made that same poise waver.

She tried to sound nonchalant. 'I never would've picked you as an accountant.' It had been bugging her ever since she'd got over the initial shock of hearing his name with the firm's secretary when she made the appointment. 'You always wanted to be a mechanic.'

'And I was a mechanic up until three years ago when I returned from travelling.'

'What made you change tack?'

'I still love tinkering with cars but I wanted to take a more corporate route. I got a traineeship with an accountancy firm in London and then, when a job came up down this way, I saw the chance to return to my roots.' A look passed between them. 'It's really good to see you, Jo.'

Hadn't he already said that?

'I'd better get on. I still have the floor to do.' She collected up the mugs and took them out to the kitchen.

'The board is getting really full.' When she returned to the café Harry, hands in pockets, was looking at the postcard collection. 'I remember when we used to come here for milkshakes and talk about exotic places we wanted to visit one day. I seem to remember Bali was top of my list and you quite fancied Portugal.'

Jo met his gaze properly for the first time tonight. 'And

I remember another type of postcard that pretty much made my world stop.'

Hands out of his pockets, one hand reached up and scraped across his jaw. 'I was wrong to do that to you.'

'Have you any idea what it was like for me?' She refused to let her voice wobble. 'It was bad enough that you ended things with us when I thought we were happy, but to do it on a postcard, on my birthday!'

He shook his head and she saw his regret, but she wasn't going to let him off the hook that easily.

'I'll never forgive myself for doing it, Jo. We were really serious, and I guess I freaked out. I've grown up a lot since then.' He cleared his throat as his excuses settled in the air. 'Would you rather I handed your account over to someone else at the firm? If you'd rather not work with me, that is.'

She thought about it. It would be easier. But then again, maybe he was the one it would be easier for. He'd be able to avoid her like he'd done back then. 'No, it's fine. It's all ancient history.' It was, but him being here had raked it all back up again.

He looked about to say something when there was a knock at the door and Steve peered in through the glass.

Jo opened up. 'Hey, Steve.'

'I brought those stencils over for you.'

'Ah yes, for the sign.'

He handed her a plastic box. 'There are a few in there that could be suitable – sea shells perhaps, even a surfboard if you like. Just let me know and I'll come and paint it on. I'll need to collect the stencils as soon as possible though – I borrowed them from a painter and decorator friend and he's down in Brixham tomorrow doing a café refurb.'

'Not a problem. Come in.'

He hesitated. 'I'm not interrupting?'

'No, don't be daft.' He was, but he had impeccable timing in Jo's opinion. 'This is Harry, my accountant. We've just been sorting through everything but we're done.' She couldn't even look at Harry now, who thankfully took his cue to leave.

'I'll be in touch, Jo.' He hovered, but when she didn't respond, her eyes glued to the stencils in the box, he left.

'He's your accountant?' Steve asked, once Harry was on his way and they'd sat at a table to go through the choices in front of her.

'That's right.'

'Looked like more than that to me, the way he had his eye on you.'

Jo suspected that despite his blond and brawn persona, not a lot got by Steve.

'Come on, out with it,' he probed.

'We used to date once upon a time.'

'That explains it. How long for?'

'A few years. Four to be exact.'

Steve whistled. 'You dumped him?'

'Why do you say that?'

'Because he's not looking at you as though he let you go, he's looking at you as though he wants to be the one to catch you.'

Was he? Was that why he'd taken the appointment, why he'd begun to apologise for what he'd done?

'Come on,' she said, putting Harry out of her mind. 'Let's choose a stencil so we can both get home.'

He let the issue go and after some debate Jo finally settled on sea shells for the sign. It was simple, fitted with the beach theme and it was the perfect accompaniment for the wording.

Steve turned in the doorway before he left. 'If you don't mind me saying, you look knackered.'

It raised a laugh anyway. 'You mean I look like crap?'

'That wasn't what I said.' He put a hand against her arm. 'Don't overdo it, eh? Running a business is hard, but you're doing a great job.'

When she closed the door and refilled the bucket with fresh hot water now that it had gone cold, she knew Steve was right. She was tired, and even the euphoria of running her own café couldn't bat it away this time.

And seeing Harry again hadn't helped either.

6

The weather had been unpredictable for the last week. Some days were bright and beautiful with nothing but clear blue skies, and others had been miserable and wetter than they'd seen in a long time. Rain had lashed the end of the pier the day after Jo's appointment with Harry and left behind gusty winds and ominous bruised clouds that had only begun to show signs of clearing this morning. Still, they matched Jo's mood now, as Monday morning came around yet again and the oven at the café had gone on the blink. She had to pay an emergency call-out fee to have it fixed, she couldn't do without it, and right now it felt as though the café was haemorrhaging money. She wasn't sure how many more unplanned expenses she'd be able to deal with. Last week she'd had to replace a stack of crockery that was chipped and stained, the week before that had been an electricity bill she'd somehow managed to miss, and receiving it in red was always so much worse.

But Jo was determined to stay positive as best she could and with the café quiet for now, it finally gave her the chance to focus on her plan to inject a little bit of magic into the lives of a couple of Salthaven locals. And at the same time it distracted her from Harry, who'd been on her mind more than she would've liked.

She took her early delivery of fruit and vegetables from Matt and they talked about the live band who'd played at the pub on Saturday night, Jo admiring the talents of the bass player but Matt insisting the guitarist had been the star focus. And when Jess came into the café, as she always did early every weekday morning, Jo's matchmaking mind was moving at warp speed.

Jess was perfect for Ben, but their lives never intersected – Jess was a weekday regular, Ben a weekend customer. Jess worked in the doctor's surgery in town while Ben worked either at home or in an office in the next town down the coast from here.

'Your door is sticking again,' Jess told Jo when she'd taken out her earbuds and tried to shut the café door behind her.

Jo shook her head. 'I'll need to get Steve onto it again. Our handyman,' she explained.

'I know, I've seen him around, either here or running in and out of the surf.'

Jo looked out in the hope of catching him as she sometimes did on weekday mornings around this time, even if the weather was hideous, but the sand was clear except for an elderly couple brave enough to walk their two chocolate Labradors. She'd have to text him instead.

'How was the run?' Jo asked. 'Miserable day for it.'

'At least it's not raining.' Dressed in SKINS and a running T-shirt, Jess's earbuds were plugged into her phone, which was safely tucked into a pouch fixed to her upper arm. 'It's a good way to start a Monday morning though. It takes a big storm to keep me away.'

'You put us all to shame,' said Jo. 'Come on, how far

did you go today?' She took position behind the counter and nodded hello to two customers she didn't know as they came in and perused the blackboard of specials and beverages. She noticed them checking out the postcard board too, trying to spot which places they'd been to and which they had on their bucket list.

'Ten kilometres, the last kilometre along the sand for an extra challenge,' Jess beamed, full of the runner's high, endorphins buzzing around like crazy.

'You make me feel guilty for never getting my heart rate out of the walking fitness zone.'

'Walking is one of the best exercises you can do. It's what I tell my patients.'

'I heard you have a walking group.'

'That's right.' Jess was spearheading the town's fitness initiative. 'Every Sunday morning, whoever wants to come along meets at the start of the pier beneath the signposts. I take everyone on a circuit of the town and finish by taking the hill up away from the pier and come back down on the opposite side.'

Jo had seen groups gathering at the signposts directing people to the café, the summer supply shop, the fish and chippery and the ice-cream place. She'd giggled the first time she'd overheard some of the walkers in the café post-exercise session. They'd covered seven and a half kilometres and were sitting there eating brownies or cookies as though they'd done a marathon.

'The usual?' Jo asked as Jess filled a glass of water from the complementary jug at the side of the room. Today she'd added some slices of cucumber to the water to make it extra refreshing.

'Please,' Jess answered. 'And what's that wonderful smell?'

'That'll be the cheese and bacon quiches I've popped in the oven.' It may have cost a bit, but at least the call out had meant the oven was fixed in no time this morning.

'I'll grab one to take away if they'll be ready in the next ten minutes.'

Jo checked her watch. 'They will be. I'll pop one in a cardboard box for you. Do you want me to add some salad too?'

'That would be amazing. I never get a chance to make my lunch. I really should.'

'I think the run and the full day at work is enough, don't you? When do you ever get five minutes to yourself?'

'I don't.'

'You need to. Do you go out much?' She needed to know Jess's availability if her plan was going to work. Cupid's arrow was almost ready to fire, but she needed to make sure she had at least tried to line up the target first.

'My evenings are mostly spent slumped in front of the television,' Jess admitted. 'Embarrassing, really. But I don't have much time for anything other than work. There are only two doctors at the surgery and our work-load is terrible. We're trying to get another person, at least part-time, but you know what it's like. It's all about fund-ing, which nobody has much of these days.'

Jo found the ingredients to make the strawberry smoothie, the post-workout drink Jess always favoured each time she stopped off after her run. 'I'm usually exhausted after the café, so the television is my only com-pany too. Apart from the nights Molly likes to feed me up with her home cooking, or Saturday nights when my friend Melissa drags me to the pub. You should come with us one time, if you'd like.'

'Thanks, Jo. I might take you up on that.'

Jo finished making the smoothie, slotted a plastic lid over the takeaway cup and handed it to Jess.

'There are so many now.' Jess began perusing the post-cards board. 'Sadly not many from me.'

'Check this one out.' Jo retrieved another postcard from beside the till. 'It was on the mat this morning.'

'Hamilton Island. Where's that?' She peered closer. 'The Whitsundays, Australia. Wow, I'll bet it's gorgeous there. May I?' When Jo nodded she turned it over to read the words. 'It's from Andrea . . . and she's engaged!'

'I met both of them a few times,' said Jo, 'and it's lovely that people are still sending postcards to the café even though it's me running the place and not Gran and Gramps.'

'Ah, but it's still the same café and you're one of us now, Jo.'

Her heart warmed hearing it from a local. 'I feel like I am.'

Jess sighed. 'I knew it wouldn't be long for Andrea and Toby. They've been together a while and are perfect for each other.'

Jo knew two other people who fitted that description and it was on the tip of her tongue to say something, but she kept quiet and just hoped her plan would work. Jess needed something more in her life than work, and seeing her reaction to someone else's happy ending proved it.

Jo took a pin from the very top of the board, pushed it into the card and fixed it in place, the beautiful blue set against the lush green palm trees brightening the dull day here on the south coast of England.

After Jess left with a takeaway quiche, Jo texted Steve about the door and Steve, being Steve, agreed to come over tonight after he'd finished at the building site. With the café quiet she looked at a few more of the postcards. One in particular caught her eye. Arguably one of the most gorgeous winter scenes Jo had ever been shown, it was from Aspen, Colorado, depicting a picture-perfect street covered in snow, with lamp posts festooned with green foliage and red ribbons, and a horse-drawn carriage with a couple tucked beneath blankets, huddled together.

She thought about Jess again. Jess, the hardworking local doctor, fit and healthy, friendly and fun, and categorically single. Jess, the beautiful woman who deserved to find happiness.

With the café quiet for now and her mischievous streak desperate to escape, Jo took out the special postcards she'd ordered to set the wheels of her plan in motion. She picked up the black calligraphy pen she'd bought especially and, after a little practice on a scrap piece of paper, it was time to pen the first invite.

Since her idea had first hatched after the Valentine's Day debacle, Jo had been too busy to get going with it, but now, filled with anticipation and a certain level of nerves, she was ready. Both Jess and Ben were lonely, both were too busy with everyday life to even look up for a minute and wonder what they could add to the mix to make themselves happy, and it was time for Jo to give them a little nudge.

She penned the postcards with a date and time on them – set next Saturday evening when neither Ben nor Jess would be at work, and if babysitters were an issue for Ben, Jo was sure someone would stand in. It would be a blind date and she hoped both of them would be willing to play along. She added a message on each postcard that said 'Come to The Café at the End of the Pier to find new love', and with a little giggle at her masterplan she popped the cards into matching red envelopes just as the bell at the door tinkled.

Steve came in, toolbox in one hand, his other scraping the hair back from his forehead. 'I'm early, I thought I'd nip here in my lunch hour.'

'You're a lifesaver.' She watched as he tried to shut the door and found it sticking much in the same way as it had before. 'My shoulder is bearing the brunt of it again.' And without Steve's timely help and availability her cash flow would be suffering too with another expense. He charged reasonable rates for everything he did and quite often threw in little extras, like today, for free. Jo wasn't sure where the café would be without his help. She certainly wasn't very hands on when it came to anything involving a screwdriver or a hammer.

'Right, well, we can't have that, can we?' he winked, bending down to take out a block of wood wrapped in sandpaper. 'Must be the warmer temperatures. I'll sand a bit more this time, and it looks like the bottom hinge could do with tightening. It won't take me long.'

She thanked him again and smiled at Angie, who'd appeared in the doorway and managed to squeeze her way past. Thankful not to be rushed off her feet, Jo could let Angie commandeer her time for a chat, although now she'd written the first invites, the red envelopes were almost burning a hole in her pocket.

7

May Day was a total washout. Surly black clouds hovered over the pier and made the sea look the colour of ebony. Rain pelted the windows of the café and drenched anyone who dared venture outside, while angry waves frothed as they rose and then thundered against the shore.

'I don't think today is going to see business booming.' Jo moved away from the window, over to where Molly and Arthur were warming their hands on cups of tea. 'What happened to spring?'

'What are you talking about?' Arthur chuckled. 'This is traditional British bank holiday weather!'

'He's brave,' said Molly as she noticed a dog walker battling his way across the sand, clutching the top of his hood to make some kind of shelter.

'Silly, more like,' Arthur replied. 'I'm only glad we got here before the heavens opened. Even the seagulls seem to have hidden today. And the dancing around the maypole event on the field at the top of the hill is cancelled. Shame, the kids love it.'

'I loved it when I was little, too.' She wished she could be pragmatic about all this but she'd pictured glorious sunshine bathing the café the entire day, kids running along the wooden planks with ice-cream wobbling precariously in cones held in their tiny hands, her not having a chance to sit down because the day marked the start of a wonderful tourist season.

Molly and Arthur kept her company for most of the morning, but even they tired of the gloomy weather enveloping the entire pier and the lack of locals coming in for a chat, so they left her to it before lunch.

Customers trickled in for the rest of the day but all it did was remind Jo of how this wasn't what she'd anticipated. She'd thought of today as being a time for T-shirts and flip-flops, the scent of sunscreen. She hadn't imagined long faces, dripping coats and footwear that left dirty marks on the café floor. Even the vases of daffodils she'd positioned around the café couldn't cheer customers up, and when Matt made an unexpected visit Jo was slumped against the counter for the first time since she'd arrived in Salthaven-on-Sea.

'You look about as miserable as the weather out there.' He shut the door behind him.

'What are you doing here?' He'd roused a smile. 'This is your day off, isn't it?'

A little girl followed him inside. She was so adorable that Jo didn't mind a jot that her cerise pink wellies left little footprints from the door mat to the table she chose. Bundled up in a matching pink body warmer with a roll neck jumper, her chestnut curls tumbled across her shoulders.

'Poppy here was all set to dance around the maypole up on the field,' Matt explained. 'We'd planned it ages ago, didn't we?' The girl beamed back at him and nodded, a flush to her cheeks hinting at her shyness. Matt leaned closer to Jo so only she could hear. 'I'm hoping you have something really naughty on the menu so it distracts her. I promised her mum I'd take her today and I want to return a happy kid if I can.'

'Is she yours?' There was definitely a resemblance.

'She's my sister Anna's daughter and with a new baby on the way, Anna is exhausted.'

How kind of him to help out. Jo wasn't sure many men would do the same, especially single men who rarely took a day off from the busyness of the family farm as it was. 'Leave it to me.' She moved closer to Poppy and crouched down to her level. 'I'm betting you know a lot about fruit and vegetables.' When Poppy nodded Jo asked, 'Do you eat plums?'

The little girl found her voice and her eyes widened. 'I love plums.'

'Well, this morning I was up bright and early and I made chocolate plum cake.' She had Poppy's attention. 'Would you like some?'

Poppy looked at Matt as he sat down in the chair opposite his niece.

'We'll take two helpings please,' he said.

'Would you like chocolate sauce with it?'

Matt laughed. 'I don't think you even need to ask.'

Jo went about warming the cake. She melted chocolate pieces in a bowl over a pan of water, added cream, sugar and water, and when it was done she poured some over each portion of cake.

She'd only just set the plates down when Steve came into the café, along with a blonde Jo hadn't seen him with before. They settled themselves at a table in the middle and Jo took their order for coffees and a slice of the chocolate and plum cake to share. She'd almost teased Steve about his wanting to be healthy and keep his body fit and toned, but she wasn't sure whether her new audience would appreciate the overfamiliarity.

By late afternoon, as the rain continued to lash down over Salthaven-on-Sea, and with no customers for over an hour, Jo made the decision to shut the café early. She took her time clearing up and for once it was nice not to rush. With Melissa unable to make the pub until later, Jo jotted down some more ideas for her plan.

To create a night of love at the café, she needed to conjure up a romantic ambience. She sketched out what she thought she might like. In her mind, she wanted to turn the far right corner, away from all the other tables, into the venue for the blind dates she was going to set up. She wanted to decorate the table with flowers and candles, and surround it with some kind of inside bower that would give privacy and add to the theme of the event. She wasn't sure how it would work, she needed something she could assemble and disassemble with minimum fuss, but this was the gist of it. And now she'd furthered her plans, she was all the more excited.

By the time Jo left the café and locked up, the clouds had parted, the rain had eased and a light drizzle mixed with salty sea spray followed her as she made her way to the end of the pier and across the road towards town.

In the pub she found Melissa sitting at the table closest to the fire that was roaring today as though it were winter, not spring. 'What's that you're drinking?'

'It's Billy's May Day punch.' Melissa lifted her glass and recalled the ingredients the landlord had used. 'He told me it has fresh strawberries, white wine, lemonade and some other herby ingredient I can't actually remember the name of. As soon as I heard it had wine in it, I was sold.'

Jo hung her coat on the back of her chair and when Billy walked past with glasses gathered between his fingers she accepted the offer of a May Day punch for herself.

The warmth of the fire took away the chill that seemed to have settled in her body all day and the punch wasn't half bad.

'Business slow today?' Melissa asked.

'So slow I was actually bored at one point. It's the first time I've been able to say that since I arrived in Salthaven.'

'That's very unlike you, or the café.'

'I know. The weather is atrocious.'

'It's the bank holiday jinx,' said Melissa. 'I had a great day off, didn't leave the house all day.'

'Don't tell me, James was with you.' Jo felt a small pang of jealousy. Cold, rainy days were always so much better when you had someone to share them with. When she'd been with Harry she remembered many a winter's day when they wouldn't see another soul, snuggled up and content with each other's company. She could tell that some people had come to the café today, despite having to battle the weather, because they didn't want to be alone, and she knew what that felt like.

'He wasn't, actually. He's away until tomorrow, visiting his parents in Wales. But I enjoyed the space on my own, making the most of it before we move in.'

As talk changed to Melissa's plans with James, they moved away from the fire.

'That's better,' said Melissa. 'The fire's a bit much now I'm completely dry.'

Jo's coat was dry and warm too as she rehung it on

another chair. Unfortunately, when she sipped her punch she turned her head and from their new position fell right into Harry's line of vision, as though thinking about him had made him appear from nowhere. He was over at the pool table and there was no hiding now; he'd seen her and was making his way over.

'Great to see you, Jo.' He stopped at their table, pool cue in his hand. 'Awful bank holiday weather isn't it?'

In a work situation she'd been prepared to see him, but now, on a social level, it was completely different. 'Not good for business.'

'I can imagine.'

'Harry, this is Melissa – you might remember her?'

Melissa said a terse hello as Harry confirmed that of course he did. And when conversation didn't really get off the ground he took the hint and went back to his mates.

'He's got a nerve after what he did to you.'

Jo shook her head. 'It was a long time ago. I've moved on.' But in the corner of her eye Jo knew he was still looking over at them every now and then. And she was annoyed that he was already beginning to get under her skin, whether it was in a purely platonic way or not.

They left the pub long before closing, as Jo wanted to get an early night so she was up and ready for her one and only full day off tomorrow. And, truth be told, Harry had looked over one too many times, prompting her to down the remains of her drink, stand and pull on her coat, surprising Melissa with their sudden departure.

They walked part of the way together, thankful that even the drizzle had finished for now. After saying goodbye Jo reached the main road opposite the promenade and crossed over to walk by the little boating lake adjacent to one of the big hotels. As a kid she'd spent hours down here with Nicholas and Timothy. They'd launched their wooden toy boats onto the water and watched as the breeze caught the sails and took the vessels on their own journey. She walked past the pier and then crossed back again at a laneway that led up to town, the sweet shop still on the same corner as it had always been. She and Harry had come here on their first date to pick up sweets before they went to see a movie at the tiny cinema at the edge of town.

Jo turned round with the shop behind her so she could see the pier once more. She saw the ice-creamery, the end of the structure where fishermen sat, the fish and chip shop and the signpost under which she'd had her first kiss with Harry. It'd been on a day when she'd watched him surfing and he'd tasted of the ocean, the sun and everything that was good in the world. She'd thought then that they would always be together, but, like many first loves, they'd gone their separate ways. She still couldn't believe both of them were back in Salthaven-on-Sea and she wasn't sure it was a good thing. She wasn't even convinced she should be keeping him as her accountant, but she'd been allocated him because he was still building up a client list, and the last thing she needed right now was to have to find another firm, perhaps someone out of town, and someone she didn't trust to do a good job. Whatever had gone on between her and Harry in the past, his firm had come recommended, and word of mouth was the strongest clue of a firm's professionalism in Jo's book.

She continued walking up the hill. This town had changed in many ways. Parking restrictions were in play, there was a bigger supermarket before you reached

Salthaven, and there were new shops popping up every now and then. But so much of it had stayed the same, including the warm welcome the community had for anyone who chose to come here. And that was what had brought Jo home. This town had a heart and that would never change.

Inside her flat she hung up her coat, turned the thermostat dial well past the meagre fifteen degrees it was set on, and made a cup of hot cocoa. And when she was done she picked up her iPad. Just because her love life had crashed and burned, never to be resurrected in the foreseeable future, didn't mean it was like that for everyone. Regardless of her own hopelessness when it came to relationships, steering others towards their happy ending was enough for now.

She Googled and planned exactly what she needed for the night of love at the café. Tomorrow, on her day off, she'd get everything she needed to put those plans into action.

With a flash of enthusiasm, and glad she'd stopped at one glass of punch in the pub, she grabbed her car keys and the two red envelopes lying in wait on the shelf in the hallway, and ducked out of the nice warm flat.

She started up her old VW Beetle – it groaned in protest at having to get going at this time of night, but eventually it obediently trundled along the back streets to the other side of town where she found Jess's place first. She deposited one red envelope in the mailbox for her flat and, filled with a sense of adventure, jumped back into her Beetle and drove on to Ben's place. She'd been given both approximate addresses by Molly, but had established the exact flat number for Jess and house number for Ben with Melissa, who was as hopelessly romantic as she was – though at first she'd said it was more than her job at the post office was worth to divulge that information. Jo had pointed out that she was friends with both Ben and Jess, and it wouldn't be hard to find out the information from anyone else in town, and so Melissa had backed down.

Jo delivered Ben's postcard and, as she climbed back into her car, he pulled into the driveway in a red Range Rover. She held her breath, waved at him and went on her way hoping he'd take this in the spirit it was intended.

Back at her flat she fired off a text to Steve, hoping she wasn't interrupting him with the blonde from earlier, but he wrote back within ten minutes and said of course he'd help with her plans. He hadn't berated her once for being a soppy romantic either, but maybe he was saving that for later.

And with romantic notions floating around in her head, Jo climbed into bed and drifted off to sleep.

The next day she met Steve at the nearest DIY shop, where they chose four treated pine logs to make a sort of inside bower for the café. He manoeuvred the logs into his van. At six foot in length Jo wouldn't have had a hope of getting them anywhere near the café. She unloaded the bits and pieces he'd put on a trolley: a set of screws, and some huge cubes of wood which she could only lift one at a time.

'You need to learn to surf, build strength in those arms,' he suggested. But he met with a look that said, *not likely*. 'I'm serious. Then you'd be able to lift the blocks like this.' He took one out with a lot more ease than she'd managed.

'Show off.'

'You're going to a lot of trouble for other people.' He pulled his shades down from the top of his head. The rain from yesterday had well and truly dried up and it was like they'd jumped into a different season entirely.

'People in Salthaven have done a lot for my family. When I was in Scotland and there were all those floods here, Gran and Gramps had so many people helping them at home and at the café.'

He patted the base of the van next to where he'd sat down and Jo sat beside him. 'Your family are well thought of. And you're well thought of too.'

'Thanks.' She was a little embarrassed.

'I remember the floods. The café might be on the pier and raised above the sea, but with the deluge came the hugest waves I'd ever seen. We ended up putting sandbags at the entrance of the café as well as all the other outlets. Bea cooked for your Gran every night for a week because your Gramps was poorly, and Angie took Arthur to the doctor – although I'm not sure how thankful he was for the constant ear bending he got all the way there. Then, when the storms took tiles off the roof of the bungalow and ripped away part of the guttering, lots of residents pitched in.'

'Including you,' she smiled. For someone so confident, he didn't like to talk himself up.

'Your grandparents do their bit too. When Maggie, deputy head at the primary school, broke her leg, Molly completely took over the school bake sale. She collected cakes, she took charge of setting up, and she bossed everyone around to ensure stalls were manned and all cakes were sold. They raised more money that year than they've ever done before.'

'Sounds about right.'

He held her gaze for a moment but then snapped out of it. 'So tell me, do you really think you can play Cupid with this night of love at your café?'

'I really hope so. Meeting people is hard.'

'Do you think they'll come, whoever you've got your eye on?'

'I don't know, but I have to try. And I have a feeling the two people I've got in mind are good sports so will give it a go. I'm very persuasive when I want to be.'

'I can imagine.'

She let the sun warm her skin, enjoying the feeling compared to yesterday. 'How are you going to make those lovely pine logs stand up?' She looked into the van behind her. 'They're rather big. I don't want them falling onto the lucky – or unlucky – couple on Saturday night. They could end up suing me and it'll be no more night of anything at the café.'

'See those huge blocks we lifted . . . or you attempted to lift—'

She pushed her elbow playfully into his ribs. 'Hey, I lifted one fair and square.'

He picked one up. 'They're weighty and deep so I'm going to make a hole in the side of each, then use those long screws we picked up to fix the logs to the bases. Screws on all sides should see to it that they stay upright. And the screws are easy enough to remove so I can take the structure down after date night and put it up again whenever you're ready.'

'Sounds good to me. And I'll stash the pieces in the storeroom which is no longer full of boxes of stray papers.'

'Oh yes, your grandparents' accounting system.' He

put the word 'accounting' into air quotes and made them both grin.

'Saturday night's event is going to be perfect.'

'Are you cooking?' he teased.

'Of course I am. Just got to firm up the menu, but the dinner will be after closing time, the date will be private apart from me, and I can hide in the kitchen. Imagine, if these two get serious, maybe even get married, it could be the start of something that people come to the café for all the time.'

'You'll be the new Tinder of Salthaven.'

'Hey! I'll be no such thing. I prefer to think of myself more as a Cilla Black type matchmaker than anything involving swiping or no-strings-attached. All legit and above board.' She worried for a moment that this could possibly be less romantic than she envisaged. But Steve was wrong. With the bower around the table, the flowers and candle-light, this was going to be a springtime sight to behold.

They returned to the café and, between them, managed to stash all the posts and the bases in the storeroom. Upright, the posts didn't take up too much room, and the bases fitted against the wall nicely.

'Thanks for all your help.' Jo fixed them both a flat white to take away. It would be lovely to sit on the window seat and gaze out to sea, but Molly and Arthur were in their element for their only day here and Jo wanted to get outside, walk along the shoreline and make the most of her freedom.

'I'll need paying, you know.'

'I've already written down the extra hours,' she explained, 'and I covered the supplies today.'

'No, not that kind of payment. Payment for being

involved in anything romantic. If anyone found out it wouldn't do much for my reputation.'

She wondered if he meant the blonde, but didn't delve further. 'What did you have in mind?'

He raised his eyebrows.

'Oh, you've got to be kidding.'

8

Ben Mulroney had been single for three years. Ever since his wife left when it all got too much, it had been a case of swimming against the tide as a single parent so he didn't sink under the weight of responsibility, organisation, trying to hold down a full-time job, and the stress of his wife's wellbeing that meant he didn't always trust her with his son, Charlie. Ben hadn't had a date since he'd started going out with Lorna, and they'd ended up getting married, so he didn't even want to think too much about how rusty he was at all this.

'Charlie, breakfast!' He set down the French toast, served on Charlie's favourite Batman plate, on the table in the terraced house he'd called home for a decade. He'd bought the house after a promotion at work and when Lorna had come on the scene she'd loved it and happily moved in to make the house a home. With the sunlight streaming through the double doors at the end of the kitchen, the spring came inside when he opened them up to the outside world.

He called Charlie again who came running, still in his dressing gown, having spent the morning watching cartoons and racing his cars up and down the wooden floors. He was always an early riser and Ben wondered at what age he'd suddenly become one of those teenagers who lay in bed until well after lunch.

With a mouthful of French toast, Charlie asked, 'What's a blind date?'

Ben nearly choked on his own piece of egg-soaked bread that had been fried to a golden brown. 'Where did you hear that phrase? And don't talk with your mouth full.'

Charlie chewed quickly, swallowed and then said, 'I saw it, written on the red paper in the re-cling bin.'

Ben knew he should've torn it into pieces before he put it in recycling. The invite had said to come to The Café at the End of the Pier to find new love, and since receiving it on Monday night the card had been in and out of the recycling box more times than he cared to acknowledge. One time, as he'd sat looking at the invite while chatting on the phone with his dad, who was wittering on about the neighbour who kept parking across the front of their drive, Ben had written 'blind date' in capital letters if only to remind him of how crazy the whole idea was. But without a chance so far to confront Jo and ask for more details, or tell her he wouldn't be going, he'd gradually begun to get more curious. He'd seen Jo driving away from his house and the date was at the café, so was it with Jo? They got on well, they chatted for ages, and she seemed to really like Charlie. She knew him more than any other woman did right now, she was beautiful with her shoulder length wavy dark hair and smile that lit up the café, and he found part of him hoping it was her, and nobody else.

Out of his daydream he said, 'Watch me, Charlie.' When his son looked at him he said, 'Re-cy-cling'.

'Re . . .' Chew. 'cy . . .' Chew 'Cling.'

'That's better. Three syllables, remember.'

'So what is it?'

'Why were you going through the bin?'

'I wanted some cardboard to make a fort for my Lego pieces.' Charlie shrugged as though it made perfect sense. 'I know we always have cardboard in the re-cling bin.'

Ben didn't bother to correct him this time. 'Well, it's a date between two people, but neither of them have seen each other before.'

'How does that work?' He gulped from the glass of milk Ben had set out on the table beside him. 'How can you have a date if you have never seen the person before?'

'Drink your milk,' said Ben and finished his own French toast before scrubbing the frying pan waiting in the sink full of water. That was another challenging thing about fatherhood: the constant questions. And even when you gave an answer, it very often wasn't the end of the discussion. Each answer led to another question, then another, and then another until you somehow managed to skilfully change the subject to escape the grilling.

After Ben had cleared the kitchen and Charlie had finally got out of his pyjamas, he faced round two when Charlie asked if he was going to The Café at the End of the Pier tonight.

'Sit,' said Ben. They were at the bottom of the stairs, about to put on their shoes and go down to the boating lake with Charlie's new boat he'd got for his birthday. Lorna had chosen it for him and he was chuffed to bits. It was deep blue with white flapping sails that had blue stars on them and a big rudder below to guide it through the water.

Charlie sat on Ben's lap. 'It's OK if you go. I don't mind. Maddy could babysit me. I like her, she lets me eat cookies and stay up past my bedtime.'

'I'm not sure you should tell me that.' Charlie put a hand across his mouth and giggled when Ben tickled him. 'I don't think I want to go,' he said simply. 'I'd rather stay here with you.'

'Why? Because you don't know the other person?'

'That's right.'

'But they might be perfect for you.'

'Out of the mouth of babes.'

'What does that mean?'

Here we go again. 'Come on, get your shoes on.'

'Are we going to the café?'

'I thought we'd grab fish and chips for lunch today instead and then walk along the beach.' With thoughts of the invite invading his head he wanted to avoid The Café at the End of the Pier for now. He kept his fingers crossed that Charlie obliged.

'And an ice-cream?' Charlie grabbed his red coat.

'We'll see.' Which usually meant yes, which Charlie probably knew, judging by the grin he was doing his best to hide. Ben looked at the red coat. 'You don't need that today, you'll be too warm. The sun's glorious out there.'

Charlie ignored him. 'If you go on this date, I promise I'll be in bed by seven o'clock exactly.'

'Is that so? And what if Maddy offers you cookies?'

He thought hard. 'Then I'll tell her I can't have them.'

'I tell you what . . . I'll go on this date if you leave that red coat here.'

Charlie's face fell but only for a moment. He held out his hand. 'It's a deal.'

Ben shook his son's hand, ruffled his hair and out they went into the sunlight and down to the boating lake.

Tonight he had a date and – completely out of character – he was already wondering what he should wear.

9

'I still can't believe I'm doing this.' Jo stood on the golden sands with the sea stretched out in front of her, thankful for the wetsuit she'd squeezed herself into before Steve had picked her up from her flat this morning. They'd driven on past the pier and around the bay to a popular spot for surfers and even though they could see the pier and dry land from where they were, Jo was still as nervous as anything.

'You owe me, remember.' Steve teased as he reached for his back zip and tugged it from the base of his spine right to his neck, shielding his tanned skin. She'd witnessed Steve without a top this morning, and it was hard to ignore the six-pack he obviously worked on. No wonder he usually turned down the alluring treats she baked at the café.

Jo took the board when he handed it to her. 'Just like that?' She looked around the beach and the handful of other people armed with their surfboards.

'Relax, we're way too early for onlookers unless they're surfing themselves. Right . . . warm up time.'

She laid her board down on the sand next to his and followed his instructions. They covered quads, hamstrings, arms, shoulders, and then he made her run up and down the sand a few times.

'Warming up will keep you safe from injuries, like any other sport,' he explained, trying to keep a straight face when he saw her frown. 'Now we'll do a lesson on the sand.'

'Can't we get it over with and get in the sea?' She could see the glow of the sun above the horizon, but there was no heat. And the water looked cold even with the faint shimmer across its surface.

'Jo, take my word for it, you need to have a go on dry land first.'

She let him take her through the steps. She lay on the board and pretended to paddle, her hands hitting nothing wetter than the damp sand on either side. Then it was on to learning what Steve called the 'pop up'.

'I'm tired before we've even got in the water,' she claimed when she popped up for what felt like the millionth time. Popping up involved putting both hands on the sides of the board next to your ribs, gripping firmly and then, with your butt in the air, somehow contracting your torso and leaping into place with your feet landing on the board at the same time in the right position. Jo was beginning to doubt she'd ever be able to stay upright without the help of dry land.

Steve looked like he'd done nothing more than lie down. He wasn't even breathing heavily. 'It's a full body workout.'

'I'm embarrassed at my fitness levels.'

'Don't be, it takes the body a while to adjust to something new. You'll be sore for the next few days.'

She looked out at the water. Her love of the sea usually stopped at the shoreline unless it was a heatwave. 'Let's do this.'

'I think I saw a smile just then.'

'I wouldn't push it.'

'Is your surf leash on properly?'

She checked the Velcro strap around her ankle that would stop the board drifting away from her not *if* she fell off, but *when*. 'It's on, I'm ready.' She'd never been tempted to try surfing, content to watch from the promenade or while sitting on the sand, impressed with the way the lithe bodies carved up the waves. Steve was good, she'd seen him once as she went on a long walk one morning before opening the café, and he clearly had the patience of a saint to be teaching her.

'It's freezing!' When her bare toes touched the water she stood still for a second but Steve had no qualms in wading out a bit further.

'I assume you can swim,' he called over his shoulder.

'What do you take me for?'

He shrugged and turned when the water wasn't even up to his knees. 'I have to check.' He lay down on his board. 'Come on, let's practice paddling out.'

She did as she was told and, apart from a face full of water when she forgot to push up over a modest sized wave, she reached him safely.

'We'll stay in the shallow water for a while. Master it here before you make it even harder for yourself.'

By the time Jo managed her first pop-up after a few falls, and actually stayed upright long enough to cruise on a small wave all the way to the shore, she was laughing.

'Admit it.' Steve shook his blond hair side to side like a shaggy dog when they finished their session and were back on the safety of the golden sands. 'You've enjoyed this morning. You're glad you came.'

Jo could see exactly why surfers got addicted to the sport: the outdoors, the smell of the sea, the freshness of the water and the endorphins from an exhilarating session. 'It was fun, I'll give you that. It might be a while before I try it again though.'

'I promise you, once you really get going you'll love it. And you could meet a surf dude, the love of your life.'

'Now who's the romantic?' she asked as they made their way back to his van.

'I'm just saying. It wouldn't hurt you to get yourself out there a bit more.'

She handed him her board to slide onto the roof rack and waited for him to secure the ties. 'You think I'm boring.'

'Didn't say that, did I? But you're working long hours, maybe give yourself a break now and again.'

She didn't really want to bare all, but she couldn't get in the van in her wetsuit, so while Steve was still fixing the boards on top she unzipped her wetsuit and pulled on the T-shirt she'd popped in a bag this morning.

'Trouble?' he asked as he watched her trying in vain to get her wetsuit unattached from her legs.

'It's like a second skin! I'm not used to these things.'

He motioned for her to lift one leg up and he yanked the suit off then they did the other. More than a little embarrassed, she wiggled on a pair of shorts and hopped in to the van.

'How did you get yours off so fast?' she asked when he climbed in to the driver's seat, minus his own wetsuit.

'Practice.' He started the engine and Jo turned the heat dial up. He turned it down again. 'I'll have you home before this thing warms up.'

'Worth a try.' She turned it back up again.

'You're a pain in the backside,' he told her.

They chugged out of the parking bay, teasing one another, but when they turned to trundle down the hill to the roundabout, past the pier and up the other side, Jo locked eyes with Harry, taking his own board down from the roof rack of his car. She should've known he wouldn't stay away from the surf for long. She waved, but by the look on his face he clearly assumed she was with Steve as a lot more than friends. By the time she got back to her flat and showered, ready to go and open up the café, she knew that was only a good thing. He needed to see she was a different person now, and there couldn't be any going back, no matter how much nostalgia crept into her mind and his.

'You're very chirpy this morning,' said Matt later that morning when he brought the delivery of fruit and vegetables over from the farm. 'What's your secret?'

Jo took the box and peered into it. It was filled with goodies from fresh eggs and tomatoes to rich-coloured blackberries. 'I went surfing this morning,' she divulged.

'I'm impressed.'

'And surprised, I expect. Me too, but Steve persuaded me. He says I need to make time for myself.'

'He's right. So how was it?'

She put the box on top of the counter and waved to Angie who had already been in for a cup of ginger tea and a fruit salad, and was off to her book club. 'It was better than I thought. I swallowed a lot of water, my arms hurt by the end of it, but it definitely woke me up and it was a surprisingly nice way to start the day.'

'So that's the secret.'

'You should try it. Steve's a good teacher.'

'I tried it a few years back.'

'You did?'

'On a holiday to Cornwall. But I'm afraid I didn't really take to it. I much prefer the dry land unless I'm in a boat.'

She rummaged through the box and began unloading ingredients. 'How do you grow such a variety, Matt?'

'With a lot of hard work. You have to create the right environment, give the produce the care and attention it needs.'

'These blackberries look wonderful.' She lifted the plastic punnet to under her nose and inhaled their sweet aroma, and when she pinched one to taste, it was slightly tart, exactly the way she liked them. 'So, what do you think . . . blackberry turnovers or blackberry pie bars?'

'Hey, I can grow things but I'm useless at making anything out of them, so either gets my vote.'

When he went on his way Jo debated what to make, and seeing as she had most of the blackberry pie bar ingredients, and she'd made them before for a school picnic up in Edinburgh, she went with that option.

She looked up to see Jess coming in to the café following a run, ear buds hanging over each shoulder. She'd wondered when she'd have to face her after delivering the invite, and it looked like her time had come. 'You're not usually in on a Saturday.'

'Another doctor is doing Saturday morning surgery today.'

'How was the run?'

Jess shook her head. 'Oh no, don't you go trying to get out of it. You know what you've done.'

'The invite,' said Jo, quietly enough that nobody else would hear. There was a low hum of chatter, but every table was full today so it was lucky Jess only wanted a takeaway smoothie.

'Yes, the invite.'

'Are you ready to kill me?'

'I was when I first got it. I'm not some lonely old spinster, you know.'

'And now? I'm assuming that if you wanted to kill me you'd have done it already.'

'I came in on Tuesday but you weren't here, and by Wednesday I'd calmed down.'

All Jo wanted to know was whether she was up for it. Ben had to be, surely, because she hadn't heard from him, and she took it as a good sign.

'So . . .?' Jo tried again, crossing her fingers behind the counter.

'I'll be here.'

Jo almost squealed but didn't want her excitement to put Jess off.

'Are you going to tell me who it is?'

'Not a chance.' And with that she went out to the kitchen to make the regular smoothie for her customer. When she returned, Jess was looking worried. 'He's lovely,' Jo assured her. 'I wouldn't set you up with him if he wasn't, and I'm really pleased you're willing to give it a try.'

'It's a lot easier than trying to arrange my own dates, that's for sure.' She closed her eyes at the first welcome sip of the thick, fruity treat. 'I never have the time. Spring colds and bugs have kept the surgery busy and I've done more hours than usual this week.'

'You won't regret it if you come, I promise.'

'What's on the menu?' Her interest was piqued, which was a good sign.

'All you need to know for now is that you'll be very happy with it.' She'd been doing a bit of detective work leading up to tonight, finding out both their favourite and least favourite foods, and building the menu around those preferences.

'I'll see you tonight then.'

'See you tonight.' Jo took a deep breath. All she needed now was Steve's help to get the café ready, and for both of the people on this date to turn up. And then Cupid would have a decent shot.

Ben and Charlie didn't come in all day, and as time marched on Jo was beginning to worry. Her positivity that Ben's silence could only be a good sign had disappeared, and she hoped she hadn't upset him. This was her way of getting more involved in the community, giving something back, making people's lives easier and happier, not harder.

Had she messed up by meddling in the first place?

Steve arrived shortly before closing so they could get started with fashioning the bower around the table in the corner, and Jo tried to stay positive. As he screwed upright log posts into bases and made sure the main structure was sturdy, Jo started food preparations. She'd already made a special aioli which was in the fridge, she'd prepared the fish elements – turned out both Jess and Ben were big sea-food lovers – and she'd already made the dessert after the lunchtime rush.

'So when's your next surf session?' Steve asked as he finished the fourth post around the table.

'Er, hang on,' said Jo, with a glint in her eye. 'Let me see, today's Saturday, tomorrow's Sunday, so . . . never?'

'Oh come on, you're floating around nice and happy tonight. I can tell you loved it.'

'I'm floating around because I'm setting up a night of love.'

He didn't buy it. 'Whatever, I'll get you back out there one day.'

'One day,' she agreed as she looked at the structure. 'It looks great. Once I get the twinkly lights and the flowers it'll look like springtime in this corner.'

After he left Jo locked the door but opened the windows, so that when everything was ready it would allow the breeze to drift in and mingle the scent of the ocean with the flowers she'd chosen. She retrieved the flowers from their buckets of water on the worktop in the storeroom where they'd been since this afternoon when Molly and Arthur collected them from the florist. They were curious as to what would happen tonight, but Jo assured them it was all in hand and they weren't to come back and try to spy. 'You'll drive both lovebirds away,' Jo had told them.

When Molly had found out Jess was one of the guests tonight, she'd gone on and on about how lovely she was, how she was kind, how she'd never once made Molly or Arthur feel like they were at the doctors too much when it seemed their visits were happening more often than not. 'Heart of gold', Molly had said of Jess, and Jo was really happy she had a chance to give something back to one of the town's most popular residents. Ben wasn't far behind in their estimations either. 'A doting father,' Arthur had described him as, before going on to tell Jo all about the time Ben had chased Arthur's hat down the pier to retrieve it for him when a gust of wind carried it away unexpectedly.

Jo set a round glass vase in the centre of table, filled it a third of the way with water, and arranged jasmine in the centre. She'd chosen just the one type of flower. Spring-like, classic, pretty, and with a beautiful scent she hoped would please her guests. She took more jasmine and the shiny leaves it came with and, using mossing twine, she fixed it all the way up each log post to the very top, standing on tiptoes to reach the last sections. She carefully wound twinkly lights around each post, tucking them between flowers and leaves; she lit candles and dimmed the lights and put on the soft sounds of classical cello as the sun began to weaken outside and hint at its descent.

Before long the spring evening would be dark, the café lit solely by the romantic lighting she'd engineered. The meal she'd planned was ready to go and would take minimal cooking time while Ben and Jess got to know each other here in the privacy of the inside bower, and she'd fade into the background as much as she could.

She put on a clean apron – white to go with the more sophisticated night she wanted to carry off. Using the mirror out back she wound her dark wavy hair up into a chignon with strands hanging down on either side to frame her face. She put on cherry red lipstick, primped her eyebrows and added a little blusher to her cheeks so she looked the part of the elegant hostess. And when she heard a knock at the door to the café her heart leapt. She took a deep breath in and as she let it out, emerged into the café and went to greet her first guest.

'Ben, come in.' She tried to keep her voice even when she opened the door, but she was so relieved he'd turned up. 'Can I get you a drink?' He didn't seem to be looking around for the other guest, and he looked almost surprised when there was a second knock at the door. 'Hold that thought.'

And with a smile she welcomed Jess. It was time to get this plan underway.

10

Ben had changed his shirt four times before he came here tonight. But as he'd gone through the ritual of trying the first in beige and white checks – no – plain sky blue but a bit worn around the cuffs – no – pale green and almost new – no, didn't want that either – he couldn't help but think he was going to be having dinner with Jo tonight. But now, dressed in his fourth choice of a black button down shirt that he'd teamed with a pair of dark ink jeans and brown suede brogues he was in front of a different woman entirely.

'It's lovely to meet you, properly, I mean,' he said to Jess, shaking her hand. Was he doing this all wrong? Should he have kissed her on the cheek?

'Hello, Ben. This is all a bit odd isn't it?'

'Very odd, and thank you for saying that. I feel better already.'

Jo had made the introductions and left them to it but now she came out of the kitchen with two glasses of fizzing champagne on a silver tray. Jess took one, he took the other and Jo disappeared off again without another word.

'Shall we?' He gestured to the table in the corner.

Jess went over first. A slender, tall blonde, she was definitely beautiful. Aside from seeing her in passing in her running gear a few times along the promenade, or a more official meeting with her when he took Charlie to the doctor's after Christmas to check out a nasty cough, he hadn't really exchanged more than a friendly few words with her before now.

Both of them hid behind glasses of champagne until Ben said, 'So, what do you do?' and immediately put a hand to his head. 'Dumb question, can't believe I asked that when I've seen you as a GP.'

'It's OK, you could've asked me if I came here often and then I might have upped and left.'

Her joke broke the ice, at least, and after Jo brought over an amuse-bouche of seared scallops with lime jalapeño aioli, they launched into conversation about Jess's love of skiing and running, and then moved to his job as an architect, his admiration for old buildings and past trips around Europe.

'Which is your favourite city?'

'Do I have to pick one?'

'Yes!'

'Well, I love Prague for its clock tower in the old town square, the unusual shape of the Dancing House, and the views of Prague Castle.'

'So where's next on your list?' she asked.

Ben was about to answer when Jo came over again.

'Sorry to interrupt, but I wanted to let you know what's on the menu tonight.'

'If it's anything like those scallops, I won't be leaving anything on my plate,' said Jess before grimacing as though she'd said something wrong.

'For the main course there'll be seared tuna with cous-cous and sugar-snap peas sourced from a local farm, and for dessert, a lemon cheesecake with a gingersnap cookie-crumb crust.'

'It all sounds great,' said Ben.

'Can I get you another glass of champagne each?'

'Keep it coming,' said Jess. And when Jo left she said to Ben, 'I probably shouldn't be on a date boasting about how much I'm going to eat.'

'Ah, that's why you made a face.'

'Doesn't make me very appealing does it? Maybe that's why I'm still single.'

'Come to think of it, I eat like a horse too.'

'We make a fine pair.'

They continued their conversation through the main, through the dessert covering all manner of topics from siblings, Charlie and his antics, to her training to be a doctor and the highs and lows, and by the end of the evening Ben couldn't deny he'd had a really wonderful time.

'Thank you for not standing me up,' he said to Jess when they were on to coffees.

'Jo should be glad we're both good sports. I'm not sure this plan would work with everyone.'

'It's a lovely idea though, don't you think? Better than using online dating, way less scary in fact.'

'You're completely right. Have you tried it?'

'Online dating? No, knowing me I'd pick some fruitcake.'

Jess was an attractive woman with kind eyes, and she was great company. 'What did you think about the menu?' And with that they were back to another comfortable conversation, this time about local restaurants – best and worst.

By the time they left the café under the cloak of darkness, chatting as they made their way along the pier, Ben knew he'd found a friend. He may even ask her to dinner in the future, but the spark wasn't really there, and he could tell she felt the same way.

At the start of the pier they went their separate ways, and Ben walked home wondering how tonight would have gone if his date had been with Jo instead of Jess.

Perhaps it would've had a different ending entirely.

II

I t was Monday morning in the café and now Jo knew what Steve meant when he'd said her body would hurt from surfing. On Saturday night she'd been on a high after the date looked like it was going supremely well, yesterday she'd felt mildly achy as she took everything off the bower and Steve dismantled it and stored it before Molly and Arthur opened for the day, but today every part of her hurt.

Jo took a cappuccino over to Melissa, who had a late start at the post office. She winced as she set the mug down, her body struggling to do even the easiest of moves.

'Whatever's wrong with you?' Melissa asked.

'I'm sore from surfing.'

'I thought you enjoyed yourself.'

'I did, until the after-effects began to appear. Lifting anything hurts and as for bending down to get things out of the oven . . .' She shook her head.

Melissa motioned for her to lean closer so she could whisper. 'Would you check those two out?' She was looking over at a group of young girls huddled conspiratorially along the window seat farthest away from the counter.

'Which two?'

'Look at the girl on the end, the brunette, then follow her eye line.'

Jo had no idea what Melissa was on about but surreptitiously observed as she cleared another table and brushed crumbs from a chair.

Back with Melissa she said, 'It's sweet. She's got it bad.' Whoever the girl was, she couldn't stop looking at one of the boys in another crowd who had taken over the table nearest the blackboard and were about to leave.

Melissa nodded to the boy as he went past to the door. 'That was Dan,' she told Jo. 'I work with his mum.'

'Who's the girl watching him?'

'That's Maddy – all I know is she just turned twenty-one because she had a big party at the pub. Oh, and she's Ben's regular babysitter.'

'Well Dan had better watch out,' whispered Jo, 'because she definitely has her sights set on him.'

'I think the feeling's mutual.'

Sometimes Jo felt as though she was always on the outside looking in when it came to new love.

Melissa got back to her magazine and Jo continued to move gingerly around the café like a little old lady. When Angie came in she noticed Jo's inability to function normally, and when Molly stopped by on her way to the library they both had a good laugh at Jo's expense. But she took it well – she could see the funny side. Jo suspected they were both glad to see it wasn't only the oldies who felt like their bodies let them down sometimes.

'I can't believe I forgot to ask. How did last night go?' Melissa asked when the mid-morning rush died down.

'I think it went really well.' Jo wiped down the low table in front of the window seat and fetched a dustpan and brush for the crumbs beneath it.

'Is that all the info you're going to give me?'

'I can't gossip, it's personal to the people who were on the date.' She gasped as she tried to crouch down and when she'd eventually managed to move her limbs and collect all the crumbs in the pan she stood again. 'And besides, I haven't seen Ben or Jess since then, so I really don't know. But they were talking all evening, and they looked happy when they left.'

'Oh, do you think it went *really* well?' Eyebrows raised, Jo knew exactly what Melissa was hinting at.

Jo shushed Melissa and tried to look casual because here was Jess, taking out her ear buds after a run. Jo took an abandoned cup out to the dishwasher and came back to greet her next customer.

'Jess, lovely to see you this morning. How was the run?' She wouldn't mention the date until Jess did. Unless Jess tried to leave without uttering a word, in which case she'd block the door to find out details. She was enjoying her role as Cupid but she was terribly impatient when she wanted to know something. Her brother Nicholas had taunted her when they were growing up, winding her up whenever he knew something she didn't because he knew she hated it. She'd found the best way to play him at his own game had been to feign nonchalance, even when it was eating her up inside, and it had worked. He'd always ended up blabbing because like she couldn't bear not knowing things, he couldn't bear not opening his mouth.

'The run was slow. I had a bit too much champagne on Saturday night, thanks to you.'

'I supplied it but I didn't force you to drink it.' She smiled. 'So . . .'

'The usual smoothie, please.'

'Coming up.' Perturbed Jess hadn't said anything, she went off and fixed the drink.

Jess, straw ready to plunge into the lid of the takeaway cup, held out her hand for the smoothie.

Jo was about to pass it over but pulled it back at the last minute. 'Did you enjoy the date?'

'Yes I did, thank you.' This time she reached out and took the drink.

Jo took payment but the second she shut the till she said, 'Oh, come on, I need to know more. Please. You can't leave here until you share.'

A local mother's group chose that moment to pile into the café and Jo knew she was about to lose her moment. 'Don't go anywhere.'

'I'll be outside,' said Jess.

When Jo had fixed coffees and teas, and handed out teacakes and her special of the day, apple turnover, she joined Jess at the single aluminium table outside. There'd be more come summer, but right now she'd put out just the one as the weather was so up and down.

From here Jo could peer through the window and duck inside as soon as she was needed. 'Please put me out of my misery.'

'It was a really lovely evening, Jo.'

Her spirits plummeted. 'But . . .'

'Neither of us felt a connection.'

'I'm sorry, I really thought . . .'

Jess shook her head. 'Don't say sorry. It was exactly what I needed, and I think Ben feels the same way too. It's ages since I relaxed with someone and enjoyed a nice long conversation and I think because neither of us felt a spark, we both enjoyed the date for what it was.'

'And what's that?'

'Friendship.'

'Oh.'

'Jo, I mean it, you shouldn't be disappointed. You did a good thing – a really special gesture to two people who are now friends thanks to you. We've already arranged to go to a movie next week, and . . .' She sighed. 'I can't thank you enough for giving me that. Romance would be lovely, and it may happen one day, but this is more than I had a few days ago.'

Jo felt the disappointment in her heart settle into something else: contentment. She'd managed to give something special to two very deserving people. So they hadn't fallen head over heels in love in the way her romantic brain had hoped for. But so what? They'd found something equally as special. So it was mission accomplished – just a different mission to the one she'd originally intended.

Jess picked up her smoothie. 'I should be going, I've got back-to-back appointments today.'

'And I'd better get inside.' Jo frowned as she watched two kiddies ripping open sugar sachets and emptying them on the table to form a little tower.

'Jo, I'd hug you for what you did if I wasn't so sweaty.'

'Raincheck?' she grinned, and when Jess went on her way Jo went inside the café to sort out the little terrors before they completely ran her out of sugar supplies.

The rest of the morning passed slowly with Jo's mind on Ben and Jess, and when the phone rang mid-morning Jo wasn't expecting her mum. They hadn't spoken or texted since the other day when her mum had basically accused her own parents of guilt-tripping her into taking over the café. She knew her mum was only looking out for her, but she was letting her own issues with her parents overshadow the relationship Jo had with Molly and Arthur.

'Have you called to tell me I'm doing the wrong thing again?' Jo asked without much preamble.

'I know you better than that. It won't change anything.'

'I am happy, Mum.' She nodded her thanks to Peter as he left, and the little bell on the door tinkled as the café settled in to quietness once more. The lunchtime rush was yet to come and Sasha had timed her phone call well.

'Why didn't you come here when Gramps was sick?' Jo asked now.

'I'm not sure either of them would want me there.'

'Oh, Mum. I wish you'd all make peace. Life's too short.'

'Jo, it takes two – or in this case, three.'

'Maybe you could be the bigger person. Come over and see us all. The café is too busy for me to visit you.'

'I'll think about it. And great to hear the café is busy. Busy means financial security.'

Jo's heart quickened. So far she hadn't told a soul about her financial concerns which seemed to be mounting by the day. This morning it'd been an insurance renewal to add to her worries, and she was slowly realising she'd grossly underestimated everything involved with being in charge of a café. Until recently Jo hadn't even thought about what was involved with the insurance side of the business. Harry had raised concerns in their initial meeting and Jo had called the company, who'd gone through the various types from product liability and employer's liability insurance to public liability insurance. She'd upped her level of cover on some of them but with that came an exorbitant premium; yet another cost to bear. And then there was everything else that came with running a café. There was the cleaning up at the end of the day, keeping on top of the maintenance side, monitoring supplies so you neither ordered too much or too little, keeping up with the tradition of making something new for the menu depending on the produce Matt delivered. First she had to be creative and think of something, then source a recipe, then manage to cook it. She wasn't a bad cook, but it was different when you were making food for others. You had to get it absolutely right.

'Jo? Are you still there?'

Her mind had drifted, filled with terms and phrases such as lost revenue if she couldn't trade, stock insurance separate to contents, responsibility for every visitor who entered the café should they hurt themselves on the premises. 'Sorry, Mum.' When the door opened, announcing a customer, she said, 'I'd better go. We'll chat more another time.'

At the counter she welcomed Hilda Jenkins who was on a break from the toy shop in town. 'What can I get for you?'

As Hilda thought about her choices, Jo put her worries about the café's finances even further out of her mind. She was here in Salthaven where she wanted to be. And that was the main thing. This had never been about making a fortune. She'd wanted to return to her roots and make a fresh start by the sea. And walking away was what other people did in her life: her father, Harry, her mum. But not Jo.

'I'll have a slice of the courgette pie, please,' said Hilda as she made up her mind, 'and a bottle of the sparkling mineral water. I'm too warm for anything else. I've had a lovely walk along the promenade so I've worked up an appetite.' Her Swiss accent had never completely disappeared. Jo wondered if perhaps, one day when the weather got colder, she could put a Swiss fondue on the menu. Maybe Hilda could even taste test it for her.

Next through the door was Matt, with his delivery. 'I'm so sorry, Jo. I'm really late today.'

She took the box from his arms. 'Is everything OK?'

A smile spread across his face, highlighting the flecks of gold in his hazel eyes. 'I'm an uncle again. My sister gave birth to a baby boy at three o'clock this morning.'

Her heart soared for him. 'Congratulations! And what a wonderful reason to be late.' She peered into the box. 'You've given me some lovely produce again. I need to put my creative hat on and come up with something new.'

'There's plenty of rhubarb in there. I know you loved it last time.'

'I certainly did, and I have a recipe in mind already: white chocolate mousse with poached rhubarb. It's simple and fresh – perfect for spring.'

'Sounds good to me. I might have to come in tomorrow to try it.'

'Any time. And bring Poppy if you can, she'll love it.'

He raised a hand to say goodbye and as Jo unpacked the fruit and vegetables into the kitchen cupboards, fridge and storage boxes, she wondered whether Matt had thought about having a family one day. He seemed to have a natural affinity with kids, going by what she'd seen with Poppy, and men like that made very good dads themselves.

Shaking her head at her romanticism she headed out of the kitchen to tackle the lunchtime rush. She'd only turned her back for a moment and two large groups had descended.

Ben came in after work that day, and in a suit and tie he looked very different to the man who'd been in so many times before. Jo stopped sweeping the floor.

'You're not here to have a go at me, are you?' Jess had responded well, but maybe Ben wouldn't be so nice about it.

'Don't be silly. I came to say thank you for thinking of me. Jess is lovely and we've both found a friendship we hadn't expected.'

Jo put a hand to her chest. 'I'm so relieved you're not upset.'

'Why would I be? Cupid's arrow just went a bit off course this time round.'

They talked about Charlie, Ben grabbed a takeaway coffee for his walk back home, and by the time he left Jo was glad she hadn't upset anyone. In fact, she was already beginning to think of who she could embroil in her plans for the next date night.

She finished sweeping the floor, mopped, and made sure everything was switched off in the kitchen. She wiped down the surfaces, cursing when the button fell off the cooker. This morning it had taken forever to warm up and she had a sneaking suspicion the thermostat was about to go on the blink. It had already been repaired once, but maybe it was about to give up for good. Great, another expense she wasn't sure she could afford. With a sigh she switched off the lights in the kitchen and then in the café itself, plunging the place into darkness. When she pulled the door open to leave, she noticed a postcard lying there on the mat.

She looked left towards the start of the pier, right towards the end and the sea beyond, but nobody was around.

She turned the postcard over. All it had was one sentence:

Dear Jo, don't be so busy worrying about other people falling in love that you miss what's right in front of you ...
remember, love can be found in the strangest of places.

Jo clutched the postcard and looked outside again, but apart from an elderly couple walking their dog along the sand down below, there was nobody.

She locked the door behind her, baffled as to whom the postcard could be from. She slotted it into her bag, and beneath a fading spring sky she walked along the wooden boards towards the promenade as a light breeze lifted her dark hair around her shoulders. All she wanted now was a hot bubble bath where she could stay and let the tiredness of her day wash off her. And she wanted to lie there and think about who could possibly have sent this postcard. She had no idea, but the excitement zipped through her, making her even more sure that her idea for bringing love to The Café at the End of the Pier had been the right one. Because if the people she chose felt as hopeful and elated as she did right now, then it could only be a good thing.

She turned to go up the hill, but realised that at the end of the pier was a man she recognised. He was leaning up against the white wooden fence, and as soon as he saw Jo he walked over to meet her.

'Hello again.' He extended a hand. 'We met the other day,' he said, as though that explained everything. 'My name is Curtis Durham.'

She held out a hand to shake his, knowing it would be rude not to return the gesture. He was the good-looking businessman who'd come to the café once before. But she had no idea why he was introducing himself now. Was he responsible for the postcard she'd just found?

'Are you the owner of the cafe?' He was looking around him – down the length of the pier, out at the sea, off up the hill in the direction Jo was about to walk – as though committing the small town to memory.

'I run it, but officially it's leased by my grandparents.' She saw his eyes light up. In fact, the legalities of changing the name on the lease were going through at the moment – but he didn't need to know that as they stood here on the pier with the sun buried deep on the horizon. Molly and Arthur had insisted upon it and after discussing it with Jo's siblings, none of whom had any desire to run the business, the move was logical. Jo would be responsible for everything from hereon in.

It was a daunting prospect, but a good long-term move, she hoped.

'What's this about?' she asked.

He handed her a business card. 'I have a proposition for you.'

Summer

12

As she set out towards the café, Jo paused for a moment, closing her eyes and allowing herself to bask in the glorious summer sunshine. The frantic feeling she'd had when she first took over the café had finally started to fade, and in its place was a sense of calm. At least, that was how she felt when it was business as usual. The only time she wavered was when something unexpected happened – the oven breaking, the fridge leaking, a clogged drain or the toaster going caput. It was those little things that made Jo question whether her mum had been right to suggest that her return to Salthaven was out of some misguided sense of duty to her grandparents, rather than purely for herself.

But there was another thing weighing on her mind: Curtis Durham's proposition. When she'd first seen him waiting for her at the end of the pier, she'd wondered if he'd put the postcard beneath the door to the café, suggesting she might find love. He was charismatic, handsome and had vision, all qualities Jo admired. And he seemed to be the type of man who would enjoy the thrill of the chase. But it was his business proposal which had really thrown her into a whirl of confusion. Curtis Durham owned a very successful chain of cafés with outlets throughout the

UK and he was on the verge of opening up another. Much of his success could be attributed to his remarkable ability to pick the best staff, but he hadn't quite managed to do that for the new venue. When he'd dropped into the café after an unsuccessful round of interviews for his new project, he'd spotted something special in Jo. He'd told her he could see her drive, her passion and her energy, and he was proposing she head up his new place in Cornwall.

Over the last couple of months Jo's morale had been boosted not only by Molly and Arthur, but also by her two younger brothers. Timothy had been to visit and, as a business owner himself, had given Jo some much-needed support, spurring her on to keep giving it her all. Nicholas had been supportive too, albeit in a different way. He'd been sending postcards from various ski resorts around the world – he was currently in Falls Creek Resort, Australia – and he'd told Jo the café was a far better business to be in than his chosen profession as a ski instructor who travelled all over the world with no base to call home. Apparently, even the pistes and the bars (and, she suspected, the women) didn't make up for his meagre income and the unreliability of finding work. Then again, Jo knew full well he wouldn't have it any other way. It was his passion, and she hoped she'd found hers. Her brothers' recent encouragement had at least gone some way to helping her believe she'd come here for the right reasons.

Walking down the hill from her flat, accompanied by enthusiastic birdsong, Jo pushed any worries to the furthest corner of her mind. She greeted Sally, who owned the bungalow next to Molly and Arthur's. 'Your roses and the cornflowers are looking beautiful this morning,' she praised, raising her voice as a lawnmower kickstarted at one of the houses a bit further down. Molly often talked about spending more time in her garden now she was retired, but she'd have to get out of the kitchen first. The woman could win awards for her baking, especially her chocolate brownies: soft and gooey on the inside, flaky on top when you dared to give them a try.

'Good afternoon, Morris.' Jo spotted Morris Eckles from number twenty-two walking up the hill with the newspaper tucked under one arm. 'How's the topiary going?'

He pulled a face. 'Let's say it's work in progress.' And, with a wave, he went through his front gate.

Yesterday, Jo had watched Morris trying to shape wire netting over a shrub, although she'd been too polite to ask what he was attempting to make.

Jo crossed the road, and a fresh sea breeze skimmed her neck as she reached the pier, the boards beneath her feet creaking with a breathtaking familiarity as she made her way to work. The fish and chip shop had joined the summer season by setting out blue and white stripy deckchairs for their customers to lounge in with their parcels of delicious salt and vinegar-coated treats, and the smell hung on the air, enticing holidaymakers and locals. The bits and bobs shop Bits and Pieces was doing a roaring trade and Jo waved hello to Lena, who ran the place, as she stacked sunshine-coloured buckets and sky-blue spades out front along with the postcard rack that spun in the wind.

Jo dodged excited children and hand-in-hand couples as she trod the wooden boards of the pier towards the café. Since her failure to help Ben and Jess find love, she'd been a little nervous about setting up another blind date, but perhaps the arrival of summer would offer a new chance to bring a little romance to Salthaven. Long evenings, days spent on the beach, everyone jovial and willing to take a chance. All she had to do now was find the perfect man, the perfect woman, and put her plan into action. Her mum, not a romantic by any sense of the word, thought it a crazy thing to be doing when she was supposed to be running her own business. Apparently that was quite enough to focus on. But her grandparents had other ideas. They loved how Jo was giving the night of love at the café the same attention as the café itself, and they had every faith that she could bring some magic to two lucky, but unsuspecting, participants.

How could she ever think about leaving this town? She was back by the sea, in the place she'd always wanted to be, working in a business that had been in her family for years. No, Curtis Durham would have to make his proposition to someone else, because her only plan was to stay put.

'Greetings!' Arthur, white apron pinned around his waist, was chatting with one of the locals who sat outside the café trying to make the pages of his newspaper behave. 'Paperweights,' he added when Jo stopped beside them.

'Excuse me?' She smiled at Bruce, seated at the only aluminium table they'd put outside so far.

'I need a paperweight, or rather Bruce does, for his newspaper.' Arthur patted the man on the shoulder before following Jo inside.

Jo hung her bag in the cupboard and then in the storeroom stood on tiptoes and grabbed a jar of pebbles from the uppermost shelf. 'Give him this for now.'

'Ah, that'll do.' Satisfied, Arthur left her to it.

Jo tied her hair up in a ponytail, ready to take over for the Sunday afternoon shift. Molly and Arthur had made it a regular thing for them to do Sunday mornings and Tuesdays, and, Jo had to say, she appreciated the lie-ins and the chance to recuperate.

Out in the café Molly bustled over from where she'd been chatting to someone sitting at the furthest table. 'How are you this afternoon, Jo?'

'Bright and breezy,' she said. All this sea air was very good for her. 'I saw Morris earlier, but I still haven't asked what he's trying to make with all that wire netting in his garden.'

'He's aiming for a bird; apparently, the wire will help train the foliage and twigs to fashion the shape of the tail. Can't see it myself.'

'You didn't tell him that, did you?'

'Of course not.' She winked. 'He'll find out in his own time.'

Jo sighed, looking outside as the sun shimmered across the sea. 'All this beautiful weather and fresh air is a great combination.'

'Not having second thoughts about being stuck in a café all day long, are you?'

'Of course not.' And she meant it.

'Did you see the latest postcard?'

For a moment Jo's heart skipped a beat wondering if Molly had picked up another mystery postcard like the one that had landed on the mat in spring. Jo still remembered the words that had told her not to be so busy worrying about other people that she might miss out on love, and that love could be found in the strangest of

147

places. All very cryptic, and she had no idea who could have possibly sent it, unless Curtis Durham really was responsible. The conundrum was oddly exciting.

'It's from Vince,' Molly continued. 'He went on a cycle tour in France.'

Jo's heart rate returned to normal. Perhaps thinking about it was a waste of time. It had been so long since her mystery admirer had left the postcard. Perhaps whoever it was had decided not to pursue the idea. Shame. She was enjoying her own matchmaking game with some of the town's locals and couldn't wait to get going with it all over again, and she wondered how much of her inspiration and her enthusiasm came from one day hoping she'd get swept off her feet herself to find her own happy ever after.

She tied on her apron. 'I'll read the card later, Gran. Right now, I need the rundown.'

'We're almost out of fresh strawberries, and I've sold the last of the white-chocolate mousse with the poached rhubarb,' Molly told her. 'I've made raspberry-swirl rolls and added them to the blackboard.'

'The strawberries are beautiful this season. And it's great to see customers are enjoying the mousse.' It always made her happy when a menu item went down well. 'And raspberry-swirl rolls sound very naughty, but very nice.' She looked over at the board. 'Let me rub out mousse from the list before we forget.'

Molly shook her head. 'I knew there was something I'd forgotten.' She took payment from a customer. 'Would you like to try one of the swirl rolls?'

'They smell heavenly. I'll have one later.' Or maybe her waistline would thank her more if she said no.

'You need to eat.' Molly shut the till and the customer went on their way.

'I have. Stop fussing.'

'I'm allowed – you're my granddaughter.'

'Did you leave the recipe for the swirl rolls, in case I run out?'

'There's a Tupperware container in the kitchen filled with another batch, but it's too time-consuming to make more. The dough would have to rise. I'd leave a fresh batch until the morning if I were you. And the recipe's pinned to the wall in the kitchen.'

Sometimes she was sure Molly forgot how new to this she really was. She'd always enjoyed baking but usually it was to an audience of housemates, not an entire town.

'You'll be fine.' Molly picked up on her granddaughter's hesitation. 'You always are, Jo.'

They went out to the kitchen and Jo looked through what was in the fridge, since Matt, their fruit and vegetable delivery guy, had delivered fresh supplies this morning to add to the extras Jo had brought in from the supermarket yesterday.

'Your gramps,' Molly tutted. 'He seems to think our one-and-a-half days a week is in order for him to catch up with the local gossip.'

Jo followed her gaze to the outside, where Gramps had given Bruce the makeshift paperweight, but was still talking with him and didn't bat an eyelid that other customers were coming into the café, including Ben and Charlie. Jo waved over at them before turning to Molly. 'He's fine. It's nice to see him taking it easy for a change.'

Molly's shoulders relaxed. 'He's finally listening to me, slowing down and eating right.'

Jo clasped her grandmother's hand in her own. 'It's time for you both to take a step back.' When her gran looked at her, slightly panicked, she added, 'Not entirely. At least not yet. I still need your support. I know it'll be just me when you retire completely, but, for now, it's lovely to share this with both of you.'

Jo served another three or four customers before turning her attention to baking quiches. She'd got quicker at cooking since she'd been here, and she was beginning to experiment with flavours as she went along, using plenty of the fresh herbs Matt brought the café from his farm. Jo cracked eggs, chopped pancetta and grated Gruyère cheese. She seasoned the mixture, rolled pastry and pushed it into quiche tins before dividing the filling evenly between them. Matt had brought in some fresh chives so she snipped the tops and sprinkled over the quiches for added flavour.

Once the quiches had been slotted into the oven it was time for Molly and Arthur to leave her to it. She kissed her grandparents in turn. 'One more favour before you go?'

'Anything for you,' said Gramps, 'as long as it doesn't involve hulling strawberries. Molly made me do a thousand of those this morning.'

'It was about forty,' Molly clarified, 'he's making up stories again.'

'Well this doesn't involve strawberries.' She smiled at Ben when he caught her eye from where he and Charlie were sitting at the window seat. 'I thought it was about time we put more chairs and tables outside now the weather's warmer. What? Why are you both grinning?'

Steve shouted a hello at the door of the café. As she

caught sight of his tall, tanned form in the doorway, Jo had to admit that she was drawn to him. He didn't seem to do long-term relationships, focusing more on the fun, but she sometimes wondered whether perhaps he could help take away her loneliness – even if only for a moment.

'We beat you to it,' said Molly. 'I hope we weren't standing on any toes when we made a business decision. But we called Steve this morning and asked him to bring all the chairs and tables from our garage down to the pier.'

Jo shook away her inappropriate thoughts about the handyman. 'All I can say is that great minds think alike.'

Arthur muttered to Steve under his breath. 'I think we may have stamped on her toes.'

'Not at all, Gramps.' Jo stepped forwards and ushered both Arthur and Molly away. 'Now off you go. Leave this place to me for the rest of the day. And thank you for pre-empting the decision with the outside furniture. Now it's all here I can clean it up.' When she saw Arthur's expression she knew he was about to offer his services. She gently pushed him towards the door and out onto the wooden planks as Molly followed. 'Oh no you don't! I'm perfectly capable of getting some warm soapy water and sorting them out.'

Leaving Steve to unstack the tables, Jo hovered near Ben and Charlie's table for a chat on her way to the kitchen. 'Hello, you two.'

'Hey, Jo.' Ben was attempting to teach Charlie how to play chess but Charlie wasn't having any of it. 'He lacks the patience.' Ben reluctantly packed away the pieces as Charlie scrambled over to the counter and came back with a piece of paper and a pot of crayons. 'Maybe in another couple of years.'

'Can I get you anything else?'

'I'll have another long black, please. Charlie?'

'A strawberry milk, please.'

'Coming right up. Hey, we missed you in here yesterday. You're usually our Saturday-morning regulars.'

'Where were we yesterday, Charlie?'

'We were at a party.'

'Well that sounds nice.'

Charlie finished drawing a picture of a sailboat.

'Sorry,' Ben whispered, 'he's not very conversational.'

'He talks more than a lot of kids his age.' She thought about Matt's niece, Poppy, and how quiet she was. Charlie wasn't talking because he was busy but Jo wouldn't mind betting that, if he was talking about a subject of his own choice, there'd be no stopping him.

Over time Jo had got to know a lot about Ben. It may not have worked out romantically between him and Jess after their blind date, but Jo had seen how kind and lovely natured he was by the way he was so content with the friendship he'd ended up with. Jo couldn't help feeling a twinge of disappointment that her matchmaking hadn't gone entirely to plan – but she had brought two people together as friends. All she hoped was that her next idea had a bit more success in the romance department.

Jo checked on the quiches, which were nicely golden, and set them on top of the cooker to cool. She fixed Ben and Charlie's order and, by the time she took the drinks to them, Charlie had started to get fidgety again.

'Come on, mate.' Ben looked desperate for a break. 'We had a nice long walk this morning, and after this we'll play on the sand.'

Charlie didn't seem convinced.

'Where did you go this morning, Charlie?' Jo had often found distraction was the best way to get through to kids acting up in the classroom, especially in the early years, when they hadn't quite sussed out how to manage their behaviour in line with their emotions.

'Walking.'

'Well that sounds nice. Where did you go?'

'The nice lady who daddy had a date with took us.'

'You mean Jess?'

'I like her. She's nice. But they're just friends,' he said seriously, causing Ben and Jo to exchange an amused smile. Charlie slumped back against the window seat, narrowly missing Ben's elbow, which would've caused a big coffee spill.

Sensing Charlie needed more than a little distraction, Jo asked, 'Charlie, how would you like to do a little job for me?' His eyes lit up. 'You see all those tables out there now?'

Charlie turned round, got on his knees and looked out of the window, his nose pressed against the glass. He counted. 'One . . . two . . . three . . . four . . . I can't see any more. How many are there?'

'There are five altogether. Now, I'm going to clean those tables, but do you know Bruce? He manages the cinema in town.' Charlie nodded. 'Well this morning he was trying to read his newspaper and it kept flapping around in the wind. So, what I need are some paperweights.' She held out a hand and Charlie jumped down. 'If you run outside, down the steps to the sand, staying where your dad can see you, there are a lot of rocks.' She reached for a crayon, drew an oval on a piece of paper and gave it to Charlie. 'Can you collect me seven or eight rocks around about this size and bring them back? If it's OK with your dad that is?'

'It sounds like a wonderful idea,' said Ben. 'And I'll watch you from the window here, Charlie. Come straight back when you're done.'

Jo found a strong carrier bag and lined it with another. 'Use this. It should hold all the rocks. Now, find me some good ones.'

'I'll time you,' said Ben. 'You've got five minutes. Now go!'

'Easy!' he called as he shot out of the door, across the boards and down the steps. He was easy to spot in his red coat and both Jo and Ben watched him from the window as he crept along stealthily trying to pick out the perfect rocks.

'I wonder how much seaweed he'll bring back,' said Ben.

'Euw! Don't say that. I hate the stuff. Kudos on the time challenge, by the way.'

'He responds well to those. If he thinks it's a game I'm much more likely to get him to do something.'

'And long may it last.'

'Hear hear.'

Sure enough Charlie was back inside five minutes with a wonderful collection of rocks and seaweed that he handed to Jo, and something he hadn't been tasked to find at all: a girl.

'Hello, Poppy.' Jo greeted the little girl in a sky-blue cotton dress and pigtails. 'Do you and Charlie know each other?'

She shook her head, quiet as ever. Jo wondered if she'd just followed Charlie.

'Is that your name?' Charlie asked the little girl, and, when she nodded he told Jo, 'She helped me find the last rock I needed.' He shrugged, as though it were all the explanation he needed to give.

When Matt came through the café door looking frantic, Jo pointed to Poppy, who was peering into the bag alongside Charlie so they could look at their treasure. 'Let me guess: she ran off and you had no idea?'

Matt tugged a hand through dark hair that had been lightened by the summer sun, or maybe by all the hours he spent outdoors at the family farm. He walked over to Poppy and presumably gave her a talk about stranger danger and not letting him know where she was.

Reprimand over, Matt came to the counter. 'I feel like I've aged about ten years in the last few minutes.' He exhaled with relief. 'Seeing as we're here, we'll take two of the raspberry-swirl rolls and two cartons of apple juice, please.' He looked over at Poppy, checking she was still in the café. 'My sister owes me big time for this. It's one thing looking after a kid, but a whole different ball game when it comes to worrying.'

Jo pulled two apple juices from the fridge and lifted the raspberry-swirl rolls onto plates. 'I think you're doing a good job. Poppy seems a lovely little girl.'

'She is. But word to the wise: beach trips with kids need more than one adult.'

'Believe me, I've been on enough school trips as a teacher to know exactly what you mean. And they don't do it intentionally. Their little minds wander off and their legs tend to follow.' She led Matt over to a spare table, where she set down the tray and unloaded everything.

After Poppy had wolfed down her snack, Jo decided it

was time to give the men a respite. 'Right, kids, come over here.' Her teacher voice was back as they joined her at the counter. 'I have a little job for you.'

'That was genius,' Ben said over an hour later. 'I can't thank you enough, Jo.' He'd finished his coffee, been for a walk along the shoreline on his own while Jo kept Charlie entertained in the busy café.

'I think you restored my sanity,' said Matt, who'd thought it best to stay near Poppy in case she went walkabout and had hunkered down at the table beside the door to the café watching the activity with interest. It wasn't hard to sit outside on a day like today and enjoy the feel of the sun, the gentle breeze, the hum of chatter from people on the sands.

For the last hour Jo had set Charlie and Poppy up on one of the tables outside, before she bothered to clean it. The kids had painted rocks in the brightest sunshine yellow and sky blue; they'd done dots and stripes, swirls, something that was supposed to be a giraffe but looked more like a piece of abstract art.

'You kids have done a brilliant job.' Jo inspected their handiwork. Molly and Arthur had walked by twenty minutes ago, enjoying an ice cream each before they went to see a movie up at the cinema, and they'd marvelled at both the kids' and Jo's ingenuity.

'When can we use them?' Poppy was desperate to know.

'I'll need to give them a couple of coats of varnish first, so I'll start that tomorrow when I know your designs have taken.' Hopefully, that would persuade them to be patient. 'How about you come by again soon and see them in action, helping my customers out when they want to weigh anything down?'

'Like their newspapers?' asked Charlie.

'Or their napkins,' suggested Poppy.

Jo nodded. 'That's the idea.'

Charlie tugged at his dad's arm. 'We'll be in next Saturday morning, won't we?'

'Of course we will.'

'Can *we* come back on Saturday?' Poppy asked Matt.

Was it terrible that Jo was almost jealous of this pair? Charlie and Poppy had formed a bond over a few rocks and five minutes on the sand, whereas she'd been hoping to meet someone her whole life and still not managed it. Still, perhaps her idea for love at the café would work better next time. She'd missed the target with Ben and Jess, but perhaps the next couple she had in mind would be luckier. And other people's happiness had a way of making your life that bit brighter, too.

No sooner had she waved off Ben, Matt and their charges than she greeted her next customer, and the very woman she had in mind for her next attempt at match-making. 'Hello, Valerie. I saw you on the sand yesterday morning practising your yoga.' Jo had got used to seeing her and was always impressed. 'How's the crow going, and the penguin pose?'

Valerie laughed. 'I'm getting there with the crow pose as long as I remember to look forwards and not down; and the *pigeon* is going well, too. I'm not sure there's a penguin pose in yoga. If there is, you know more than I do.'

Jo shook her head. 'I don't know how you remember all those moves. Do you work out your routine every day?'

Valerie scanned the blackboard and chose a bowl of fresh fruit salad with Greek yogurt on top. 'I usually do roughly the same but my body seems to tell me which move to follow on with when I get to the end of one.'

'That's funny, my body tells me to sit down or stand up, sleep, and that's about it.'

'You're a good age to give it a go. I didn't start until a few years back, and now I'm fifty; but I find my body's learning new things all the time.'

'I'm not all that flexible.'

'I bet you'd surprise yourself once you started.'

'Take no notice,' said Steve, who had just stepped inside the café. 'Jo's flexible enough. And she's a natural on a surfboard. Which reminds me, when's the next lesson?'

Jo looked at Valerie. 'I'm not a natural at all, it's really hard.' She looked at Steve. 'Rain check?'

She left Steve shaking his head in frustration and Valerie talking about balance techniques and core strength. Valerie wasn't immune to Steve's appeal, either, and Jo noticed her eyes dip more than once from his face to his tanned and toned chest. When he'd come through the door he'd brought with him the smell of the sea on his skin, and now it was time to distract herself by filling a bowl with fresh fruit for Valerie and delivering it to her table along with a pot of peppermint tea.

Back at the till she asked Steve, 'Do you walk around like that all day hoping you'll pick up?' It was hard to drag her eyes away from Steve when he leaned against the counter, wetsuit unzipped to the waist as though walking around half naked were second nature. Or maybe she was a prude. Maybe she needed to loosen up, live a little.

'Very funny. I surfed this morning, then went out on

a jet ski. Awesome, total buzz.' He peered in the glass-fronted cabinet. 'But now I need sustenance. I'll take a slice of the quiche to go please. And a portion of the fruit salad.'

'No coffee today?'

'Nope. This is lunch. Then it's back to the beach.'

Jo sailed through her work right up until she answered the phone. She frowned at the sound of Harry's voice reminding her of their appointment on Wednesday.

'Yes, I'm still OK for six o'clock, thank you, Harry.' She kept it formal. 'I can't talk now: I'm rushed off my feet.' Thankfully, the next group to enter the café were noisier than most, which backed up her claim. She bet Harry hadn't called anyone else about their upcoming appointments. What accountant did that on a beautiful, summery Sunday afternoon? Somehow, fate had played a game with Harry and Jo and made him her accountant, but Jo refused to run from the problem.

By closing time her body was begging for a rest. On a wave of customers, more and more sand had been trodden into the café, she'd swept up whenever she had a free moment, wiped down every surface, served up cold cans of drinks to people who finally gave up on the sands and admitted it was time to go home. When she opened up the front door ready to leave for the day, she noticed a crack in the glass. Pressing lightly, she felt it give beneath her fingers. She swore under her breath. 'How did that happen?' It wasn't tiny, either, and, although tempted to ignore it, she knew from a safety point of view she couldn't. It was below the handle, a place a lot of hands went during the day, and the last thing she wanted was someone hurting themselves. She made a mental note to

Google glaziers when she got home, but her head was already filling with pound signs. Here was another expense on top of all the rest. And, yes, the café was managing, but she could understand Molly and Arthur's utter exhaustion. It wasn't merely the physical working in a café but the upkeep and the stress that came with it, something they'd neglected to mention. It wasn't as though they'd kept anything from her. It was more that their love for the place had masked anything negative, and she supposed she couldn't blame either of them for that.

As she trod the planks of the pier that she'd run across as a kid without a care in the world, Curtis Durham's proposition wheedled its way into her mind once again. The remuneration he'd quoted was far more than she'd ever earn here in Salthaven. It was financial security with a hell of a lot less stress.

If the going got even tougher here, maybe it could be time to give Curtis's offer some serious thought?

13

The sun was out in full force all week, Salthaven having well and truly turned its back on the heavy rain from a fortnight ago. But, on Wednesday morning, thoughts of her latest matchmaking scheme, the bright blue sky and even the blooming abundance of delicate pink roses in the beds beyond the boating lake couldn't lift Jo out of her lacklustre mood as she headed towards the café. She'd paid a ridiculous sum to have a glazier come out first thing Monday morning to measure up for the pane of glass, and today he was meeting her before the clock in the town even chimed 7 a.m. But what choice did she have? It was either pay out now or face legal action if someone injured themselves.

Since Monday the cracked pane had been covered with sheets of cardboard and tape, completely dragging down the look of the freshly painted café. But this morning the glazier was speedy and replaced the glass in no time. Jo had let him do his thing while she hung out on the pier, looking over the white-painted fence and down at the sands where Valerie was taking Hilda through some beginners' yoga moves. Hats off to Hilda for being brave, but it gave Jo an idea of how she'd look if she ever tried it herself, and she made a mental note that even surfing would be the better option.

Jo paid the glazier and he went on his way while she tried not to think about the expense. At least now she didn't have to stress about getting sued, and the only thing troublesome on her mind for the rest of today was her appointment with Harry at six o'clock. And, when she saw Matt's bright smile along with today's produce come through the door, she got busy with what she was best at: distraction.

She breathed in the heady smell of fresh fruit and vegetables as she put her hands out to take the box.

'It's heavy today,' he warned. 'I'll take it to the kitchen for you.'

'Thanks, Matt.'

He pushed the box onto the side of the worktop. 'You're definitely getting through more now it's summer, which is great for your business and mine.'

'Exactly. Now let's see what wonderful ingredients we've got.' She looked through the box.

'The strawberries are sensational right now, so you've lots of those.'

She leaned in and pulled out one of the enormous punnets. 'Nothing says midsummer like a bowl full of strawberries.'

'I need you to write captions for our farm's ads.'

'Your farm's produce speaks for itself. I'll bet business is booming.'

'Actually, it really is. I can't complain at all. I have another box for Molly and Arthur. Are they at home today?'

'Molly should be there. And she'll be happy if you've got more strawberries for her. She was only saying the other day that she wanted to make an Eton Mess as she hasn't made one in ages. Unfortunately, I think I'll be her next victim.'

'You don't like Eton Mess?'

'That's the problem: I love it! But it's full of cream and sugar and she's on a misguided mission to feed me up.' However, much as she joked, Jo had started to crave the evenings she had with her grandparents more and more. She'd bought the flat she'd been renting, jumping onto the property ladder at last, and having her own place was great, but sometimes she missed talking at the end of a day, chatting over a cup of tea come morning. But she knew she needed to make her own life, and, besides, they'd fret if they thought she was lonely. And part of being in Salthaven was about easing their worries, not adding to them.

'Before I forget, Poppy asked if I could check on their rocks. It's almost like she's thinking of them as pets.'

'Well they're no longer rocks,' Jo explained as she led him through to the storeroom, where they were all lined up, 'they're now fancy paperweights. I've given them one coat of varnish and I'll do a second later today or tomorrow. Do you think she'll be in at the weekend?'

'I expect so. Will Charlie be around?'

'Is Poppy hoping he will be?'

'Between you and me, I think she has a big crush on Charlie. He's a whole year older, and, at their age, that's quite something. Why are you shaking your head?'

'You know, I've realised those two have more of a love life than I do. Sad, isn't it?'

'Hello, anyone there?' A voice came from the café.

'That sounds like Angie to me,' said Jo before she

embarrassed herself any more in front of Matt. Talk about being saved by the bell.

When they emerged from the kitchen, Angie had her eyes fixed on the postcards board. 'I read Vince's card,' she said. 'He sounds as though he's having the time of his life. Although I do wish he'd use sunscreen. He says he got badly sunburned the first day.'

Angie loved nothing more than a good gossip, and she'd become one of Jo's favourite customers. If she ever did consider that offer down in Cornwall, Jo wondered, what would the community be like? Would it be small and friendly like this one, or big and impersonal? Would there ever be another Angie, who might talk for England but was one of the kindest and sweetest people Jo had ever had the pleasure of meeting?

Back in the kitchen she took everything out of the produce box, marvelling at its quality, not like buying fresh fruit and vegetables from the supermarket, where you often got home to find half of it was mouldy, limp or simply not up to scratch. Now she was the boss of the café, Jo appreciated each ingredient all the more when she saw it in its raw state. She knew the flavours would pop in your mouth no matter whether you were eating rhubarb or raspberries, lettuce or beetroot.

She took out the salad leaves, gave them a wash and chopped a mixed bowl of red Russian kale, rocket and spinach leaves in the richest of greens, and added in spring onions. She roasted chunks of sweet potato and pieces of beetroot, and, when they were cooked, chopped them even smaller and added them to the salad she set in the glass-fronted display cabinet along with the other dishes she'd made already.

The bell on the door tinkled and in walked Geoff, fisherman and regular.

'Beautiful day,' he said to Jo, as courteous as ever. To be fair, he was such a positive person that he pretty much said those same words or similar on most days, unless it was teaming down with rain, in which case he was usually huddled beneath an umbrella or didn't venture onto the pier at all.

'It's lovely,' she agreed. 'I'm making the most of it. I was off yesterday, so I went for a lovely long walk and watched the surfers around the bay. I also treated myself to a facial, which was heavenly.'

'Sounds wonderful. Can I take a large black tea, please?'

'You don't need to tell me, I know your order by now. Although you're in very late today. Not fishing?'

'I've already been.'

'Wow, you must've been super early.'

'It's the sun. It wakes me up and then I can't get back to sleep, so I make the most of it. It's a wonderful time of the day.'

As Jo set about making the tea, her mind instantly went to another person who had a love for the early hours down by the pier. Someone she saw most mornings.

'What are you grinning at?' Geoff took his tea, wary of Jo's expression. 'You're up to something.'

Her eyes widened. 'I don't know what you're talking about.' But when he went on his way she was brimming with excitement because he and Valerie could be the perfect match. She'd heard on the grapevine that Geoff had been divorced for a while, and she'd never seen him with anyone else or heard of his dating anyone. And Jo had overheard Valerie once telling a friend she'd celebrated her fiftieth and was determined to stay positive. So what if I'm single? she'd said. A lot of people are. It doesn't mean I can't have a life. At the time Jo had thought, Good for you, you don't need a man. And maybe she didn't, but maybe, if Valerie gave dating a go, she might see what she'd been missing.

Molly and Arthur stopped by early that afternoon on their way to the bookshop in town.

'This heat is incredible.' Arthur used a newspaper to fan himself. He'd never coped with any rise in the temperature above twenty degrees, his fair skin susceptible to burning, unlike Molly, whose skin was the complete opposite, turning conker brown as soon as the summer months were upon them.

Arthur perused the postcards board to check whether there were any new additions and instantly picked out the latest. On the front was a photograph of Bath, showing a view of The Royal Crescent, synonymous with the city.

'It's from Sally,' Jo explained, before he'd had a chance to remove the pin and turn the card over. 'Came this morning.'

'Isn't she sweet!' Molly smiled. 'She only went there on Monday for the day to see her sister.' She huddled next to Arthur so she could read the card at the same time. 'She knows how much we love a postcard to add to our collection.'

'That's really nice of her,' said Jo.

Arthur batted his wife away, complaining he was stifling and at the same time asking her to fetch him a cold drink.

Molly rolled her eyes at Jo as they met at the table with

166

the jug of iced water sitting on top. 'Never has been one for a hot day.' She picked up the two glasses Jo poured for her.

'He's more hot chocolates and slippers by the fire, is Gramps.'

'Oh, I like this.' Molly was referring to the slice of cucumber that had tumbled into each glass. 'Trying something else new, I see.'

'Do you approve?'

Molly took a sip. 'It's very refreshing, a nice touch to the café. Bravo, my darling!'

Jo swished away the praise and joined them both while they talked about Sally and about Bath, a place both of her grandparents had visited many a time in their younger days.

'You should go off travelling again,' Jo suggested. 'I've got things in hand here, you don't need to worry about this place any more.'

'Are we visiting too much?' Molly asked.

'No, that wasn't what I meant. I love seeing you, it's why I came back to Salthaven. But I'm serious. You need to enjoy your retirement and you've been so busy with this place over the years. When did you last get away?'

Molly couldn't remember, and neither could Arthur.

'My point exactly,' said Jo. 'So how about it?'

'We could get a coach or a train to Bath,' Molly suggested. 'Or maybe venture up to Norfolk. Remember our trip to Cromer Pier?'

'How could I forget?' Arthur chuckled. 'It poured with rain and we had a ridiculous argument. I was doing my best to use my coat to stop Molly getting any wetter, and when I lifted it above her head all my loose change fell out of the pocket. I got soaked fumbling around for coins, and then I heard your gran laughing. By then, I didn't see the funny side.'

'Oh, I did,' Molly admitted. 'His face was a picture. I'd been so horrible to him because I'd had my hair done that morning and it was completely ruined. We were supposed to be going to see a show at the theatre and I'd been looking forward to it for ever.'

'Gran, I don't think you should've blamed him for the weather.'

'I'd brought a raincoat and umbrella and he'd insisted on holding both of them for me when the sun shone and the clouds were holding steady. We paddled in the sea, he won me a pink teddy bear from one of those ridiculous machines and it was only when the heavens opened that he realised he must've left them in the café where we'd had lunch.'

'Gramps!' Jo giggled. 'Well how about you two venture somewhere a bit more exotic this time round? You deserve it.'

'Nowhere hot,' Arthur insisted.

So did that rule out a trip to Majorca to see Jo's mum?

'I've always wanted to go to Ireland,' said Molly.

This wasn't quite what Jo had had in mind when she'd suggested a holiday. Memory Lane was all well and good, except they'd taken every road apart from the one leading to Sasha. Neither of them was ever willing to divulge details when it came to what had gone on between them all, but, since taking over the café, Jo's need to know more had grown.

Jo served another run of customers, mostly tourists this time, and, with so many taking food and drinks down to the sand or to the tables outside, she decided it was time to say what was on her mind. 'Gramps . . .'

'Sit down, love. Make the most of the lull. It's what we always told ourselves, isn't it, Molly?'

Molly had been gazing out of the window to the sea, the sun shimmering across its surface. She turned her attention to her granddaughter. 'He's right. Why don't you get us three raspberry-swirl rolls and come and sit for five minutes?'

This was as good an opportunity as any, and Jo knew she didn't have long before another customer would come in, so she quickly grabbed the food and a can of sparkling elderflower juice and rejoined her grandparents.

'I spoke to Mum again last night,' she told them.

'I hope she's not still worrying,' Molly replied. 'But I do realise it's her right as a parent. We were always the same.' Something about her comment made Arthur look uneasy.

'I've been trying to convince her to visit,' Jo continued.

'To visit Salthaven?' Arthur made it sound as if Jo had asked her mum to visit a prison camp rather than the town she grew up in. 'Don't tell me, she said no?'

Jo had wondered if he'd been upset when Sasha didn't show after his stint in hospital, but that wasn't the issue at hand. Jo changed tack. 'I've been thinking. Now that I run my own business and I'm on the property ladder, I guess you could say I've properly grown up.' She'd done that a long time ago but was sure they both forgot sometimes.

'You're doing so well, we're really proud,' said Arthur.

'Thank you.' She didn't want to bring them down but it was about time she got some answers. 'I think it's time we all talked. Properly.'

'I'm not sure I know what you mean.' Molly broke off another piece of raspberry-swirl roll.

'I'm talking about what went on between the both of you, and Mum.'

Her probing fell flat and she willed the door to the café to stay closed a little while longer.

'We had very different ideas, that's all.' Arthur was as diplomatic as ever with his answer, but Jo wished he wouldn't be.

'Don't you think I have a right to know? I've not asked too much before because I didn't want to upset anyone, but I'm always on the outside looking in. What if I have questions about my early years, about my father?'

That got their attention.

'He was a waste of space.' For once Arthur had spoken before he really thought about what his words should be and Jo saw the trepidation on his face. 'I'm sorry, that was uncalled for. Are you saying you want to find him?'

'Not at all – honestly,' she added when they both looked so panic-stricken she felt guilty for even mentioning him. 'But I always get the feeling that, even if I did, you'd close every door you could and make it difficult. I know he was bad news for Mum – she told me so – but over the years nobody has ever offered me any details about what happened between her and my grandparents. The three people I love the most in this world don't even talk to one another, and I feel that, if I don't try to move things forward, then that'll be it.'

The sheen in Molly's eyes was enough to tell Jo that this was breaking her heart too. Even if she didn't show it.

'Like I said, we're very different people.' Arthur's diplomacy was back and, when the bell above the door to the café tinkled and twin toddlers trod in sand in front of their tired mum, Jo had no choice but to focus her attention elsewhere.

As Jo was in the throes of listening to the twins chopping and changing their minds, Molly and Arthur saw their escape route and gave Jo a cursory glance when they left. She'd rattled them, but it was about time. How did the saying go? If you didn't ask you didn't get? Well, if she pussyfooted around for ever, there was no way anyone would shed any light on what was going on in her family.

Come three o'clock Jo had just finished wiping up a spill beside the counter when she stood up and came face-to-face with the most beautiful bouquet and behind it a delivery man. 'Are you Jo?' she heard from behind the arrangement of tall, long-stemmed pink roses, sweet-smelling palm and gorgeous oriental pink lilies.

From the back of the café Jo could hear Angie and Hilda gossiping about who they could possibly be from. 'Yes, I'm Jo.' She took the bouquet, laid it on the counter, signed for them and thanked the man, who went on his way.

'Who're they from?' It was Angie, patting her tight curls to make sure nothing was out of place.

'I don't know yet.' Jo's heart leapt. They were absolutely beautiful. Were they from the mystery admirer who'd sent the anonymous postcard? She'd never found out who it was, but maybe the person had been biding their time, waiting for the right moment.

She pulled out the tiny envelope that was nestled in among the blooms.

Hilda clapped both hands together. 'Oh, come on, tell us.'

Jo opened up the little envelope but when she pulled out the card the excitement slid from her face.

Her heart sank, and all of a sudden the flowers didn't seem so beautiful any more.

14

Jo was in a bad mood for the rest of the day and it got worse when Harry arrived for the accounts appointment. Although she'd promised herself she'd keep this strictly professional, the first thing she said to him when he arrived was, 'What are you playing at?'

His confusion faded when he saw the flowers arranged in a vase on the counter with the rest in another vessel on the side table near the blackboard. 'I thought you'd enjoy the flowers at home rather than work.'

'That's not what I meant and you know it.' She shut the door behind him and gestured to the table where she'd already set herself up with surplus paperwork, notepad and pen.

'You're angry.' He sat down.

'Our relationship is strictly professional.'

'Would it help if I told you that we often send gifts to clients?'

'Flowers?'

'Sometimes.'

'And because you do their tax returns?'

'OK, so we don't make a habit of it unless it's a really big account, but I thought it might go some way to building bridges between us.'

Jo frowned, tapping her pen on the notepad. 'What happened with us is past. There's no need for apologies or talking about it.'

'I disagree.'

Well, he would, wouldn't he?

'Let's focus on what we need to do, Harry.'

'Fine.' He relented but she didn't miss the familiar expression he was left with. It was one that said she may have got her way this time but the battle was far from over. Once upon a time, she'd admired that very same confidence, but now she wasn't so sure.

Personal issues aside, they went through the figures Harry had already collated and he explained everything in layman's terms so Jo knew what was what. She passed on extra receipts, she asked in-depth questions, and within an hour they were all done.

'So you'll put it all together and file the return?' Jo stood.

'Of course, I'll let you know when I've filed it and email you the final copy for your records. Then you'll get the usual tax bill, which will be due by the end of January.'

'What do you mean, tax bill? We've been paying a quarterly amount. I've seen it. We discussed it at the last meeting.'

'The bill will be the extra. The café's made more money this year and so it'll incur an extra tax charge.'

Her spirits slumped. She knew the café had made an extra profit, although a modest one, but she hadn't factored in having to pay more tax. She'd bought her flat at a knock-down purchase price partly because the owner wanted a quick sale but also because the kitchen needed redoing to deal with the damp. She'd assumed it would be something she'd just about be able to afford with the café starting to see an increase in profits, but costs were being fired at her from all directions and, with an additional bill now looming, it looked as if she'd be stuck with the grotty kitchen for the foreseeable future.

'Your instalments will be adjusted for next year.' Harry broke into her thoughts. 'The idea is that you won't end up with a bill at the end like this time round. Although remember, the extra tax is due to extra profits, so try to focus on that. It's a good thing.'

She tried to stay positive. 'Will the instalments increase by much?'

'It'll be relative to the extra income the café's made over the tax year, so it won't be too drastic. And, as we progress through the next tax year, we'll keep an eye on turnover and expenses and you won't be hit with any more surprises.' He paused from pushing paperwork into his briefcase. 'You look worried.'

'I am.' She let a sigh escape. 'Molly and Arthur wouldn't have had a mortgage on the bungalow to keep up with; they don't own a car any more; they stay local; and their life is in Salthaven. When I took the café over I kind of assumed that, because there was only one of me, I'd cope fine financially.'

'It's still making a decent profit, Jo.' Why did her name on his lips sound so intrusive? 'With any luck it'll get a real boost this summer, especially now the place has had a facelift, and I think you're opening longer hours than Molly and Arthur ever did.'

'I am, and I'll increase the hours more once the school holidays set in.'

'It's a lot to take on, on your own.'

'I know, but I enjoy it. It's hard work but very different when it's your own pride and joy.' She hadn't thought about it that way before. She wondered: if she managed a venue for someone else such as Curtis Durham, would she ever be able to feel the same passion?

'Molly and Arthur did longer hours back when we were kids, remember?'

'They had more energy then. Sometimes I used to wonder if they'd sleep here if they could.' Perhaps she would. Going home to her flat, alone every night was starting to make her realise that this could be it for her. Happy in her town, happy in her job, but was she destined to have a personal life that revolved around only those two things?

His hand covered hers. 'Try not to worry too much. It sounds as though you have plans for this place, and you definitely have the fighting spirit.'

She snatched her hand away, the skin on skin contact a reminder that their relationship crept over the boundaries of accountant and business owner. 'I need to clean up now, Harry.' She turned her back and picked up the cloth from the side table and wiped that area first, even though there was nothing but a stray petal that had already fallen from the flowers he'd bought.

'Jo, I'd like it if we could still be friends.' His voice made her pause, but only long enough to turn and go through to the kitchen.

She rinsed out the cloth, set it aside and filled a plastic box with ingredients so she could get a head start on tomorrow's menu items by making another goat's cheese and rocket tart tonight. She'd bring it to the café in the morning and then her mind would be free to dream up something new when Matt brought along the latest box of ingredients.

When she rejoined Harry she'd had a chance to gather herself, stand firm. 'I'm not sure that's going to work. If you can't separate business from personal, we need to re-think this arrangement.' She'd taken her time packing up the ingredients, hoping he'd leave without her having to ask him to. But she should've known he wouldn't. It had been the same when they'd got together. He first asked her out one afternoon near the boating lake, but she'd said no, not because she didn't like him but because she did. Her mum had always told her not to be too eager or men would take her for granted, and so she hadn't agreed to go out with him until the third time he asked, when, rather than just asking whether she'd like to go out with him, he had a plan. He'd asked if she wanted to share a fish and chip supper down on the beach and he'd been impossible to resist. The date had been that very same night and they'd sat on the sand, looking out to sea, the taste of salt on their lips, the smell of vinegar and hot potato on the air.

Unbidden, another memory leapt into her mind. It was of the night she'd drunk tequila on the beach on her own and her mum had found her stumbling up the hill. She'd never forgotten the night and the row that came af-terwards, but all the yelling, the words thrown back and forth, had morphed into one until now. 'We don't want Jo to end up like you.' Her gramps had said it, she was sure of it. Somehow, until this moment, she'd blocked the de-tails out, but thinking of her mum's advice on men had unlocked the memory kept in some bizarre box in her mind.

'Jo, Jo, sit down.' Harry was beside her and she hadn't realised, but the colour must have drained from her face in that moment. 'Let me get you a glass of water. No, an orange juice – you need sugar.'

It was almost comical watching Harry fussing around and it was nice to have someone take care of her for a change.

He passed her an orange juice from the fridge and she gulped it down. How had she forgotten those spiteful words between her grandparents and her mum before Sasha left Salthaven for good? And what had they meant? It wasn't Sasha's fault that Jo's father had walked out. And what was so wrong with Sasha, anyway? At the time she had a respectable job working in a bank. She'd raised a daughter on her own. They should've been proud rather than throwing accusations her way.

'Are you all right?' The concern etched on Harry's brow reminded Jo of times gone by and, much as he'd wronged her, it was strangely comforting.

'I'm fine. Thank you.'

Harry ushered her over to the table tucked into the far corner so that, if anyone peered in, they wouldn't think the café open for business. Jo ate a slice of leftover quiche at Harry's insistence and it was only as the sun began to fade outside, plunging the café into darkness, that Jo realised how long they'd been sitting there.

'I'm sorry to have kept you, Harry.' She stood, back to thinking straight. 'I'm fine, really.'

'You don't want to talk about it?'

'No, I don't.' She regretted her lofty manner and managed a smile. 'But thank you for being kind.'

'I'm not all bad.' His comment hovered in the air. 'I'll

be going, then.' He gathered his things together.

Jo prepared to cash up. She'd get the money in the safe and switch everything off, and the floor could wait until the morning. She was spent.

Harry turned when he pulled open the door letting the warm breeze and the smell of the sea trickle inside. 'Jo . . .' He waited until she looked at him. 'Have you ever thought that maybe we could still be good together?'

He lingered for a moment but, when she didn't respond, he left, and she leaned against the counter wondering what direction her life could possibly take her in next.

Was he right? He'd broken her heart once before, but could he still be the love of her life?

15

Jo lost herself in thought as she mopped the floor of the café the next morning while Steve fixed one of the chairs for her. The seat had come loose from the legs and Jo was paranoid about someone trapping their fingers and doing real damage.

She'd tossed and turned last night thinking about her confrontation with Molly and Arthur. And then there was Harry. The flowers were lovely but she wished he hadn't sent them; she wanted to turn back time so he didn't touch her hand as they talked about her accounts; she wanted to go back and not show her vulnerability as she remembered the conversation between members of her family that until now she'd pushed out of her mind. And, most of all, she thought about what he'd said last night, and how she'd been left wondering whether he could still be the love of her life. It was how he'd described her from the very first time they'd shared those three little words: I Love You. The important words that had told her he'd never hurt her, he'd always be by her side. But that had changed in an instant and, although she knew better than to hold a grudge, it was still hard to move past his ending things and the way he'd done it.

Jo was convinced now that Harry had to be the man

behind the mystery postcard she'd received in the spring. And her heart had plummeted at the realisation. He had form when it came to communicating that way, telling her their relationship was over on a postcard sent with a second-class stamp. For someone so confident he'd shown his insecurity but at least this time he'd delivered the card personally, albeit without her seeing him. Perhaps he was trying to make up for the insulting way he broke her heart all those years ago.

But, whatever motives she tried to build into it, it was still a huge disappointment. Since the postcard had arrived in May, the romance in Jo had longed for it to be the start of an epic love story. It would be from someone she would end up falling for, he'd sweep her off her feet, they'd live happily ever after. When Harry had suggested they could still be good together, it was as though his words were a huge wave that engulfed her and took away the magic.

But was she crazy to dismiss him? He had been the man for her, once upon a time. Had she inherited the same stubbornness that stopped Sasha and her grandparents from resolving their issues, so that now she was ignoring someone who had turned into a together, handsome, responsible man?

'Earth to Jo.' It was Steve, looking her way.

'Sorry.' She hadn't realised she'd stopped mopping and was staring into the murky water in the bucket. 'One second, I'll just get rid of this.' She took the bucket outside, walked along until there was sea below the edge of the pier rather than sand, and tipped the water over the side. She needed to stop obsessing about her own love life and instead turn her attentions to a couple who had a chance. She waved at Geoff as he baited his hook at the end of the pier. He and Valerie were a good match, she could feel it.

She took the mop and bucket back to the café and left it in the kitchen ready to put away.

'Chair's all fixed.' Steve began to pack his tools away when she joined him in the café.

When Jo had texted, he'd come as soon as he could, which meant he wasn't exactly dressed for the occasion. He was bare-chested, his wetsuit unzipped to the waist, and it was all Jo could do not to stare. A group of teenagers had just come in and were doing enough of that, under the pretence of perusing the menu, and Steve was oblivious.

The cogs in Jo's mind had begun to turn, seeing Geoff and thinking about Valerie. 'You know the beach where you gave me a surf lesson?' she asked Steve as he shut his toolbox.

'You want a second go?' He stood up, his body even more distracting.

Jo shook her head as she went to the counter and took payment for two cans of cola from the teenage girls still giggling away as they elbowed one another and eyed up Steve. She rolled her eyes as they bundled out of the door. 'Thank goodness it's a school day!'

'Why? Not like you to want customers to leave quickly.'

'So you didn't notice how much they were ogling you?'

He shrugged and she could tell he'd been none the wiser. 'They're young, having a bit of fun, that's all. Don't be such a misery arse.'

'Hey!' He earned himself a playful tap on the arm and Jo shivered at the feel of his skin beneath her fingers.

'Anyway, back to my question about the beach. How busy is it in the evenings at this time of year?'

'Strange question, but I'll go with it.' He leaned on the counter. 'It's much quieter than the mornings. Most people like to get out there early. Why, you thinking of an evening surf lesson?'

'Forget the surf lessons for now. I want to know how crowded the sands will be, about an hour or so before the sun goes down.' The look he gave her told her she'd get no more information out of him until she told him why she wanted to know. 'It's for my next love at the café idea.'

'Ah, I wondered how long it would be before Cupid came out to play again.'

His flirtatious demeanour was as distracting as his muscly arm, and she was thankful when Ben and Charlie appeared in the doorway. 'I'll tell you more later,' she whispered.

'My lips are sealed,' he said, and Jo tried to resist the temptation to look at his mouth when he drew his fingers across his lips in a zipping action.

She turned her attention to her other customers as Steve went on his way. 'Hey, Charlie. Hey, Ben.' Why was Ben looking at her as though she'd done something untoward? She hoped it wasn't obvious that she'd been thinking about Steve in a non-platonic way. Lately, all she'd been able to think about when she saw him was how he flitted through life so carefree and he'd be perfect for a no strings attached fling. It'd been so long since she'd been with a man that she was wondering whether she'd even remember what to do.

She shook away the thought. 'I don't usually see you two in the week.'

'I promised Charlie he could check out the paper-weights,' Ben explained, back to his usual friendly self.

'You certainly can. One more coat of varnish today and they'll be fully ready to use. Go out to the storeroom, Charlie, and you'll see them all lined up.' He didn't need telling twice. She leaned closer to Ben. 'Please tell me you'll be back Saturday too.'

'Of course. Why?'

'A certain young lady may want to see a certain young man.'

He tapped the side of his nose as Charlie reappeared gushing about how good the paperweights looked and dragging Ben by the hand to see for himself.

'Is it OK?' Ben asked.

'Sure, go through. Mind the mop and bucket – I was too lazy to clean the floor last night so only did it this morning.'

They went through as Matt appeared with today's produce box. Jo marvelled at the colourful selection, noticing the cherries, plump and shiny and asking to be eaten.

'What's going through your mind?' Matt asked. 'I love hearing what ideas you come up with.'

The deep red fruit already had her imagination going. 'I'm thinking: cherry-almond cookies or cherry-oat scones?'

'Both sound good to me.'

'Me too.' Ben appeared from the kitchen. He didn't seem to want to miss out.

'Me three,' said Charlie who was already eyeing the treats behind the counter and the jar of chunky cookies with Smarties that sat next to the till.

'Come on, we need to get you to school,' Ben told him, 'and I have to work.'

Jo dropped a cookie into a small pink-and-white-striped paper bag for Charlie. 'As a thank-you for the paperweights,' she explained.

Matt had taken the produce through to the kitchen and, when he reappeared, Jo asked, 'What about cherry-ginger scones?'

'As I've said before, I grow the stuff, I don't cook much out of the ordinary. All the suggestions sound great to me.'

'Well thank you for my daily inspiration.'

'My pleasure.'

She waved him off distractedly as she concentrated on trawling through the collection of recipe books from beneath the counter. She swore she'd seen something in there for scones so it would be easy enough to substitute a fruit and a spice to make what she had in mind. 'Bingo!' she called as the door opened and Jess came in.

'I don't mind our nights at the pub,' said Jess, 'but I'm not so old I need to start going out to play bingo.'

'Sorry, just found what I was looking for, that was all.' She showed Jess and explained the flavour she had in mind.

'That sounds too yummy, very bad for the waistline, and of course something to put on the menu. Pub, to-night?' When Jo frowned she added, 'Oh, come on, Billy will be back tonight from his break in Cornwall and he's doing Happy Hour at eight.'

Billy was the landlord at the Salthaven Arms and, although she'd heard on the grapevine that pubs weren't making as much money as they used to, he seemed to be able to bring the punters in with more than his fair share of happy hours. 'You're on. I'll see you later. Check out his postcard, it's on the board.' When Jo had picked it up yesterday morning from the doormat, the sweeping coastline and beautiful landscape with jaw-dropping views had made her take pause, Curtis Durham's proposal gnawing its way through her mind once again.

Jess didn't hang around for long and by early afternoon Jo was busy. She'd been back and forth with coffees, slices of raisin toast and sandwiches with assorted fillings, and had been yo-yoing between serving and cleaning up, and so the lull, when it came, was welcome. At last she had some time to herself and, with one small group filling two tables and happy for now, she went into the kitchen and found out the red postcards and the calligraphy pen. It was amazing how doing something special for other people could lift her tired spirits in seconds. She thought about Geoff, a lovely man but clearly lonely. She thought about Valerie and her yoga, which kept her youthful now she was in her fifties.

She peeked out to check that her customers were happy and then penned identical invites, shaking them a little to dry the ink each time. She'd checked the weather forecast for Friday evening and also knew from the extra information she'd gleaned from Steve via text that the beach would be even quieter then, as a lot of youngsters went out on a Friday night or saved their surfing for first thing Saturday morning without the hassle of work to worry about.

Back in the café, Jo had only just popped the postcards into her bag when Molly and Arthur came in, bringing with them the scent of coconut sunscreen. Jo could imagine Molly bossing Arthur about every morning when the sun was out, telling him to put it on, grab his hat, drink plenty of water.

The smile they shared with her told Jo they wanted peace as much as she did and she went around to the other side of the counter to hug each of them in turn. It was impossible to stay angry with either Gran or Gramps for long.

'We're sorry, Jo.' Molly was first to speak as she handed Jo a big plastic container. 'It's a peace offering – broccoli-pasta salad.'

'It sounds delicious. I'll get it in a bowl in the display cabinet ASAP. And I'm the one who's sorry. I shouldn't have pried.'

They settled themselves at the window seat while Jo fixed them a cup of tea and cleared a table that had just been vacated.

'I need to talk to Mum about it, don't I?' She pulled up a chair while she had the opportunity.

'It's not that we're trying to be awkward.' Arthur winced at his first sip of tea. He still wasn't used to taking it without sugar as part of his health kick. While he was allowed treats every day, he apparently had too many brews to justify the sugar in each one, so it'd had to go. 'But our relationship with Sasha is already strained and neither of us wants to push her away even more.'

So that was why they'd kept schtum. They were afraid of making it worse.

'We're worried.' Molly's eyes were fixed on Jo. 'We don't want to get to the point where she never comes back. There's still hope she will one day, at least to visit, and if she does then perhaps we can move past our argument.'

'Talk to her, Jo,' said Arthur. 'I know, I should try the same, but I think you'll be the one who can get through to her. You could get the answers you need and maybe . . .' The hope in his eyes faded. 'Well, start there and we'll see what happens.'

Jo put her hand on his. 'I'll do my best.' And she would. 'I'd better get on.' She turned at the tinkling of the bell when the café door opened and in came a party of five – tourists from Scotland by the sounds of it.

Molly and Arthur went on their way, hand in hand, and Jo watched them as the group who'd just come in pulled another chair up to the table by the blackboard.

Could she ever find what her grandparents had: a relationship where togetherness was second nature and longevity came as standard?

When Jo had made sure all her customers were happy she went out back to organise herself. She wanted to make those scones and get them on the menu ready for the after-school and after-work crowds, always ravenous.

Customers floated in and out steadily for the rest of the afternoon and, during the time in between serving, Jo managed to give the paperweights their second and final coat of varnish. Finally, in the time preceding the after-school rush, Jo took the opportunity to call her mum.

They spoke about Majorca, the new line of jewellery Sasha was making and Jo's management of the café, and, when Jo told her about Harry's reappearance including the flowers, Sasha leapt on it instantly.

'He hurt you, Jo.'

'I know he did. And now he's my accountant.'

'Oh, Jo, don't go making a huge mistake because you

think you can't do better. I know all about that.'

Jo looked out of the window across the sands at people laughing and playing, children too young for school jumping up and down as the waves crashed against the shore and disturbed sandcastles they'd taken so long to make. 'I won't, Mum.'

'He might say he's changed, but we've all heard that before.'

Harry seemed to think they could still be good together. He was different from the boy he'd been back then. He'd technically been a man but it was the only way Jo could distinguish between the person he seemed to be now and the person she'd dated and who had dumped her in such a horrid way.

'Jo, I mean it. People can change, but, from my experience with men, it's unlikely.'

This was her chance. Talk to her, her grandparents had said. And her mum was bringing up the subject of men all by herself this time, trying to use her own experience to warn Jo off. 'Can I ask you something?'

'Sure, anything. Go ahead.' She sounded open, receptive, ready to let Jo in.

'What exactly happened between you and my grandparents? Why were they so adamant I wouldn't turn out like you?'

Silence.

'Mum?'

'Who told you that's what they think?'

'You and Gramps had an almighty row, the night I drank all that tequila – which, you should know, I haven't done quite so badly since – and I'd forgotten until recently that Gramps yelled how he didn't want me to turn out like you.' The words probably stung, but it was time to get them all out there.

'It's all in the past, Jo.'

'No, Mum. It's not.' The bell above the door was definitely working because it tinkled now and Jo indicated to the customer by holding up a finger, that she'd be one minute. She took the phone out to the kitchen, where she could keep an eye on the café but was out of earshot. 'When you don't speak to your parents and you no longer visit the town that once meant something to you, then it's not in the past.'

'Jo, I will never measure up to who they want me to be!' Sasha's voice rose quickly but then fell an octave. 'They're ashamed of me, have been for a long time.'

'Then they need to get over themselves.' And her customer was now waiting at the counter, which was her cue to go. 'I have to go, Mum.' She wished she didn't. Her mum was on the verge of explaining everything, she knew it.

'We'll talk again soon, Jo.'

'I'd like that.' And when she hung up she hoped they would. Usually, her mum refused to dust the surface of things she hadn't told Jo, any questions making her close up tighter than a fresh clam.

Perhaps they were finally getting somewhere. Because what Jo wanted more than anything in the world was for her family to be happy. And that meant every single part of it.

16

The mornings were so light, now summer had come to the south coast, that Jo had enjoyed a saunter around Salthaven before she started work this morning. The streets were deserted so early on and it was a great way to begin the day. It also helped her clandestine delivery of the latest two invites for a night of love. She'd deposited a red envelope through Geoff's mailbox in the foyer of his block of flats opposite the surf beach, and pushed the other through the door to Valerie's terraced house not far from the pub.

She'd been at the café only ten minutes when Matt rocked up with the produce. She peered into the box, always anxious to see what he'd brought from the farm. It had become one of the most special parts of Jo's day.

'There are another couple of punnets of cherries,' he told her, 'so I hope you're not fed up with those . . . gooseberries, strawberries, and plenty of lettuce leaves. A good supply of eggs too, so you've got lots to choose from.'

Matt took the box out to the kitchen – he was kind that way as it was sometimes heavy. When he came back she handed him a Tupperware container.

'What are these?' He pulled open the lid. 'Wow, they smell good.'

191

'Cherry-ginger scones.'

'For me?'

'They're not fresh this morning, but they're less than twenty-four hours old and still pretty good. I've been making them for the last few days and they're hugely popular.' Golden brown in colour, the scones gave lightly in the centre when pressed and every customer who'd had one yesterday had said how good they were.

'You're just like Molly.'

'I'm not as good a cook as Gran.'

'I meant with the way you try to feed people up.'

'Ah, yes. We do like to look after friends and family with food, and you supplied the cherries, so it's also a big thank you.'

'Well I appreciate it. I'll bring the container back tomorrow.'

'Great. Oh, before I forget, could I please order extra strawberries for Friday?'

'Of course, I'll be sure to put in as many as I can. The café's one of our favourite customers up at the farm.'

Jo's heart warmed to hear it. 'Really?'

'Poppy's trying to recruit the entire family to come here at the weekend. I'm not sure what's driving her more – the paperweights, the delicious food or the prospect of seeing Charlie.'

'They're so cute, aren't they?'

'Love is easy when you're so young.' He turned his attention to the paperweights lined up beside the till. 'They did a brilliant job. These look great with a decent shine.'

'They sure do. I don't like to leave them outside but when customers seat themselves at the outdoor tables I usually take a paperweight out to them. Angie even used one to hold her book's pages down when she was seated inside, so they'll always come in handy.'

'I can't imagine Angie reading.' He looked around to make sure she wasn't in the vicinity. 'I'm not sure she'd stop talking long enough to be able to concentrate on a story.'

'Actually, I think you're right. She spent most of her time chatting to me or telling people how wonderful the cherry scones were.' Jo wondered if she'd ever get the chance to set Angie up with anyone at her café, but Angie was a hard woman to work out. And the last thing Jo wanted to do was cause any offence.

'I should get going,' said Matt. 'I'm delivering to the school next, then a couple of businesses in town, then it's back to the farm.'

'Sounds full on.'

'It is, but it's all good. And my sister will bring Poppy in on Saturday.' He waved goodbye and left Jo to it.

By mid-morning, after a brief shower from the bruised clouds that had since moved on from the pier, Jo enjoyed a steady clientele. People were opting to sit outside more and more now the summer months were upon them, and it was time to give the tables a good clean. With a bucket of hot, soapy water, her Marigolds and a cloth, Jo got to work.

'Not much point in doing that, is there?' It was Geoff, fishing rod in hand, finished for the day as Jo moved to the last table.

Her heart leapt. He'd be going home to find the red envelope in his mailbox. Time to cross her fingers, toes and whatever else she could that his reaction was a good one.

She got back to the job in hand. The weather hadn't

washed away sticky patches of jam or clumps of sugar, but she'd scrubbed hard enough to get rid of those, and now it was time to tackle what was left. 'No amount of rain will shift this.' She gestured to what could be crayon, paint or even nail polish. It hadn't been there after the kids painted the paperweights, so she had no idea what it was.

'You'll do better with a scrubbing brush,' he suggested.

She sighed heavily. 'You're right. Are you coming in for a cuppa?'

He leaned his rod up against the café and put down his fishing gear. 'I might make the most of the sun before the heavens open again and grab a black tea to drink out here.'

'Coming right up.'

'Oh, and one of those cherry-ginger scones if you've got any left,' he said, hopefully.

'We certainly have, they're very popular. I'll whip up another batch later today. You're not getting bored of them yet?'

'I'm not, and I don't have another half to nag me about my waistline, either.' He grinned.

With any luck, his love life could soon improve dramatically, if she had her way.

It was Wednesday evening and Jo hadn't heard a thing from Valerie or Geoff about the invites, so she had to assume it was still all systems go. She'd found out the beautiful cornflower-coloured blanket she'd got three Christmases ago, which hadn't been cleaned since last summer when she'd gone to Portobello beach in Scotland with Tilly. They'd spilt Prosecco over it as they toasted the start of the school holidays and six weeks off. Now, in her flat, she pushed the blanket into the washing machine, added the special wool detergent and made sure it was set on the right cycle.

She thanked goodness Molly and Arthur were as romantic as she was – perhaps that was where she'd got the trait from – because when she told them her idea of the romantic picnic, Arthur had used the long pole in the cupboard to pull open the loft hatch at the bungalow, manoeuvre the ladder until it squeaked to the floor, and he'd gone up there to find their old-fashioned picnic hamper. 'We haven't used it for years,' he'd told her, then added something to Molly that now they were retired they could get a coach down to Cornwall for the day. Molly had said that everything she had was right here in Salthaven and she didn't see the need to haul a big basket of food to another county, and Jo marvelled at the way she told him straight. The niggling reminder of an opportunity in Cornwall didn't bypass Jo, either, although she did her best to dodge it. When everything was running smoothly at the café she didn't give Curtis Durham's offer a thought, but, every time she felt doubt creep into her mind that she could make this a long-term success, there was his face again. Still, it was a handsome face. That gave her a bit of pleasure at least.

As the washing machine filled with water Jo tried to ignore the funny squeaking sound it was making and prayed it wouldn't ruin her beautiful blanket, nor that it was on its last legs giving her yet another expense. She picked up a cloth and wiped out the picnic basket. Lined with pale-blue linen with brown leather fasteners for plates, bowls and glasses, it was traditional and perfect for a night of romance. Jo had already asked Sally down the road if she could possibly have a few roses from the plentiful bush at the front of her bungalow, and, when she'd told Sally the reason, Sally had told her to help herself as long as Jo promised to tell her the out-come of the night of love. Jo had kept the couple's names to herself so far, and anyone who asked about her plans seemed to respect the need for discretion. She hoped that one day they could shout it from the end of the pier so the whole world would know how the nights of love at the café had brought such happiness into people's lives.

With the picnic basket all clean and the blanket washed and, thankfully, still in one piece after its traumatic visit to the washing machine, Jo laid the blanket complete-ly flat over the airer she'd put in the bedroom. It smelled beautiful and she couldn't wait to lay it out on the sand on Friday night. She'd already collected a few larger rocks from the beach on her walks over the last week so they'd serve as weights for the blanket, and the picnic basket could do the rest.

Out in her little kitchen she poured herself a glass of wine. She put on another load of washing, the drum filled with water and the squeak continued, more ear-piercing than before, when the phone rang. It was Molly to tell her she'd made some buttermilk cookies for the café and Arthur had made a loaf of banana bread.

'I'll collect them in the morning,' said Jo above the din. 'What on earth is that racket?'

'It's the washing machine.' She had to repeat it three times and then took her wine, shut the door and went through to the lounge. 'Goodness knows what's going on, but it works – just about.'

'You need to get it checked.'

'Yes, Gran.'

They talked some more about the cherry scones that had been such a hit, and Gran laughed when Jo told her how Angie had been selling them to everyone who came in by going on and on about how tasty they were.

'Gramps found a recipe for gooseberry-meringue tart,' said Molly.

'Great. Although I've not cooked with gooseberries before, and I don't think I've ever made meringue, either.'

'It's a doddle. Maybe Arthur can show you on Sunday when you take over. We'll wait for a quiet time, if there is one.'

They talked about an upcoming book signing that Molly was dragging Arthur to, her Gran moaned about Arthur's obsession with bowls, wanting to take her there, although Jo could tell she loved this new, less stressful side of the man she'd married. And, after she hung up, Jo flung open the windows in the lounge so she could hear the gentle sighing of the waves as they curled and crept towards the shore, and inhale the freshness they brought with them.

She relaxed in the lounge, glass of wine in hand. Apart from the bedroom, which shared the same view as she had now, this was her favourite room. Walls painted in white with a hint of lilac were bordered by glossy white skirting boards. She'd bought a light-grey sofa, which had white scatter cushions, but her favourite piece of furniture, which she'd flopped into now, was the deep, round chair that allowed her to curl up on it and gaze out at the sea in the distance. Down below she could see the golden sands beyond the grassy banks that sloped down towards the pier, and on the window ledge outside a seagull perched, scanning for leftovers.

When she heard her doorbell ring Jo put down her wine. She didn't mind being alone so much with the amazing view, the pier iconic to Salthaven reminding her of why she'd returned, but she supposed it was still nice to have visitors.

Surprised to see Harry when she pulled open the door, her first question was, 'How did you know where I live?'

'You gave me your home address when we did the accounts.'

Oh. 'Harry, what are you doing here?' He wasn't carrying any papers, so he couldn't be here under the guise of more accounting work.

'Can I come in?'

'I didn't make a mistake on the tax return, did I?' She had sudden visions of his telling her she owed a lot more than they'd thought.

'I've not come about the accounts, no. God, what's that noise?'

'The washing machine.'

'Should it sound like that?'

The squeaking seemed to increase a decibel or two. 'Probably not. I don't suppose you're handy with white goods, are you?'

'Sorry. Now, if your car was having problems, I'm the guy to call, but washing machines aren't really my thing.'

She'd almost relaxed enough to let him chat away, but not quite. 'Why are you here, Harry?' Her mum's warning words came back to her and she kept Harry at the door rather than invite him in. If he came in she'd feel she had to offer him a glass of wine and she was so heady about her romantic plans for others that she wasn't confident the wine wouldn't go to her head and she'd do something she might regret.

He extended a hand and produced a white paper bag with something inside.

'What's that?'

'Take a look.'

She took the bag and whatever it was jostled together making little tapping noises as they moved. She peered inside. 'Aniseed balls?'

'From Salthaven Heaven.'

He'd remembered. On their second date they'd bought sweets from the local sweetshop and on the way home the challenge was to suck the aniseed ball until all you were left with was the tiny seed in the middle. She'd won every time.

'Bet you can't do it,' he challenged now.

She handed the packet back. 'Harry, what are you playing at? First the postcard and now this.' His lack of denial told her she was correct in her assumption, and disappointment flooded through her body. Up until now there'd been a possibility that the postcard was from some secret admirer, but the fact that he didn't say anything told her she'd found the mystery sender.

'Jo, I—' But he was interrupted by footsteps on the stairs.

Jo leaned around the door jamb to see who it was. 'Steve?'

'Molly called.' It was then that Jo saw the toolbox in his hand.

'Not the washing machine.' She shook her head. 'She only knew I had issues—' she checked her watch '—less than an hour ago. I can't believe she summoned you already.'

Steve nodded to Harry and then turned his attention back to Jo. 'Can I take a look? This toolbox is getting heavy now I've carried it up three flights of stairs.'

She stood back and let him go in through the front door.

'You seem to see a lot of Steve.' The wobble in Harry's voice belied the laid-back attitude he was attempting to pass off.

Harry had never once made his jealousy obvious when other men showed an interest in Jo, but she'd always known he felt it. He'd tried to cover it up by acting casual and she'd spent many a time reassuring him back then that her attention was only on him. She almost felt like doing so now, but, when she thought how much he'd hurt her, she knew it wasn't her responsibility.

'I should get in there, see what's what,' she said instead.

In one last attempt Harry held out the paper bag filled with one of her favourite sweets. 'Here, take them. I never liked them as much as you did.'

'Thanks.' She watched him walk back along the landing and returned his smile as he turned at the stairwell and made his way down.

Back inside she dropped the bag of aniseed balls on the shelf in the hallway and went to find Steve. 'What's the damage?' Please say minimal, please say it'll cost nothing, please don't make me have to call a specialist, she thought desperately.

He'd pulled the washing machine out from its position beneath the bench in the kitchen and had removed the back to take a look. Thankfully, he'd left the load of laundry inside the drum. It was stuffed full with bras and knickers, and not her nicest ones, either.

He pointed to the piece of rubber that went round something that looked like a pulley. 'It looks like your drive belt needs replacing. I'll have to get another one for you but it's cheap. I'll pick one up when I'm passing the hardware shop and have it fitted in the next day or so.'

Jo sighed with relief. 'Thank you, you're a lifesaver.'

He fixed the back of the machine on once again before manoeuvring the whole thing back into place.

Jo only hoped her gran's concern had been for her finances and her washing machine rather than anything else, because she wasn't sure how she'd feel if she was being set up. And she didn't know how Steve would react, either.

17

It was Friday morning and Matt had dropped off the box of produce with the extra strawberries Jo requested. The fruit was exquisite. Their characteristic colour held a juicy sweetness and Jo washed and stashed enough of them for tonight's picnic and set them aside in a separate bowl beneath kitchen towel. She'd chosen not to hull them, leaving the stalks on for more colour and to make them easier to pick up.

Steve knocked on the door shortly before opening time to return the keys she'd lent him so he could fit the new drive belt to her washing machine, and Geoff came in shortly after. She'd not spoken to him since he must've found the invitation back at his flat and, when the bell tinkled to announce his arrival, she knew by his face that he was about to mention it.

'I'm flattered,' was the first thing he said.

Her heart sank. 'But . . .'

'No "but".'

'Really?'

'My daughter was there at the flat when I opened the invite.'

'Oh, no. I hope I didn't embarrass you too much.'

He smiled, something he needed to do more often, and

maybe after tonight he would. The weather had cooperated and already a blue sky with the odd cloud floating on past promised a fine start to Jo's plan.

'You didn't embarrass me, but my daughter seemed to think her dad needed some help, so she's been fussing over me ever since.' When Jo giggled he said, 'Easy for you to see the funny side, but I felt like a hopeless geriatric as she dragged me from shop to shop to choose me a shirt that was suitable, a pair of trousers and some new shoes. I'm not really sure what was wrong with the clothes I already have and my trusty flip-flops. Although I think my legs in a pair of shorts may have had something to do with it.'

Jo grinned. 'Well whatever you wear, I'm glad you're on board.'

'You know, when I heard about you setting up the night of love for Ben and Jess, I thought it was ridiculous, that it would fall flat on its face and the participants would hate the idea. But, even before I got my own invite, I'd begun to change my mind. I kept thinking back to Valentine's Day and the event you'd tried to hold here at the café.'

'That didn't exactly go as planned when nobody turned up.'

'No, but what I like about you, Jo, is that you don't give up. And, lately, every time I walked past the café, I thought about what might have happened had I or anyone else shown up that night in February. My addled mind had begun to weave stories and dare to hope I could've met someone.' He seemed to suddenly remember he was opening up to a girl likely to be closer to his daughter in age than his own. 'Then I told myself nobody would want a lonely divorcee fisherman.'

'Don't put yourself down.'

'I am curious,' he admitted. 'Who's the other party?'

'All will be revealed, don't worry.' The mystery was all part of the adventure and so she showed him to a table, made him a black tea and with the rest of the café quiet apart from Jess, who'd come in briefly to buy a strawberry smoothie after her run, she asked him why he thought nobody would be interested in getting to know him.

'I was divorced ten years ago, Jo, ten years. I'm fifty-three, I fish on my own, and the only reason I still work as a mortgage consultant is because I'm scared that if I take early retirement, which I can easily afford to do, that'll be it. I'll spend the rest of my days sitting on the end of that pier with nothing but mackerel, mullet and bait for company.'

'Oh, dear, you've got a bad case of the sads.'

'You sound like my daughter, Tracey. She used the exact same phrase before dragging me to every clothing outlet in Salthaven. Do you know, she set me up with a blind date last year? The first time I've been out with another woman in a decade. It's true.'

Jo couldn't see it. He was early fifties, a full head of hair with a distinguished sprinkling of grey and the kindest blue eyes. She was surprised someone hadn't snapped him up sooner, but she knew better than most how hard it was to meet people and put your trust in someone new. As a teacher, she didn't have a plethora of work colleagues to choose from. Most were either female or already married. And then the only other people she socialised with hadn't even been in double figures.

'What was it like, the date?' she asked.

'Terrible. We had nothing in common. I swear she turned her nose up when I said I enjoyed a spot of fishing.

And she was one of those women who order salad and then steal all your chips.'

Jo couldn't disguise her amusement. 'I'm sorry, it doesn't sound too pleasant.'

'She even complained I'd drenched *my* chips in too much vinegar. And she had the loudest laugh I've ever heard, which, believe me, wasn't good. I didn't want to say anything remotely amusing to encourage it.'

'All joking aside, Geoff, I can promise you that this woman tonight is wonderful, and has a very quiet laugh.'

'What if we don't get on?'

'Then maybe you'll find a friend.' It wasn't what Jo wanted, but it had worked for Ben and Jess. They met up regularly. Last week they'd been to a new seafood restaurant that had opened up two towns along the coast from Salthaven. And friendship was a lot better than loneliness.

As more customers filed in, Jo patted the top of Geoff's hand, hoping that, this time round, her plan would work its magic. 'Eight o'clock tonight, don't be late.' And when she looked at Geoff he seemed as keen for this to work as she did.

Jo had half expected to see Harry again today, bringing her some other gift, but he didn't show. Maybe he'd decided he'd made his feelings clear and now it was up to her. He was confusing her more and more and she knew part of the issue was that since Harry she'd never found anyone else so special that a relationship had lasted more than a few dates. Maybe Harry was right: perhaps they were right for each other, and the only thing standing in their way was their history. Was her determination to punish him preventing her from seeing the bigger picture?

By early afternoon after a steady stream of customers, Valerie appeared, yoga mat over her shoulder in its special carry case.

'Late session today?' Jo asked. When she was confronted by the chosen ones for her blind dates, it was always an anxious moment. Would they appreciate it? Be excited? Say they couldn't possibly be involved in such a crazy scheme?

'I'm so uptight. I did yoga this morning on the sand and then again at the studio in town.'

Jo hoped this wasn't a bad sign. 'I didn't mean it to make you stressed. It's supposed to be something nice, especially for you and one other.'

Valerie relaxed a little. 'Actually, despite being anxious, I'm looking forward to it, Jo. I feel happy you picked me.'

Relief didn't even come close, especially after seeing how enthused Geoff was this morning. She didn't want to let either of them down. 'I'm glad.'

'But . . . I've never ever been this nervous in my entire life.'

Jo showed her to a table. 'Camomile tea coming up – it'll calm you down.'

She made the tea and let Valerie settle and find her equilibrium because it was all over the place at the moment. She hadn't picked Valerie as the nervous type – she was always so serene as though she had the secret to inner confidence – but here she was fiddling with the corner of a napkin and, when she'd finished doing that, she changed to drumming her nails on the table.

Jo set down the cup of tea. 'Mind if I join you?'

'Please do.' She wrapped her hands around the cup.

'I can understand you must be anxious,' said Jo. 'I don't

want to tell you who the date's with, though. Can you trust me on that?'

'Anyone who comes and makes Molly and Arthur as happy as they are now is trustworthy in my book.' She took a deep breath. 'Doesn't mean I'm not apprehensive. I usually zone out when I practise yoga and I'm at peace, but this morning I struggled. I almost fell over doing a crescent lunge, a move I mastered quite a while ago.'

'What on earth is a crescent lunge?'

Valerie stood up and demonstrated the best she could, one leg bent at the back, her other stepping forwards, her arms in something resembling a crescent shape. Back in her chair she said, 'You need to come to the beach one morning, try it. It'll do you good.'

'I don't know, between you suggesting yoga and Steve trying to make me take up surfing, are you saying I'm really unfit?'

'Not at all. But here you are fretting about other people's lives, Jo, when you've got your own to consider. It can't all be about work. Otherwise you'll get to my age, look back and wonder where on earth your life went.'

Jo decided a change of subject was the best way to avoid any focus on her pretty sad, lonely life. 'Well the man I've chosen to be there tonight is lovely, kind, handsome—'

'Oh, no, you haven't picked a toy boy for me, have you? Because I might do yoga, but some things still head south no matter how much you try not to let them, and I don't think he'd appreciate it.'

Getting ready to serve her next customer, Jo assured her, 'He's a good match, I promise.'

*

Jo had just wiped down the only available table inside when another familiar face appeared at the door.

And a handsome face at that. Jo didn't miss a nod of approval from Valerie, who had ever so discreetly given Curtis Durham the once-over as he walked towards the counter.

'Good afternoon,' said Jo, determined to treat him like any other customer but suspecting it would be near to impossible.

'Hello, Jo, lovely to see you again.' This time he wasn't in a suit but instead he wore chino shorts in a warm grey with Nike trainers and a black crewneck T-shirt that brought out his olive skin, tanned from the sun.

'Are you in town on business?' She thought she'd keep it casual with lots of sets of ears around that had the power to absorb information and set tongues wagging.

'Pleasure.' Something about the way he said it made Jo uneasy.

'I thought you'd be busy down in Cornwall.'

'I'm still looking for that elusive manager to run the new place.'

'What can I get you?' She didn't want to give anyone the ammunition to start the gossip mill turning. She'd met with only niceness in Salthaven so far, but every small town had the ability to start rumours and keep them going.

Curtis went for a can of fizzy drink and a sausage roll and nabbed the last table. Jo wished someone else had got in there first and he'd be forced to take his order away with him. But she supposed she should be grateful for how busy it was because it meant she didn't have time to stop, or for him to corner her and ask whether she'd thought any more about his proposal. He'd emailed her a few times since he'd come to her with his idea but she'd never felt as much pressure as she did right at this moment.

'He's a bit young for me,' Valerie whispered on her way out, 'but you could use a bit of an injection for your love life. Go for it.'

'Stop,' Jo giggled. 'He's a customer, nothing more.' He was a good-looking guy but far too serious for her liking. Then again, seeing him in casual clothes did make a difference. Maybe the man had a side she was yet to see.

When the café began to empty and it drew closer to the end of the day, Curtis Durham had got through two cold drinks, a cup of tea, a slice of quiche and one of Molly's buttermilk cookies. 'Can I get you anything else?' Jo asked him.

'You could agree to my proposition. Then at least I could stop eating all this food. I'll have to run miles to burn all this off.'

For some reason it made her pleased to know he'd been as uncomfortable as she was, albeit in a different way. 'I really don't see why you can't find dozens of people as capable as me to run a café in Cornwall.'

'I've interviewed dozens, and all are capable, yes, but you have something else. Something I had when I started my own business.'

'And what's that?'

'Vision. Energy. Drive. You're committed to this place for more reasons than money. It's a part of you, I can tell.'

'It really is.'

She listened to him talk about his vision for the new café, where it was located, which sounded heavenly, Jo had to admit. He spoke about profit margins at each of his premises, talked about the salary she could expect, told her of the freedom she'd have to develop the menu and run the café the way she wanted except without the additional worry and overheads she had now.

'It all sounds very attractive.' She'd already pulled out a chair to join him.

He sat forward. 'You're tempted, I can tell.'

'I am. But . . . you said it yourself. This café is a part of me.'

He rubbed a hand around the back of his neck. 'I did say that, didn't I?'

'You know what I think?'

'What's that?'

'I think you've got the recruitment process all wrong. I know you're the entrepreneur with all the fancy ideas and ways of doing things, but this time I think you need to do it differently. You go around the country trying to recruit for new cafés and up until now it's worked.'

'It's worked very well, that's why I keep doing it that way. I get the best of the best.'

'Who says you have to stick with the same method? Surely, part of being an entrepreneur is adapting to your environment.'

'I'm not sure I get where you're going with this.'

'You said that this café is a part of me. It is. And that's why I have vision and energy for it. You need to go to the area in Cornwall and start recruiting locals instead of looking for the next big thing in management.'

'It's not how it's worked before. I've taken on graduates, people who have a background in management studies and who know about all the extras in running a business.'

'I have a degree, Curtis. But not in management. I was a primary-school teacher.'

'Now that I can imagine. I bet you didn't take any stick.'

She wondered: had Curtis been looking for the perfect person for so long that all he wanted was to relax and talk and sit and appreciate a quiet seaside town for once? 'My point is that I knew nothing about managing a business when I took over the café. It all came from in here.' She put her fingers against her heart. 'The passion I had for this town and the special memories I had for this café drove me to want to succeed.'

'So I need to find a local.'

'I think so, yes.'

He leaned back in his chair. 'Why didn't I see that before now?'

She stood up. It was time to get on and clean up, because she still had another event to organise, something she was just as passionate about. 'You didn't see it, because you needed to step back and look at the bigger picture.'

'So you're a definite no. Worth a try,' he added when her look told him he'd got it in one. 'Remember, if you ever need a change, just give me the nod. I've always got a new plan on the horizon.'

She wouldn't mind betting that was true. 'Good luck, Curtis. I hope you find someone soon.'

He held her gaze. 'So do I.'

Uncomfortable beneath his watchful eye, she began clearing his table.

'Jo . . .' His voice stopped her before she got to the counter with his empty cup and a plate covered in crumbs. 'If you ever change your mind . . .'

'I won't.' She smiled, and when the bell tinkled to

announce his departure she knew it was the absolute truth. Salthaven was where she wanted to be and Salthaven was where she was going to stay.

A little before eight o'clock, around the bay at the most popular area for surfers, Jo set up the romantic picnic. After finally telling Curtis Durham she wasn't interested in his offer, she couldn't wait to get back to her own plans for her café. Because that was what it was now. Her place, her responsibility, and, even when the going got tough, she wasn't going to run. Ever.

This section of the beach was more or less deserted apart from a couple of surfers paddling out to try to catch the last few waves before sunset. A family beyond the break-waters were cheering loudly at the end of a game of beach cricket and a gull perched on top of one of the pieces of dark wood protruding from the sand, wrestled with something in his beak and took flight. The waves continued to froth and caress the shore, turning pale sands to a deeper hue, the sea's steady rhythm in keeping with the perfect atmosphere for tonight.

'Good evening, Jo.'

She hadn't seen Geoff approach. 'You're prompt.'

'I've never been one to keep a lady waiting. What do you think?' He swept his hand down over his pale-blue linen shirt and beige trousers. He even looked as if he had on a new pair of leather deck shoes. 'Will it do?'

'Geoff, you look really good. You'd never know you were a fisherman.' Some mornings she'd seen him he hadn't bothered to shave and he was one of those men who didn't carry the stubble look off very well. Instead of looking slightly sexy it tended to make him look as though he couldn't be bothered. But tonight he was smooth-shaven and Jo caught a waft of subtle cologne mixed with the salty air surrounding them.

'Did you carry this all down yourself?' He helped Jo manoeuvre the picnic basket further along the edge of the blanket that was flapping in the breeze.

'Took me two goes. I'll give you my phone number and you can call me at the café when you're done. I'm off for an extra-long walk to make the most of the evening, and when you call I'll collect everything. My car's parked up there.' She pointed to the car park at the top of the cliff and noticed Valerie coming their way. Geoff hadn't spotted his date yet and Jo's stomach began to turn somersaults.

'Don't be daft. My flat's up there on the other side of the road, as you know after delivering the invite, so I'll take everything there and bring it to the café tomorrow morning. How does that sound?'

'Perfect, thank you.' In the corner of her eye Valerie was almost with them, her white summer dress with the long skirt floating around her. She quickly took the roses out of their paper wrapping, poured water into a tiny vase and arranged the stems inside. She set the arrangement beside the hamper to complete the picnic and then, crossing her fingers, at least in her mind, said, 'I'll leave you to it.'

Geoff turned and the look on his face was a mixture of relief and anticipation. Valerie managed a smile but she was still terribly nervous and Jo thought it best to leave them to it. She opened up the picnic basket and rattled off a list of what was in there: strawberries, cream, a bottle of champagne and a block of luxury chocolate she'd bought from the sweetshop.

Jo's feet negotiated the sands, the cool surface welcome

after the heat of the day. Gulls soared noisily across the sky as she took the steps up the cliff face to the car park, and at the top she looked back, just once.

Geoff's face was tilted to the sun and he was laughing, Valerie too.

Could it be that a little magic had at last found its way to Salthaven?

18

'Well, there were no dead bodies on the beach this morning,' said Steve when he came into the café early on Saturday to buy a post-surf snack. Wetsuit un-zipped to the waist but with the salt water already dried on his skin from a walk beneath the sun, he paid for a bowl of fresh fruit salad with Greek yogurt, blissfully una-ware, again, of the admiring glances from the teenage girls behind him.

Jo dropped the coins into the till and pushed the drawer closed. 'Whatever are you talking about?'

'The date last night. Looks like neither of them killed each other.'

'Ha-ha. Of course they didn't. As a matter of fact I do believe it went rather well.' She spooned out the mixture of melon, grapes, orange and strawberries and topped it with the yogurt. 'Geoff brought the picnic basket and everything back this morning and told me they'd had a lovely time.'

'Do you think it lasted all night? I didn't see them on the sand this morning.' When he saw her give him a look he added, 'You know, I hope it does work out well. I really do. Valerie's friends with my parents and she's a lovely lady, and Geoff keeps himself to himself, but he seems a nice chap. Who knows, maybe love is on the horizon.' He took his bowl over to the nearest table, where he sat to refuel himself.

Sometimes Steve surprised Jo. One minute he was flippant, a lad, muscly and tanned, and the next she saw a deeper level, someone who cared more than he let on.

Ben and Charlie were the next people through the door and Jo could see straightaway that Charlie was looking around for Poppy. She was keeping everything crossed that his friend would be in soon. 'Take a seat anywhere and I'll be over shortly.'

Ben showed Charlie to one of the tables and, under the pretence of grabbing a pot of crayons and some paper, came to see Jo. 'Is she coming in today?'

'Let's hope so,' she said conspiratorially. Matt had already delivered the box of fresh produce, and had told Jo his sister Anna would still be coming, but, with the baby, she wasn't sure what time.

'Charlie hasn't stopped talking about her all morning. Poppy this, Poppy that – it's sweet, really.'

'Young love.' Jo smiled. Ben looked about to say something else until one of the kids who'd come in to the café vied for Jo's attention. It was Dan, a local boy, and he might be over six foot in height with a presence that assured confidence, but he was softly spoken when he ordered a can of Coke and a chocolate-chip muffin before going back over to his mates. Jo thought of the lot of them as teenagers, but she already knew a few of them had turned twenty-one because Angie had filled her in on pretty much every resident and Molly and Arthur had done the same over time, although it was hard to remember every detail. Jo supposed in another year or so she'd

216

be as up-to-date as every other person in Salthaven, more so if it were possible, with the café being the hub of the community.

Next in were a group of girls and Charlie wasted no time running over to hug the one in the blue petal-print sundress. From the conversation that ensued Jo remembered this was Maddy, Ben's regular babysitter for his son. Charlie showed Maddy the paperweights as Jo lifted one up to take outside for Billy, who was mid-fight with the wind in a quest for who got to take control of his newspaper.

Jo hooked her hair behind her ear when she came back inside and by now Charlie had let Maddy get back to her own friends while he sat with his dad and concentrated on drawing. Every now and then his little eyes would look up, especially if the bell above the door tinkled, hoping and wishing to see Poppy.

Jo filled the girls' order, made another round of drinks for the boys plus extra snacks, wondering whether some of them had hollow legs. She swept up when the group in the far corner left behind more cake crumbs than there had been cake in her opinion, and when Poppy came through the door she looked over at Charlie. He'd given up looking out for his friend, so he'd been concentrating on his drawing, but Ben had noticed and was waiting for his reaction, just as Jo was.

The second Charlie saw Poppy his smile could match the brightest of suns.

'I've left the buggy outside,' said the woman carrying a baby boy dressed in blue shorts with a mustard T-shirt. Jo hadn't had much to do with babies over the years, but she had to admit he was cute.

'You must be Anna.' Jo came round to the other side of the counter as Poppy finally let go of Anna's skirt and went over to join Charlie. 'I'm Jo. It's lovely to meet you.'

'You know, Molly and Arthur used to talk about you all the time. I feel as though I already know you.'

'I didn't know you were a regular.'

Anna gently patted the baby's back as he rested his head against her shoulder. 'I used to come in a lot before I had Poppy, so a few years ago now. Once upon a time I helped deliver the produce from the farm. It's a real family affair. Molly and Arthur are lovely. Haven't seen them in a while. Are they well?' She'd turned the baby so he nestled in her arms, all happy and gurgling now he'd woken up enough to take in his surroundings.

Jo reached out and let the baby squeeze her fingers, mesmerised by her chilli-red nail polish. 'They're very well, thank you.'

'Matt used to worry about them.'

'Really?'

'He'd tell me how tired they looked some days.'

'I think Gramps was worn out by the time I arrived to help. He tried to pretend he wasn't, that we were fussing too much. But, while he worked with me to hand over the reins, I could tell he needed a proper break. He'd leave the café each day and barely make it up that hill to collapse on the sofa most days.'

'Well it's a good job you came when you did. And is Arthur listening to doctor's orders, or Molly's?'

'Just about, and he hasn't had any more dizzy spells.' She visibly crossed her fingers in front of Anna. 'We're hoping we caught his exhaustion and high blood pressure before it became anything worse. I really want them to enjoy the café from a different perspective now.'

'With your own business it's easy to get so engrossed trying to make it a success that we neglect what's going on around us.' Anna gave the baby a soft toy that he squished between his hands, making a crinkling sound. His little arms and legs jostled about as though doing a merry dance. 'You know, I wish Matt would start thinking of himself.'

'He seems pretty happy,' said Jo. 'Come to think of it, I don't think I've ever seen him miserable.'

'Pah! I've definitely been witness to his moody side, growing up together. But mostly he's a positive person. It's just that, when Poppy kept on and on about Charlie, she turned to Matt and asked him when he was going to get a lady friend.'

'You know, I think Poppy and Charlie are making us all feel a bit inadequate.' But Jo's mind was already starting to work overtime. Perhaps Matt could be the next person to set up for a night of love at the café. Then again, she'd heard him talking with Steve once about her mini-project and, while both of them seemed happy for it to happen to others, she wasn't sure either of them would be too enthusiastic if they found themselves unwitting victims.

Jo chopped more fruit and filled a new bowl to set in the display cabinet. She loved the colours – the red of the strawberries, succulent pieces of pear, cubes of bright orange and the smooth green of the grapes she'd halved and added. When she looked up, the café was oddly separated into two sections with the left side of the room made up of five young girls and the right side housing a group of four boys. She remembered a similar scene a while ago when her friend Melissa was in here and what was happening now was exactly the same. Every now and then, Dan would look over at the girls' table, right in Maddy's direction. Then, moments later Maddy would pretend to be engrossed in conversation but sneak a peek back at him. Whenever their eyes met they both looked away quickly.

How did you go from being a confident kid like Charlie, arranging to see a girl and spending time with her, to awkward and finding it impossible to share more than a couple of words? This pair clearly liked one another, but how many years was it going to be before one of them did anything about it?

Jo was clearing up the stray petals that had dropped from the flowers Harry had delivered and thinking about throwing the spent blooms out, when she looked at Maddy, then at Dan. The next part of her plan had been staring her in the face. Could they be perfect candidates for her next night of love at the café?

She shook her head. At twenty-one she wouldn't have wanted some café owner meddling in her love life, even if all she was doing was trying to help. Then again, you didn't know until you tried. And these two were going nowhere on their own.

'Hello, anyone there?' came a voice the other side of the kitchen door.

Jo recognised it at once. It was Valerie, and she couldn't wait to ask how it went with Geoff last night. She put the vase down and dumped the spent stalks in the sink for now, wiped her hands and went out to the front.

Valerie was smiling. It was a good sign.

'How did it go?' Might as well come right out with it.

But Valerie said nothing. She simply walked around to

Jo's side of the counter and enveloped her in a hug.

'That good?' Jo asked.

'I'd seen Geoff around, we'd exchanged the odd greeting, but I never even thought . . . Well, I never thought he'd be interested in me. To tell you the truth—' she pulled a face – 'I thought he looked boring, mooching out there to the end of the pier every morning with a fishing rod to sit on his own. But he's not the man I thought he was, not at all. I think all that quiet time must help him think and destress because it was the best fun I've had in ages.'

Jo dared not get too excited. 'Tell me more.' She willed customers to stay away a while longer and for the kids at the back to hold off if they wanted top-ups.

'It wasn't awkward at all,' Valerie gushed. 'I think it was his smile that did it. I'd never really seen him so happy before. Oh, and when he popped the champagne cork, and it fizzed everywhere as he tried to get it in the glasses, I couldn't stop laughing. We talked about everything and I didn't even realise how late it was getting until the sky grew dark, dotted with a million stars.'

'Oh, you'll have me crying in a minute. It sounds like the scene out of a soppy romance novel.'

'I almost have to pinch myself to realise it was real.'

Jo was getting into this. 'So did you kiss him?'

'Now, Jo, a lady doesn't kiss and tell. But I will say this: he has the softest lips.'

Jo couldn't contain her excitement. Geoff had traipsed this pier many a time. He'd always seemed content but never complete. And Valerie was always chipper, but now she was showing a contentment that seemed to have been hidden until something had managed to coax it out into the open.

The night of love at The Café at the End of the Pier had succeeded in bringing two lonely people together. Her plan was working!

At the end of the day as the temperature cooled and the sun began its descent, painting the sky red and casting the pier in a different light, Jo decided to leave the mopping of the floor until after a walk. With rain forecast for the next week, she wanted to make the most of the long summer nights and endless days that made her fall in love with Salthaven all over again. Besides, she needed a moment to think about her next foray into the night of love at the café. She already knew who to go for. All she needed to do was observe both parties, from a distance, to make sure she wasn't going completely off course. Then it was a matter of putting together a plan, which was the best part.

She locked the door to the café and took the steps down from the pier to the small patch of rocks below. She stepped over them and onto the sand, her toes sinking with every step she took. She nodded hello to holiday-makers who were finally dragging their towels and belongings away at the end of another day, and she walked all the way round to the surfing beach where she sat and watched a couple of surfers ride the waves into shore as the breeze carried salty spray in her direction.

She walked back via the steps to the top of the car park, down the hill and past the boating lake, and paused beside it, dipping her fingers into the water as the moonlight took the sun's place and cast shadows across the surface. If she hadn't been sitting so still she probably would've missed Geoff and Valerie sitting on a bench near the sign at the start of the pier, and this time they weren't holding hands: they were sharing a kiss.

Jo's heart leapt. Valerie had told her how much they thought of one another but now she'd seen it with her own eyes.

Anxious not to disturb them, Jo walked back around the boating lake, down to the sands and up the steps partway down the pier, which came out almost in front of the café. Sometimes the tide came in so far that these steps weren't usable, but for now she could discreetly slip back inside to finish up for the day before she went home.

She mopped the café floor, wiped down the kitchen bench and did the floor in there too, and, when everything was safely stowed in the storeroom at the back, she noticed the wooden posts and bases waiting for the next part of her plan. She wondered, what flowers could she use this time? What would be in season? What would suit the next couple she chose? Maybe some lavender-blue clematis, or perhaps pale yellow dahlias. Whatever she chose, it had to be beautiful, it needed to say romance.

Her thoughts elsewhere already, it was time to head home. She grabbed the keys from the hook near the microwave, picked up her bag, but, after switching off the lights and weaving between the tables in the café, she stopped. Because there on the mat was another postcard.

Plain, the same as last time. She didn't have to turn it over to know what this was.

Surely Harry wasn't still playing games?

Unless it wasn't from him at all.

Her hopeful heart thumped as she turned over the card and read the words:

223

Dear Jo,
Sometimes love is where you least expect it . . . Keep your
heart open and your eyes on the horizon . . .

Now that didn't sound like Harry. Or did it?

Just as she'd done before, she opened the door to the café, looked out, left towards the town, right towards the sea, but nobody was around. Whoever was doing this had perfected the art of delivering the cards without ever being seen.

Was she foolish to hope this could be someone other than her ex, a love all of her own, brand-new, uncomplicated?

She stepped out onto the pier and locked the door behind her, her heart still pounding as she clutched the card. She walked towards the start of the pier. Last time she'd done this Curtis Durham had been waiting for her but with a different proposal entirely.

Wait a minute. She thought about his little visit to the café the other day. What was it he'd said? Something about his ideas and how he always had something new on the horizon.

So it had to be him, didn't it?

She stopped beside the ice-creamery, which was well and truly shut for the evening. It was that one word that was troubling her: *horizon*. She'd heard it somewhere else too, and she couldn't quite think where.

She moved to the wooden fence of the pier looking out across the sand, watching as the tide crept ever closer to the rocks it would cover completely in an hour or two. The steps she'd taken up earlier were already submerged and stars punctuated the sky with the moon keeping them company.

Her mind picked up another fragment from the last few days. Hadn't Steve said something about love being on the horizon too?

Then again, this wasn't Steve's style. If he was interested, surely he'd come out and say it to her face. And what if he was? What would her answer be?

Oh, this was so confusing. But the excitement was exhilarating and made Jo realise exactly what she was giving to other people in Salthaven with her matchmaking plans.

She breathed in the salty sea air, the environment that always banished her cares away, and she wished life were simple.

She pushed the card into her bag, continued on until she'd stepped off the wooden planks of the pier onto the footpath, and, when she heard her name on a voice that was all too familiar, she wasn't sure what to feel.

She turned round and there he was, standing with a single red rose and an expression that asked her to give him a chance.

A chance to fall in love.

Autumn

19

Dry, chestnut-and-purple leaves skittered across the road as Jo made her way to the pier, long before the sun made an appearance on this crisp morning in mid-October. The bits and bobs shop had shut for the season, the ice-creamery knew what times to open to make the most of the post-school rush, and the fish and chip shop had begun to do a roaring trade. There was something about vinegar and salt, mixed with the warmth of potato, that on the air had people ordering their small parcels of comfort in droves. Gone now were the hordes of people vying for the best spot on the sands in the summer months, the clusters of tourists gathering on the pier, and in their place, locals steadily trod the boardwalk, greeting one another and using the café as their regular hub.

Jo pulled her scarf more tightly around her neck to ward off any chill from the gusts of wind coming off the sea, letting her mind drift back to that summer day when she'd received the last mystery postcard. That flicker of hope she'd felt as she heard a man's voice call her name had soon been extinguished when she turned and saw Harry, standing with a rose in his hand and a smile that only reminded her of what they'd once had, and lost. She was flooded with disappointment that the postcards hadn't been from a mystery man who would turn out to be the special person she'd been looking for. Instead, it appeared they'd come from the ex-boyfriend who'd broken her heart. She'd almost wanted to run far away, tell him he was wasting his time, but given their history she felt she owed him the chance to at last be completely open about the way he was feeling. And Jo knew, deep down, that it was the only way either one of them could move forwards.

'What's this?' She'd taken the rose and leaned in to smell its fragrance. 'What's going on, Harry? Don't try telling me you do this for all your clients.' She tried to make light of the confrontation when it couldn't have been more serious. For such a long time she'd wanted someone to take notice of her, to feel special, and here was Harry trying his best.

'Can we talk?'

She'd sat on the low wall surrounding the modest-sized boating lake and the cold concrete didn't take long to make its way through the denim of her jeans.

'Jo, I made a mistake.'

This again. 'Harry, I—'

'Let me say what I need to say. I was an idiot all those years ago. I saw that pretty much straight away. But back then I was young, we both were. I didn't want to be tied down. I wanted some excitement, to see a bit of the world.'

'Without me.'

His hesitation confirmed it. 'I guess so, yes. But more so, I wanted to do it without *anyone*.'

'So a bit of a case of "it's not you, it's me" then?' She fidgeted as her skin began to tingle from the cold surface they were sitting on. 'What makes you think you want me back, Harry?'

He put a hand over hers and she didn't move. 'When I first saw you again, I felt all my feelings come rushing back. Simple as that.'

Rather than sounding confident, his voice trembled and it was enough to make Jo take pause. She toyed with the rose between her hands, the silky deep red petals and their heady aroma. She ran a finger along the stem, stopping when it caught on a thorn. 'Harry, I think there's too much nostalgia wrapped up in your feelings for you to know that you still love me.' When he looked away she said, 'When we're both single it's probably easier to think we should get back together than wait to meet anyone else.' Only now, with him confronting her and laying his heart out there in the open, did she realise how right it was to leave things where they belonged: in the past.

'So that's it?' It wasn't really a question, because the tone of his voice showed he knew the answer. 'It was worth a shot, I guess.'

She had to put an end to this. 'I mean it, Harry. No more games. No more sending me flowers, calling round to the flat, or buying me aniseed balls.'

'Did you even eat them?' The atmosphere between them settled.

'Every last one.' She stood, held out a hand to shake his. 'Let's forget this happened and keep things strictly professional from now on, shall we?'

But he didn't shake her hand. He stood too and leaned in to kiss her once, kind of like a goodbye. 'Deal.'

She reached into her bag and took out the postcard she'd found on the mat and handed it to him. She was about to walk away, get home up the hill, when his voice stopped her.

'What's this?'

'The postcard, Harry.' She was growing tired of this. 'Another part of your game.' The postcard didn't say much but it told Jo love could be found where she least expected, and that she should keep her heart open and her eyes on the horizon. A similar postcard back in the spring had told her not to get so busy helping other people fall in love that she missed what was right in front of her.

'What postcard?' Harry asked.

Exasperated she began walking away.

'Jo, stop.' He caught up with her. 'I mean it. This wasn't from me.'

'Really?' She stopped, trying to read something through his bewildered expression. 'Because all the signs are kind of staring me in the face – especially now you've told me how you feel, given me this rose.' She held up the flower, careful of its thorns this time.

'I promise you, Jo. The postcard wasn't from me.'

And that's how they'd left the conversation. She'd dismissed the postcard as some kind of joke from someone in town, poking fun at her after her foray into the nights of love at the café, and neither of them had mentioned it since. Harry had maintained a respectable distance, been friendly, and only contacted her as necessary when it came to the accounts.

Life had returned to normal once again.

And the postcards had ceased.

Now, in the warmth of the café, Jo hung her coat on the hook in the cupboard at the side of the kitchen. You knew it was getting colder when the space was used for more than umbrellas and the odd stray cardigan.

She'd only just switched on the lights when Steve

knocked on the door. He'd come prepared, his ladder already leaning up against the café wall for him to fix the guttering on the roof. It had sagged and finally given up yesterday which meant a stream of water running unattractively down the window. Not a very appealing view for whoever was cosied up on the window seat.

She opened the door. 'Thanks for coming.' Rubbing her arms against the cold she pointed to the problem area and then took him to the opposite side of the building. 'I think the same is going to happen here too.'

He stretched up to touch the base of the gutter. Funny, a few months ago, watching him would've set Jo's pulse racing, but now he was firmly in the just good friends category. After finding out that Harry had nothing to do with the postcards, Steve had become her prime suspect. But now she wasn't so sure. It wasn't really his style and she suspected he valued their friendship as much as she did.

'I'll go fetch my toolbox,' he said, 'but I'll need to nip to the hardware store first and pick up the right screws and a couple of brackets to replace the ones that are spent.'

'Put it on my tab and I'll settle up later.' Her finances were on the up, finally, and Jo hoped it was a sign of things to come. She'd survived summer, the busiest season, and her confidence had bloomed along with the profits. Now, if self-doubt came her way, she was more equipped to bat it well out to sea and carry on doing what she loved.

'You're freezing.' Steve was watching her. 'Go inside, leave this with me, and I'll check right the way around. Best to do it now, before winter sets in.'

'Thanks, Steve, I owe you one.' She held up a hand, pre-empting his response. Last time she'd had to repay him for his kindness, he'd roped her into a surf lesson. 'Don't even suggest it! It's way too cold for me to be in the sea – I'm thinking more of your financial payment plus a slice of cake on the house.'

'Throw in a hot coffee and I won't mention surfing again. At least until next summer,' he called after her as she went back in to the café.

Jo put the float in the till and emptied the small plastic bags of cash into the relevant sections. She was glad she and Steve were such good friends. She might one day try her hand at setting him up on a blind date, but perhaps she'd wait until summer rolled round again, when she had plenty of tourist surfer chicks to choose from. And besides, she still had her sights firmly set on Maddy and Dan. She'd caught them glancing surreptitiously at each other across the café so many times, but she clearly needed to give them a push in the right direction.

She switched on the coffee machine and took out utensils and ingredients to make a strudel, lining up raisins, sugar, cinnamon and butter. The menu choices on the blackboard had gradually evolved to reflect the season and gone were the bright, colourful berries and cool crisp salads of summer, while in their place were darker, richer vegetables. Jo's sweet potato frittata had been an instant hit with Sally, who'd been the first customer to taste test, and with Maisy from the post office. The minestrone soup had also sold more since the weather turned and Jo's first attempt at making a beetroot chocolate cake had gone down well. At least, far better than the broccoli and salmon lattice tart she'd attempted last week. The broccoli had started out as verdant green but as Jo multitasked serving customers and forgot about the pan on the stove top, the poor vegetable slowly turned grey and inedible.

'Knock knock.' It was Matt's voice coming from the door to the café. 'Anyone home?'

She wiped her hands on a tea towel and went through to find him waiting with a box of fruit and vegetables, to-day's supply from his family's farm. 'You're just in time. I'm making a strudel this morning, so I hope you have those apples I was after.' She put both palms together in front of her, praying that he did.

'As requested.' He lowered the box enough for her to look inside. 'I'll take this through to the kitchen.'

She went ahead of him. With ingredients spread out and utensils on the bench tops, it wasn't a big enough area to include the produce until she cleared a corner. 'Will it slot in here?'

'Perfect,' he said, pushing the box into the gap. 'And Hilda will be pleased.' He'd spotted the recipe pinned to the wall. 'She hinted about you making a strudel enough times.'

'Not only that,' said Jo, taking out a good collection of the plump, pale green apples flushed with deep orange on the skins where the sun had got to them, 'it's her recipe. She wrote it out for me and brought it here.'

Matt peered more closely. He ran a hand down the list of ingredients. 'She'll be even happier when she knows I've given you Bramley apples.'

'They're the best, according to Hilda.'

He put a hand to his stomach. Even beneath jeans, a jumper, and a Barbour jacket, you could tell his job was a physical one because he was in pretty good shape. 'It's not even fully light yet and my stomach is craving baked goods.'

'Sorry about that.' She lined up half a dozen apples for the strudel. 'I need to steer clear of baked goods myself after Molly gave me a double helping of her steamed syrup sponge last night.'

'Sounds brutal.'

'It was hard to resist, put it that way.' She went back to looking through the produce to see what else Matt had brought for her café.

'No broccoli this time.' She didn't miss the teasing in his voice. 'It was too scared to come out the ground after what you did to the last crop.'

'Cheeky! Don't worry, I've learnt my lesson.'

'Glad to hear it. Those are Cape gooseberries.' He stood beside her as she took out a small punnet and inspected the Chinese lantern-type fruit. 'You need to pull apart the light brown papery skin . . .' He plucked one to do the honours. 'And inside, we have the gooseberry.'

'It looks wonderful.'

His laughter filled the tiny kitchen. 'You've got no idea what to do with it, have you?'

'Do you blame me? You've knocked my confidence since broccoli-gate.'

'Don't be silly. Here.' He put the berry towards her mouth. 'Try it.'

She popped it in and bit down on the firm flesh. 'Oh . . . they're kind of incredible.' She picked up another and peeled it herself.

'Don't eat so many that you run out before you dream up a recipe,' he warned.

'I won't, I promise.' They were mildly sweet with a slight crunch and her mind was already turning, wondering how she could use them.

'They're Poppy's favourite.'

'I'm impressed. Most kids avoid eating anything that looks unfamiliar.' She wouldn't even dare use them for her menu when she set up the blind date for Maddy and Dan, just in case they weren't willing to try anything unusual. 'I don't think I'd have touched these at her age.'

'You probably would if you'd grown up on our farm.'

'Fair point.'

'My sister often uses them in a crumble, or makes a pie, or you could make a sauce to go with a dessert. Mum used to do that. I'll ask around, text you later. But I thought I'd drop a few in the produce box today, keep you on your toes.'

'Thanks, Matt.' She loved the challenge. It was part of the fun of being the boss, and she could never imagine changing it so the café had a fixed menu all year round.

She saw him to the door, lingering when he left along the wooden boards, so she could enjoy the beauty of sunrise over the pier as the sky turned burnt orange.

Back out in the kitchen she unloaded the rest of the produce: onions, sweet potato, a surprise punnet of raspberries, eggs and a melon. As she waited for Steve to return from the hardware store and get going with the repairs, she peeled, cored, quartered and sliced the apples, before mixing them with the sugar, raisins, lemon zest and cinnamon. And being able to focus before opening time meant she had the apple strudel ready to slot in the oven before her first customer of the day.

Geoff was first through the door. 'Good morning,' she smiled.

'Good morning, Jo.'

'Usual black tea for you?'

'And an extra hot hot chocolate for me,' came a voice behind him.

'Valerie, you're early today.'

When she stepped inside, Jo noted the waterproof jacket, the floral wellies and the absence of a yoga mat.

'I'm going fishing.' She looked like she'd already caught her fish when she hooked an arm through Geoff's.

As they chatted, Jo made the drinks and slotted take-away lids onto each cup. 'These will keep you warm this morning. So, tell me, Geoff, when's your first yoga session?' She shared a conspiratorial wink with Valerie. 'If Valerie is trying fishing, it's only fair.'

'We'll see.' But his response told Jo he'd be willing to try anything now he'd found a new love in his life. It was good to see them together, the first successful match in her nights of love at the café. And now, it was time to take aim with her Cupid's arrow again and get Maddy and Dan together on a date that could change everything for them.

20

When Jo shared her idea with Molly and Arthur it turned out they'd both noticed Dan and Maddy tiptoeing around each other since last Christmas. Back then, even the mistletoe hadn't been enough to bring them together, and Molly agreed they needed a helping hand.

Jo was buzzing at the thought of setting up the next date night and the euphoria kept her going all morning. The apple strudel was a hit and so she made another, then a third after that. Lucky for her, Matt had brought plenty of apples with him, but she'd run out by the time Molly and Arthur came in for their share of dessert.

'But Hilda said you were cooking them one after the other,' Molly moaned.

'I was, but I've almost used an entire orchard already.' Jo took payment from Vince for a banana smoothie to take away. 'You'll have to wait. I've put in a text order with Matt, but meantime, can I interest you in lemon tart with cape gooseberry compote instead?'

'Now that sounds fancy.' Impressed, Arthur sat himself at the table in the corner.

'A small piece for him,' Molly whispered. 'He can't resist treats, so I have to make sure he doesn't overdo it.'

Since his health scare earlier in the year, Arthur had been resting more, eating healthily – and enjoying life without a business to worry about now Jo had taken over.

'And for you?'

'I'll try some, but not too much or it'll make Arthur jealous.'

Molly joined Arthur and Jo cut a section of tart from where it was in the display cabinet before heading out into the kitchen to add the compote. She was braver with her recipes these days, trying new suggestions, spending longer getting them right.

'Can I pin this up?' Molly took a postcard out of her bag when Jo emerged from the kitchen.

'Sure, who's it from?' She set down two plates of lemon tart onto her grandparents' table where Arthur was engrossed in his newspaper.

'Our former accountant.'

The postcard showed an idyllic shot of Bolam Lake in the Northumberland countryside, the water glistening beside a backdrop of autumnal trees in rich chestnut, rust and bronze. Jo thought of Harry, the accountant she'd ended up with instead, as she turned over the card to read the chatter about long meandering pub walks, nature and all the sides of life that came with retirement. When she'd first arrived in Salthaven, seeing Harry had been hard, but at least it meant they'd both worked through their feelings and finally moved on.

'Pin it up,' Jo encouraged. 'It's our first autumn card in a long while. The board is kind of overrun with summer scenes.'

Molly pinned it front and centre. 'I'm sure we'll have some different postcards soon. There aren't many warm, sunny places around at this time of the year unless you're willing to fly for hours.'

'Mum says the temperature has fallen in Puerto Pollensa.'

Molly turned at the mention of her daughter and a look of sadness passed her by before she pinned on a smile again. 'I'll bet it's still quite pleasant.'

'Chilly at night,' said Jo, before greeting Angie when she arrived. She knew both her grandparents would avoid the subject of their daughter entirely if they suspected they might have an audience. Since confronting them all about the feud, Jo had let it lie. Because if there was one thing she knew about this family, it was that stubbornness had always prevented them from sorting out their differences and she had no intention of making it any worse.

The day passed quickly for Jo and by the time the sun began to set and she closed the café doors for another day, it was time to get the wheels in motion for the next part of her plan.

In the kitchen she took out the red postcards and envelopes along with her calligraphy pen. She pulled the tortoiseshell hair claw from her hair and let the dark waves hang loose after another hectic day. Young love in the making was exhilarating, full of possibility, and she hoped Maddy and Dan saw it that way rather than something the older generation thought a good idea but not them. If she was right about this pair, they'd see the opportunity. But if she was wrong, the gossip mill could be laughing in her face come early November.

She penned each invite for next Friday night at seven o'clock, after closing, when the pier was covered in darkness except for the lights in the Victorian lamp posts illuminating the boardwalk and the café. She added her phone number to each postcard, suspecting Gen Y would be more likely to text a response than let her know in person.

She wanted to give both Maddy and Dan every opportunity to make this work.

In the pub that evening, over a glass of Merlot each, Jo, Jess and Melissa lowered their voices as they discussed Jo's plan.

'I'm worried about this one,' she confessed.

'Why?' Melissa set her wine back onto the table. 'They're obviously into each other, but they need a bit of a nudge.'

'A shove, more like,' Jess claimed. 'Oh, I remember those days, eyeing up boys across the classroom but never daring to talk to them.'

'You never talk properly to them now,' said Melissa, 'unless you're discussing their ailments that is.'

'I'm not that bad.'

Jo harrumphed. 'Apart from Ben, who's no more than a friend, when was the last time you made an effort to speak to a man, a possible love interest?'

'Right back at you, Jo.'

Jo sighed. 'You've got me there. We're both pretty useless. Not like this one.' She nudged Melissa. 'You're all loved-up with James and we're jealous. There, I've said it.' She made it sound like a joke but sometimes, sitting in her flat in the evening with nothing for company but the television or the sound of the waves crashing to the shore beyond the window, she wondered what it would be like to have a special someone.

'Don't be,' said Melissa. 'And the right man is waiting

around the corner, for both of you. I know he is because he was for me.'

Utterly unconvinced, Jess turned the conversation back to Jo's plans. 'Do you think they'll go for it? They're a lot younger than us.'

'It worries me they'll think it's a bit of a joke,' said Jo. 'I mean, it's supposed to be fun, but not the type of fun that involves ridicule at my expense or each other's.' She looked up and saw Geoff and Valerie come in through the door, bringing the autumn chill with them, but they took up the cosy booth seat on the other side past the pool table. 'At least my plan has worked once.' One bullseye was better than none at all.

Talk dissolved into the romantic picnic Jo had set up on the beach, Jo's exact plans for Maddy and Dan, and when Jo's phone pinged with a text she began to laugh.

'Oh dear,' said Jess when Jo showed her what was on the screen.

Jo showed Melissa. 'Dan thinks it's a wind-up. He's asking which one of his mates is behind this.'

Jo bashed out another text telling Dan it wasn't a joke, and this was Jo from the café, as the message had originally claimed. She recounted his latest order when he'd come in and the brief conversation they'd shared, so he'd know this was for real.

Melissa opened the cheese and onion crisps she'd bought from behind the bar and passed them round.

'There's more air in the packet than there are crisps,' said Jo.

'Ripped off,' Jess agreed. 'Jo, how's Arthur feeling now?'

Apparently, he'd managed to drop a cup on his foot that afternoon and his toes had bruised up a treat. Molly had sent Jo a text to say they were off to the doctor but she wasn't to worry. 'He's sore and feeling sorry for himself, hobbling about and determined not to let us fuss.'

'Sounds about right to me. I don't think he would've come in if Molly hadn't insisted.'

'Should he literally be putting his feet up?' Jo took another crisp.

'As much as he can, but that doesn't mean he can't move around. It's only superficial, so he'll be back to 100 per cent before we know it.'

'Gran was worried it was more than clumsiness. Oh, I know, doctor–patient confidentiality and all that,' she added when she saw Jess's expression. 'But do I need to be worried?'

Jess discretely shook her head and Jo let it drop for the rest of the evening as they were joined by Maisy, who worked in the post office with Melissa.

But it didn't stop Jo from heading to the bungalow on her way home, under the pretence of picking up some oatmeal and raisin cookies she knew Molly had rustled up for the café.

Stubbornness ran in her family and Jo knew by now that if she wanted to keep on top of what was going on, she'd have to do a little digging.

21

The next morning flew by, and she was experiencing her first lull when Matt appeared in the doorway. 'Twice in one day?' she asked him. He'd already brought her that day's fruit and veg, and she was surprised to see him again.

'Sometimes this café feels like my second home.' He joined her by the windowsill. 'You look tired.'

'I don't think autumn showers or the cold are putting people off venturing along the pier.' She gestured to the box on his lap. 'What do you have there?'

'This is something a bit different.'

She looked inside. 'They're gorgeous.' In the box were twenty or so miniature pumpkins. 'Did you grow them?'

'Of course.'

'I've never seen such small pumpkins. They're so cute!'

'Not how I'd describe them, but I'll go with it.' He smiled back at her, delighted he'd made such an impression. 'And I know they make a good pumpkin soup, especially with a touch of chilli added.'

Jo's mind conjured up bowls of thick, hearty, orange warming soup served with crusty bread. Or she could make pumpkin scones, even pumpkin pie like they had in America. But then, amongst the yummy recipes, came another concept.

'I have an idea,' she said.

'I can taste test if you need someone.'

'I'm afraid this isn't of the edible kind. Do you have larger pumpkins?'

'Lots . . . why?'

'How big are we talking?'

He moved his arms and hands to give her an idea of some of the bigger pumpkins up at the farm. 'We're open for pumpkin picking right now.'

Jo toyed with one of the tiny orange fruits. 'How do I not know this already?'

'It's the first year we've done it.'

'Are you getting much business?'

'Steady.'

'Right, then I'm putting in my order now.'

'Go for it.' He took out his phone and tapped in her request for four large pumpkins, twenty medium and another box of the miniatures. 'What's the idea? Because that kind of supply will have you producing vats of soup, not bowls.'

'I'm going to run a theme night on Halloween.'

'So date nights aren't enough?'

For some reason she blushed. 'I like to be busy, you know me.'

He sat back against the table top. His sister had told Jo he was lonely, but looking at him now, she couldn't understand why he hadn't been snapped up already. He was good-looking, had a great physique which his denims did nothing to detract from, he had an entrepreneurial mind to be admired, and what's more, he was kind. If Jo thought he'd go for it she'd set him up with someone for a night of love at the café, but she suspected out of the two of them, Steve would probably be the more willing participant of the male cohort, so probably safer to target him first.

'Earth to Jo.' Matt's voice grabbed her. 'You're off in your own little world. Tell me what your plan is?'

She switched her head back to pumpkins rather than blind dates. 'I'm going to hold a pumpkin-carving night. I still get customers drifting in after school and then in the evening, but this will remind those who think the café is all about the summer, that we're open year round.'

'Good idea. Bring you more customers who might keep coming back.'

'Exactly. Perhaps I could ask Poppy and Charlie to design some posters.'

'They'll love that.'

'We'll put one in the window here and Molly can take one to the school when she delivers more of her cakes and biscuits; I can get one displayed in the pub, and I'm sure Jess will pop one on the surgery noticeboard.'

When a group of customers invaded the quiet café, Jo took the miniature pumpkins out the back – they'd keep in the storeroom until next week – and Matt went on his way, promising to fill Poppy in on their plan. Jo texted Ben who said he'd arrange to have Poppy over for tea with Charlie tonight and Jo would have the posters by morning.

It was true, what she'd told Matt. She loved to be busy, so having another plan was ideal. The more she had to do, the less time she had to think about her personal life which was underperforming compared to her work life. And so, at the end of the day, with the floors and table sparkling clean, Jo grabbed a notepad and pen. It was time to plan the menu for the next night of love at the café.

'It's so great to see you!' Jo hooked her arm through Tilly's. Her best friend was visiting from Scotland but only en route to her cousin's hen night and wedding in Exeter, and they'd already spent the last few hours talking at a rate of knots, both competing to get everything out and cram their long overdue catch-up into such a short space of time. 'And well done for picking a Tuesday to visit because it's my day off.'

'I'm glad to be here too.' Tilly bit into the waffle cone now the rum and raisin filling had gone from the very top of her ice cream. She'd insisted they buy an ice cream despite autumn being upon them, because it brought back memories of their schooldays when they'd hung out on the pier all summer long without a care in the world except which flavour to go for. 'I'm sorry it's such a quick visit, but I couldn't come all the way down south without popping in. Except now Mum has roped me in to help her shop this afternoon.'

Tilly's text had come through late last night to tell Jo about her spur of the moment decision to stop in town on her way to the impending nuptials. 'Surely she's got everything she needs by now?' said Jo.

'She wants me to help her find a hat, says the wedding won't be the same without one.'

They made their way further along the pier, trod the wooden boards that would always be so familiar to them both. 'Well, any time spent with my best friend is invaluable, so I'll take what I can today. I'll see you more at Christmas, I'm sure.'

'You can count on it.'

'What do you think?' Jo asked as they reached the café and turned their gaze from the shimmering sea to the sign she'd had repainted back in the spring.

'I'll bet the repaint made it really feel like your own place, didn't it?'

'That, and the thorough spring clean, not to mention sorting out the paperwork, marked a real fresh start for me.' Jo's raspberry ripple had been demolished all the way down to the last bite of the cone.

'Well, I for one think Salthaven agrees with you. You look fantastic, the most relaxed I've seen you in a long while. I was a little worried at some of the early texts you sent me. You sounded a bit stressed.'

'Becoming a business owner was a shock at first.' She popped the final piece of cone into her mouth.

'And now?'

'And now it feels like a part of me and I can't imagine not having the café. It was a steep learning curve, but Gran and Gramps have been great. They give me a bit of time off too, which really helps.'

Tilly waved through the window to Molly who had already given Tilly the biggest hug when she saw her earlier. 'You know, I always knew you'd come back here.'

'Do you think you will?'

Tilly shrugged. 'I really don't know. I'm settled up in Edinburgh, but when I see you, my family, and the beach, I do get a pang of desire. One day, maybe.'

Molly opened up the café door. 'Jo, Gramps has gone

home for a rest, I don't suppose you could help me out this afternoon, could you?'

'Is he OK?' Jo was ready to leap into action either here or back at her grandparents' bungalow.

'He's fine,' Molly dismissed, 'just not pushing it.'

'Do you need me now?'

'No, you two enjoy yourselves, but I need to get out into the kitchen soon so it would be useful to have another pair of hands.' She disappeared back inside when a customer came looking for a takeaway coffee.

'How is your Gramps?' Tilly asked.

'He's doing really well, but like Gran says, he's not supposed to push it too much. Neither of them need to be working crazy hours any more, which is why they wanted me to run the café in the first place.' She suspected it wouldn't be long before they stopped helping out on a regular basis, but rather than that scare her, Jo was ready for it now.

Jo and Tilly spent the next hour walking along the sand, inhaling the scent of the sea that even in cooler temperatures held a certain magic, before finishing up when it was time for Tilly to make a move and meet her mum in town for a spot of shopping.

Jo went straight to the café and Molly gave her an update of what was selling today, what she wanted to cook next.

'Thank you for coming in.' Molly finished wiping down the low table in front of the window seat.

'No need to thank me.' Jo hung her coat and scarf in the cupboard. 'As long as Gramps is OK.'

'Of course he is – I'd tell you if he wasn't.'

At mid-afternoon Arthur came into the café and

wanted to hear all about the pumpkin-carving event and Jo happily told him, if only to get a chance to observe his behaviour and be sure it was only clumsiness that had caused his accident rather than anything more. But apart from limping slightly, he seemed normal, if a little grouchy when you tried to imply he was anything other than fully functional.

Jo wondered what would happen in a real crisis. If he lost his faculties like his own mother had, would her mum return to Salthaven then? And if it was going to take something so major to get her back here, wasn't that the saddest thing you'd ever heard? Because by that stage, it would mean it was too late for them to have any kind of relationship ever again.

It was Molly and Arthur's turn to save the day the following morning when Jo woke up with the worst headache known to man.

'I'm sorry, Gran.' Even using the telephone this morning felt as though a marching band had climbed into Jo's head and given it their all. 'Are you sure you can manage?'

'Of course we can. Ben brought round the posters that Poppy and Charlie made – they're perfect – and I put one up at the school, Arthur arranged for one in the pub, and I saw Jess this morning who took one to put up in the surgery. I also gave Matt a couple of cookies to take for Poppy as a thank you for her help with the designs.'

'Thanks so much.' Slumped over the phone she couldn't bear to even open her eyes. 'Now all I need to do is get better.' She also needed to recover in time for Maddy and Dan on Friday night because she had no intention of letting them down. 'How's Gramps's foot?'

'Don't you worry about that. And I'll have him sitting to chop and peel ingredients for me to use, while I do the running around.'

Jo didn't chat more. All she wanted was to crawl back under her duvet and hibernate until she felt anything close to normal.

By lunchtime she'd at least transferred from bed to sofa. Her headache was still there, but instead of raging it had dulled into something far more manageable. She'd drunk more water than ever before but the rest was probably the biggest cure of all. Since she'd taken over the café it had been all systems go. Perhaps her body had decided it was about ready to call time out.

Her tummy grumbled, but on the way to the kitchen to make some toast there was a knock at the door. At least she could answer it now without the fear that her head might explode.

'Steve, what are you doing here?' She tried to think if she had anything at the flat that needing fixing, but luckily nothing had gone wrong since the washing machine episode. 'Excuse the pjs.' Suddenly aware she was wearing her favourite berry plaid bottoms with a slouchy marl grey top, she felt she had to mention it.

He gave her the once-over. 'You don't look bad to me.' He pulled out a parcel from behind his back. 'I heard we had a man down.'

'My hero.' Although she winced when she tried to smile, she took the parcel of warm paper and by the smell of the vinegar seeping through she was left in no doubt as to what was inside. 'I was just about to get some food.'

'You do look a bit peaky. How's the head?'

'Better than before. But don't get me too excited or tell me any funny jokes, or the pounding starts up again.'

'Sounds like a parcel of chips might be exactly what the doctor ordered.'

'Come in.'

'Are you sure? I don't want to make you any worse. I could tell you a hilarious joke and you'd be in pain all over again.'

If she could've rolled her eyes without it hurting, she would've done. Every time she moved her gaze without turning her head at the same time it hurt. And she may have made it to the door but standing here was taking all her energy and she worried she might end up falling down.

'Would you like to share?' She'd opened up the parcel on the kitchen benchtop, ready to take out one plate or two from the cupboard.

He leaned across and took a chip. 'I wouldn't want to deprive you. Go on, you tuck in. I'll keep you company for a bit.'

'Help yourself to a drink, there's some in the fridge.' She emptied the chips onto the plate, discarded the wrapping, and grabbed a bottle of water.

In the lounge she curled up on the deep round chair with her plate on her lap while Steve took the sofa and cracked open a can of Coke.

'These are so good.' She bit into another chip – crisp and golden on the outside, delightfully fluffy in the centre. 'How come you have time to hang around? Work quiet again?'

He stole another chip before settling back against the sofa cushions. 'It's been really quiet with all the rain. Great for having some time to myself, not so great for the bank balance.'

'I can imagine.'

'It's not too big a deal. You and the café keep me busy and I've been doing odd jobs for people in town to keep me out of trouble. I fixed the shelving in the toyshop, put up a new display stand in the library. Lena even had me redo the shelves in the bits and bobs shop, ready for summer. I'm keeping busy, don't worry, and hopefully the autumn rain will be over soon.'

Jo pulled a face when she looked out the window. Usually, from her position, she'd be able to look far out to sea, watch seagulls soar up into the sky, and down below to search the sands. But today she couldn't even make out the pier and the café because it was shrouded in mist. She supposed she could've picked worse days to be tucked up inside.

'And how's your love life?' The question was out before she had a chance to ram a chip in her mouth to shut herself up. They were friends, but it was still nosey.

'Bit personal.' But he didn't seem offended.

'I'm sorry. But weren't you seeing someone a while back? The blonde?'

'Ah, Ruby. Nice girl. And we had a few casual dates, nothing more. She's gone off to Singapore to work as an au pair.'

'Shame.'

'It was only ever a bit of fun.' He watched her cram the chips in, one after another. 'You really are hungry. Is eating helping get rid of the headache?'

She nodded, her mouth full. And after she swallowed, said, 'I think the food has hit the spot. Maybe they're magic chips.'

'Maybe they are.'

'I nearly forgot to ask, are you free Friday night?' She put the empty plate down on the table beside her and before he thought she meant anything else, added, 'I need those heavy posts put up again to make the bower for the café.'

'Sure. Count me in. What have you got planned this time?'

'You know I can't share specifics.'

'Spoilsport.'

'But you'll help?'

'What time do you need me?'

'Six o'clock?'

'Done. And I'll report back to Molly and Arthur that you're surviving.'

'Are they coping OK?'

'You know, it's almost like they've worked in a café before.'

She leaned forwards and shoved him on the arm. 'Very funny.' She winced.

'Headache back?'

'If I move suddenly.'

'Hah, that'll teach you.' There was another knock on her door. 'I'll leave you to it, you're in demand today.'

'Thanks to you and the magic chips I'm almost back to normal, so ready to be sociable again.' She took her plate to the kitchen on the way to the door.

'Glad to hear it. Hey, Ben,' he said as she opened the door and he passed the familiar face. The two men nodded to each other and it was almost comical. If she didn't know it was platonic between her and Steve, and the same with her and Ben, it would be like a set-up, each man having time with her so she could appraise them and judge who she liked the best.

'Something smells good,' said Ben after Steve went on his way.

'That'll be the chips Steve brought round.'

'I should've known. That smell grabs me every time I step onto the pier. How are you feeling? I went to the café but Molly said you weren't well.'

'I had the worst headache ever when I woke up but it's slowly getting better. Excuse the pjs.'

He grinned and she hoped it was in kindness rather than because she looked a state. 'I came to ask if I could sign Charlie up for the pumpkin carving.'

'Of course; it's fine for anyone to come along.'

'He's worried he won't get a pumpkin. He thinks you might sell out. And he wants it to be special. He'd like to bring his mum along but she won't be able to get to the café earlier than the start time because she'll be working.'

'I tell you what, I'll reserve a pumpkin out the back for him if it looks like we're running out.'

'Thanks, Jo. He's really nervous about everything going right. I didn't want to assume you'd have space for them.'

'Are you kidding? He's the reason people are hearing about it. I hear he and Poppy did an amazing job with those posters.'

'They're quite the team. Make us single oldies look like rookies.'

'They certainly do.'

'It's almost like Charlie is in tune with how delicate things are with Lorna and I, so he's anxious to please and puts this pressure on himself. I thought I'd come here and make sure I could help him with his plan so it goes as smoothly as possible.'

'I'm sure it will.'

Ben leaned up against the doorjamb. 'I'm sorry for off-loading on you. The least I could do was save it till I came into the café.'

She swished away his concern. 'Don't be silly. I'm happy to listen whenever.'

'I'd better be going, leave you to recuperate. Although you've got a bit of colour in your cheeks, that's good.'

She certainly did because she felt herself blush now as he stayed leaning against the doorjamb, his actions not matching the claim he was leaving. He looked like he wanted to say something else and Jo had an uneasy feeling in the pit of her stomach.

'Tell Charlie I said hello,' she told him.

He gathered himself and, with a friendly wave, followed the corridor and took the steps down to the hallway, ready to leave the building.

And he left Jo wondering whether perhaps Ben was looking for something more than friendship.

22

Jo didn't bother with a doctor's appointment but when Jess came into the café on Friday morning to collect her post-run smoothie, she pointed her in the right direction of over-the-counter medication if the headache from hell chose to visit again.

'It sounds like a migraine,' said Jess, pushing a straw into the lid of the takeaway cup.

'I had one a couple of years ago when I was teaching,' Jo admitted, 'and it knocked me out for a couple of days, but it wasn't quite so bad this time. I didn't have so much blurry vision at least.'

'I'd avoid driving if you get visual disturbances.'

'That's the great thing about Salthaven,' said Jo, 'I barely use my car unless it's to go to the supermarket; everything I need is here in town.'

'You need to be mindful of what triggers your migraines,' Jess advised. 'I'd say yours is probably as a result of your busy workload – am I right?'

'Probably.' Jo felt as though she'd been running on empty for a while. 'The day off did me the world of good. By early evening the dull ache behind my eyes was merely irritating rather than painful.'

'You look after yourself. Don't overdo it,' were Jess's last words before she headed out into a dry yet blustery day. Autumn could be gloriously pretty with coloured leaves showing off their golds and deep reds like dried-up jewels. But not today. Today the wind had blown Jo along the pier so fiercely she'd almost been worried she wouldn't be able to stop at the café entrance, or that it would take the fresh baguette she was carrying way out to sea. The outside tables were still there because sometimes customers liked to bundle up and enjoy hot drinks next to the wild sea, but no amount of coffee or hot chocolate and colourful paperweights to hold their books, newspapers and napkins in place, would convince anyone to want to be out there on a day like today.

Jo took the delivery of fruit and vegetables from Matt, made two quiches and a fruit salad, juggled a mid-morning rush as she made a ginger and pear upside-down cake to serve with crème fraiche, and in the late morning she grabbed some time to prepare the menu for the night of love at the café. She'd picked up Molly's slow cooker from her bungalow yesterday and brought it to the café so it would be ready and waiting. Now, she chopped carrots, mushrooms, pulled out a couple of sprigs of thyme Matt had popped into the produce box today, and sliced garlic into tiny pieces. She set the heat on the stove to high and browned all sides of the piece of beef she'd bought for tonight, and then, along with wine and all the other ingredients, popped it into the slow cooker. It would take seven to eight hours to cook, which fitted in perfectly with Maddy and Dan's arrival time of 7 p.m. They were in for a real treat with beef stew served with crusty bread, followed by a fun apple and caramel cheesecake shooter dessert.

'Good afternoon, Jo.' It was Geoff, much later than usual.

'I was beginning to think I wouldn't see you today.' She couldn't miss the huge bunch of the most delicate orange roses, sitting in their bouquet with greenery and sprigs of tiny deep purple flowers, the display giving her a surge of satisfaction that her plan had brought him together with Valerie.

He blew out his cheeks. 'No way was I fishing in this weather.'

'I think Valerie had the same idea. I saw her with her yoga mat first thing, heading towards the town hall.'

'She left very early this morning.' When she raised her eyebrows he must've realised he'd dropped himself in it. 'Things have progressed,' he clarified.

Jo put him out of his misery. 'I think it's wonderful! I'm happy for you. Will she be joining you today?'

'Not today, but we'll be taking a walk later and then having dinner tonight.' He stepped forwards and handed the bouquet to Jo.

'For me?' She almost joked that taking things to the next level must've put him in a really good mood, but she'd embarrassed him enough.

'We owe it all to you, Jo. I would've kept sitting at the end of the pier doing nothing with my days but fishing if you hadn't jumped in and made me see sense.'

'They're beautiful, and I'm incredibly touched.' She leaned in and smelt the stunning autumn blooms. 'But most of all I'm pleased it all worked out for you both. I'm going to take these home to my flat tonight, to enjoy them all to myself.' She'd put them on the windowsill that looked out across the sands with the sea in the distance and that way she'd enjoy the flowers along with her favourite view.

'I almost forgot to ask . . . how are you feeling? Molly said you were a bit under the weather, but you've got the colour back in your cheeks now.'

'I'm much better, thank you.' She'd never tire of being part of a community where people asked after each other on a daily basis and were ready to step in and help. She hadn't really noticed it when she was younger and living here, but now it was plain to see.

'I'd better be off, then,' said Geoff. 'But I'll grab a takeaway tea if I may. Jess's Sunday walking sessions are rubbing off on me and Valerie and I have been walking here, there and everywhere. Today it'll be over to the fields at the edge of the town to meet up with the council team organising this year's fireworks event.'

'Oh yes, that's almost here already. I can't wait.'

'You know, a lot of people congregate on the pier.'

'So I've heard. Don't worry, I'll be ready for them.'

'I hope you get to enjoy some of it yourself. Pretty spectacular across the water. The sea lights up and it's a sight to behold.'

'I'll make sure I see plenty.' She made his black tea and waved him on his way, suspecting this new poetic, talkative side from the man who'd said very little before, was down to the blossoming romance with Valerie.

By the time Steve came in, Jo had finished assembling the desserts, layering soft creamy cheesecake with caramel apples all the way up the tall glasses that she'd topped with whipped cream and slotted into the fridge.

Jo and Steve manoeuvred the posts into place, he fixed

them with the screws, and she brought through the flowers from the storeroom.

'Admirer?' Steve nodded towards her beautiful bouquet next to the till as he packed his tools back into his toolbox.

'They're from Geoff. A thank you.'

'He and Valerie seem happy.'

'I think they've sealed the deal too.'

'I won't ask how you know that.' He followed her over to the makeshift bower.

Steve took a set of lights and wound them around the first post for Jo as she followed the pattern with the flowers. For this date she'd picked clematis and, using gardening twine, she secured the white, bell-shaped flowers kissed with purply-pink edges so they mingled with the fairy lights to create the perfect romantic atmosphere for tonight.

'I think the lovebirds will like this and whatever's cooking,' said Steve as he helped her wind the last of the lights around the very top of the post.

'It's Maddy and Dan,' she told him. She didn't share the identity of the people she'd chosen with many, but she had with Steve when he was willing to put in so much effort to help prepare the café.

'Dan's a top lad.'

'He does seem nice. Do you know much about him?'

'Only that he surfs. And does it very well. We tend to know one another over at the surf beach, watch each other's backs.'

'Sounds like a safe idea to me, especially on days like today.'

He wound the lights around the second post. 'What's on the menu?'

She reiterated what she'd chosen as she fixed more clematis to the second post. 'And I've got red and white wine, plus beers, all in the fridge out in the kitchen. I had no idea what they'd like.'

'Good to cover all bases.' Steve was busy stringing lights across the top to form a pretend roof so Dan and Maddy would be eating beneath the fairy lights, a magical illusion of stars. 'So how about you?'

She pulled a face. 'What do you mean?'

'I figured you asked about my love life on Tuesday when I came to see you at your flat, so I can ask about yours too.' He started on the third post and she followed, taking more flowers from the packaging she'd opened up on the table top.

'Nothing to tell, I'm afraid. All very dull.' She tugged a piece of foliage and wound it round as he took the lights all the way to the top of the post.

'What about the man I saw hanging around back in the summer?'

It took a while for it to dawn on her. 'You must mean Curtis.'

'Fancy name. So was he interested?'

'Actually, he was.' They moved on to the final post. 'But not in the way you think. He was after me for business, not pleasure.' She explained all about Cornwall. 'It's a good offer.'

'You wouldn't desert us, would you?'

'I was tempted for a while.'

On his haunches as he checked the lights were tucked in at the bottom, Steve looked up at Jo. 'Really?'

'At the start I thought I'd taken on too much. Gran and Gramps weren't the best with the accounts and the café wasn't doing as well as I'd hoped. But by claiming for what I should and bringing a bit of attention to the café with the nights of love, business seems to have improved steadily.'

'You'll always have peaks and troughs.'

'I expect you're right.'

'Don't do a runner.' He touched a hand to her arm. 'I think I speak for the whole town when I say we kind of like having you around.'

'You're really sweet to say so. I kind of like being around here too.' She tied the last of the clematis flowers to the fourth post. She'd once suspected Steve had been behind the mystery postcards, but it wasn't his style at all. He'd tell her how it was, like he was doing now, and it was for the best that he wasn't interested, as she didn't want anything to jeopardise their friendship. At school, Tilly had been best of friends with a boy called Warren, and as they'd all settled into sixth form he declared he was head over heels in love with her. After that, their friendship was never the same again. Gone were the easy lunches they'd shared, the days at the beach where they'd hung out. A few words had seen to it that everything changed. They'd gradually drifted apart and Tilly hadn't heard from Warren once they both left school.

She stood back and admired their handiwork. 'Thanks for all your help tonight. I've got it from here, you're free to go.'

He picked up his toolbox. 'Time to get the atmosphere right eh?'

'Something like that.'

'I don't expect the local handyman hanging around fits in with the image.'

'I think these two need all the help they can get.'

'I'll be by first thing tomorrow to help take the posts down. You can fill me in on the night of love then.' And with a wink, he went on his way.

With the bower ready, Jo laid out the pristine white tablecloth, napkins, cutlery and a vase of blush pink lilies for the centre of the table. She switched on all the twinkly lights up high on the interior walls of the café as well as those on the bower. It was almost time.

Out in the kitchen she cut the long baguette into pieces, ready to serve with the stew, and placed a couple of blocks of butter onto a plate. And when she looked at the stew it not only smelt wonderful but the beef was tender and the vegetables perfectly cooked.

All that was missing now was her third set of participants and it would be all systems go. And the only slight chink in her happiness armour was that, one day, she longed for it to be her turn to be a part of a whirlwind romance.

Dan was first to arrive at the café and Jo sent up a silent prayer of thanks that he'd turned up and was prompt. Nothing would deter a potential girlfriend more than a guy who didn't show up when he should.

'Come in, Dan. How are you?'

'All right.'

Jo didn't suppose she'd get much out of a guy in his early twenties, especially one who looked so nervous. Gone was the wetsuit, his hair was dry and styled neatly, he'd shaved, and a light scent of cologne wafted in with him. Jo was about to try and make conversation when Maddy appeared outside the café.

Top points for Dan who opened the door for his date, but he didn't say anything apart from 'Hello.'

Maddy returned the sentiment and Jo got busy showing them to the table beneath the bower.

'Thank you.' Maddy took a seat and Dan sat opposite her.

It felt as though they were in one of those posh restaurants with a stilted atmosphere rather than a relaxed affair with good food, and the latter was definitely the mood Jo was aiming for. 'Can I get you some drinks?' Maybe that would be the answer. Alcohol would relax them and while Jo was away from the table it would give them some space to talk.

But it didn't work. Even with wine at hand, the date was almost half an hour in and it was not going well.

Out in the kitchen Jo spoke into the phone in hushed tones. 'They're barely talking,' she whispered to Steve. She'd called him as he was closer in age to them than Molly who would usually be her first port of call for advice, and also because Steve knew Dan from the surf circuit. 'What am I going to do?' Maddy and Dan were both clearly glad to be here, Jo had seen that on their faces the moment they arrived, but they were really uneasy with one another.

'I'm on my way,' said Steve.

'What are you going to do?'

'Sit tight. I'm in the pub, I'll be there in fifteen minutes.'

Jo hung up and spied on the couple once again. She'd found a soundtrack from the most romantic movies of all time and it played softly through the docking station, she'd delivered the stew that they were eating happily, and she'd already topped up their glasses with red wine. But all the food and drink had done was given them something

266

to hide behind in lieu of the conversation they needed to have so they would realise their feelings for one another. Maddy was usually outgoing, chatty, unafraid of conversation with a stranger from what Jo had seen over the last couple of weeks in the café. She chatted with Ben and Charlie whenever they were in, Jo had even heard her talking to a stranger last week, recommending local places of interest when it was raining and their kids were heading towards meltdown. Dan, on the other hand, seemed painfully shy unless he was with his friends. Deceptively, at first glance he was a man, tall, muscly and every bit as grown up as someone like Steve, but the second you spoke to him you realised he was still unsure of himself and needed time for his head to catch up with his physical appearance.

Jo discreetly passed through the café where Maddy and Dan were tucked beneath the bower in the corner. She opened the door when Steve appeared and stepped outside where they couldn't be seen.

'Is it going any better?' he asked.

'Not really. The talking on this date is less than at a sponsored silence.'

'Give Dan this.' He handed her an envelope. 'You called at exactly the right time. I'd just picked up the newspaper. Pretend you saw it yourself.' Jo picked up an aftershave that wasn't always there when he came into the café after surfing. 'Focusing on something other than each other and how nervous they are will help. Trust me.'

Jo took the envelope and crept back inside and when she was safely in the kitchen she pulled out the contents to find a newspaper article. With Maddy and Dan still eating the stew she read it from start to finish.

She went out, armed with the bottle of Merlot, ready to jump in now they'd finished their main course. Their coats were piled one on top of the other on the table behind, and Jo hoped the stilted atmosphere would disappear by the time they had to put them on again and venture outside. The date was in danger of fizzling into nothing and she didn't want that at all – and deep down, she suspected neither of them did either.

'More wine?' Jo topped up both glasses at their approval. 'I'll give you a break before dessert.'

'Thank you, Jo.' Maddy's dead straight blonde hair that hung almost down to her bottom had been curled with a subtle, soft wave for tonight and in jeans with a ribbed, Bardot-necked top showing off slender shoulders, she looked stunning. No wonder Dan was stuck for words, although he looked good enough himself in jeans and a navy Oxford shirt.

Jo took the plates away to the kitchen and it was time to do as Steve suggested. She only hoped this would work.

Back at their table she put the article on the table in front of them both. 'Dan, I was flicking through the newspaper. Is this you?' She wanted it to seem as though she'd been casually reading while they had their meal. She'd checked the date was today's so it wouldn't be an unreasonable assumption.

Sheepishly, he nodded. 'Yes, it is.'

Jo flattened the article with the title 'Surf's Up at Salthaven Primary', as Maddy took the bait and leaned over to see it for herself. 'When were these taken?' Maddy asked as she looked at the photographs accompanying the narrative. Dan, on the sands of Salthaven beach, had his surfboard propped up with an arm casually holding its tip, wetsuit leaving nothing to the imagination when it came to his body.

'A few days ago,' he confessed.

'Is that Charlie? He mentioned he'd tried surfing.' Maddy's smile spread wide as she peered at the photograph of the little boy she knew so well standing alongside his peers, all in little wetsuits, all with their own boards.

'I've been running lessons for the local primary school,' Dan replied. 'It was a trial run last week and they're hoping to introduce the programme for all years in the school next summer.'

'That's brilliant, no wonder the newspaper gave good coverage,' Maddy replied. 'I wish things had been so exciting when I was at primary school.'

Jo sneaked off and left them to it. Steve had been so right to suggest this. With the spotlight on something other than their date, both Maddy and Dan relaxed and chatter came naturally as they discussed the newspaper coverage.

Back in the kitchen she fired off a text to Steve: '*You're a genius!*'

He replied quickly with a laughing face emoji and a message telling her to get the awful music off right now. '*Total passion killer,*' he texted. '*Put on something lively, they're 21 not 71!*'

And so she served the apple and caramel cheesecake shooter desserts with the wooden ice-cream spoons she'd nabbed from the ice-creamery and left Maddy and Dan chattering away with the radio blasting out lively Friday night music that seemed to buoy them along better than any playlist she had on her phone.

Despite tonight's rocky start, Cupid's arrow seemed to be on course for another bullseye after all.

23

The morning after the night of love at the café was beautiful, with a soft autumnal golden glow taking over the sky as Jo got organised for the day by baking miniature pear crumbles in individual ramekins. She served cups of tea to Geoff and Valerie who wanted to sit outside and enjoy the sea air, using the bright giraffe paperweight plus the one painted with purple and sky-blue dots, to hold down their newspapers. And by the time Jo got under way with the other recipes she'd earmarked for today, bruised clouds had ganged up in the skies overhead, ready to unleash whatever they had planned.

'What did you do all evening?' Steve arrived and got to work dismantling the bower. He unscrewed the fourth pole from its base as Jo steadied it until he could reach up to take its weight.

'I lurked in the kitchen. Awkwardly, until your genius plan broke the ice.'

He hoisted the first post from the back of the café to the storeroom with Jo's guidance. Jo had already removed the clematis flowers, most of which were unscathed, and she'd filled a few small vases with them and set them on tables to brighten up the café.

'They were talking constantly after I put the newspaper

article in front of them,' she told him.

'I'd seen the piece in the newspaper on top of the bar when you phoned me in a panic.' He got to work dismantling the next part of the bower. 'Billy was talking about it and when I got your call he gave me the nod to tear out the page. I told him it was all for a good cause, but he said he'd already read it so it'd be used for lighting the fire before long.'

'Well, you saved the day. I really felt for them both up until that point. They so obviously like each other but couldn't seem to get over the first hurdle of actually talking. Love's hard when you're that age.'

'Love's hard at any age.'

She bundled up the fairy lights and set them in a deep box to stash in the storeroom until next time. 'They left hand in hand, so I'm taking that as a good sign.'

'You know you're the talk of the town?'

She wound up the last set of lights. 'I am not!'

'You are. These date nights are becoming legendary.'

'I doubt it.' She picked up a stray clematis petal from the floor.

'In the pub last night, Geoff was meeting other council members about the fireworks night, and the conversation didn't take long to turn to what you're doing here. Of course, he's a fan. You're well thought of, Jo.' He lifted out another post. 'You're special.'

Glad of their solid friendship, she excused herself when Matt came in with the second delivery of the day.

'Heavy,' was all he said. The strain in the tendons of his arms and his expression said the rest and she led him through to the storeroom which was filling up by the second.

'Pop it down there,' she told him. And when he set the box of assorted sizes of pumpkins down she tried to shift it to the side but it didn't budge an inch.

Behind her, Matt laughed. 'I told you it was heavy.' He gave it a shove for her. 'Is there room for a few more boxes?'

'It'll be a squash in here for a while, but come Halloween all these pumpkins will go home with whoever carved them, so for now it's fine.'

Steve came through with a post, stepped over the box of pumpkins, and leaned the post against the far wall.

'Can I help you with the rest of the pumpkins?' Jo asked Matt. 'Where's your van?'

'Parked on double yellows at the start of the pier. And no offence, but I might grab Steve if you don't mind. Muscle power and all that.'

'Hey,' Jo frowned. 'What happened to gender equality?'

'They're all as heavy as that one.' Matt nodded to the first box.

'Point taken,' she said as Steve volunteered his services. 'Why don't you two unload, then move your truck to somewhere legal, Matt, and come back for a coffee on the house. Cappuccino?'

'That'd be great.' He and Steve went off to do the honours and between them they transported the pumpkins to the storeroom in no time.

'It's going to be some pumpkin party.' Matt took a grateful sip of the steaming hot cappuccino Jo had made him. Steve had gone on his way to another job, darting down the pier to stay reasonably dry despite the drizzle.

'I'm really looking forward to it,' she confessed. 'Gran and Gramps were always big on Halloween.'

'Really? I thought it was only a recent development over from America.'

'Not for us. And Gramps is brilliant at carving. He's told me he'll get here early for the event, bag himself the best pumpkin.'

'I'm pretty good myself. Sounds like I could have some competition on my hands.'

'Really?'

'One of my many talents.' He took out his phone from his back pocket, swiped the screen a few times and showed it to her.

'You did this?' Staring back at her was a medium orange pumpkin, more of an oval shape than round. The spooky symbol had the traditional hollowed out face of a ghoul but Matt had also etched leaves and branches around the skin of the pumpkin. 'I don't suppose you'll be coming to the carving night, will you?'

'Actually, I will. I'm bringing Poppy.'

'And hanging around?' she asked hopefully.

'Why?'

He was right to be suspicious. 'Because it would be great to have a professional on hand to give tips.'

'Happy to. What tools do you have?'

She took him out to the kitchen and went through what she intended to use. 'I don't want anything too industrial, it'll be mostly kids, so I don't want to risk accidents.'

'Yeah, a sliced-off finger in a pumpkin might be a little bit too far.' He smiled. 'I tell you what. These scoops and small knives are great, but I'll bring along some stencils. Do you have greaseproof paper?'

She pulled open a drawer to reveal an industrial-sized roll. 'Plenty.'

'Great. We can trace the stencils onto greaseproof paper and then more kids can use them. We'll keep the designs reasonably straightforward.'

'Fantastic! You're my partner in crime for Halloween.'

'Do I have to dress up?'

'I hadn't thought of that. I suppose we should.'

'Definitely.'

As much as she loved running her own business, it was nice to do something with someone else now and then. The storeroom was filled with bright orange pumpkins, the posters had brought plenty of enquiries, and talking about it now was getting her even more excited. 'We don't have long to organise anything.'

'Anna has costumes from last year. I'll send pictures and drop something in later if you're interested. You look about the same size as her.'

A little uneasy under his scrutiny, she agreed and with a wave he went on his way as Jo turned her attention to Hilda, her next customer, who requested a pot of tea while she waited for Angie. And by the time both women were ensconced in the corner enjoying Molly's infamous brownies which Jo had collected first thing this morning, Jo was juggling cooking with serving and clearing up, buzzing with the job she felt she'd almost been born to do.

With Angie and Hilda playing chess at their table, Jo kept the tea supplies flowing and greeted Ben and Charlie next, on their regular Saturday morning visit. Since suspecting Ben had been behind the mystery postcards, Jo flitted between feeling awkward and thinking how utterly ridiculous the notion was. She'd tried looking at him through the eyes of a single woman, but as with Steve, she couldn't get past their solid friendship that would be at risk if anything ever changed.

This morning, Charlie only had eyes for the brownies and eating one was the only way he stopped firing off questions about the pumpkins – how many did she have? How big were they? How hard was it to cut shapes?

'What do we do with the guts?' he wanted to know as Ben handed him a napkin to clean the chocolate off his chin. 'I don't think my mum wants to put her hands in. But I do.'

'How about you scoop them out yourself, then we'll put them aside and I can use them for soup or a pesto?' She cleaned the table beside them and gave the giraffe paperweight that had been used outside a quick wipe.

'Do I get to use a saw?' Charlie asked.

Jo and Ben exchanged a look. 'You'll use tools, but knives will do the trick.'

Charlie seemed disappointed and ran to get the crayons and a piece of paper to design his pumpkin.

'Thank goodness you won't put him in charge of a saw,' said Ben, 'or it could be like a chainsaw massacre. You saw what he was like with his brownie, bits everywhere.'

'It'll all be very safe in here. How's his reading going?' She wanted to ask before Charlie sat down again.

'Actually, not bad. After I spoke with you I tried to think a bit outside the box. Lorna found some Captain Underpants books in the bookshop and I think he's getting into them. I think jokes about nostrils, stinks, underpants and turbo toilets help.'

'Ah, boy humour.' She grinned as Charlie came back to join his dad and she left them to it.

*

When her phone pinged after the lunchtime rush, Jo took it out to see the photos Matt had promised to send. The first was of a costume for Catwoman, a slinky all in one black suit complete with mask. Jo wasn't sure she'd ever be able to squeeze into that. The next photo was of a skeleton costume next to which Matt said he'd be wearing the male version on the night, so up to her if she wanted to match. Third was a photo of a stripy all in one prisoner costume, fourth was Anna wearing a zombie outfit, her face painted white with black eyes and red colouring to represent blood. And the final photo was of Anna wearing a witch's outfit with a very short skirt.

Jo took away Hilda and Angie's plates as Hilda concentrated on the chessboard and how to play her next move, and when she'd put them in the kitchen she dialled Matt's number to thank him.

'I haven't called at a bad time, have I?' she asked.

'No, just supervising pumpkin picking and making sure nobody tries to leave without paying. You never know, they might try to shove one up their jumper.'

'Not the kind of thing you can steal very easily,' she surmised.

'What did you think of the costumes?'

'I think it's safe to say I won't be coming as a zombie.'

'No, don't want to give the kids nightmares, do we? I've got a mask for my skeleton costume but we'll see how we go with the little kids at the pumpkin carving. I may have to take it off.'

'I don't think I'll fit into the Catwoman costume, so I was thinking the witch.'

'You don't sound sure.'

She hesitated, but he was a friend, she could say it. 'It

might be a bit risqué for a night at the café. The skirt's rather short.'

'Anna wore that to a very adult Halloween party last year, but I know she went out the door in a pair of red and white striped stockings. I was babysitting Poppy and seem to remember my sister coming home, complaining how hot the venue had been, how she'd had to take off her stockings so she didn't pass out. Always was a drama queen.'

'Does she still have the stockings?'

'I could text and ask.'

'That'd be great. Then could you do me a favour and drop the costume in later on, or tomorrow morning?'

'Of course I can. I'll drop it over in the morning. But will you still want it if she doesn't have the stockings?'

'I'm going to be brave and say yes. I'm sure I've got some black tights lurking around somewhere.' She'd worn them in her teaching days but not much since she'd enjoyed the freedom of being able to dress down and wear jeans every day.

'Shame.'

The bell to the door of the café tinkled. 'Thanks, Matt. I've got another customer, I'd better go.' The costume would be fine, she was sure it would fit, and Matt was right, it would be a shame if she had to wear black tights rather than something more fun.

She served her customer and then busied herself tidying up a bit. She took discarded plates and cups to the kitchen, picked up a jam-covered knife that had been left on another table, a napkin from the floor by the window seat. The windowsill had sticky finger marks all over it so she grabbed a cloth, ran it under hot water, and returned with the surface spray to clean them off. She listened to Hilda and Angie chatting away in their own little world, faces fixed on the chess pieces, contemplating their next moves. Hilda was talking in chess language – something about rooks and pawns and how Hilda had once got her brother in checkmate and it had been the first time she'd ever won a chess game. But it was the next part of her conversation that stopped Jo in her tracks.

'I hope Sasha knows what she's doing,' said Angie. 'Molly and Arthur aren't getting any younger. She'll regret it if she never mends their relationship.'

It made Jo sad to hear how other people were aware of the trouble in her family, relationships that sometimes felt beyond repair. She wiped the rest of the windowsill, careful to stay tucked behind the wall so they wouldn't think she was eavesdropping.

'How can she?' Hilda asked. 'She's ashamed of what happened – and from what Molly told me, so were they.'

Jo froze. Not only did they know there was trouble, but it seemed these two outsiders knew more details of her family dynamics than Jo did.

'Molly and Arthur are pillars of the community.' It was Angie's voice again. 'I'm not surprised it drove them apart, what she did with that man.'

Jo couldn't leave it any longer and as she stepped into their line of vision it was Hilda who looked up from the chessboard first.

'Jo!' Hilda looked like she'd been caught pilfering the till.

'What man are you talking about?' Jo toyed with the cloth between her hands. Both women suddenly focused all their attentions on the hand-crafted chess pieces that had been part of this café almost as long as Jo's family had. 'Do you mean my father?'

Hilda bit down on her bottom lip. 'It's not our place to say anything further, love. We should've kept our mouths shut.'

The bell above the door tinkled and in came Maddy with a girlfriend. Jo longed to ask her how her date had gone but how could she with what she'd just overheard playing on her mind? She served Maddy and her friend with one eye on Hilda and Angie to make sure they didn't try to escape. And when she saw them packing away the chess pieces she stood over by their table.

'You need to talk to Molly and Arthur.' Angie's voice was soft when she pre-empted Jo's request for more information.

'Don't you think I've tried?'

'They're proud people, Jo.'

'And Mum brought shame, is that what you're saying?'

Hilda looked at Angie and put a hand on her friend's arm. 'You go on without me. I'm going to talk to this one. It's time she knew the truth.'

Angie shook her head. 'Molly and Arthur won't like you meddling.'

'Someone has to.' She sat back in her seat and Jo pulled out the chair opposite. 'I remember you as a little girl,' Hilda began.

'I loved the toyshop. I came in there all the time.' Jo frowned. 'But Mum never took me. It was always Gran and Gramps. I don't know, perhaps she thought toys were a waste of money.'

Hilda didn't comment on Jo's remark. 'Your mum got in with a bad crowd and a bad boy.'

'I know all that, I've been told enough times what a waste of space my father was.'

'There's more.'

'So tell me.'

'I think I'm going to need a very strong black coffee.' Her hands clasped in her lap Hilda was having trouble sitting still and Jo knew she'd have to fix her a drink if she wanted answers.

As the coffee machine gurgled and clicked away, depositing the dark liquid into the waiting cup, Jo watched Hilda. She obviously didn't want to be the one to tell Jo anything, but here she was, risking Molly and Arthur's wrath by doing so. She was a kind lady who Jo wished she could remember. Her Swiss accent had a way of putting you at ease, maybe because it was a pleasant lilt, different to the norm. As a little girl Jo had loved saving her pocket money to go into the toyshop, and her mum couldn't have thought all toys were a total waste of money because she'd loved coming home from work to Jo's miniature café where she'd made frozen treats with her Mr Frosty Ice Maker.

Jo took the coffee over to the table and Hilda reached for it, blowing across the liquid. 'Your dad was a handsome devil,' Hilda began. She was obviously starting with the good points. 'He was very attentive to Sasha, and I think we all wanted to give him the benefit of the doubt. But it was soon obvious she idolised him so much she'd be willing to do anything.' She sipped the hot coffee, its temperature unwavering without the addition of milk. 'He had one of those tattoos all the way up his arm and I remember your mum getting one too.'

'A tiny dolphin on her left calf,' Jo recalled.

'Molly and Arthur were furious, but they knew better than to say anything. It was almost like they were treading on the finest of seashells every time your mum did anything out of the norm, as though they were scared she'd run away. Your father had a manipulative way about him that they weren't entirely comfortable with. I heard them arguing once, in the café, but your mum wouldn't hear anything bad about him. She accused your grandparents of wanting perfection – and that just because they'd lived their lives a certain way, it didn't mean everyone else's methods were flawed.'

'Sounds a lot like Mum. So how did my mum's relationship with someone who wasn't quite what my grandparents wanted, lead to a feud that put a permanent wedge between them all?'

Hilda looked relieved when a customer came in, but Jo wasted no time serving them, relieved the visitor to Salthaven wanted two cups of takeaway tea and didn't seem to want to hang around. Back with Hilda she urged her to continue.

'Your mum was out late most nights. All the youngsters were, but this was different. For a start, your mum was pregnant with you. And your father had a lot of friends older than Sasha. I don't think your mum dabbled in drugs, but I know some of the people she hung around with did. Perhaps even your father.'

'She always told me he was bad news,' said Jo.

Two young mums brave enough to be out walking with their babies came in next. They'd left the strollers tucked inside the front door, and Jo assured them they needn't worry about droplets tumbling off the rain canopies and puddling onto the café floor. 'I've plenty of old towels in the cupboard,' she told them as she ushered them to the farthest table from Hilda and took their order, anxious to get back to her own conversation.

Jo left the mums chatting away over hot chocolates and a chocolate brownie each – sod the calories they'd said, looking out at the dismal weather enveloping the pier – and joined Hilda again. 'I want to know how bad he was,' she said. 'I've waited to find out the truth for a long time.'

Hilda kept her voice low. 'A lot of people in this town suspected Alan of being behind a spate of thefts and vandalism: the ice-creamery was wrecked one day and the takings went, the sweetshop was graffitied – vile words for kids to see the next day – and the school was broken into once, although nothing was taken because the caretaker showed up and chased whoever it was on their way. The police had Alan in their sights, along with his friends, but could never prove anything.'

'So maybe it wasn't him?'

Hilda shuffled in her chair. 'We caught your father mid-burglary of my toyshop.'

Jo's mouth fell open. 'I'm so sorry, Hilda.'

'Don't be, love.' She covered Jo's hand with her own. 'He's not your responsibility.'

'So what happened? Did you report him?'

'Your mum was with him.'

Jo had been standing in case her customers needed anything further, but now she slumped into the chair next to Hilda. 'Mum was a criminal?'

'She was the one spraying the paint over my shop window. She was drunk, maybe even high – up to her eyeballs in something, I wouldn't know what – and when I caught her she didn't run, she froze.'

'Was she arrested?'

'I told Alan I'd got the whole event on CCTV and if he buggered off out of her life I wouldn't take it any further. I was livid. She had a tiny human being growing inside of her and put her baby – you – at goodness knows what risks. And I knew she'd been coerced, you could see it in the way she idolised him.'

How could her mum ever do anything like that? How could she commit a crime, take drugs or alcohol, especially when pregnant? 'How could she?' Her voice soft, Jo shook her head in disbelief.

'Like I said, he was charming, persuasive, and your mum was vulnerable. Who knows what he told her when they were together, how he made her look at things from his point of view? I didn't give him the chance to walk away for his sake. I did it for your mum. He could've rotted in jail for all I cared. Actually, I didn't really do it for Sasha, if I'm completely honest. I did it for Molly and Arthur. They'd been to hell and back, trying to keep their daughter away from that man, facing her wrath when they so much as voiced their opinion.'

'You make it sound like Mum was a monster.'

'Of course she wasn't. She got in with a bad crowd, that was all, and I could see what it was doing to your grandparents.'

'So what happened?'

'I think your mum sobered up a bit and was waiting for him to fight for her, insist he'd never walk away from her. I think the way he agreed so readily to my request hurt and shocked her more than anyone realised. It shattered her illusion of having a rosy future with him, and with you. He was being given a get out of jail free card and using it without a bloody concern about his partner or baby.'

Jo had never held a very high opinion of him, but what little respect she'd had fell away in an instant. The only people she cared about were her mum and her grandparents whose lives he'd affected without giving a toss. 'Excuse me, I need to see if they want anything else.' She gestured towards the two mums but really she needed to walk away for a moment, let her heart rate return to normal, deal with the shock of what she was uncovering.

The mums requested bottles to be warmed for their babies and Jo, glad of something to do, went out to the kitchen to sort them. It was one thing her dad walking out of her life, but doing it in such a cowardly way was even worse.

'Nobody told me any of it,' Jo told Hilda when she sat down again. 'My mum could've been put in prison if it hadn't been for you.' Tears sprung into her eyes and she felt Hilda's arm across her shoulders. 'Thank you. Thank you for looking out for us.'

Hilda handed her a tissue. 'Hey, it's what we do in this town, and you're a part of it now. The question is, can we ever get your mum back here?'

Jo dried her tears and shook away any more. 'Has Mum ever spoken to you about what happened?'

'Never. Since that day she avoided me, at the shop, in the street, wherever I was she very quickly made sure she wasn't.'

'So what happened after Dad did a runner?'

'He left there and then without so much as a goodbye to your mum. I took Sasha to Molly and Arthur's place. I thought maybe they could talk some sense into her.'

'But they didn't?'

'I really don't know much more, Jo. All I can tell you is that Molly came to see me the next day. She and Arthur shut the café, and helped me clean up the shop. We scrubbed the windows and when other people stood there blaspheming over the awful people responsible and what they'd do if they ever caught the culprits, none of us said a word.'

Jo was almost glad when the door tinkled again, but not when she saw it was Molly and Arthur. It was Hilda who stepped in and ushered them over to the table where Jo was waiting. 'Why don't you make a big pot of tea,' she suggested.

'What's going on?' Arthur hadn't even taken his coat off yet and Molly was already fussing around insisting he elevated his foot on an extra chair.

Jo's heart thudded at the realisation that this was it. The truth was out and her grandparents had no idea what was coming. She took the pot of tea to the table and set out three cups with saucers. Hilda patted her on the arm, then hugged her goodbye.

'What's wrong with Hilda?' Molly didn't miss the odd behaviour as their friend left. The two mums were too busy clipping up baby harnesses and fussing with rain covers to care what was about to go down in the café.

'Hilda's fine, Gran.' Jo poured three cups of tea. She left a small jug of milk and a pot of sugar lumps for those who wanted them. She supposed Arthur would be heaping them into his drink when he found out she knew their family history. 'But you should know, she told me everything.'

Molly poured milk into her tea. 'About what?' She

offered milk to Arthur and it seemed the truth had dawned on him before it did on his wife. But all it took was his hand on hers to still her fussing with the tea none of them really wanted, that silent understanding between married couples, to let her in on the secret.

Molly shook her head. 'So you know.'

'You could've just told me,' said Jo.

'What good would it have done?' Arthur's face was a picture of pain, representing the hurt Jo's mum, their daughter, had caused over the years, perhaps the pain he'd been a part of making worse.

'I don't understand why, though. Why keep it such a secret when I'm sure most of the town already knows?'

'Keep your voice down,' said Molly as she and Arthur looked around them. There weren't even any customers, it was almost as though they thought the walls had suddenly developed ears. 'And that's not true. Hilda didn't gossip about it to all and sundry. Only our closest friends know anything about it.'

Jo stood, sudden realisation dawning. 'Oh, I get it. I can't believe I didn't see it before now.'

'Get what?' Arthur pushed his tea away as though even the sight of it made him recoil.

'You kept quiet, the both of you, because you were embarrassed! It had nothing to do with what the truth might have done to Mum.'

'We'd sorted the mess out,' said Arthur, head in his hands. 'It was in the past.'

'But you never let her forget it, I bet!' Jo said angrily.

'Don't shout at him, Jo.' Molly put a hand to her husband's arm. 'It became very hard to trust your mum after what happened at Hilda's shop.'

'She never felt good enough, you know.' Jo had lowered her voice but it wasn't easy to keep it level. 'She was defined by a mistake she made. It shaped your opinion of her forever, and you know it.'

Arthur patted his brow with a napkin. 'We didn't ask her to leave Salthaven. We never wanted her to do that.'

Watching Gramps reminded Jo of what happened the last time he looked like this; he'd wound up in hospital and she didn't want to be responsible for that, no matter what he had or hadn't done. She sat down again. 'Did you even try to stop her leaving?'

'Your Gramps begged her not to go.' Molly's eyes pleaded with Jo to hear them out.

'Is that true?' She looked to Gramps, small and vulnerable in the chair next to her.

'She's my daughter.' He cleared his throat to scare away his own tears. 'But things had gone too far and she refused to listen to me. She'd made up her mind and that was that.'

Jo didn't say it, but she imagined that with two of them as stubborn as each other, there wouldn't have been much room for negotiation.

Molly, content her husband had calmed down enough and wasn't going to have a dizzy spell, turned to Jo. 'After your father left, all we wanted was for your mum to keep her job, keep you safe – and stop hanging out with those people who were just like Alan.'

'Don't tell me she refused to give up her friends?'

'Flat refused,' Molly confirmed. 'You know your mum, strong-willed, tough, a survivor. That man broke her heart and she lost her way. We tried to show her but she didn't want us.'

'She's a good mum,' said Gramps, surprising Jo with his remark. 'But one night, when you were a young toddler, we suspected she was involved in the latest spate of town burglaries. She couldn't account for her whereabouts and everything pointed at her guilt. I'm afraid we jumped to conclusions and she never forgave us for doubting her.'

Jo, head in her hands, shook her head. 'I can see that one from both sides. I can understand how angry she must've been to feel you thought so badly of her, but I can also see how, without a defence, it would've looked like history repeating itself. I remember the night you had a big argument and Gramps told Mum he didn't want me to turn out in the same way she had.'

Gramps's jaw fell. 'You heard that?'

'I'd tried not to think about it until recently, blocked it out. I was embarrassed at the state I'd let myself get in that night after too much to drink, horrified at the hateful words exchanged in our family.'

'They were words I regret saying, Jo. I'd take them back if I could. But you were right.'

'About what?'

'We were embarrassed too.' Jo saw him reach for Gran's hand. 'This community is everything to us. It's where we want to live out the rest of our days and the town's support and respect means a great deal to Molly and I.'

She put her arms around him. 'I love you, Gramps. And I love you, Gran. But I also love Mum.'

'So do we, pet,' said Molly.

'Salthaven was always too small for her, Jo,' said Arthur. 'She wanted adventure and now she's found that in Spain, and I think . . . and I hope . . . she's happy.'

He seemed to accept that this was it. They had Jo, they

24

It was Halloween and, along with Steve's help, Jo had put the bower up and decorated it with cobwebs covering the wooden posts, along with plastic spiders and skull string lights. She'd put a little cemetery RIP tombstone at the side of the room with more spider webs and a huge black and orange tarantula-sized arachnid, and along the walls were more twinkly lights, while each table was covered in a bright orange paper tablecloth, and she'd even found a plastic black cauldron at Hilda's toyshop that she'd filled with sweets to hand out at the end. Between them, Jo and Steve had hauled the pumpkins from the storeroom to the table beneath the bower and everything was ready to kick off the pumpkin carving event in half an hour.

When Molly and Arthur arrived at the café, Jo was glad to see them looking happy. It seemed getting everything out in the open was a relief for them all, no matter that it hadn't mended the rift between her grandparents and her mum. Jo just wasn't sure how they'd react if they found out Jo had lied to her mum in an effort to move forwards. Not that it had come to anything. Sasha had dug her heels in as she always did, but Jo knew that telling her Arthur's health was worse than it really was had rattled her mum.

Perhaps one day she'd come home and they could sort this out once and for all.

'Jo, this is all so wonderful!' Molly enthused as she nursed a cup of camomile tea in a black and purple paper cup with a skeleton on the front. Jo had brought matching plates too, ready for the Halloween treats later on.

Molly took Arthur by the hand and went out to the kitchen as Jo draped more cobwebs in the windows. 'Where are you two going?'

Molly called back. 'Don't come in, we're getting changed.'

'You're dressing up?' She got down from the chair she was standing on and moved it over to the other window. 'What as?' she called after them, but no reply.

She checked the time. She'd have to get changed too if she wanted to be ready for the guests. She'd been so busy decorating and preparing snacks with everything from bright green popcorn, devilled eggs dusted with paprika and a chive sticking out of the egg mixture to mimic the stem of a pumpkin, to sticks of liquorice for kids to snack on and a hopeful healthy option of a carved-out watermelon with a ghoul's face spewing out chunks of melon and pineapple.

'Ta-da!' came Molly's voice.

Jo turned round to see not Molly and Arthur, but Popeye and Olive Oyl. 'Wow, you look amazing!' Gran, hair scraped back in a low bun, was dressed in a red shirt with white lacey cuffs, a black skirt with a yellow trim and Ugg boots in brown with white furry tops. Gramps had on jeans and a yellow belt and a black sailor shirt with a red collar and gold buttons. He wore tan foam armbands to cover his forearms, each with an anchor symbol.

'I never expected you two to dress up.'

'What, miss out on all the fun?' Gramps flexed his biceps. 'No way were we going to do that, were we, Molly?'

She winked at her husband and then ushered Jo towards the kitchen to get herself ready.

Away from prying eyes, Jo took out the bag with the costume Matt had dropped over for her. Luckily, he'd found the red-and-white striped stockings, which were so much better than plain black. She pulled on the dress with its layered tulle petticoat, put on the black flapper gloves, a very pointy black hat to cover her hair which she'd let loose for the night and finally the stockings. Anna had been wearing heels in the photograph Matt sent and so Jo had gone for the same, seeing as it was a party.

'Now, don't you look quite something?' Arthur appraised his granddaughter when she joined them in the café and did a twirl.

But she didn't have long to chat and reminisce about her younger days when she'd dressed as everything from a fairy godmother to Frankenstein, because her first guests arrived.

It was time to get this party started. And time to forget the lie she'd told.

The café was filled with lively chatter and the soundtrack Jo had put together on her iPhone last night. They'd had 'Somebody's Watching Me', 'I Put a Spell on You', 'Monster Mash', and now it was on to 'Time Warp' which had people of all ages bopping along: Gramps could barely sit still now he'd finished his superb carving of a Halloween witch and cauldron on a medium-sized pumpkin, and he and Molly were swaying in time to the tune. Poppy and

Charlie, both dressed as ghosts in enormous white sheets that made pumpkin carving a real challenge, had downed tools and were giggling away as they danced around the café. Charlie started doing some funny breakdancing spin on the floor until Ben pointed out it might be dangerous with knives and other implements lying about.

'The costume is a great fit,' Jo told Matt as he took off his skeleton mask for a breather. The kids hadn't been at all scared of it, unlike when Billy from the pub turned up as a freaky clown and had kids cowering under the table. He'd quickly whipped off his mask to reveal his true identity and, after insisting Jo do the rounds with the ghost bagels she'd made from bagel halves, tomato paste and melted ghost shaped mozzarella, they'd restored some sort of order before he declared his punters would appreciate it more and headed back to the pub to serve Halloween cocktails to anyone willing.

'I'm glad you like it,' said Matt, 'and the stockings look good.' His eyes followed her legs from her heels to the bottom of the skirt.

Poppy tugged at her uncle's arm. 'Uncle Matt, can we please have some of the fruit?'

He indicated Jo. 'You're asking the wrong person. The witch is in charge of the food, remember.'

'I'll bring you over a bowl. One for Charlie too?'

'Yes please.' Poppy ran back to her friend.

'They must've got thirsty after all that dancing,' said Matt.

Jo scooped up melon and pineapple – she'd already removed the flapper gloves which made food prep and hygiene far too difficult – and took the dishes over to Poppy and Charlie, but not before Matt straightened her witch's

294

hat for her. 'It's got a mind of its own,' she frowned.

Over at Ben's table she checked out how the carving was coming along. Matt had supervised the event as much as she had and the kids as well as the adults had been having a grand time using the stencils and carving some spectacular shapes.

'Impressive.' She looked at Ben's work of a bright orange pumpkin now sporting evil eyes and a mouth stitched shut. 'Where are you going to put it?'

'On the front doorstep as soon as we get home. And I'm armed with a very unhealthy supply of chocolate and sweets for trick or treaters.' Ben made an excellent Fred Flintstone tonight in the trademark orange tunic with black spots that made him instantly recognisable. He hardly needed the plastic caveman club he'd brought along with him too.

Jo watched Lorna helping Charlie. He'd got halfway through carving the word 'Boo' in his pumpkin then lost interest in favour of Poppy and dancing, but now he was sitting with his mum again. Jo wondered whether one day she and Ben would be able to sort out their differences and give it another go. Jo herself had been the child of a single parent but she'd never known any different for many years until Stuart, her stepfather, came on the scene. Charlie on the other hand saw each of his parents and probably had a permanent cloud of confusion hovering above his head, wondering why his parents couldn't be together, especially as they seemed to be enjoying themselves. And Lorna made a great Wilma Flintstone alongside Fred.

Jo handed round the Halloween tucker. She offered creepy-crawly bugs from a platter – she'd cooked sausage rolls, chopped the ends off to reveal the meat, dotted on two yellow eyes made from mild mustard and finished them by giving each one thin, tubular breadsticks for legs. She offered thick black sticks of liquorice, handfuls of demon green popcorn, Molly's graveyard chocolate cupcakes topped with toffee shaped as tombstones, the devilled eggs, the spewing fruit melon, and Arthur's devilish cupcakes with vivid red icing.

Melissa and Jess came to offer their support, neither dressed up apart from their devil bopper headbands. 'I can't believe you'd rather go to the pub than hang out here,' Jo had laughed when they'd said they were off to see what was happening in town. But she'd shooed them out the door when they thought they'd offended her. It was chaotic in the café tonight, a lot of fun, very loud, and she knew by the end of this she'd want to flake out. They'd invited her to join them but she'd never have enough energy left.

Next in through the door were Maddy and Dan. 'Hey, you two.' She'd found it best not to even mention the date night that had brought them together, and thankfully they never seemed short of conversation these days.

'You look fab!' Maddy told Jo.

'So do you. Wow! I'm guessing, Morticia . . . ' she said, pointing at Dan next, 'and Gomez Adams.'

'Told you.' Maddy nudged Dan who was desperately trying to scratch an itch beneath the fake moustache he'd fixed above his upper lip. He put a hand to his black wig too. 'He thought nobody would have a clue who we were,' Maddy explained. She'd covered her own blonde hair with an ultra-long black wig, perfectly Morticia.

'You both look fab. Pumpkins?'

'Please,' said Maddy.

'Do you mind what size?' They followed her over to the bower. 'We don't have any of the huge ones left, I'm afraid.'

'Any size is fine,' said Maddy, and after they picked up the last two medium pumpkins Jo settled them at the edge of the table by the window.

Jo helped a couple of local schoolkids with the stencils and the cutting of their pumpkins. Between her and Matt and the parents and adults in tonight, everyone seemed to be mucking in and helping so things didn't get too crazy. It was turning out to be a real community event and Jo had already decided she'd be doing the same next year. People had got into the spirit with the dressing up, the themed food, she'd served what felt like hundreds of cups of coffee, tea and hot chocolate and, above all, she'd had a brilliant time too, despite being in constant demand.

'Tell her about some of the outfits we saw on the way here,' said Dan, when she passed by their table again. He was already carving the top from the pumpkin, ready to scoop out its innards.

'I saw someone go into the pub dressed as a bunch of grapes,' Maddy giggled. 'Basically covered in purple balloons with a purple knitted beanie on their head.'

'Interesting costume.' Jo handed a bunch of orange napkins to Molly to go and mop up a spill at the table beneath the bower before it crept towards the remaining pumpkins.

'There were also a couple of guys dressed as mummies. Actually, I'm sure you know one of them. Harry, I think his name is. Anyway, he'd used toilet roll and wound it around himself from head to toe and so had his mate.'

'At least if they run out of loo paper at the pub, there's

always backup.' Jo left them to it. She was glad Harry seemed to be getting on with his life without trying to make her a part of it. As promised, he'd kept things strictly business and from now on she suspected he would start to find his own version of happiness. And Curtis Durham had sent her an email last night, out of the blue, telling her he was in full swing with interviews and he was right to say she had vision because the locals in Cornwall were better than any of the graduates he'd interviewed so far.

The door opened again and in came Dracula before Jo had made it back to the counter. 'Hi, Steve. Nice outfit!'

'Who's Steve?' He did his best to look menacing, bared his fangs and did a swish with his cape before grabbing her and tilting her backwards. 'I'm Dracula and I vant to bite your neck, suck your blood, turn you into a vampire!' As Jo giggled he set her back to upright and took out his plastic teeth. 'I can hardly speak with these things in.' He whistled. 'You make a good witch – love the stockings.'

She straightened her hat again. 'If only this thing would stop moving.' Flushed from his antics she offered him a tombstone cupcake.

'Not for me, thanks. Just eaten at the pub.'

'There's some pumpkins left over if you're interested.'

'Actually, I am. Wouldn't mind one to take home and put on the windowsill in my flat.'

While Steve got going with a pumpkin, Jo topped up cups of water. 'Everything OK?' she asked Ben when she reached his table and saw him looking over at her.

'I was going to ask for water but you beat me to it,' he smiled.

She topped up his cup and then quickly whipped around to tidy up. Kids were beginning to tire; most of the pumpkins had been carved and pretty much all the food had been demolished, so Jo clapped her hands together to grab everyone's attention. She adjusted her witch's hat when it fell lopsided. 'We've got some amazing pumpkins here tonight, but now I think it's time to start putting on the finishing touches.' When kids grew impatient she held up a finger to tell them to wait. 'I need you to all stay sitting down and put your hand up in the air if you've finished. I'm going to come round and pop a small tealight into each of your pumpkins. Then, when everyone is ready, we're going to light the wick and I'm going to turn off all the lights. How does that sound?'

She almost wanted to cover her ears at the squeals of excitement as kids fidgeted and tried to reach high up into the air, desperate to be first to get a candle as she made her way around the café. When everyone was ready, she and Matt went around the room again, with a box of matches each, to light the candles as promised.

'Are we ready?' she called loudly as she stood, hand poised on the light switch. It had been dark outside for hours but the twinkly lights around the edges of the café and the lit-up skulls on the bower would be perfect alongside the tiny flames that would soon flicker against nightfall. 'OK . . . count with me. Three . . . two . . . one!' And she switched off the lights.

Squeals had been replaced by sighs of wonderment, faces full of excitement in the soft glow of illuminated pumpkins. She took a couple of photos on her phone, so she could capture the spirit of the evening and shared a conspiratorial look with her grandparents who had clearly enjoyed tonight as much as she had.

With everyone more than ready to go home, Jo grabbed

the plastic cauldron filled with sweets and chocolates and stood by the door to say goodnight to each and every one of her customers.

'I'm putting my pumpkin beside my bed,' Charlie proudly told her, although Ben suggested his windowsill was a better place to attract trick or treaters.

Matt had Poppy in his arms but set her down so he could carry the pumpkins. 'Thanks for tonight, Jo, we had a great time, didn't we?' Poppy managed a nod and a murmured thank you. 'I need to get this one home to bed.'

'Thanks so much for tonight, Matt.'

'It was my pleasure.'

'Can I help you carry the pumpkins to the car? Then you can carry Poppy.'

'I think you've got enough to do here. You'll need someone to carry you up the hill.'

'You're not wrong there,' she sighed, and waved them on their way.

Everyone left with their bright orange pumpkins clutched protectively. Jo had handed out an extra couple of tealights to each person so they could have their carvings shining long into the evening, and when the last person had gone, except for Steve who was chatting to Molly and Arthur as he began to remove decorations from the bower, Jo grabbed another bin bag and walked around the café depositing in the empty paper plates, cups and pieces of pumpkin she'd missed earlier.

Between Jo, Molly and Arthur, and Steve, the bower was down, the decorations packed away, surfaces were gleaming, floors washed, and the café put back to normal ready for tomorrow.

Arthur went through to the kitchen and came back with something behind his back. He'd taken off his Popeye armbands and left them with his tin of fake spinach on the counter.

Jo slumped onto a chair next to Steve. 'What have you got there, Gramps?'

'The first bottle of mulled wine for the season.'

'Bring it on,' said Jo. She'd already taken off her witch's hat and wound her hair up into a chignon. 'Steve, you deserve one for all your hard work.'

'I'm not going to say no.'

Arthur waved away Jo's help, insisting he was quite capable of warming some wine, cutting up an orange into slices and serving the drinks.

Jo kicked off her heels. The twinkly lights had set the atmosphere in the café to one of calm, tranquillity after all the madness. 'My feet are killing me.'

Molly looked at the culprits. 'Not the best choice of footwear.'

'I approve,' said Steve.

'You would. You're a man and never have to wear heels.'

He lifted up her leg, his touch sending shockwaves through her body. 'Relax, I'm going to give your tired, aching, hardworking feet a rub until the mulled wine is ready.'

'OK, Dracula,' said Jo doubtfully.

'Hey, I've been told by some that I've got a magic touch.'

Molly sniggered. 'I think the less we know about that the better.'

Jo managed to relax and had to say Steve was as good as

the reflexologist she'd seen as part of a spa day with Tilly last year.

'I'd like to make a toast,' Molly announced, as soon as they all had their drinks. She got to her feet and Jo claimed hers back from Steve's grasp, marvelling at how relaxed she felt already. 'To Jo, who made not only tonight a huge success, but every day since she came back to Salthaven. We truly don't know what we'd do without you.'

'To our wonderful, talented, amazing and beautiful granddaughter,' Arthur added, raising his glass next.

'To Jo,' Steve chorused along with her grandparents.

They weren't in any rush to leave the café. This was their reward for a hectic day, a manic evening, and all the cleaning up. Steve had well and truly earned it too with all his hard work putting up the bower, taking it down. And not only tonight, but every time Jo wanted to convert the café for a night of love.

They talked about Jack-o'-lanterns, costumes – the good, the bad and the ugly – and when Steve got a text from a mate up at the pub they all wanted to know why he was so amused.

'Tell us,' Jo pleaded.

'It's Harry.'

'Go on, you can mention his name, we're both mature adults. We've both moved on.'

'You know his mummy costume consisted of lots of toilet roll wrapped around and around his body? Well, apparently, he was sitting at the bar and a girl next to him sneezed and reached out for a tissue. The closest tissue.'

'Oh no, not his costume?'

Steve nodded. 'Apparently she had a streaming cold

and a bit of tissue was flapping off his shoulder and she just went for it.' Jo waited for more. 'Then, when he was leaving, he collided with a smoker outside and the cigarette set his costume on fire.'

'Oh my God!'

Molly put a hand across her mouth and Arthur set down his mulled wine. 'Is he OK?'

'He's fine.' His voice wobbled. 'But people stepped in to help him by tearing the tissue off. He was only wearing a pair of pants underneath, and they had a hole in a place where nobody wants a hole if they're out in the elements, if you know what I mean.'

Jo started to snigger now. 'So he had to walk home on a cold October night, more or less naked?'

Even Molly and Arthur saw the funny side.

'Imagine if he hadn't put those pants on,' said Arthur making them all fall about some more.

'It would've been one of the liveliest nights at the pub yet,' Jo giggled. 'And there was I thinking I'd come to a quiet, unsuspecting town.' She left them all laughing away at Harry's predicament, but on the way to the kitchen to warm up some more mulled wine something caught her eye. It was someone at the door.

'What's up, Jo?' Steve called over. 'You look like you've seen a ghost.'

'Maybe it's Harry and he found more toilet paper to wrap himself in,' joked Arthur. 'Don't let him near the stove!'

But it wasn't Harry. Jo unlocked the door and let their visitor in and when Molly and Arthur saw who it was their laughter faded as did the smiles on their faces.

'Well, *he's* hardly at death's door!' Sasha yelled, pointing at Arthur. 'You had me believe he was on his deathbed, Jo. What the hell is going on?'

Jo froze. Steve left his glass where it was, mumbled a brief goodbye and scarpered.

25

'Is it safe to come in?' Steve poked his head around the door to the café early the next morning. 'Never mind Bonfire Night in less than a week, I reckon you had enough fireworks here last night, didn't you?'

'It's safe,' said Jo. 'None of them are here.' She was at the counter emptying coins into the till, ready to start her day. Thank goodness they'd cleared everything up last night and the only thing she had to face this morning was washing up four glasses and emptying the stained orange pieces into the compost. 'Have you been surfing this morning?' She'd rather steer the subject away from her family.

'Couldn't face it. The mulled wine made me want to lie in, what can I say? Although I admit I did go for a cheeky pint at the pub on my way home. I wanted to hear more about Harry's predicament and they were all talking about it in there.'

Jo took out a tub of gingerbread cookies Molly had made before the Halloween event last night and emptied them into the wide-mouthed jar on the counter.

'Come on, Jo. Are you going to tell me what went down last night?'

'Like you said, fireworks.' Her mum hadn't wasted

much time before booking her flight from Spain to come here, so Jo's lie had worked. She gave Steve a brief explanation of what she'd done.

'Are you in trouble?'

'I was for about five minutes until Mum, Gran and Gramps launched into a screaming match about things that didn't involve me.'

'I could hear it from the end of the pier, and in the pub too.'

At least he'd made her see the funny side, sort of. 'Mum is staying at one of the guest houses on the other side of the hill, so at least there's separation between us all.' As much as she often got lonely at her flat, the mood her mum was in, Jo was relieved she didn't have to share a space with her. She didn't even know how long her mum was staying in town. The conversation hadn't developed much further than accusations being slung left, right, and centre.

'I'm sure they'll all sort it out,' Steve offered.

She didn't share his optimism. 'I guess we'll have to wait and see.'

Steve went on his way and she greeted Geoff who came in for his regular black tea. 'No Valerie today?' She slotted a plastic lid over the takeaway cup.

'I think it's too cold for her.' He counted through his spare change to check it was correct and handed it to Jo.

'She's still doing yoga on the beach some mornings. I'm always impressed.'

'She prefers to be outdoors, does Valerie.' He said it as though they'd known one another all their lives. 'I told her she should've been born in a warmer climate.'

When he left, he passed Matt coming through the door with today's delivery.

'You seem happy today,' she commented. It was good to see a friendly face that didn't bring trouble along with it.

'The sun's shining,' he said, 'which is more than I can say for myself.'

'Not feeling well?' She followed him through to the kitchen to nosey through today's produce box.

'I'm exhausted. Poppy and I had so much fun last night at the pumpkin carving.'

'I'm glad – and thank you again for all your help with the little ones, making sure they used the tools safely and left with the correct number of fingers and toes.'

'I'm getting quite good with kids. So much so that Poppy insisted on a sleepover last night at Uncle Matt's place.'

Jo had taken out the fresh eggs and was in the middle of placing them carefully into the bowl on the bench in the kitchen. 'So that's why you're tired.'

'She had me making a camp when we got home. Somehow, she got her energy back. So there we were until almost ten o'clock last night, moving furniture, draping over sheets and fixing them with clothes pegs.'

'I love making a camp.' Jo lifted out a bag filled with pears. 'We had the best fun doing that as kids. Me and my brothers would convert the entire dining room using all of Mum's sheets.' She took out another bag filled with sweet potatoes. 'Come to think of it, I don't think she found it as much fun, having to wash all the linen after we'd finished with it.'

'Maybe I'll volunteer your services next time.' He put a

hand to the small of his back. 'I'm the wrong side of thirty to be sleeping on the floor.'

'I think kids have a way of keeping us young.'

'Do you think about it?'

She paused from pushing the sweet potatoes into the vegetable rack. 'Having a family?'

'Yeah.'

'Sometimes, although I'm beginning to think Mr Right only exists in my imagination.' She took out another punnet of Cape gooseberries. 'I remember these,' she smiled.

'I thought you'd appreciate some more. And I'd better tell you that's the last of the pears today and the last of the courgettes.'

'Winter really is on its way. Will it be a busy time for the farm?'

'I'm never quite sure what to expect. October's been a good month for sowing and planting crops that don't mind the cold and frost, November is a good time to plant new fruit trees and get some vegetables going in the greenhouse, and December tends to be the quietest month for sowing and planting. But I love the cyclical patterns, keeps me on my toes.' He pinched a couple of Cape gooseberries, peeled one for Jo and another for himself. 'Do you realise you've almost been here for every season now?'

She stopped what she was doing. 'I hadn't thought about it that way.'

'Are you settled?'

'I can't imagine being anywhere else. And like you, I love the seasons when they change, the difference it makes to the café and the customers on the pier.' She deliberated how far she'd come in such a short space of time before getting back to her job. 'Now, what do you think . . . carrot cake . . .' She held up a carrot, 'plus zucchini tart . . .' she held up one of those next, and looking at the Cape gooseberries asked, 'And what about gooseberry and apple crumble? I still have a few apples left.'

'All sounds good to me.' He raised a hand in farewell. 'I'd better go before I eat my way through more of those gooseberries.'

'See you later, Matt. Say hi to Poppy for me. And if she's interested, I was going to ask her and Charlie to make some Christmas paperweights for me.'

'She'll love the idea,' he called over his shoulder. 'I'll tell her.'

Jo got straight to work and had the carrot cake mixture prepared and in the oven in no time at all. She made pastry between serving customers in for early morning coffees on their way to work, and Jess when she popped in after her run for her usual smoothie. She chopped courgettes, onion and garlic, and grated Gruyère before putting together her courgette tart which could be served with salad leaves, strong and fresh from Matt's family farm.

Jo was busy writing up the list of specials on the blackboard when Angie came in.

'What delights do we have here?' Angie pulled on the reading glasses that had been hanging beneath her coat. 'Carrot cake is a winner for me.' She sniffed the air. 'And it smells like I'm just in time.'

Jo slotted the chalk back onto the lip of the blackboard. 'It's cooling down but it'll be fresh and warm especially for you. Can I get you some tea to go with it?'

'Peppermint, please. And a pot for two – Valerie's joining me. She's talking about getting a group of us to try yoga on the sands at the weekend but I think I'll pass. Actually, bring her a slice of cake as well; I'll bet she won't say no.'

Amused, Jo made up the pot of tea, glad that running the café meant she couldn't spend a lot of time mulling over how her mum was going to react when she saw her again. She'd half expected her to be in the café first thing this morning, and every time the bell above the door had tinkled Jo had looked for her face, but she was lying low, and perhaps that was a good thing. Molly and Arthur were too, and Jo wondered which one of the trio was going to make the first move to sort this all out. Last night the shouting had gone on long enough, until all of them went their separate ways. They'd traipsed along the pier in complete silence, and as far as Jo knew there hadn't been a word exchanged since.

When Valerie came in the two women lost themselves in conversation and Jo went through the motions of running the café and keeping her mind off of everything else. Steve came in late afternoon, his hair salty and damp from the sea and claimed two slices of the courgette tart with salad.

'Where do you put it all?' Hilda wanted to know. Only Hilda could get away with asking him that.

He patted his stomach. 'It's the wild seas of the south coast, Hilda,' he winked. 'An hour of surfing after a hard day at work gives me quite the appetite.' He gave her a hug and she wrestled him off making everyone around them laugh.

'Love's young dream,' he whispered to Jo on his way

out. She'd just served Maddy and Dan one of the crumbles with a dollop of ice cream on the side and they were cosied up at the corner table, the same location their first date had been.

'They're a lot more talkative now,' she whispered, trying not to stare at them as she wiped down the counter near the till.

'People around here really appreciate what you've done.'

'I'm enjoying doing it.'

The only thing she wasn't enjoying right now was wondering when she was going to hear anything from her mum or her grandparents, and whether there'd be a resolution or an even bigger wedge driven between them all after the lie she'd told.

The water in Jo's bath back in her flat hovered precariously near the level of the overflow as she sank down into the bubbles. The air outside as she'd left the café tonight had turned; autumn was well and truly upon them, and not a leaf on a tree remained as she'd traipsed up the hill.

As she lay immersed in the bubbles, a glass of wine within reach, she pondered Matt's question about whether she'd like a family one day. When she'd first arrived in Salthaven her loneliness was a big focus, but she'd got so busy these days that it was only when she slowed down or when someone asked her personal questions that she started to wonder if it would ever happen. She was strong, independent, all the things Curtis Durham had said made her so good at running a business, but sometimes it would be the ultimate dream to have that little bit more.

She thought about Matt who reliably brought the

produce to the café each day. She'd watched him with Poppy and she could tell he'd loved every minute of it. He clearly wanted to be a family man, and Jo thought hard about who she could set him up with. At first, she'd thought he'd baulk at the suggestion, but now perhaps he'd go for it. He deserved someone nice – he was quite a catch and she had the power to do some good.

She'd planned to watch a film, but as she climbed out of the bath she realised there was something else she had to do. Her family was finally together in Salthaven, something she'd wanted for such a long time. And OK, so the way she'd brought them together wasn't ideal, but surely it was a starting point?

Jeans and her chocolate brown jumper on, she un-pinned her hair, gave it the once-over with a hairdryer and grabbed her coat and keys. She'd left it almost twenty-four hours and enough was enough.

She started down the hill. Past Sally's place, past her grandparents' bungalow – ignoring the lights that were on – past Morris Eckles's failed attempts at topiary on his front lawn that would have to wait until spring to be res-cued now. She reached the foot of the pier and was about to head up the other side towards the Swallow guest-house where her mum was staying when she saw Sasha, her back to her, walking down the boardwalk past the ice-creamery. And before Jo knew it, her legs were taking her the same way.

The wind was so strong tonight that it took four at-tempts of saying her mum's name to get her attention and she finally came to a standstill beneath the Victorian lamp post right before the café.

'Mum, can we talk?'

Sasha took a deep breath, her sigh swallowed on the wind. And she leaned up against the wooden fencing, her back to the sea, facing the café. Jo joined her and for a while neither of them said anything.

'I loved this place as a little girl,' Sasha confessed. 'I'd come in every day and help out. I'd play cafés at home, at playgroup, with a babysitter if Mum and Dad were working all day, and when I was older me and my friends would hang out here with our milkshakes and hot chocolates or cups of tea. I loved it if it was really busy and Mum and Dad asked me to help out by manning the till or taking orders. I thought that one day I'd take it over and it would be Sasha's Café by the Sea. That was the name I was going to change it to, when I was the boss.'

'I never knew you were interested in it.'

'I wasn't, not really. It was a pipe dream. When I was a teen it was all very attractive, but I didn't like cooking or dreaming up recipes, I definitely didn't enjoy accounts – still don't – and I started to wonder what other places there were in the world other than Salthaven.'

'Like Spain,' said Jo.

'Not just Spain. Anywhere. England, abroad, farther afield. My passion at school was in art and craft; I loved sewing and making new things. I remember I'd make some of my own clothes or accessories for my friends. And then Julia, a close friend of mine, moved to the Middle East with her family. We wrote to each other and she began sending me photographs. Her mum worked in the jewellery business and they'd visit the most exquisite markets. I was in awe of another world that felt so far away from what I could ever reach.'

'Did Gran and Gramps mind that you didn't want the café after all?'

'They didn't. I don't think they'd have ever stifled my dreams.' The wind picked up and she pulled her coat tighter around herself, her hair, the same shade as Jo's but cut into bob length and less vibrant now she was older, blew across her face and she hooked it behind her ears. 'I'd always been independent and your gramps said he admired that in me, that he'd always been the same. I got a job at the bank in town as a stopgap. I always knew it wasn't me, but it would do to raise some funds. I had plans to save up, go and live in London with the buzz of the city and the nightlife. I wanted to support myself and study the intricacies of jewellery design, making exquisite pieces, maybe working my way towards selling them at markets like Camden or Brick Lane, even having my own shop eventually.'

'So where did it all go wrong?'

There was no trace of the anger she'd shown last night at Jo's ploy to bring her back to England when Sasha looked at her daughter. 'I met your father.'

They both turned to look out across the sea, the choppy surface visible beneath the moonlight and the lamp posts from the pier. It was such a different place to be at night when darkness fell, as though whatever had happened on the sands during the day had just been a figment of their imagination.

'I know what happened,' Jo admitted. 'At the toyshop in town.'

'The truth's out.' Sasha shook her head. 'I'm still so embarrassed about what we did, how I behaved. They were my wild days and I got carried away, thinking your father was someone he wasn't. When he walked away so easily he broke my heart. But not only that, I was ashamed. Even more ashamed than I was about graffitiing and robbing the toyshop.'

'Were you involved in the other thefts?'

'That was my first.' She harrumphed. 'I say that as though it was a lesson to learn, a profession to grow in. And if he'd hung around I think I'd have been persuaded to do more.'

'Did you do drugs with him?'

She didn't answer straight away. 'I drank, when I was pregnant. I was terrified your grandparents would think me such an unfit parent that they would take you away from me. I became paranoid, and the more I worried, the more I tried to drive them away, from me, from you. And the more I did that, the more the rift widened and we couldn't get back to being the normal family we once were.'

They both let the words settle as the wind whistled along the pier, past the café and out to sea. 'I'm glad they told you everything,' Sasha said. 'I should've done it a long time ago.'

'It wasn't them.'

'Then who?'

'I overheard Hilda talking one day. She wasn't gossiping,' she added before her mum went in another direction with her anger and went to find Hilda. 'She was worried about you, about Molly and Arthur.'

'People around here look out for each other. It's a special place.'

For some reason it pleased Jo to hear her mum admit it. 'I'm sorry I lied to you about Gramps.'

Sasha's hair refused to stay behind her ears and she turned so the wind at least blew it off her face. 'I was very angry when I got here and saw you all bundled into the café, joking about. I felt like it was all at my expense.'

'Mum, no. It wasn't like that at all.'

'I know it wasn't. From the look on your face I could tell you had done it out of desperation. Do you remember that time you cut down most, if not all, of Sally's roses?'

Jo gasped. 'I did no such thing.'

'You did. I was having a very bad day and you'd done everything you could to cheer me up and you handed me a big bunch of roses wrapped in some birthday paper I'd had at home. You told me that on the television, if someone was upset, they got given flowers and everything was always much better. At first, I thought you'd bought them with your pocket money, but when I asked you, you turned all sheepish and I finally wheedled out the truth.'

'Oh my goodness, I don't remember.'

'You were only seven at the time. I yelled a lot that day, but Sally wasn't angry. I think she'd heard enough from Mum and Dad about their wayward daughter and the mess she'd made of her life and felt sorry for me. She simply got on with pruning what was left of her rose bushes and assured me they'd flower next year and every year after. We took her some oatmeal and raisin cookies by way of an apology.'

'I'll have to say sorry to Sally again when I next see her.' Jo cringed. 'What a little monkey I was!'

'You did all right. You haven't given me much grief over the years and for that I'm grateful. Oh, but you did scare me when you said Dad had had an accident. You didn't give any details, only that he was badly hurt and you were worried it was something more. Very cryptic. And all along, it was only a cup falling on his foot.' For some reason the words made them both burst out laughing, probably more in relief at finally having this long overdue conversation than anything else.

'Seriously though, Mum, they're not getting any younger.'

'I know. And I'm glad you lied to me. It's what I needed to get me on that plane to come over.'

'Have you seen them since last night?'

'No, we all went our separate ways and I've been stewing all day. I could've murdered a cup of coffee from your café first thing this morning but I've spent the day in the next town, walking by the beach, going to far more inferior places let me tell you, but I needed the space. I was out tonight to clear my head and I was going to see you and your grandparents tomorrow, finally talk after we'd all calmed down. What are you smiling at?'

Jo braved the cold and lifted her face from beneath her bright red scarf. 'You said "your café".'

'I did, didn't I?'

'I'm not making a mistake by being here, Mum.'

Sasha put her arm around her daughter's shoulders. 'I know you're not. You know, I overheard someone talking about your café in the next town.'

'You did?'

'They were talking all about the nights of love that you run.'

A surge of pride flowed through her. 'I'll give you all the tiny details on one condition.' She hooked an arm through her mum's. 'You come to see Gran and Gramps with me, right now. I don't want to wait until morning.'

'I suppose I can do that for you.' She kissed the top of Jo's head and as they made their way back along the pier, leaving the café until tomorrow, past the bits and bobs shop and the fish and chip shop, Jo told her mum everything.

'I'm not sure I'm ready.' Sasha stopped a couple of doors away from Molly and Arthur's bungalow.

'They'll be glad you came.' Jo urged her to keep going as they paused by Sally's home. 'Come on, or I'm going to go straight into Sally's garden and rip out every single one of her roses.'

Jo managed to get her mum to her grandparents' gate and along the path to the front door. She usually went straight in, using her own key and calling out that it was only their favourite granddaughter. But not tonight. This time she rang the doorbell and they waited.

Arthur opened the door and saw Jo first, but the second he saw her mum his expression changed from delight to trepidation.

'Can we come in?' Jo asked when neither Sasha or Gramps spoke a word.

'That depends.'

Oh no, was a row about to kick off already? was he about to suggest Sasha go away? Because if she flew back to Spain without sorting this out, Jo suspected that would be it, for good.

'Molly's brownies have just been sliced,' said Arthur, 'and you know she won't take no for an answer.'

Jo hugged him and stepped inside. 'Thanks, Gramps.'

She turned back to see her mum hovering on the

doorstep and tentatively step onto the concrete porch step, then take another step into the hallway, but before she could pass her dad he put a hand out and grabbed hold of her arm. Sasha looked down at skin on skin and time stood still; then, when Sasha looked up, her eyes were filled with tears and she wrapped her arms around her dad for the first time in years.

26

The storms of the last couple of days that had blown a layer of sand along the pier and the promenade and kept people battling the onslaught of high winds as they fought to get to the café, were replaced on bonfire night by a chill that said winter wasn't far away at all.

'Thank goodness it's dry.' Sasha bustled through the door of the café as the sun went down and the sky turned from deep orange to a mixture of pale blue and pink.

'You're early; I wasn't expecting you for another hour.' Jo collected stray empty cups from the table closest to the counter. It wasn't too busy yet and she'd had plenty of time to prepare food for tonight's big firework event that took place up the hill on the big fields at the edge of town, but that attracted crowds to the pier for the best view across the water.

Sasha pulled an apron from her bag. 'I'm here to help.'

'Are you serious?'

'Hey, I know the ropes well enough – I grew up here didn't I? But I know you're the boss. Mum and Dad told me not to interfere and do as I was told.' There was fondness in her voice rather than the defensive tone that usually accompanied conversations about Gran and Gramps.

On the night Jo had taken her mum up to her

grandparents' bungalow, Sasha, Gramps and Gran had finally sat down and talked. More than that, they'd all apologised for the part they played all those years ago and ever since. There had been a couple of wobbly moments when Jo had had to mediate, when they didn't see eye to eye, but that evening each of them finally saw how different they were. And more than that, they realised that differences didn't mean anyone was right or anyone was wrong. Molly and Arthur had raised Sasha to be an independent woman and that night Arthur had told his daughter how proud they were of her, words that Jo suspected had meant the world to her mum. 'Now, if you'd just told her that a decade ago, we'd never have let it get this bad,' Jo had said, breaking the ice enough for them to sit and chat like a normal family, catch up on what they'd been missing for years. And Sasha had been doing it ever since. She'd been with Molly and Arthur for the last few days; they'd gone out of town, walked along neighbouring beaches in their own little unit with no outside interference. And it was exactly what they'd all needed to let go of the past and move on. Sasha's life was in Spain now, and Jo wasn't sure, but she thought Molly and Arthur were even beginning to come around to the idea of visiting one day.

Jo wiped her hands. The café was empty once again but she knew it wouldn't be long before it filled up. People were already starting to gather on the pier, vying for the best spot to watch the fireworks. 'Mum, how are you at basic assembly?' She took out a flat, cardboard shape. 'This will make a miniature hot dog stand, complete with stripy awning on top. Do me a favour and pull across a table to put next to the counter would you?'

Her mum did the honours. 'Do you think you'll sell many?'

Jo gestured to outside the window. 'People are gathering early, they'll be hungry.'

Between them they busied themselves erecting the cardboard stand and when that was done they chopped onions, began cooking the sausages, sliced rolls lengthways. They piled up napkins, got the takeaway cups and lids ready. Sasha took control of making platefuls of toffee apples which were as popular as the savoury food.

'Gramps said that the café is dead quiet during the display, so I'll finish up ten minutes before kick-off, giving me enough time to get out there.' Jo had started the first batch of sausages, the oven hot and ready to stash them inside so they could cook up some more. They wanted everything ready to feed the hungry locals and visitors to Salthaven, but most of all Jo wanted tonight to be about family, together again at one of the town's most popular events.

The crowds multiplied quickly along the pier and, between them, Jo and her mum served what felt like a thousand hot dogs to hungry husbands and wives, siblings, lovers and kids. And they'd poured as many cups of tea, stirred as many mugs of hot chocolate.

When Steve came through the door the wind reminded Jo that it was a very different temperature outside, now the sky had grown dark. 'Ten minutes until fireworks. You'd better get out there.'

'Almost ready,' she assured him as she served another mug of hot chocolate topped with cream and sprinkles. They'd run out of takeaway cups – the demand was so huge she'd reverted to using their heavy-duty white mugs for the hot chocolate with customers assuring her they'd return them afterwards.

'Come on, Jo,' Sasha urged, removing her apron. 'Leave the clearing up. It'll still be here afterwards.'

Wrapped up in coats, scarves and gloves, and armed with hot chocolates, Jo and her mum huddled together outside the café. Molly and Arthur called out to them from beneath the lamp post in front of the bits and bobs shop, and they joined them, ready for the fireworks. Jo had been to the display in Edinburgh many a time, but there was something extra special about being here in her home town this year, surrounded by so many familiar faces, so much love and kindness.

A little voice called Jo's name and tugged at her arm. She turned round to see Poppy, eyes dancing in expectation, hand clutching a half-eaten toffee apple. It looked like she'd savoured all the caramel and left the fruit but hadn't yet been allowed to dispose of it. 'Where's your mum?'

'She's at home. It's no place for a small baby,' she said, unintentionally mimicking an adult tone. She'd obviously heard the grown-ups talking. 'Uncle Matt brought me. And we're going to have sparklers afterwards.'

'Now that sounds good.' She couldn't see any sign of Matt. 'Did you tell your Uncle Matt where you were going?'

The little girl pulled a face. 'I got lost.' Only now did she look upset.

'Don't worry. You stay here with Gramps and I'll find him for you.'

Gramps held out a hand. His other arm was linked

with Sasha's and Molly was on the other side. 'You can join our chain.'

Poppy found it fun enough to be distracted rather than upset and Jo left them there. She squeezed through throngs of people chattering and excited, eagerly anticipating the launch of the first stream of colour to light up the night sky. It wasn't long before she saw Matt coming the other way.

'We found her,' Jo said before he could even ask if she'd seen Poppy.

He took a deep breath in, ran his hands through his hair and let out a humongous sigh of relief. 'I had hold of her hand but someone knocked into me and when I turned round she was gone.'

Jo tilted her head back in the opposite direction. 'This way, she's waiting with Gramps.'

As soon as he saw Poppy, Matt scooped her up and the little girl kept her arms wrapped possessively around his neck. There was no way she wanted to lose him again tonight.

Ben found them next and anchored himself and Charlie with their group, Steve chatted with Molly and Sasha, and Gramps was commandeered by Hilda who wanted to know how cold it had to get before Jo would put fondue on the café menu.

Hilda looked at her watch as she moved to say hello to Jo. 'It must be nearly kick-off time.' It was when her eyes met Sasha's that Jo was reminded how long it had been since the pair had come face-to-face.

Jo nudged Sasha and whispered in her ear. 'Remember how you made me go and apologise to Sally about her roses?'

Sasha swallowed any nerves hovering on the surface and asked Hilda if she could have a word.

'It's all water under the pier now, Sasha,' Hilda concluded. 'I don't need any apologies. I've seen how happy you've made your family and that's enough for me. Fresh start?'

'Sounds good to me.'

'You got off lightly,' Jo teased her mum. But she couldn't have been happier at how things had changed for the better.

Poppy and Charlie had managed to squeeze through the adult legs to get the vantage point in front of the fence and Matt wasn't taking his eyes away from his niece this time. He smiled over at Jo before she was distracted by a voice.

'Hi, Jo.' It was Harry, a tray of chips in hand, walking with his mates towards the end of the pier. He obviously hadn't spotted Sasha who was standing behind Hilda now. 'I heard about the pumpkin carving.' He offered her a chip but she declined. 'My nephew raved about how good it was. You know, you could run parties from the café if you ever need to boost business.'

'Thanks, I'll think about it.'

'I have a bit of news of the work variety myself. I'm moving on.'

'From Salthaven?'

'I've got a new job in Philadelphia.'

'Wow, that's quite a move.'

He shrugged. 'I needed to move forwards, make some changes.'

'Then I'm very happy for you.'

'Thanks – and don't worry, I'll hand your accounts over to someone very capable.'

Jo hadn't even thought about it, but perhaps it was the best thing in the long run. Leave the past exactly where it was with no overspill into the future. 'Thanks, Harry.' When her mum squeezed through to join her she seized another chance. 'Harry, you remember my mum?' She looked to him and then Sasha who looked tense. To her, Jo guessed, Harry would always be in the same category as Alan, her father, a heartbreaker and someone to avoid.

'Er . . . yes . . . hello.' When he stammered over his words it reminded Jo of the boy he'd once been all that time ago.

When her mum said nothing Jo leaned in to whisper in her ear for the second time tonight. 'Remember how Hilda gave you another chance?'

'Nice to see you again, Harry,' her mum managed and he returned the smile but went on his way. 'See, I was polite.'

Jo's laughter mingled with the salty air, the aroma of hot chocolates and fish and chips from revellers lacing the boardwalk. 'You may have said hello, but he scarpered pretty quick.'

'What's all that smoke?' Poppy asked, poking her head through adult legs so Jo could just about see her face.

'It's coming from the fields where they'll launch fireworks from. It's a big bonfire – perhaps you could go next year.'

'It's wonderful,' Sasha told the little girl, 'the heat of the bonfire is so much you can't get too close and the flames crackle and spit.'

Poppy and Charlie's faces lit up but not as much as the first firework launched into the air. The crowds quietened as everyone turned to look over at the fields and sighs of ooh and ahh replaced conversation as the first white fireworks wiggled their way up into the inky sky before exploding to send showers of shooting stars spurting in all directions. Next came purples, golds, reds, with the magical pause between the hiss and whizz while the fireworks climbed higher and higher and the moment they sent out shards of multiple colours. It was right to think that the pier was the best place to watch the fireworks from. Watching them across the water made them all the more special, and the entire pier, above the café and beyond, was lit up in a surreal glow.

The next fireworks felt like a billion shooting stars going off all at once, the sky lighting up as though part of it was suspended in daylight, until the colours and lights descended once again and dissolved in the distance with an enormous bang that had Jo jumping in fright, and the plumes of smoke accompanying dazzling fronds of gold had children watching on in amazement. The whole town had come together in one event that showed this community for what it was: solid, welcoming and a part of who Jo had always wanted to be.

'That was spectacular,' Sasha beamed as the fireworks reached their crescendo before darkness wrapped around them and the skies calmed to what they'd been before. She hugged Jo to her. 'Thank you so much.'

'For lying to you?'

'Thank you for . . . well, for being you. I love you and I'm incredibly proud of you. Seeing you here in Salthaven, you fit completely. And as for the café, you look like you were born to be in charge.'

'Talking of the café, I need to get back to it and clear up,' Jo announced after saying goodbye to Matt and

Poppy and Ben and Charlie and Lorna who'd joined them by now.

'Come on, between us we'll have it done in no time,' said Sasha.

Jo put her hands up to stop the rest of her family. 'It's my business and I want to do it. I'd rather you all went back to the bungalow and were together.'

It took her a bit of persuasion but she got there in the end. Steve insisted he help her at least bring in the cups that had been left on the tables outside, and Jo found it impossible to turn down his help. He even bagged up the rubbish for her while she wiped down the tables inside and got rid of the cardboard hot-dog stand.

Steve went on his way and Jo mopped the floor, ensuring everything was set to go again in the morning. As the floor dried, she wiped down the surfaces in the kitchen, cleaned the top of the cooker and thought about the nice glass of wine she was going to pour and enjoy on the big comfy chair looking out across the sea. The sky had quietened so quickly after the onslaught of pops, bangs and colours, and now it was back to reality.

She turned off the lights to the kitchen and to the café, turned off the twinkly lights that ran along the walls and, hooking her arm into her coat sleeve, almost missed the postcard lying on the doormat.

'Another one.' She spoke out loud, because after last time, she'd thought it was over. The writing was face up this time and she picked up the card.

Dear Jo,
The fireworks lit up the sky tonight, but you light up my
heart . . . xxx

She opened the café door and looked right but there was nobody else on the pier apart from a group of teenagers using sparklers to write their names in the air. She looked in the opposite direction but there was nobody there apart from Maddy and Dan, walking hand in hand away from the café.

So who was sending these postcards? First the one in spring, then another in the summer, and now a third.

Should she dare to even hope that whoever was doing it would reveal their identity and it would be the start of something really special?

Winter

27

Jo had every light in the café switched on today, including the twinkly Christmas lights. Winter had well and truly set in and she'd barely been able to make out the pier on her way down the hill to work as thick fog enveloped the town and hung over the sea like a thermal blanket.

At the start of December Gramps had brought in his trusty Advent calendar and handed it over to Jo, passing on the café's festive tradition to her. Arthur and Molly had gradually eased into retirement over the last few months, delighted that the café was in such good hands. She'd set the calendar on the ledge near the blackboard so people could see it the second they came in, joyful with the spirit of the season, anxiously counting down the days together. With a taupe and white snowman at its centre, the calendar's wooden cubes could be changed to reflect the number of days left, and below the numbers the wording read: *Days until Christmas*.

Jo turned the cubes to a two, then a one, with three weeks to go until the big day. Beside the till she set up the lamp she'd brought from home, another touch of Christmas and a touch of her personality. Shaped like a small tree, its illuminated petals added to the twinkly lights already strung around the café walls. All she wanted now was some fresh holly to fix to the corners of the menu blackboard and the postcards board. She'd already set out the finished Christmas paperweights that Ben's son, Charlie, and Matt's niece, Poppy, had worked so hard on. They could be used at the tables she'd left outside for dry days, or simply used as Christmas décor at the tables inside. Poppy had painted a wonderful Santa on the top of one stone, a snowman on another, and Ben had helped Charlie to paint reindeers on top of the largest stone they'd collected from the seashore.

Today Jo was as busy as ever, but the café was running like a well-oiled machine. It was her personal life that still lagged behind. It seemed to have ground more or less to a halt, apart from the odd night out at the pub with Jess and Melissa. Molly kept telling her she needed to put herself out there, a phrase which made Jo shudder, because somewhere out there, waiting in the wings, was her mystery admirer. She was beginning to wonder if he would ever make himself known, or whether the whole thing would turn out to be a huge wind-up.

She opened the door to the café when she saw Matt arriving with today's produce. 'Good morning.' She shut the door firmly behind him. 'It's freezing out there!'

He took the box straight through to the kitchen at the back of the café, calling over his shoulder, 'You're not wrong. The sun's on its way up but I don't think we'll see it through all this fog.' He left the kitchen quick enough. 'I left something outside, hang on a minute.'

Puzzled, she followed him, and when he brought an enormous Christmas tree in a pot, through the door, a smile crept across her face. 'You're growing trees up at the farm now too?'

He set the tree down. 'No, but the farm down the road from us is, and I picked up a tree for Molly and Arthur last year, so I figured you'd want to carry on the tradition. I usually add it to the next invoice, if that suits?'

'Of course, and it's gorgeous.' She leaned in to smell the pine needles, nostalgia flooding through her at Christmases past. She almost opened her mouth to ask about getting another tree for her flat, but somehow it didn't feel right. She would be on her own there and something about getting her very own tree was even worse than buying a microwave instant meal for one. It was depressing. Last year she'd been in a shared house and they'd clubbed together to get a Christmas tree from outside the local pub which had been so tall it had bent over on the ceiling, causing their inebriated selves to laugh hysterically until one of them borrowed a neighbour's shears to take the top off. But this year a tree at the flat would only remind her she didn't have anyone special to be with on the day. Gran and Gramps had at last decided to make the most of their retirement, as well as their reconciliation with Sasha, and were heading off to stay with her in Majorca over Christmas and a couple of weeks into the new year. And they'd only agreed to go because Jo had told them Tilly would be in Salthaven over the festive season and had already invited her to her parents' for the big day. Jo was grateful to have somewhere to go, but at the same time, she'd rather have spent it with her own family – or, truth be told, snuggling up on the sofa with her own special someone, listening to Christmas music beneath twinkly lights, enjoying mulled wine or hot chocolates.

'Jo . . .' Matt's voice prompted her to stop daydreaming. 'I was asking where you wanted it?' He picked up the bucket at its base, his face battling the needles and branches as his arms took the strain.

'Right. Sorry.' She looked round. 'Hang on, I'll drag the middle table away from the wall and we can stand it next to the blackboard. Will you need the bucket back?'

'No, it came with the bucket.' He seemed amused at how scatty she was. He probably thought she was a complete idiot. She wasn't usually this bad, but Christmas seemed to bring out the very best and very worst of her. It was a time of celebration, happiness, but also a time where you began to think beyond the bright lights and wrapping paper, to what really mattered. Still, at least her family were back together once again. She'd got something right along the way.

She helped Matt manoeuvre the tree into the space she'd made and directed him as he turned it left and right to get the best side. 'Right a bit more . . . no, left . . . sorry, right again.' She let a giggle escape. 'There. Don't move it again.' When his head emerged, flushed from a face full of pine-scented greenery, she said, 'It's perfect, I really appreciate it.'

'Glad to be of service.'

'I'm putting the decorations up this afternoon, so your timing is spot on.' She'd decorate the bucket at the tree's base with some crêpe paper and a bow, make it look really dazzling.

'I'll look forward to seeing what this place looks like when you've finished,' said Matt. 'It's always like a little bit of treasure at the end of the pier for locals and visitors to town when so many places are shut during the winter months.'

'I'm glad.' She might be lonely when she was at home,

but she had as much company here at the café as she could ever want, and sometimes she knew she needed to count her blessings. 'I'm really excited about my first Christmas here.'

'I can see that. You can't stop smiling.'

She turned to look at the tree. 'Do *you* like Christmas?'

'I love it.' He manoeuvred some of the lower branches of the blue spruce on one side so the tree was better shaped. 'These things are hypnotising before they're even decorated.'

'The smell is heavenly.'

'I'm hauling one in for my sister, later, and another for my parents. I think I'll smell like a Christmas tree myself by the end of the day.'

'You could smell of worse things,' she teased. She went out to the kitchen to unpack the produce and Matt followed. 'Driving must've been hazardous today, so I'm doubly grateful you delivered here.' She watched him as he leaned against the door jamb. Perhaps she should've told him not to come although she knew he'd be bringing what she'd requested.

'I went very slow,' he assured her. 'And the café is one of our best customers – we can't let people down.'

Jo took out the enormous green stalk with the rounded vegetables attached to it. 'I've never seen them this way before.'

'I could've harvested them one by one, but I knew you wanted a fair few so it was easier to uproot the entire plant. It'll keep for a few days if you stand the stalk in a bucket of water.'

'Thanks for the tip.' She immediately found a bucket from the storeroom, added a little water in the base and set the two stalks he'd brought into the plastic container.

'I assume you're a love 'em kind of girl?'

'The sprouts?' She grinned. 'Definitely. I love them, not sure all the customers will but I like experimenting.'

'What's on the menu?'

'A winter salad using the sprouts, some shallots and pomegranate seeds, drizzled with a dressing made from balsamic, apple cider vinegar and maple syrup.'

'Where do you dream up all these recipes?'

'Gran and Gramps give me pointers, or I know roughly what I want and dig out the recipe books. Sometimes I take tips from different recipes on Google, other times I wing it.' She went through the rest of the box. 'This all looks amazing, Matt, thank you again for driving out here.'

'My pleasure. Better go – off to the school next.'

'Delivering sprouts?'

'Would you have eaten sprouts when you were a kid?' He raised a hand and off he went, out into a day where the sun had risen but was still wrapped in a slate grey fog.

As Jo unpacked the rest of the produce – a plentiful supply of eggs for her baking and savoury dishes, winter radishes which would challenge her thought process when it came to a recipe, leeks which would go perfectly in a frittata, plus some basil leaves and sprigs of thyme – she wondered if the weather would make business slower this month, because so far, it hadn't seemed to. As Matt had said, other businesses shut their doors out of the tourist season, but according to Molly and Arthur, unlike some of the seaside resorts on the south coast, Christmas wasn't quiet here but rather one of the busiest times when locals came together.

Jo set about making puff pastry and had just wrapped it in cling film to let it stand when she heard Jess's voice calling through to the kitchen.

'Good morning, Jess!' she called from the sink. 'I'll be out in a sec!' When she'd finally got all the remnants of flour and egg from her fingers she wiped her hands and went out to the café. 'You're not running in this hideous weather, are you?' She took in her friend's running gear, the autumn long-sleeved top now with the addition of a body warmer, a knitted hat, and gloves.

'Can't always use weather as an excuse,' she puffed, a faint sound still coming from the earbuds that hung waiting around her neck. 'I'd get far too lazy if I did.'

'Well, I'm in awe,' Jo admitted.

'It's so cosy in here.' Jess took in the twinkly lights which stood out all the more when it was so miserable outside. 'And the tree smells beautiful.' She sniffed in the scent that would soon be mingled with the smell of baking. 'I almost don't want to venture outside again, but I must, so it's a banana smoothie to go for me, please.'

'Coming right up.' Jo went out to the kitchen and chopped the fruit, poured milk, drizzled honey and had the takeaway drink whizzed up in no time.

Jess was perusing the postcards board by the time Jo came out with her smoothie and a paper straw to push through the lid on top. She was repinning the card that had come today. Locals were invited to read the cards at their leisure – it was a big part of the community feel in the café. 'Harry seems to be having fun,' she said, closing her eyes briefly at the refreshing first sip of her drink.

'It was sitting on the mat this morning when I got here.' It had fallen through the letterbox at the bottom of the door and landed writing side up and Jo's heart had skipped a beat when she unlocked the door to the café, hoping with everything she had that the card was from her secret admirer, but when she'd seen Harry's name she'd shaken away the thought, glad she could pin up a card from someone who would always be a friend. She was so pleased he'd found a fresh start and seemed happy and she was even happier she hadn't let nostalgia steer her back towards him. It never would've worked.

'It looks like he's seeing America while he's working,' said Jess.

Jo looked at the photograph which depicted a street scene in Denver, Colorado. 'He always did want to see a bit of the world.'

'Do you think he did a runner because you told him you weren't interested?'

Jo smiled as her next customer came in and whispered, 'I don't think so, but it's the best thing all round. Hopefully, he'll meet someone on the same wavelength as him.' Salthaven had never been big enough for Harry Sadler. They were completely different people now.

'Good morning, Hilda. You're early today.' Jo took up position on the other side of the counter as her next customer went straight over to the tree. Without any decorations it was still stunning and Hilda took a big inhale of the scent before joining Jo near the till.

'Lots to do at the toyshop,' Hilda explained, bidding farewell to Jess who had to get going to the local surgery to see her patients. 'This season is manic; I feel like Santa Claus. Or maybe Mrs Claus . . . yes, that has a better ring to it.'

'You need another elf.'

'I do. Shame your mum doesn't live closer.'

By way of apology for vandalising Hilda's shop years ago, Sasha had insisted she work for free in the shop until she returned to Spain.

'She'll be enjoying the milder climate back in Majorca, I expect,' Jo replied. For the first time in a long time she was content with her mum living in a different country. Now the family had put the past to rest, the present was so much nicer. 'Gran and Gramps can't wait to get out there.'

'I'm impressed they're going.'

'I think, with it being winter, Gramps can face the temperature. I'm not sure how he'd react if Gran wanted him to go over in the summer months.'

'You're right, he doesn't much like the heat,' Hilda agreed. 'Talking of which, I'll have a takeaway rhubarb and green tea please. It'll warm my hands on the way to work.'

'Coming right up.'

'Is the fondue still on for tomorrow?' she asked as Jo pulled a takeaway cup from the stack next to the coffee machine and found the appropriate tea flavour.

'Sure is. I'll be out tomorrow, but Gramps is ready to kick off the first Fondue Tuesday and we'll make sure to do it every Tuesday from now until the end of winter if it's popular enough.'

Hilda pulled on her lilac gloves. 'Tell Arthur I'll be in for Fondue Tuesday tomorrow at midday sharp.'

When she went on her way, Jo got back to it. The pastry was almost ready to roll out so she prepared the filling for the creamy leek and cheese pie, a hearty, warming addition to her winter menu for the day. She sautéed the leeks in butter, added flour and seasoning as well as the milk to form a sauce, and then finally added cheese, fresh parsley and chunks of potato.

With its pastry top on, she slotted it into the oven and, not long afterwards, Gran and Gramps came through the door with a couple of boxes of Christmas decorations, Steve with a third.

'You knew about the tree,' Jo concluded.

'Of course,' Molly shrugged. 'Matt brings one every year and he gave us the heads-up last Tuesday. We thought we'd let it be a surprise for you.'

'It's a great tree.' Steve nodded his approval.

'These boxes aren't getting any lighter,' laughed Gramps. 'Where do you want us to put them?'

'Leave them on the table in the corner, I'll put the decorations up when I get a chance. I still have a winter salad to make as well as a frittata.' She looked at Steve. 'Are you sure you're OK to be carrying anything with your arm?' He'd injured it at the building site last month and had been wearing a sling for some time, although Steve being Steve, had insisted on helping her out, one-armed, whenever he was needed.

'Relax, Jess gave me the all-clear over a week ago,' he told her. 'It was only a strain so a bit of rest was enough. And she's said I'll definitely be good for the Christmas Day swim.'

'Well, you don't want to miss that, do you?'

He didn't miss the sarcasm in Jo's voice. 'Careful, or I'll drag you in the sea with me.'

'Come on, you two, stop messing about,' Molly warned. 'If we get started with the decorations we can get them done in a jiffy.'

'Oh no you don't,' Jo warned, 'this is my job. Your job is to go home and pack. You're looking after this place for me tomorrow and then leaving first thing Wednesday morning. What's with the face, Gramps?' She thought they'd worked through their problems with Sasha.

'I'm a bit out of my comfort zone,' he admitted as Steve went on his way to a house development on the perimeter of the town. With the time he'd had to take off over the last few weeks he said he'd have to put in the hours now before they finished up for the Christmas period.

'Come and sit down.' Jo ushered both her grandparents onto the chairs beside the window, their favourite spot. 'I'll make you some tea.' She went out to the kitchen and brought back a pot of Earl Grey. 'Now tell me, what's the hesitation, Gramps?'

'I haven't been away for Christmas in years.' He looked at Molly. 'Neither of us have.'

'He's right, we're Salthaven locals, we like it here.'

'But you'll be with Mum – and you all need this time together.'

'He's worried,' Molly admitted as she sipped her tea and then set the cup down again.

'About what, Gramps?'

'We left things with your mum in a good way when she left town this time. Since then we've had lots of phone conversations which have been like all our Christmases bundled into one.' Jo listened, puzzled. 'We're in a good place. And besides, there's you. This place is a lot to manage for one person.'

'It is, but I'll cope.'

'You're not panicking about us being away?'

'Not at all. If you'd done this to me back in the summer

then yes, I would've been. But not now.'

'There's also the big day,' said Gramps. 'Molly wanted to cook for you on your first Christmas back home.'

'Well, that's lovely.' She was disappointed not to be sitting down with them to enjoy a Christmas feast. But she wasn't about to make them feel guilty. They'd always been there for her and now it was her turn to do the same for them. Whatever it took. 'Don't you worry about me, I'll have Tilly and it'll be lovely to catch up with her.'

Molly wasn't convinced. 'But it's still her family, not yours; it's not the same.'

No, it wasn't. 'Come on, you can't tell me one minute that community and the friends within it are like an extension of family, and in the next breath tell me it isn't the same.' It took seconds for the real reason for doubt to dawn on her. 'Are you worried that going over to stay with Mum is going to be too much too soon?'

'Do you think it will be?' Molly asked.

'I think all three of you have learned a lot over the years and now you've come together, none of you will jeopardise that. I know Mum is very keen that this visit goes well. She's also very excited about it.'

'She says she is,' said Arthur.

'Whenever I speak with her,' Jo continued, 'she talks about something else you can do together. She wants to show you her life out there. She wants to take you to the jewellery markets, show you the business she's built up – with the business acumen she no doubt got from the pair of you – and she wants to go on a boat cruise, eat at the fabulous restaurants she's discovered. Gramps, she wants to share her life with you.'

'And you'll really be OK?' Gran asked as some

out-of-town customers bustled through the door.

'Not if I don't rescue my leek and cheddar pie with its braided edges from the oven,' she joked.

'Listen to you!' Molly exclaimed. 'The fanciest we got to was crimping the pastry.'

'Finishing touches make all the difference,' Jo said, winking as she went off to the kitchen.

This time last year, Gran and Gramps would have been on their own running this place full time. Jo had been here almost a year now, and had to admit, despite the initial panic and the pressure of not having a guaranteed income each month, she hadn't looked back once. She had purpose, close friends, a place of her own to live – and she felt settled. All she wanted was for the mystery sender of the postcards to come out and say who he was. The cynical voice inside her head said it would fizzle into nothing, but the hopeful and romantic side that believed in happy endings like the one Molly and Arthur had found, said a little bit of magic was about to come her way.

28

On Wednesday morning Jo switched on the main light in the café, followed by each set of white twinkly lights strung along the tops of the walls. She was used to this, illuminating the place the second she arrived now that winter had the town in its grasp.

The temperatures had dropped further, with icy patches along the pier this morning, but soon, Jo knew, the sun would make the surface of the sea sparkle and the frost on the grassy banks between the pier and the town glisten on what was a rare clear day in December. The forecast threatened snow flurries for Salthaven in a few short weeks, which had sent the locals into a tizzy. But not Jo. As much as she loved summer, she believed you couldn't beat the magic of snow in the Christmas season, and here in her café she was at her happiest. Even if she soon had to trudge here in wellies, battling the histrionics of the sea as it beat against the posts of the pier and sent icy spray her way, she would never lose her love for this place.

And now, it was straight to work. It was time to finish what she'd started. Gramps had given her some beautiful holly from his garden this morning, so first job was to fix it to the blackboards. Watching her fingers on the needle-like prickles she hooked a piece at each of the top corners, securing the twigs with a little bit of Blu-Tack. Holly never failed to add cheer to a cold and bleak wintry day, adding a touch of beauty with its glossy leaves and ruby red berries.

She picked up the second cube on the Advent calendar and changed its number for the Christmas countdown, and then, before any recipes could be dreamt up or dishes prepared, it was time to decorate the tree. The poor thing had been standing here since Monday morning when she'd been so frantically busy that she hadn't had the chance to do anything with it, apart from give it a generous glug of water into its base before she went home. Molly and Arthur had kept it watered yesterday but had been under strict instructions to leave the trimming to her. She wanted to do it to mark her first Christmas as the boss.

She had a small box she'd brought from home, and along with that she'd dragged the boxes her grandparents had brought in from the storeroom out the back. She took out the lights, which thankfully didn't take long to unravel. They matched the bright white lights strung around the walls and which snaked up the posts of the bower when it was in operation for Jo's nights of love at the café.

With the aid of a chair, Jo could just about reach the top of the tree, and she began winding the lights round and round until she got to the bottom where she reached behind the tree and pushed in the plug. She stood back and inhaled the lingering pine scent coming from the silvery blue-white iridescent blue spruce that brought Christmas well and truly to the cafe. She wished she had time to make a morning coffee and sit here to appreciate it, but very soon customers would descend and she had no time to waste.

Raiding each and every box she had more than enough decorations to choose from. She added silver and white baubles, some matte, others shiny. Next it was on to another box Gran and Gramps had brought in with them on Monday, and with each ornament she pulled out, she enjoyed the special memories they evoked, one by one. There was a wooden mouse dusted with glitter and a hedgehog to match, both chosen on a trip to the Cotswolds with her mum. She hung up the squishy felt reindeer with a scarf she remembered choosing in town with Gramps one day after school when she'd been under the weather and desperately needed cheering up. She hung the three delicate glass bell ornaments, each with a white ribbon and silver frosting, and put those at the higher branches of the tree, away from inquisitive hands. She eased a penguin in a Santa hat with ice skates on its feet onto a branch. Then came a collection of candy canes, a packet of miniature toy drums, a silver ice skate with a furry top around the boot. She found a small felt stocking, another ornament in the shape of a hearth with a roaring fire, then a silver VW Beetle. She watched it dangle after she passed the white ribbon over the green needles on a branch, realising how far she'd come since she'd gone into the little shop near her shared house in Edinburgh to buy the decoration for her first Christmas in Scotland.

When her phone pinged, she took it out to see a text from Tilly. Excited, she swiped the screen, but the words weren't what she had hoped for. In fact, they were the exact opposite and threatened to send her into a flap. 'Great,' she muttered. Tilly had cancelled visiting Salthaven over

Christmas because of the weather. She was about to call to see if there was any way her friend would change her mind, but it wouldn't be fair to make her come all the way down from Edinburgh in the snow and so she wrote a quick message back telling her friend she wasn't to worry, it couldn't be helped, and they'd get together in the new year. Tilly texted again to say that Jo was still welcome to go to her parents' as she knew them well, but Jo said she'd make other arrangements. It was lovely of them to be so welcoming but without Tilly, she'd rather do her own thing. Maybe she'd take a well-earned rest and flop on the sofa watching her choice of Christmas movies all day long, eating whatever she wanted. The freedom of doing so suddenly seemed appealing.

Jo took out the last decoration to go on, an exquisite angel in the sort of dress that every little girl dreamed of wearing. Glittery, with sparkles and lace, this angel had been a gift from Gran when Jo had left Salthaven for Scotland. Jo had wondered then if they'd thought she was doing what her mum had done and was leaving for good and that the angel was a way of keeping watch over her, or to remind Jo of who they were. But they couldn't have been more wrong. Jo had never drifted apart from her grandparents emotionally – and she never would. This was where she belonged and even if she now faced Christmas on her own, she'd handle it – and nobody else needed to know her plans had fallen apart.

She stretched for a second time, but even standing on top of the chair Jo couldn't reach the top branch. She almost wanted to cry. Nobody to share Christmas with, her grandparents out of town, and she couldn't even do this right.

'Looks like I'm just in time,' a voice came from behind her, accompanied by the gentle tinkle of the bell on the café door.

Jo stepped off the chair. 'You certainly are. Could you do the honours?' She hoped Matt hadn't seen her face which gave it all away, the feelings of loneliness, hopelessness even.

He set down the box of the day's produce and took off his gloves, handled the angel delicately and, once on top of the chair, put it on the highest branch of the tree with ease. He adjusted the lights too. 'This will highlight her all the more. Lucky she's all the way up there,' he said, climbing down, 'because when Poppy – or any other little girl – sees her they'll be wanting her for themselves.'

'It's beautiful, isn't it? Gran and Gramps gave it to me.'

'They don't often make tree toppers like that any more,' he said, 'some are cheap plastic and they're never as good, but that . . . well, she's the star of the show.'

She turned her attentions to the produce box. 'Thanks for all this. How's business up at the farm?'

'Slow, compared to the other seasons, but still enough to keep me out of trouble.'

'Glad to hear it.'

'How did the Brussels sprout salad go down?'

'If you call it that, it'll never sell.' She pushed him on the arm. 'Winter salad.'

'I do apologise. How did the *winter salad* go down?'

'Very well. Vince had some, Maddy and Dan enjoyed it, and a couple of out-of-towners said they hoped it would be on the menu again soon.'

'Good job I brought you more sprouts, then,' he winked.

She pulled out the enormous stalk. 'These look beautiful. I think I'll have the salad for my own lunch today.'

The bell over the door tinkled again to announce another arrival and the voices left Jo in no doubt as to who it was.

She went straight out to the café and enveloped Gran, then Gramps, in a hug. 'I'm going to really miss you. But you'll have an amazing time, I know it.' No way was she going to let it drop that Tilly had cancelled on her or they'd never leave to go visit their daughter in Spain. And Jo had been trying to get them to do it for years.

Gramps couldn't hide the tear in his eye. 'Steve will be in soon to fix the cupboard next to the cooker.'

'It broke again?' Jo asked.

'The kitchen is old.' It was one of the renovations Jo longed to have enough money to do, along with the kitchen in her own flat, but a quick fix would have to do for now. 'Hilda's already spread the word about the fondue, by the way.'

'It went down well?'

'She brought Angie along as well as Bea from the fish and chip shop and Maisy from the post office. They all said they'd be back next week.'

'Looks like I'd better ensure I've got the ingredients ready, then. Fondue Tuesday might be a regular fixture on my menu.'

'Matt here will keep the produce coming I'm sure,' said Molly, 'and you've got lots of friends here now if you get into trouble.'

'I'm not going to get into trouble, Gramps, I've been running this place very smoothly.'

'Just let me know what you need,' said Matt. 'Now I

need to rush off to another delivery, but have a wonderful holiday, Molly.' Gran blushed when he kissed her on the cheek. 'And you Arthur.' He shook Gramps's hand. 'And Merry Christmas to you both.'

'You have a wonderful Christmas, Matt,' said Arthur, adding an uncharacteristic wink. Holidays and Christmas obviously agreed with him.

'I hope Santa brings you something very special,' Molly added, and Jo wasn't sure but she thought she saw her gran wink too. What was with them both? They were like a couple of big kids conspiring to get up to no good.

'What are you like?' Jo laughed when Matt went on his way. 'He may be younger than you, but I don't think he believes in Santa Claus any more.'

'Maybe he believes in magic,' Arthur answered, his mood not in the least dampened.

'Maybe. Now, do you have everything you need? Passports? Tickets? Money?'

'Jo, stop fussing,' said Gramps. 'We've not lost our marbles yet.'

'I know you haven't, but I worry about you as much as you worry about me.' Molly had told her last week that Gramps was doing well with his healthy eating and he was getting more rest and enough exercise now he'd taken up bowls, and he'd had an appointment with Jess up at the surgery and she'd given him a clean bill of health. 'When's your taxi coming? Do you have time for a cup of tea?'

'We can't stop. The meter is ticking. The taxi is waiting in the drop-off zone at the bottom of the hill.'

'Then off you go!' She gasped. The meter would not be working in their favour! 'Bon voyage!' She hugged both of them so tight. They weren't going to be gone for all that long and she'd encouraged this, but still, it was hard to say goodbye.

She bundled them out of the door. This would be the first time they'd left the café in her capable hands when they couldn't pop down the hill to check on her, weren't within easy reach for any problems she might have, and she knew it had to be hard for them. She stepped outside and waved to them all the way to the end of the pier, Molly bossing Arthur about something, the sight of the two of them tugging at her heart as she watched them go.

Steve trotted up the steps from the sands below. In a wetsuit. 'Aren't you cold?' He looked at Jo in jeans and a jumper which was nowhere near enough for today's temperature.

'I should be asking you that question.' She stepped inside the café, shivering and rubbing at her arms. 'Don't tell me you've been in the sea?'

'Of course I have, I'm no wimp.' He followed her inside. 'And I need to maintain my stamina for the Christmas Day swim.'

'You're crazy.'

'Plenty of us doing it, still time to sign up.'

She ignored him. 'What can I get for you? I assume you haven't come to fix the cupboard quite yet,' she said, smiling.

He cast his eyes down his wetsuit. 'Not sure where I'd put my tools.' When she blushed, he added, 'and don't change the subject.' He took in the tree. 'Great job; it was bare yesterday. You had me worried you were into this whole minimalist approach people go for nowadays.'

'Not a chance. Coffee?' She'd love to chat but already her mind was ticking over the recipes she wanted to get through and pop up onto the blackboard.

'Yes, please.' He looked at the glass cabinet, usually filled with offerings. 'Where's the food?'

'I'm about to get started. I wanted to do the tree first. I can do you some fruit toast if you like.'

'Sounds good to me.'

She made him the coffee, worried that if he stood around in a wetsuit for too long he'd catch a cold, but he seemed far too robust for that to happen. She put the bread into the toaster and, when it was lightly golden, added a couple of portions of butter and took it through to where he'd settled at the front table.

'Is there anything else?' she asked.

'Why do you ask that?'

Because he looked like he wanted to ask her something. 'No reason. I'll be out in the kitchen, so if you need me, holler.'

'Right you are.'

Weird, that was the only word for it. He'd been normal when he first came in, joking and talking in his cheerful way, but he had something on his mind and Jo had no idea what.

She left him to it before she ended up with more customers who couldn't be fobbed off with a couple of slices of toast. Matt had brought in a good collection of produce so she went ahead and made the winter salad again – some of the teens had turned their noses up the other day, but she'd had lots of takers too – and along with it, she planned to whip up a banana bread, using the eggs Matt had supplied plus bananas from the supermarket, and with the pumpkin he'd included she wanted to make a batch of pumpkin scones.

'Customer,' Steve called from the café.

'On my way.' She wiped her hands and went out to greet Jess. She took in her friend's running gear, the sheen on her forehead after her workout. 'I don't know, between you and Steve, you're making me feel really lazy.'

'Nonsense.' Jess took out her earbuds. 'How's the arm, Steve?'

'It's good.'

'Must be if you're back surfing.'

He looked puzzled but must've realised her powers of deduction came from seeing him in a wetsuit. He really was on another planet today.

'How was it?' Jess asked him.

'How was what?'

It was her turn to pull a face. 'The surf.'

He muttered something about catching waves, a drop, a crest, and then left the second he finished his coffee.

'What's with him?' Jess asked.

'You noticed it too? I really don't know, but he's out of sorts. Away with the fairies, almost.'

'Maybe it's Christmas that's done it to him,' said Jess as Jo made her regular takeaway smoothie. 'It affects people in weird ways. Talking of Christmas, I've decided to do the Christmas Day swim.'

'You're not!'

'I sure am. This year it's raising money to help fund the local hospice.'

Jo whizzed the ingredients in the blender and poured them into a takeaway cup. 'How about I sponsor you rather than get wet myself?' she suggested, handing Jess the drink. She'd already got talking to a crowd of locals about the event and they'd each taken on responsibility for something. Some were lifeguards in the water, others were in charge of drinks, some people were bringing extra towels and blankets, and her contribution would be to make mince pies on Christmas morning and then stand on the sands watching people brave the waters, ready to hand a treat to them as soon as they'd finished.

'You're on.' Jess plucked a straw from the dispenser by the till. 'I'll send you the link for JustGiving. And make sure you come and watch before you go off with Tilly for the day and have your Christmas feast.'

'Don't worry, I will,' she smiled. She didn't want anyone to know she now had nowhere to go for the big day. She didn't want to be factored in to anyone's plans because they felt sorry for her. No, she'd be a grown-up and deal with it. Nobody else needed to know, her grandparents certainly didn't. Lonely meal-for-one it would be, and she'd survive. 'I'd better get into the kitchen and start cooking.'

'I'm running away in case you try to force me to eat any of those green things you keep putting in a salad . . . they're evil.'

'Sprouts are delicious!' Jo hollered good-humouredly after her as she left the café, holding her cup aloft to say cheers.

Back in the kitchen it was time to make the scones. Between serving customers she chopped pumpkin and popped it in a pan to cook, measured out buttermilk, made a sticky dough once the vegetable was cooked and cooled, prepared the other dishes, and wrote them all on the blackboard. Melissa came in, complaining that the pandemonium at the post office was giving her a headache,

Hilda stopped by to grab a portion of the winter salad for lunch and drop another hint to ensure Fondue Tuesday hadn't been a one-off, and Geoff and Valerie snuggled together beneath a blanket at an outside table, gossiping over hot lattes topped with cinnamon. Customers came and went, business was steady, and by the time Steve came back with his toolkit and fixed the cupboard later in the afternoon, Jo had even had enough time to make her first batch of mince pies for the season.

'Careful, they're hot,' she warned, but Steve had already bitten into one and wide eyes plus the steam coming from between his lips had her laughing.

'You're cruel,' he said when he'd finally finished the bite.

'I did try to warn you. And you didn't wait for the brandy butter I've stashed in the fridge.'

'I'm sure this won't be the last mince pie I have, so next time.' He picked up his toolbox. 'Can you believe this is your first Christmas here?'

'I can't.' Jo leaned against the counter. The months had flown by through busyness and the chaos of running her own business rather than working for someone else.

'To think, when you first arrived, you were scared of what summer would bring you.' He calmly popped the rest of the mince pie into his mouth now it had cooled. 'I'd say there's nothing you can't handle. Is there anything you'd change, if you could?'

'Actually, I really wouldn't.'

He nodded approval. 'Catch you later.'

She waved him off and turned to serve a crowd of locals who'd just been to the school nativity play. She made the kids hot chocolates and used her special stencils to make a Christmas tree out of chocolate powder on one, a snowman on top of another and a Santa figure on top of the third. The group had her busy for almost an hour, mince pies and brandy butter selling fast, as did the scones, and by the time they left the night had drawn its curtain over the café and she was about ready to drop.

She turned the sign on the door to 'Closed' and flopped down on the window seat. She took off her shoes and put her feet up on the low table and shut her eyes for a moment, before she faced the clearing up. Christmas was on its way and the anticipation, the excitement of the season, was a lot to take on.

When Jo felt her breathing calm and her body relax, she knew she had to clear up before she fell asleep right here. With a deep sigh, she looked over at the tables the group who'd just been in had occupied. There were spills and crumbs and the chairs were all haphazard. Everything seemed such an effort right now. She should never have sat down.

She turned her attention to the Christmas tree. The tidying and cleaning was still waiting, but with her eyes wide open again she was at least on her way to getting going again. The lights shone behind the ornaments, a pine cone squirrel shimmered and glistened on the end of a branch, a silver bauble was glossy enough that Jo could almost see her reflection. And there was something else.

She sat up and leaned forwards . . . what was that, on one of the uppermost branches, right near the angel in all her glory?

She stepped between tables, around chairs, and plucked an envelope with her name on it from the tree. Her heart melted. Perhaps it would be a Christmas card from one of the kids at the school. So many of them had come to her pumpkin-carving party at the end of October, others she'd served hot dogs to on Bonfire Night, and it seemed people of all ages were happy to see her in Salthaven – the Christmas biscuits she'd put out on December 1 had apparently been the talk of the playground, according to young Charlie.

She tore open the gold envelope and pulled out the Christmas card, expecting to see a snow scene, or a Santa or something festive. What she hadn't expected to see was a postcard with a fancy holly border, its red berries gracing each of the four corners, and another anonymous message.

Her heart beat faster. Because this was no ordinary postcard . . .

Date: Christmas Day
Place: The Café at the End of the Pier
Time: 2 p.m.

Dear Jo,
This Christmas it's time to let someone else take care of you;
Come to the café at the end of the pier for all your wishes to
come true xxx

Jo's heart beat faster and she felt excitement flood her body. This was it! She wondered how she'd managed to miss someone putting the postcard on the Christmas tree, but then again, traffic in and out of the café was constant. It could've been anyone.

She clutched the card against her chest and looked over at the Advent blocks. Nineteen more days to go. Nineteen

29

'I don't know,' said Morris Eckles who lived a few doors down the hill from Molly and Arthur, 'Maybe I should give up entirely.'

Jo's mid-morning customer had been talking about his attempts at topiary in his garden but Jo's mind was barely able to have her hand over a mince pie and a mug of coffee, let alone multitask to talk about hobbies. All she could think about was that postcard and, so far this morning, she'd topped up the coffee with orange juice instead of milk and had to start all over again; she'd decimated the first batch of mince pies by forgetting about them and almost burning the café down in the process – and she'd forgotten to give Hilda her change this morning when she came in for a cup of tea and a gossip with Angie.

'Keep at it,' she told Morris as he removed his coat and sat down to enjoy the mince pie. 'I doubt anyone is a master until they've practiced enough. Get on the Internet, do some more investigation, and then go for it.'

'You youngsters are all the same, you've got gumption. Shame it's not infectious.'

'Rubbish.' She flipped her tea towel over her shoulder, picked up a cloth and wiped down the table next to him. 'Why don't you shape what you've made into a ball? It's basic, but a good start. When I first took over the café, toast and straightforward recipes were my repertoire,' she told him as she straightened up the napkins in the chrome dispenser. 'But now I'm happy to give most things a go.'

She went off to serve another customer, glad to be busy. Cooking, serving and cleaning up all served their purpose at distracting her from that postcard. Because she had no idea who had sent it, and it was exciting and terrifying all at the same time. She knew now how Valerie and Geoff, Jess and Ben, and Maddy and Dan must have felt when she'd set them up for blind dates. They must have felt the same levels of anxiety, yet none of them had backed out, and she wouldn't either. Whoever this was, she needed and wanted to know.

That evening Jo had arranged to meet Jess at the pub. Melissa was all loved-up with James, enjoying a cosy night in, and she'd told Jo that after a day on her feet at the post office, sorting through more mail and parcels than Santa probably had in his workshop, all she wanted was to put on her fluffy slippers and snuggle up with her other half by the fire.

Jo left her flat and, out in the cold, pulled her scarf higher up on her neck. A howling wind came in off the sea in an icy blast, evergreens and winter foliage shivered in fright, and the roads were quiet. A complete contrast to the high season with out-of-towners searching for parking spaces, kids running freely as daylight stretched into the later hours, and people making the most of the sunshine by spending their waking hours on the beach, along the pier, or sitting in their gardens at home.

She smiled when she passed Morris's bungalow, because

he must've done exactly as she'd suggested earlier today; fuelled by her mince pies and coffee, he'd fashioned the topiary bush he'd tackled with something else in mind into a sphere bedecked with soft white lights – OK, so it wasn't perfect, but sometimes life's imperfections were the most beautiful of all.

Jess was waiting by the bar when Jo arrived. 'What are you having?'

Jo had seen the blackboard outside with the holly and ivy drawn in coloured chalk and the wine glass coloured red in its base. 'Mulled wine sounds good to me.' She pulled off her gloves, shoved them in her pockets and draped her coat over the stool before she sat down.

'Two mulled wines please, Billy.' Jess got the landlord's attention with a wave of a ten-pound note.

'Coming right up.' He asked how things were at the doctor's surgery, they talked about the Christmas Day swim, and both of them tried to persuade Jo to be a part of it.

'Do it for the town,' Billy urged.

'Do it for your wonderful friend,' said Jess.

'This year you have my sponsorship,' Jo replied. '*And* my mince pies.'

'Can't argue with that, I suppose,' said Jess.

'I might think about it next year.'

Jess was on her feet straight away. 'Did you hear that? Everybody, Jo here says she will be doing the Christmas Day swim next year.'

A big roar went up and Jo cringed into her bar stool. 'I can't believe you did that. And I only said I'll *think* about it.'

'You'll back out, otherwise.' Jess plonked herself back down.

'But who will serve mince pies on the sands afterwards? Tell me that.'

'You can make them beforehand and we'll pass them to someone else; I'm sure there'll be willing volunteers.'

It looked like she was committed. Usually Jo hated being cajoled into anything, but weirdly, not this time. It seemed the more you put in to being a part of something, the more you got out of it. She thought again about how Curtis Durham had offered her a job down in Cornwall and wondered how she could've ever considered leaving this place. The café was making a bit more money at last, and although not huge amounts, enough to let her relax and not panic. And after holding the pumpkin-carving party on Halloween and receiving so many compliments, she knew what her backup plan would be if she needed to generate more income. She'd run parties, themes of all kinds, and she knew she'd be good at it.

Jess chinked her handled glass with white snowflakes decorating the outside against Jo's. 'So . . . it's almost Christmas, and here we are, two lonely old spinsters—'

'Enough of the old!' Jo sipped the wine, the ginger and cloves warming her right through.

'Anyone even on the horizon for you?'

The word horizon gave Jo a jolt, because it had been used in the postcard she'd received in the summer. But she knew it was wishful thinking that Jess knew something. Every time another postcard had come to the café, Jo had analysed the vocabulary of pretty much every Salthaven resident, even the tourists, but as time marched on she'd gradually let her obsession go and assumed the mystery writer was too shy to come forwards. 'No, nobody on the horizon.' She'd toyed with the idea of telling Jess everything, but in case it came to nothing, decided to keep it to herself. And whoever this was, they wouldn't want an audience, and neither would she if the person decided to back out at the last minute.

Thankfully, Jess let the subject drop. 'How are Molly and Arthur doing?' She cradled her warm glass, her fingers slotted through the handle.

'They're having a wonderful time. We did a FaceTime call this morning over the iPad, and they're sitting outside, in glorious sunshine – nothing like the wild weather here, at least not yet.'

'And how's it going with your mum?'

'They all seem to be coexisting very happily. Gran said Gramps had bitten his tongue a couple of times, but he's slowly getting used to the fact that their daughter is all grown up and makes her own decisions. She doesn't need them to mollycoddle her. Although I think they'd both like to.'

'You sound very similar to your mum. You're both independent, you go after what you want.'

'For some reason Gran and Gramps always admired me for being that way but fought my mum for being the same.'

'Perhaps they learnt their lesson the first time, and it sounds as though she did get into a bit of trouble. You, as far as I know, never have.'

'I'm like the angel on top of the Christmas tree,' said Jo with a cheeky grin.

'Well, from what I saw, your mum loves her family as

much as you do, even though she doesn't live close by any more.'

'She really does. I think that's what stopped her coming back for so long. She had the same fear as Gran and Gramps that any little thing could be a trigger point to making everything worse, meaning they'd never see or talk to one another again. And I know I was the buffer between them all. I don't mind so much now; I'm just glad I could be because it brought them together in the end.'

'I'm really happy it all worked out. You're living the dream.' Jess toyed with the cinnamon stick in her glass and then set it onto a napkin so she could enjoy her drink without it spearing her nose any longer.

Jo thought about what she'd managed to achieve, moving forwards in a different direction and managing to keep her balance. It was a hell of a lot to do in under a year, and she wondered where she'd be in another year from now, how the café would be running, what events she'd take charge of and bring to the people of Salthaven.

'So, who's next for a night of love at the café?' asked Jess.

'I haven't really thought about it yet. What with the Halloween mayhem, then bonfire night and now Christmas fast approaching, I've not quite got around to arranging the next date night.'

'You know, there's always me,' Jess suggested. 'You could set me up again.'

Jo put down her glass. 'Is that the wine talking or are you serious?'

'I'm completely serious. I'm hopeless, I really am. The last date ended up with a wonderful friendship, but I need something more. I really do.'

Jo suspected there would be plenty of men she could set Jess up with and they'd probably be chuffed to bits to have a date with a doctor who was not only beautiful but lovely on the inside too. 'I don't know, you've already had a turn,' Jo teased.

'That's true, wouldn't be fair on all the other single people out there. But promise me, somewhere down the line, if I'm *still* single and you've been through everyone else in Salthaven, you'll sort out something for me.'

'It's a deal.'

'We need to set you up too, you know.'

Jo dismissed the suggestion. 'With who exactly?'

'I don't know . . . there are a few nice-looking locals and some lovely ones too. What about Matt? He's gorgeous and I've seen the way you two are together.'

'We're business associates.'

'OK, if you insist. But you have to admit he's good-looking.'

'He is, and a lovely person. And his sister says she wishes he'd put himself first some more.' Jo wondered whether Jess could be good for Matt. Mind you, she'd seen them talking often enough, and there hadn't been any trace of a spark between them. Or maybe Vince, local and a keen cyclist, could be just who Jess was looking for, given he also liked to stay fit and healthy. He was good-looking too – not many men could carry off Lycra cycling gear, but he managed it. There was always Steve of course, handsome and a lot of fun, and there were a few locals in the pub to-night that Jo was slowly getting to know. Any one of them could be a possibility. Perhaps love was right under Jess's nose, and all she needed was one more turn at the café's nights of love.

'Even if I was attracted to someone,' Jess went on, 'I'm not sure I'd ever have the nerve to ask anyone out. How bad is that? I'm thirty-three and too chicken to ask a man on a date.'

'I've never asked anyone out either.'

'We're not doing much for women's rights are we?'

'We're setting them back fifty years,' Jo giggled. She was definitely fuelled by the wine which had gone down a treat and when Billy passed by, offering them top-ups, they gladly accepted.

'What's so funny?' It was Steve who'd come through the door and nodded at Billy's offer of his usual, a pint of Kilkenny.

'What's your opinion on feminism, Steve?' Jess turned to him and all at once he was flustered by the question.

'I might go and join the lads,' he replied, watching Billy pull his pint with a look in his eye that said please make it swift.

'I'm serious,' said Jess. 'Has a girl ever asked you on a date before?'

He pulled out some coins from his wallet, sifted through them and handed over the correct amount to Billy. 'Maybe once . . . not often.'

'Do you think it should be the man who does the asking?' Jess demanded. She was on a roll and it was fun to watch.

'I . . . er . . . never thought about it.'

'When did you last ask someone out, Steve?' It was Jo's turn to fire a question.

'Thanks, Billy.' He scooped up his pint, clearly unable to leave fast enough. 'See you ladies later.'

'Cinnamon rolls tomorrow,' Jo called after him, amused

at how he couldn't wait to get away. 'He's been hanging out for me to make them, said he'll let me know if they're as good as Molly's,' Jo explained.

Jess was preoccupied, clearly taking this whole asking men out thing seriously. She even went over to the pool table and challenged Steve to a game, cheering away with a couple of locals when she sank three balls in succession – a complete fluke by her own admission.

Jo called over to Billy and asked for two more mulled wines, one to be delivered to Jess over at the pool table where it looked like Steve would have to start pleading that his arm was playing up to withstand the ribbing he'd get for losing to a girl. Leaning in to smell the heady Christmas spices from the glass in front of her, she discretely looked over her shoulder to see Maddy and Dan snuggled up in the corner.

'Love's young dream,' said Jess, coming back over to join Jo and noticing the happy couple too. 'Am I ever going to meet someone?'

'Stop being so maudlin,' said Jo. 'Your time will come.'

And so would Jo's. Soon.

30

Matt delivered the day's produce beneath a graphite sky, plagued with clouds. 'Good morning, Jo. I'll pop these in the kitchen shall I?'

She'd opened the door but kept both hands on it lest the wind took it from her grasp. 'Wait up, I'll clear a space.' She followed him into the kitchen and moved her recipe from the end of the bench.

'What's cooking up here?' He peered into a bowl which didn't look much right now. 'Doesn't look all that appetising.'

She gave him a shove on the arm. 'Cheeky. It's work in progress . . . I'm proving the yeast ready for cinnamon rolls.'

'I think Molly made those last year.' His eyes lit up.

Jo crossed her fingers on both hands. 'I hope I can pull this off, I've never made them before. The first sticking point will be leaving the yeast too long before I use it, so . . . ' She picked up the timer and set it for ten minutes.

'I'm sure you'll pull it off, and I'll be sending Poppy in later to get some of those if I don't have a chance myself.'

'Busy day?'

'I've got one delivery to go to the pub, another to the hospice and a third to one of the guesthouses up the hill on my way out of Salthaven. Then it's back to the farm for dreaded paperwork.'

'Ah yes,' she said as she began unloading the produce. 'There's no rest when it's your own business.'

'Definitely not. I'll be delivering right up until Christmas Day.'

'I'm sure you will. There'll be parties and big family gatherings to cater for.' Saying those words made her swallow hard. She was no longer going to be on her own for the day, but something much bigger was going to be happening, and sometimes she needed to take pause and stay brave. She never allowed participants of her blind dates to know who the other party was, she'd told Jess it was all part of the fun, and when she began to panic that she might be setting herself up for a fall when she found out who her mystery admirer was, she tried to tell herself to get in amongst it, go with the flow, all those annoying words of wisdom that were so easy to dish out yet no-where near as easy to abide by.

'Would you like a cup of tea, coffee?' she offered Matt, checking the timer which still had seven minutes to go.

'Actually, I will today. If you're sure I'm not interrupting. I'm in no rush to go outside, it's miserable.'

'At least it's not raining . . . yet.' She picked up a mug. 'What can I get you?'

'Word is you're doing wonderful cinnamon topped lattes, so one of those, to have here if I'm allowed?'

'You're really up for taking it easy, aren't you?' She purged the steam wand on the coffee machine, ready to get started in a routine she was all too familiar with. But she was glad Matt was hanging around. He was good company and she enjoyed their chats.

'Putting off the inevitable is probably a better way to describe it,' he replied as she poured the espresso she'd made, into a mug. 'But hey, it's almost Christmas . . .'

'. . . and you've earned a rest,' she finished for him. She took the homemade cinnamon syrup from the fridge and poured a little in the bottom of a jug before topping it up with milk. The steam wand would turn the mixture into a cinnamon froth ready to pour onto the espresso.

'Something like that.'

She picked up her stencils and fanned them out. 'Take your pick.'

'Santa, for sure.' He really did have a nice smile, and she'd never heard a bad word about this man who flew under the radar.

She positioned the stencil across the top of the mug and from the container next to the machine, dusted a mixture of cinnamon and chocolate powder. 'Ta-da!'

He peered at the results. 'Wow, really looks like a Santa.'

'Of course it does!' The timer beeped and she snapped to it. 'I need to get on.'

'Can I watch? Or would you rather I headed out to the café?'

'Actually, you could be my eyes and ears.' She picked up the pre-measured out buttermilk to mix with the yeast. 'If anyone comes in, hold the fort. Molly did warn me to make time-sensitive recipes at home, but I was too exhausted last night after the pub. Jess and Maisy had me chatting till all hours.' She mixed the wet ingredients together and added them to the flour.

'This is good,' he admitted, after sipping the cinnamon latte. 'Very festive. What's next?' He nodded to the mixture in her bowl that she'd begun to knead lightly.

'I'm working this gently and then it'll rest for an hour. And that's when the magic happens and they rise.'

'I'm hungry just watching you.'

The bell above the door to the café tinkled and Matt ducked out to see who it was. 'It's Steve,' he called back.

She put the mixture to one side, cleaned her hands and went through to join them.

Steve had his toolbox with him. 'Show me this dodgy tile, then.'

For a moment she'd forgotten her text to him first thing this morning. She walked past the Christmas tree and behind the lower branches put her foot on the tile to demonstrate the wobble. 'I don't think I would've noticed if I hadn't had to pick up a decoration that fell off yesterday.'

'Not a problem, I'll have it sorted quick enough.'

'Is the tree in your way?'

He felt around the tile. 'No, I should be able to work around it.'

'Can I get you a coffee?'

'Go on then, I think you can twist my arm,' he winked. 'Flat white for me, please.'

'Coming right up.' She left the men talking tiles and glue and grout as Steve took out a drill and marked places on the tiles ready to make holes. She had no idea how this all worked but thank goodness he did. The café wear and tear would be way worse without Steve in her corner.

She made the coffee and warmed a mince pie for him and when she emerged the men looked deeper in conversation. They went quiet when Steve saw her and she sensed she'd interrupted something. 'Here you go.' She set down the plate and the cup.

'I'd better be off.' Matt gulped back the rest of his coffee, bid them goodbye and off he went.

She left Steve to it so she could attend to her next lot of customers. She chatted with Geoff and Valerie about their morning yoga session. 'You'll get better,' Valerie assured Geoff when he said he didn't have a hope of ever being able to master it. 'It's too many years of sitting down at the end of the pier waiting for those fish. Mark my words, you'll be a new man after this.' When Valerie went to get glasses of water from the complimentary jug and was out of earshot, Geoff told Jo, 'I think she's trying to finish me off.'

'I need to do some sort of stretching myself,' Jo told him. 'But I've no time, not until Molly and Arthur return.'

'You must always make time for yourself,' said Valerie as she set down two glasses, each with a slice of cucumber. 'It's important, Jo.'

As Jo went out to the kitchen she thought about Valerie's words. Molly and Arthur had commented the same recently, so had her mum, and she knew if Tilly hadn't cancelled Christmas she'd be hearing the same advice from her friend. Jo had given the business her all since she'd arrived, but was there room for something more now?

She rolled out the dough that had doubled in size until she had a rectangle shape. She brushed it with melted butter, creating a layer on the dough for the cinnamon and sugar to stick to, and once she'd sprinkled over both, she rolled the rectangle into a long sausage shape. With a sharp knife she cut it evenly into slices that she turned out onto a greased baking sheet.

'All done here.' Steve's voice came from the café so she

went out to meet him. He handed her the bucket. 'If you could empty that, I'll put it across the space.'

'Will do.' She emptied the bucket and then scribbled a sign which she pinned on it saying not to walk on the floor tile beneath. 'I'm not sure how I'll go keeping the kids from inspecting the tree when they come in, but it's only twenty-four hours, we should be fine.'

He seemed hesitant to leave. 'I can't smell anything yet. What's happened to the cinnamon rolls?'

'Patience! They need another forty minutes to rise, then I cook them, then it's onto giving them a good glaze, and we're done.'

'How long do you expect a man to wait?' He closed his toolbox and picked it up, a bemused look on his face. 'You should be beating men away with a stick, Jo. How come nobody's snapped you up already?' She wasn't sure what to say to that. 'They do say the way to a man's heart is through his stomach,' he added.

'Right . . . thanks?'

'So, have you or Jess asked anyone out yet?'

'What? Gosh, no. Absolutely not.'

'It's just that in the pub you both seemed set on the idea.'

'We were kidding, trying to be all in support of women's rights, you know how it is.'

'Right.' There was that nervous look on his face again, the same look as the other day. 'Actually, Jo. Do you have a minute?'

'Sure, what's up?'

He put his toolbox down again and opened his mouth to begin, but the bell tinkled to announce a group of teenagers, one of them Dan, who immediately launched into a conversation with Steve about the perils of winter surfing and their moment was lost.

She wondered, not for the first time, what Steve had been about to say.

31

There was definitely something weighing heavy on Steve's mind, and Jo had wondered whether, if Molly and Arthur were here, they'd be able to get to the bottom of it. He was close enough to her grandparents to be able to chat to them, but she'd hoped, in their absence, he'd be able to talk to her instead. One minute he seemed to want to, the next, a distraction had dragged his attention away. He'd left this morning after talking to Dan but had made Jo promise to save him a cinnamon roll for when he popped in later that afternoon. Perhaps they'd get a chance to talk some more then.

With the cinnamon rolls filling the café with their sweet aroma, Jo wrote the item on the blackboard in the café.

'Comfort food at its best,' said Angie, who'd just come in the door. She clapped her hands together. 'I've been waiting for these all year.'

'Well, I hope I do them justice.'

Angie dismissed her concern. 'I've no doubt you will; they smell wonderful.'

Hilda was next in. Her nose lifted in the air and her eyes zoned in on the words in chalk. 'My favourite. How long, Jo?'

'They're out of the oven. All I need to do is add the

glaze. I guess I don't need to ask for your order when it comes to food.' The pair settled down at the table in the far corner and Jo fetched them a pot of camomile tea.

Back in the kitchen Jo looked at the cinnamon rolls. They were nice and plump, soft to the touch, and smelt the same as she remembered from her gran's home cooking. And when she poured over the white glaze made from confectioner's sugar, they looked just like Molly's.

'Now those look wonderful.' Hilda's eyes widened as Jo approached with two cinnamon rolls and set them down on the table. 'Are you waiting for me to taste?'

'Of course.' Jo lingered by her customers' table, hands clasped together, hoping she'd pulled it off. 'You know Molly's cinnamon rolls, so you can compare the two.' And she really wanted her customers to remember this, her first Christmas in town, for the right reasons.

Hilda's eyes fell back into their sockets and when Jo looked at Angie her reaction was about the same. 'Good?'

Hilda eventually swallowed. 'Yes! Now go away so I can devour it in peace.'

Jo did a little jump and clapped her hands together. And when her phone pinged in her apron pocket and she saw a message from Tilly, apologising again that she wouldn't be making Christmas Day, she was on such a high that she couldn't be upset. She tapped out a quick reply to tell her friend it couldn't be helped and that staying safe from the wild weather was far more important. She was tempted, yet again, to mention her mysterious date, but for now it was her secret and it made it all the more exciting.

Ben and Charlie appeared while Jo was wiping down the display cabinet. 'Ah, must be school holidays if you two are in here in the middle of the day. Are you glad to have a break, Charlie?'

'I miss my friends.'

'His friend Zac will be over for tea tonight,' Ben explained, 'and tomorrow he's seeing Poppy and they'll be sailing their boats on the lake, weather permitting.'

'Boats still go out in storms, Dad,' Charlie admonished before grabbing the pot of crayons and a sheet of paper and settling himself at the table bang in the middle of the café.

'Well, that told me.' Ben sniffed the air. 'What's that wonderful smell?'

'Cinnamon rolls,' she said.

'I'll take three please.'

'Three?'

'Lorna is joining us today.' He checked his watch. 'In about fifteen minutes. And I'll take two hot chocolates for Charlie and I, but I'll wait to order Lorna's drink. It's crazy, isn't it? We were married and I'm not even sure what to order her.' He seemed frazzled, nervous even.

'It's not crazy, it sounds as though it's going really well.' It seemed like he was falling in love with his ex-wife all over again. Jo could tell by the way his voice softened when he mentioned her name and the slight hesitation at admitting he didn't know her as well as he perhaps should.

She made the hot chocolates and took them to the table, and on her way back to the kitchen Ben caught up with her so they were out of earshot. 'I wanted to thank you, Jo.'

'Me? What for?'

'For being a very good friend.'

'The feeling is mutual.' She went through to the kitchen

and returned with the cinnamon rolls but Ben was still waiting. He was hovering, a bit like Steve. What was it with the men in this town that they couldn't come out with it and say what was on their mind? 'Is there something else?'

'You remember setting me up with Jess, on a date,' he began.

'Of course, it was the start of the nights of love at the café.'

'Well, that night I thought ... well, I thought it was going to be a date with you.'

Jo's face fell when she realised he wasn't joking. He was a good friend but she'd never thought of him in any other way. 'Really?'

'You and I seemed to hit it off the second you moved back to Salthaven and took over the café, and I think I attached myself to you. In a non-stalker way, of course.' His voice wobbled with nerves. 'Your kindness, your friendship and starting a friendship with Jess, all of it has helped me be a better person and to look at the situation with Lorna with a bit more perspective.'

'The female perspective?' she teased.

He finally relaxed. 'Yes, I suppose it was. The night I came to your flat to sign Charlie up for the pumpkin carving was so lame. I wanted to confide in you about Lorna, but got cold feet. Then again, at the pumpkin carving event, I wanted to try to get you on your own and tell you that Lorna and I had turned a corner. But it's hard for us guys to confess our feelings – fear of ridicule or something like that.' He shrugged. 'I wanted to say thank you, Jo. Lorna and I had a rough time but your encouragement that I was doing the right thing in letting her spend more time with Charlie, and Jess's reassurance too, well, it opened another door in my life.'

'Are you saying what I think you're saying?'

'We're going to give it another go, Lorna and I. Not just for Charlie, but for the both of us too. The more time I spend with her the more I realise I actually miss her and want us to be a family again.'

It seemed appropriate. Jo put down the plates and wrapped Ben in an enormous hug. 'I'm over the moon for you, I really am.' The night of love at the café may not have quite worked out in the way either of them had expected, but it had led to strong friendships and his ability to see through the fog and reunite his family. That was a win in Jo's book.

'Dad . . .' Charlie was growing impatient. 'My tummy is making noises, Dad.'

'That's my cue.'

'And here's your other half.' She looked over at Lorna who'd pushed open the door, the little bell tinkling enough to make Charlie leap up out of his seat and run over to her. He dragged her by the hand over to the table.

Ben joined his ex-wife and son and Jo, a tear in her eye, almost missed him mouthing the words 'cinnamon latte'.

Ben and his family stayed a while longer, before tackling a bracing walk along the pier. Other customers came and went and the rain held off, with regulars Hilda and Angie making no move to leave their game of chess.

Steve popped his head in just as the sun went down. 'How long have they been here?' He nodded to the two women in the corner, eyes down at the board, deep in concentration.

'Hours, but it's great for business,' said Jo.

'Any cinnamon rolls left?'

'I saved you one.'

He leaned against the counter. 'You're an angel, Jo.'

She went out the back and reappeared with a plate. 'I'll need to make another batch tomorrow – they're big sellers.'

He bit into the delicate dough. 'As I said before, you give these to a man and he's yours, you mark my words.'

'Coffee?' She restarted the playlist on her iPod which was sitting on the docking station. Filled with Christmas tunes, and the air plumped with a buttery cinnamon aroma, Jo looked at the wooden block Advent calendar sitting there counting down the days until Christmas. Seventeen. And with Christmas, this year, would come her mystery date. All she hoped was that whoever this person was, he'd read the situation right and Cupid's arrow would have a good aim.

'Yes, please. Takeaway cinnamon latte if it's still going.'

'Of course, every day until winter is over. What do you reckon?'

'Good idea. Billy has said he's keeping mulled wine on the pub menu all winter long too; I think you need your comforts when it's so cold.'

'You been surfing today?' He seemed to be talking happily enough and she wanted to give him the opportunity to confide in her about what was bothering him, but she got the impression he needed to feel comfortable first, so she'd picked one of his favourite topics.

'Yep. I go as much as I can, especially when I'm eating so much of your tempting creations.'

Her insides did a happy loop the loop every time someone referred to the café as hers. She wondered if she'd ever get used to hearing it. 'I think you need to stock up on all this Christmas food, ready for the big and very cold swim. The temperature of the water should burn about a million calories.'

'You'll be doing it next year,' he mocked. 'I still can't believe Jess got you to agree. I can't even persuade you to have another surf lesson.'

'I can't believe I agreed, either. The sea and I don't mix in the winter months unless I'm wrapped up in a dozen layers, watching it from the sands.'

Jo made his cinnamon latte and they talked about the swim over the glugs, hisses and whooshes of the coffee machine. 'You wanted to talk to me, the other day,' she added when she handed him his takeaway cup.

'Did I?' He really did appear to have forgotten.

'You did, but the café got busy. Is there something on your mind?' Ben had said she'd become a good friend and she liked to think Steve felt the same way.

He'd finished the cinnamon roll and sipped his latte. 'I can't remember what it was.' His face said that actually he did but had thought twice about mentioning it. 'I'd better go. I'll see you soon. But keep making those cinnamon rolls and you'll never get rid of me,' he said and winked.

When he left, Jo had a slow stream of customers, mostly school kids glad to be out of the confines of the educational environment. She chatted with a couple of mums, ushered youngsters away from the bucket covering the dodgy floor tile, and by the time Hilda and Angie finally finished their chess game and Jo turned the sign on the door to 'Closed', she was exhausted.

A fog had closed in over the pier, making it impossible to see the sea, but the twinkly lights and Christmas music were enough to buoy her along as she cleaned up at the end of another long day. She swept the floor, humming away to Christmas songs from years ago, others more recent. She refolded the blankets she kept in the café, ready to hand out to anyone wanting to sit outside, and stowed them on a shelf in the storeroom, next to the posts from the makeshift bower.

Once everything was as it should be, she left the café and locked the door behind her, but instead of walking straight home, she hovered on the pier, leaning against the wooden fence, her face absorbing the mist, a foghorn sounding on the horizon protesting at the grey blanket it was up against. Even in the bleak depths of winter, this town was heaven. She could just about make out the faint lights that, on a clear day, shone brightly on the huge Christmas tree in the centre of town, above the pitched roofs of the houses. Closer were the white lights wound around the Victorian lamp posts all the way along the length of the pier, and the café, even without being illuminated, standing reliably behind her, spoke of everything she worked so hard for: to be a part of this town, a part of people's lives, to have a place to call home.

It was almost time for the mysterious person to show their face and Jo couldn't wait. She had no idea who it was, but in a peculiar way she felt as if they knew her so well. Perhaps they'd hesitated at doing too much too soon because they knew she was finding her feet, had been ever since she returned. If she'd been in this position a few months ago, she would've panicked, been flustered with everything that was going on in her world. And then, of course, there'd been Harry. She'd needed to work through her feelings about him, both past and present, and whoever this mystery admirer was, he seemed to have sensed the same. He'd given her time to get to grips with the business, time to make new friends, all the while waiting in the wings until the moment was right and she had begun to see for herself that work wasn't everything, that she needed an injection of something special in her personal life.

And now that moment had come. This Christmas could change her life more than it had been altered already.

Was it too much to believe she was finally going to find her happy ever after?

32

The weeks rolled on and a fortnight after Gran and Gramps had taken off to visit her mum, Jo was busier than ever before. The Christmas season at the café had her making festive treats, keeping the hot drinks flowing, and as she chatted with customers, she rode the wave of the festive period as she waited for the big day to draw nearer.

She left the main lights off and hung up her coat and scarf, changing out of her knee-high boots and into a pair of sparkly black trainers for her working day. A bit of comfortable Christmas bling, she'd decided. She whipped up a treat, a cinnamon latte, to start the day, using the snowman stencil to make a shape on top with the spice and chocolatey sprinkles, and took it into the café to enjoy the Christmas ambience. It was one of those days to stay indoors if you could and cosy up in front of a log fire, staring out of the window if you were lucky enough to have a view of the sea or of the town with its shops and streets decorated in coloured lights for the season. But without a tree at home, this was her treat, being here.

Once she'd finished the latte it was back to reality and on with the cooking. First up was making gingerbread men. She had a reliable recipe from Arthur and had already pondered the idea, for next year, of holding a gingerbread-making party for some of the local kids: or adults, should they so desire. The town would love it. They could even make gingerbread houses if she could get hold of some templates, and she looked around, wondering how she could turn this place into a gingerbread house for the event, perhaps with giant cardboard candy canes, big painted gingerbread figures on the walls and gingham tablecloths on the tables.

Buzzing with her ideas, Jo made the gingerbread in time to take the day's delivery from Matt.

'Not long to go now,' he said, rubbing his hands together to warm them up after he'd taken the produce through to the kitchen.

For a moment she thought he'd heard about her clandestine date and almost asked if people had been gossiping, but then realised he was referring to Christmas. Of course. This whole postcard thing had her on edge and it was making her far too jittery.

She pulled out a few small cauliflowers. 'I'm impressed – these look great.'

'What's whirring around in that head of yours?'

'I'm thinking . . . a cauliflower soup – we're well into soup season – or perhaps a cauliflower rice, with eggs, mushrooms . . .' She delved through more of the box. 'Carrots,' she added, 'and a bit of ginger and soy sauce.'

'Sounds good to me. Or you could make something sweet.'

She took out today's batch of fresh eggs. 'I don't think so.'

'I mean it; my sister Anna's into all that cooking with weird and wonderful ingredients. I think a lot of her passion comes from spending time with mums who struggle to get their toddlers and kids to eat anything resembling a vegetable. She made cauliflower brownies once.'

Jo finished putting the eggs into the china bowl at the rear of the kitchen benchtop. 'Don't let Molly hear you talk like that. Her brownies are legendary – I can't see cauliflower making it into the recipe anytime soon.'

'Anna used me as a guinea pig to test the things and I have to say batch one nearly had me running for the nearest bucket.'

'If it's all the same with you, I'll be sticking to Molly's version.'

He shook his head. 'The brownies would never replace Molly's, but it's something new to think about. Talk to Anna next time she's in – she'll surprise you with her weird concoctions and how good they are. You may even want to add them to your repertoire if you're brave enough.'

He went on his way and left her pondering the challenge, the thought of cauliflower brownies. Who knew, maybe he was right. Perhaps it was time to step out of her comfort zone and give something different a go.

When Jo had wiped down the recently vacated tables after lunch, she looked up to see a group of carollers gathering on the pier. She turned off the music from the iPod and opened up the café door. The salty sea air milled around but the soft voices in harmony singing favourites such as 'Good King Wenceslas', 'Silent Night', 'We Three Kings' and 'Deck the Halls' were enough to warm anyone. She handed out blankets as the tables outside filled with customers, and made an endless supply of cinnamon coffees and hot chocolates as the carollers lingered between two of the lamp posts which someone had festooned with red ribbons.

'It's magical, isn't it?' Matt trod the wooden boards of the pier over to where she was standing.

'Amazing.' She leant against the door jamb. 'This is what it's all about, you know.'

'Christmas?'

Mesmerised by the carollers she said, 'Life. It's all about this, the town, friendships, the magic when everyone is together.'

'I wouldn't leave here, that's for sure.'

'Me neither.' Shaking away the emotion, she asked, 'What brings you back here?'

'We're quietening down at the farm so I've helped Mum do some last-minute shopping in town – I left her gossiping with a friend while she waits for Dad to collect her and all the bags – and now I'm having some down time.'

'Coffee or hot chocolate?' With the rush of customers dispersed and only a few tables occupied as people crowded outside to hear the carollers, Jo suddenly liked the sound of down time herself.

She made two hot chocolates and they hovered in the doorway drinking them as they listened to 'Hark the Herald Angels Sing' and 'I'm Dreaming of a White Christmas'. And only when the carollers moved on did Jo snap back into work mode. She took her empty cup and Matt's inside.

He followed her and pulled a piece of paper from his pocket. 'My sister's recipe for cauliflower brownies. I called her and she recited it from memory. Poppy is pretty good with her fruits and vegetables, but apparently hates cauliflower and this was Anna's way of overcoming it.'

'Wow, she certainly rises to a challenge.'

'And I'm sure you can too.' He looked at the list on

the blackboard behind her. 'Look at what you manage to rustle up every day – each time I come in it's a surprise. You're the talk of the town, exactly as Molly and Arthur were when they ran the show.'

She gulped at how far she'd come so quickly. 'I draw the line at stinky cauliflower spoiling a delicious chocolate treat.' He proffered the recipe again and this time she took it. 'You're determined to show me how good they are, aren't you?' She gave the ingredients the once-over, still not convinced.

'It took her a while to perfect it, but you've got a good recipe there and plenty of cauliflowers, so why not?'

Matt went off to prepare for a family gathering up at the farm and Jo looked at the ingredients again. But no matter how many times she read through it, cauliflower stood out like arsenic on a list of ingredients.

But then again, sometimes things that felt wrong at first could turn out to be the best things in the world.

With two days to go until Christmas Eve, Jo had dived into the café half an hour earlier than usual, not only to escape the rain but to get a head start on her cooking. Since Matt had given her the recipe, she'd decided to bat away any misgivings, and even though making soup had been her intention this morning, she was going to give those brownies a go.

She smiled her way through her cooking session, blending cauliflower, chocolate, eggs, making a mousse-like batter. There were ingredients everywhere, Christmas music turned up to the max, and long before opening time the intensely chocolatey smell snaked its way through the café. It was heavenly, and soon she'd be adding the smell of gingerbread plus cinnamon rolls again. Her customers were being treated to the best, but she wanted to keep busy, anything to keep her mind from Christmas Day. Because, in approximately eighty hours, she'd know who had been waiting in the wings, sending her postcards.

While the brownies cooled she got to work on the gingerbread dough. She mixed together sugar, syrup, treacle, spices and zest, stirred in butter, flour and left the mixture to firm up when a knock at the door told her that her produce had arrived for the day. There wasn't as much in winter, but Matt kept up the supplies of whatever he could, and they'd laughed the other day that if the worst came to the worst, she'd just take the eggs as she seemed to get through hundreds in her recipes.

'Good morning, Matt. I see you have a helper today.' Jo smiled at Poppy, who was carrying a big stalk of sprouts.

'Hello, Jo.' Poppy marched straight through to the kitchen when Matt led the way, the produce box in his arms. 'I'm earning extra pocket money.'

Matt leaned closer to Jo and she caught a whiff of aftershave rather than the usual fresh-soil man smell that usually accompanied him. It was never unpleasant, almost a part of him, but the change took her by surprise. 'I'm keeping her out of her mum's way, more like it.' He tapped the side of his nose. 'It's time for Santa to wrap the presents, if you know what I mean, so my task is to keep her occupied.'

Poppy was already investigating what was going on in Jo's kitchen, her eyes fixed on the brownies. 'I love Molly's brownies,' she admitted.

'Then you should have one,' Jo insisted, taking her

chance to have them blind-tasted. 'On the house, but on one condition.'

'What's that?' The little girl looked up at her in trepidation as though she was going to ask for something wholly unrealistic.

'You help me cut out the gingerbread when my dough is ready, and perhaps hang around long enough to decorate them. How does that sound?' She looked over at Matt for approval. 'She can stay here if you have deliveries; just pop by and collect her in an hour or two.'

'Are you sure? I don't want to palm off my uncle duties if you're too busy.'

'Nonsense.' Jo had already found out a pink apron with white spots and looped it over Poppy's head. She helped her tie the bow at the back. 'Happy to help – and if she can decorate the gingerbread men it frees me up to do other things around here.' She lifted a brownie onto a plate for Poppy and another for Matt.

'Bit early for me,' he said.

'Oh no, it's a requirement I'm afraid, in return for the favour I'm doing you.' She'd already tried them and could vouch for their deliciousness.

He lifted up the chocolate morsel. 'Well, if you insist. Can I grab a cappuccino to go then please, and I'll drink that as I carry on with my rounds. Hospice next, then on to the pub.'

Jo let them both enjoy the brownies while she made Matt's coffee and it was only as Poppy devoured hers and said, 'They don't taste like Molly's,' that Matt twigged what Jo had done. He shared a conspiratorial wink, their secret safe from his niece who insisted she wouldn't touch cauliflower if you paid her all the pocket money in the world.

'You like them, Poppy?' Jo handed Matt his coffee, but the little girl didn't need to answer, her chocolate-coated lips said it all.

'I might have to make them when we have a mother's group in,' she told Matt.

'You'll be a saint in their book.' He winked and off he went.

It was time to roll out the gingerbread dough and Jo found the special cutter for Poppy who cut out six-teen man shapes and gently lifted them onto the greased baking sheets as Jo started on the cinnamon rolls. Jo even shared her secret ingredient for the brownies and Poppy took it well considering she'd eaten her most-hated veg-etable. Jo had the odd customer in for a hot drink, the order of the morning with the frost on the ground out-side. The winter sun made it glisten in an angel white that made Christmas feel as though it was really coming. When the doorbell tinkled as Jo had set the dough to rest and settled Poppy at a table to draw Uncle Matt a Christmas picture, she looked up to see a face she hadn't seen in a while.

'Curtis, what are you doing here?' She beamed at him. The last time he'd been into the café he'd still been trying to persuade her to come and run a café in Cornwall for him. 'What brings you to town?'

'Christmas, of course.'

'In Salthaven?' She collected an empty mug from the windowsill before it toppled down of its own accord and mopped up a spill on the low-set table in front of the window seat.

'The next town along, but I thought I'd pop in.'

The man was good-looking, she gave him that, and dressed in a suit he looked like he'd stepped out of the *Next Directory*. If Hilda saw him, she'd be getting all sorts of ideas and probably dropping massive hints that Jo's love life needed a lot of help to get off the ground.

'I have family down this way,' he went on to explain. 'I'll be spending a few days with them.'

'What's with the suit?'

'I came straight from a meeting.'

'Business going well?' She admired Poppy's drawing of a questionably skinny Santa and a tree about half the man's size, but she didn't criticise before making her way over to the blackboard to write Gingerbread Men on the menu. She wouldn't pop the cinnamon rolls on there yet as they still had a way to go.

'Business is going very well. I came in today to say thank you.'

'Really?'

'Really. If you hadn't suggested I try a different approach, tackle the locals, I think I'd still be looking for that perfect candidate to run my new venue in Cornwall.'

'So it worked?' Jo's eyes lit up.

'Like a charm. In the end, it was almost hard to choose because I had more than one candidate.'

'I'm really pleased for you. And I'm glad I helped. Now, can I get you anything to eat or drink? This is a café, after all.'

He returned her friendly smile. 'Actually, I'm ravenous. I'll take a brownie please and a takeaway black coffee.'

'Coming right up.' She served the brownie on a plate and he sat down to enjoy it while she made his coffee and by the time she came out he'd got through half of the chocolate treat and Poppy was by his side.

'Excuse me,' Poppy said politely.

'Hello, young lady.' If Curtis was confused at why she was talking to him, he didn't let on.

'Do you like cauliflower?'

With a bemused look at Jo he went with it. 'Hate the stuff,' he told Poppy as he scraped up the last few crumbs from his plate. 'An evil, smelly vegetable if ever there was one.'

Jo tried to keep a straight face when Poppy winked over at her.

'What was that all about?' Curtis asked when he returned his plate, paid Jo, and picked up his takeaway coffee.

'I really couldn't tell you,' she answered, doing her best not to giggle. It seemed they could fool adults as well as kids with the chocolate treats.

Steve came through the door, his wetsuit zipped up now it was in the winter months. He only treated on-lookers to his fit body when it was about twenty degrees warmer than it was right now. His hair was still wet, ruffled from a quick towel dry, and he gave Curtis a cursory glance.

Curtis thanked her again, took the takeaway coffee to keep him going on the way to his family's home where he'd stay for Christmas, and Steve was straight to the counter. 'What did he want?'

'To see me.'

'Not trying to take you away from us is he?'

'You sound as though you're in the playground, not wanting me to have any other friends apart from you.'

'I don't like to see you taken advantage of, that's all.'

'Relax, Steve. He was here to thank me for helping him out with a staffing issue. I'm not going anywhere; you're stuck with me I'm afraid.'

'Well, I for one, am glad about that.' He lingered and for a moment Jo thought he was about to say something else.

'Poppy, looks like time's up,' said Jo when Matt came through the door. The little girl rushed to give him the picture she'd drawn and if he thought the Santa looked dodgy, he was too kind to mention it.

'I'll be going.' Steve was off and yet again, Jo had missed her chance to ask what was going on with him.

There was something on his mind but she wondered whether he'd ever just come out and say it.

33

It was Christmas Eve and childhood excitement had flooded Jo's mind from the moment she woke up, spurring her on past the festooned lamp posts of the pier through the morning drizzle and the grey day to her haven at the end.

Christmas Eve had always been her and Gran's favourite day, her mum's too, with all the excitement still to come. She wished she knew whether they were awake yet, over in Spain, but at only five in the morning, she doubted it. Last night Gramps had sent her a photo on his iPad of a big jug of Sangria and the four of them sitting outside a local tavern. And it hadn't only been the smiles on their faces that convinced Jo their family was slowly repairing itself, but the way those faces spoke of genuine happiness and warmth.

With a cup of coffee on the go, Jo sorted through papers – Steve's invoices and matching receipts for the café repairs, supermarket receipts for extra supplies and cleaning products, another electricity bill to add to the collection, Matt's latest invoice from the farm. She pushed them all into an envelope, ready to send to the accountant in the next couple of weeks. It was weird to be forwarding them to anyone other than Harry, but weird in a good way.

After tackling the accounts it was straight out to the kitchen to prepare for the day. She made mince pies, more brandy butter to put in the fridge, another round of cinnamon rolls, fruit salad, quiche and an enormous winter salad. Customers drifted in steadily, one after the other and by mid-morning the café was full, not a free table in sight. When Jess came in from a late run, Jo was standing there, staring into the fray. A group of teens were chatting away at a volume more akin to a nightclub, Angie and Hilda had commandeered the far table and were yet again playing chess – clearly, whoever had lost last time wanted to win this match – and Ben, Charlie and Lorna were laughing away at the middle table over hot chocolates and mince pies.

'So the lights are on, but nobody's home,' Jess observed from the other side of the counter. She'd already taken out her earbuds.

'What?' Jo came back to the present.

'You were daydreaming; are you that exhausted?'

'I am, but in a really good way. I was just thinking how wonderful it is. When it's frosty outside with the threat of snow, I wondered whether people would hunker down at home and enjoy togetherness on Christmas Eve rather than venture out.' She was daydreaming about her date tomorrow too, but nobody apart from her and the mystery postcard writer knew that.

'Are you kidding?' With a smile as bright as her blonde hair, she told Jo, 'This is where people have gathered for years. I always knew it had something to do with Molly and Arthur and the way they welcomed everyone with open arms, and you've kept the same vibe going.'

'You really think so?'

'I know so. Ask anyone: they'd far rather be here, in amongst it with the other locals, than at home. Tomorrow will be different, of course, being Christmas Day.'

'Usual smoothie?' Jo was keen to steer the conversation well away from the big day for now, in case her face gave away the fact she had something exciting brewing.

'Yes, please. I'm working a half day today. What time are you meeting Tilly tomorrow?' Bad luck, Jess seemed intent on talking about it. 'I'd love to say hello although I'll be with my parents right after the swim. I think they're concerned I'll get hypothermia. They'll be fussing over me constantly despite my medical training. But I guess that's what family do.'

Jo chopped fruit and whizzed it in the blender with yogurt, ice cream and honey before pouring the mixture into a takeaway cup and grabbing the plastic lid. 'Lunch is at two o'clock.' It wasn't a lie; that was the time on the postcard and she assumed whoever it was would be asking her to lunch somewhere. Maybe the pub? Her cheeks warmed; could it be Billy? He was single, not much older than her, and a lovely chap. But not really her type. She swished away the thought . . . it couldn't be, could it? 'I'm not sure what Tilly's plans are with her family,' she added, to avoid the complication of having to explain why Jess couldn't say hello to Jo's best friend.

'Well, that's a shame . . .' She plucked a straw from the dispenser next to the till and pushed it into the see-through lid of her smoothie.

She looked about to say something else but Jo cut her off. 'Sorry, customer.'

'Catch you later,' said Jess and went on her way.

Jo looked up when the postman came through the

door. She took her mail but didn't let him leave without handing him a couple of cinnamon rolls wrapped in a stripy paper bag.

After serving a cinnamon latte and a couple of slices of raisin toast to a family visiting Salthaven for the first time, Jo removed the elastic band from the bundle of letters. And between all the other bumf, she found a piece of treasure. A postcard from her grandparents. She skimmed over the words – how Gran and Gramps had been to the markets where Sasha sold her jewellery, how they'd enjoyed dining out most evenings, how the winter sun was mild, how beautiful a place their daughter had fallen in love with. She took a pin from the top of the board and pushed it through the card, a photo of the sea with boats, the sun setting over them. She could almost imagine the lapping of the water, the tranquillity of sitting there beneath the sunshine when the warmer months allowed.

'And now, anyone can read it,' she said softly to herself.

Christmas Eve passed by in a flash. Cinnamon rolls were ordered, mince pies devoured, hot drinks supplied and the atmosphere filling the modest space was heady and filled with joy. In between her usual routine, Jo made batches of mince pies, stashing them in Tupperware tubs once they were cooled, ready to take to the sands tomorrow. Maddy and Angie had both agreed to make more and between them they'd be able to feed the masses. With two hundred swimmers taking part and most likely almost as many watching, that meant a whole lot of baking.

Jo looked at her watch as the sky turned overcast and an icy blast and spray from the white-crested waves greeted her as she wiped down an outside table after clearing the remnants from her hardier customers who'd sat there beneath blankets. She was organised for tomorrow but her insides fluttered as though a skittish butterfly was desperately aiming for an escape route. Because now it was after two o'clock on Christmas Eve, which meant in less than twenty-four hours, she'd have her answer.

She'd know exactly who wanted to meet her at The Café at the End of the Pier.

34

'Merry Christmas, Jo.' Geoff and Valerie nipped in on Christmas morning, earlier than anyone else. Geoff insisted the fishing habit meant he was allergic to lie ins, Valerie said she much preferred to get going with a yoga routine as soon as the sun came up. They were a match made in heaven.

Angie was talking about sun salutations or something, but Jo could barely hear a word of it. Her mind was on that postcard, her date, this afternoon. Christmas Day, one of the most magical days of the year, but would it bring magic her way?

There were hugs all round when Hilda came in an hour later as Jo was propping up a blackboard outside the café to say they'd be closing at 10 a.m. sharp and would reopen first thing tomorrow morning. Jo had contemplated opening up for longer today, but when she'd received that postcard, she'd decided to put herself first, for once.

'You'll be busy tomorrow,' said Hilda, hugging Jo. 'People will be lining up for their Boxing Day respite in here.'

'The more the merrier,' she replied. 'I love it when it's busy. Can I get you anything?'

'Not for me, love, I only came to see if I could help

you with the mince pies. Maddy and Angie have already made their way down to the surf beach with theirs and Angie has taken a supply of blankets in case anyone forgets towels or warm wraps – the sea can be treacherous at this time of year, you know.'

The sky was clear and bright, but with frost lining the pavements this morning, the winter chill had Salthaven in its grasp. 'Jess is making me take part next year.'

'Then you should consider this your inauguration.'

Jo's laughter filled the empty café with its wonderfully illuminated Christmas tree, the lights strung across the walls, the crisp holly with rich berries on the blackboards, the empty corner where the bower would stand when she set up another lucky couple of locals for a date night. 'Then that means everyone else must do it, including you.'

'Oh dear, I've done it!'

'No way.'

'Yes, way.' She mimicked Jo's youthful expression. 'Six years ago to the day. Angie did it with me. Your grandparents sponsored us very generously and kept everyone fuelled with food.'

'Ah, so they haven't done it?'

'You know, I don't think they have.'

Jo and Hilda shared a conspiratorial look. 'Maybe we'll have to persuade them for next year too.'

With the time only a few minutes before ten o'clock, Jo turned off all the lights, ensured the oven was off, picked up the tubs of mince pies and handed some to Hilda and then locked up the café. In four short hours, she'd be back here to meet someone in this very doorway. And who knew what would happen then.

Hilda wasn't keen to walk all the way round to the surf beach on the sands so they walked the longer way, past the boating lake, up the hill and to the main car park which was jam packed. The local press were there, a radio station, and several people arriving in fancy dress, ready for the off.

'It's manic.' Jo couldn't believe the crowds drawn by the event.

'It's like this every year,' Hilda beamed proudly.

'Jo!' It was Steve, running towards her, clad in a jumper and jeans.

'Where are the swimming trunks?' she teased.

'Don't worry, I'll strip off when it's time.'

'We'll look forward to it,' Hilda flirted as though she were forty years younger before she went down to the beach to join Angie who was manning the trestle table filled with food and drinks.

'She's got a soft spot for you,' said Jo.

'Hasn't everyone?' He put a hand on his chest. 'I was getting your attention, because see that man over there . . .' He nodded his head and Jo followed his gaze.

'Should I know him?' She had no idea who he was.

'No, you shouldn't, but he's heard, on the grapevine, about the nights of love at the café and was asking about the owner. I told him who you were and he said he's interested in hiring the café one night . . .' He leaned in close and whispered in her ear, 'For a proposal.'

'As in a marriage proposal?'

'Apparently so. He heard about this pier café that ran nights of love, and with his other half being from a town beside the sea – but one without a pier – he thought it sounded like the perfect place.'

Jo beamed. 'I'm flattered.'

'And you should be. It's amazing what you've been doing, thinking of everyone else and making them happy.'

She felt herself colour at the thought of her own plans later. 'Come on, the swim will happen without us if we're not careful. We'd better get down there.'

Battling the sand when it blew her way, Jo delivered the other containers of mince pies. They were quite organised at the trestle table which was somehow fixed in place with the help of rocks and guy ropes and now Hilda was there to boss people about until they established some kind of order.

'Hi, Jo!' It was Charlie, who'd raced across the sands ahead of his parents. His red coat looked like it was getting too small for him, especially now the weather demanded extra layers, but by wearing it today, at least it would be hard for him to get lost in the crowds. 'Guess what I got for Christmas!'

'Santa came?'

'Of course!' He shrugged, as though being on the naughty list was incomprehensible. 'He brought me the best thing ever.'

'And what was that?'

'Mummy was there when I woke up.'

Things must be going very well for Ben and Lorna and Jo waved over at them. 'Well, Charlie, I think that's a mighty fine present.'

'And I got a Lego air show jet, chocolate coins, socks, and a new cup with a snowman on it!'

'You're a very lucky boy.'

Charlie raced off to greet another of his friends and Jo chatted with Ben and Lorna. Frank, the postman, was there and she was introduced to his wife Nicola; she talked with Bea from the fish and chip shop about how Grant was insisting they open New Year's Day for anyone sporting a hangover, and she chatted with Maisy who was on a well-earned break from the post office until January. Jo hoped that by the time she organised the blind date for Maisy, the girl would be rested and ready to embrace something new.

Crowds slowly expanded on the sands, the weather distinctly wintry yet kind in its delivery with very little wind now and plenty of accompanying winter sun. People were taking selfies, before and after shots, wishing one another Merry Christmas, sharing the sentiment of the season between them.

'You're all so brave,' she told Jess when her friend came over to say hello.

'Crazy, more like.'

'Now, now, doc,' said Geoff, 'we'll be raising good money doing this. And think of the mince pies at the end and maybe a big mug of hot chocolate.'

'That sounds like bliss,' said Jess turning to look at the waves but distracted. 'Oh my word, would you look at Steve?'

Jo turned to where she was looking and he was jumping up and down on the spot to keep warm. In a pair of swim shorts with an image of Santa on a surfboard, he was bare-chested and the only other thing to keep him warm was a red Santa hat. 'He must be freezing! I've got a coat and scarf and gloves on, plus a jumper, and a top under that, and I don't want to even remove one layer.' Jo didn't miss Jess give him an approving once over either.

Swimmers were milling and more and more people

were peeling off their layers. Jess had only another ten minutes before she had no choice but to join them and take off her puffy coat, with Jo promising she'd be there to cheer her on.

A group of carollers had come down to support the townsfolk and were gathered near the far breakwater, away from the mayhem but close enough to be heard, kids were racing about on the sand, overexcited, swimmers were eager to get into the water, and the radio and newspaper crews were interviewing whoever they picked at random.

The carollers came to the end of 'Joy to the World' and launched into 'Let it Snow', which had the crowds on the sands singing along. Jo got into the spirit too, singing lyrics she remembered from long ago, and when she looked round the beach bonfire was crackling away. It didn't take long to feel the heat coming off it, and it would no doubt be a welcome sight for anyone braving the water today.

By the time the voice came over the loudspeaker to announce they were five minutes away from the crowds making a splash on Salthaven beach, the lifeguards had already braved the sea, positioning themselves strategically in the waters to keep the event safe. Men, women and children gathered and spectators flanked them on either side, Jo on the sands next to Hilda, others wearing wellies and in the shallows of the seawater, ready to cheer on the swimmers.

Everyone joined in the countdown, joy written across their faces, starting at the number ten and yelling every number thereafter until the crowds yelled, 'Go!'

Swimmers *ran* into the freezing waters – it seemed the

only way to do it. Jo had no idea how cold it could be, but she could imagine that if you didn't run, you'd never get in there! She laughed at some of their faces – the fright, the feeling of doing something so different and daring, all part of being a member of this wonderful community. She saw Steve splashing Jess head to toe when she froze at mid-thigh. Jo cheered her on when she dived into the oncoming wave and came up with the biggest grin on her face. Many of the swimmers wore Santa hats; Maddy and Dan were dressed as Christmas elves and ran into the water hand in hand while some of their friends were dressed up as snowmen and another group had come dressed as Christmas crackers, their heads poking out of the middle of body-long tubular costumes that Jo thought would probably float all on their own. Watching this was really something else, and Jo had never spent a Christmas morning like it.

The dangers of cold-water swimming in the sea, with its tides and currents, meant most people were in and out of the sea quickly, swapping an icy bath for the comforts on dry land. Onlookers congratulated every single swimmer and Hilda and Valerie took charge of ensuring everyone had a towel or a blanket to warm up, while Billy and Geoff were delivering hot beverages at a rate of knots and Jo handed round mince pies to ravenous locals who were already talking about doing it all over again next year.

The event was one of the best things Jo had ever had the privilege to be a part of. It had raised over two thousand pounds for the hospice and showed how much of a difference people could make when they all came together.

But by the time she left the sands – and the carollers belting out 'We Wish you a Merry Christmas' – and was walking up the path to the clifftop towards home, Jo was ready for something else entirely.

It was time to find out who was going to be meeting her at The Café at the End of the Pier.

Jo was all fingers and thumbs, trying to put in the spiral drop earrings her mum had made especially for her and sent over for Christmas. She'd had a long, hot shower after spending so long in the bracing cold on the beach and had washed her hair with her most expensive shampoo, then she'd changed outfit three times before settling on a cosy, comfortable, knitted dress in burgundy that finished just above her knees. And now, with her opaque tights and knee-high boots pulled on and a spray of her favourite Chanel perfume, from the bottle her grandparents had bought her for her birthday earlier in the year, it was time to go.

Was she really going to do this? Meet a stranger – at least in her mind – to go somewhere with him on a blind date?

Her heart thumped against her chest. And before she could change her mind she grabbed her keys and phone and opened the door to winter in Salthaven.

She walked down the hill, past the familiar gardens now bare in the season. She could see windows along the way, dotted with the low glow of Christmas lights, families brought together for the day. The town's tree in the distance stood high above the pitched roofs, its coloured lights a warm contrast against the cold.

She reached the start of the pier, deserted now, and when she felt a snowflake land on her nose she couldn't believe it. Snow hadn't been forecast today, but as she felt another flake and then another, she twirled around on the spot as it fell, feeling happier than she had in a long time.

But then she stopped. What if whoever had sent those postcards was a weirdo luring her here under false pretences?

Jo berated herself, and whether it was simply a feeling she had deep down, or the magic of the snow falling all around her now, she wasn't sure, but she kept on walking along the wooden boards that would soon be covered in a white dusting if the weather got its way.

It was only as she got closer to the café, trying to see whether there was someone waiting there already, that she saw lights inside. The bright, twinkly lights along the windows glistened and she heard the faint sound of Christmas music coming through the glass. As she moved slowly towards the door, she saw the bower set up in the corner. Decorated with silver baubles up the sides, deep red calla lilies mixed with soft white roses, greenery and pine cones tipped with a frosty finish, the arch was surrounding a table with a large matching floral arrangement in the middle, a white tablecloth with place settings for two. It was the most romantic setting Jo had ever seen.

And it was all for her.

And there was only one person who knew how to set that bower up.

35

She hovered at the door. What on earth was she going to say to him? This man who was a true friend but nothing more and it was a relationship she never, ever, wanted to ruin. She was tempted to leave, but how could she? Look at all the trouble he'd gone to.

She looked out to sea, at the waves that had calmed down after their earlier excitement and listened to their gentle rumble onto the shore as they fizzed against the sand and drew back, ready to build up again. She shut her eyes and breathed in the salty air, the shampoo and perfume she'd used as she got ready for this date. She'd wanted to seem calm and casual, yet sexy, and like she'd made an effort.

She wasn't even sure she wanted to go in there now. She felt sick, nervous, scared of what was going to happen. But when she heard her name on the lips of a man she hadn't expected to open the door to the café, she knew she'd been right to come.

'It's pretty cold,' he said, standing at the door and looking up at the feather-like snowflakes fluttering down from above. 'You could always come in if you like.'

She stepped inside the winter wonderland. Not only was the bower set up and the table beneath ready for a cosy lunch for two, but the Christmas tree and the lights she'd already set up were twinkling away and he'd added more across the ceiling and silver sparkly snowflakes were fixed to the windows. 'You did all this? For me?' She stood in the middle of the café – *her* café – and took in the transformation, breathed in the smell of a home cooked meal coming from her kitchen, and the realisation that all along he'd been planning this for the two of them.

'Let me take your coat.' He stepped forwards as she unbuttoned it, her eyes not leaving his.

She handed it to him, along with her scarf. 'I don't know what to say.'

He hung up her things and walked back over. He reached out and she felt his fingers lightly touch her. 'You had a snowflake in your hair. If I'd known the weather was going to give us a white Christmas I wouldn't have bothered asking Poppy to make all the pretend snowflakes. She was cutting those out with Anna and Steve for ages.'

'Wait, so that's how you did it?'

'Don't be angry with Steve.' He touched her cheek, his hand warming her skin now she was inside. 'He helped me set up the bower and I made him promise to keep his mouth shut.'

'I'll bet that took some doing.' Jo gulped, nervous beneath his touch, because his hand was still right there. 'And you've made Christmas lunch, in my café?'

'You're not angry, are you?'

'Not at all.' She couldn't think of how she felt. Surprised, happy, excited, nervous. So many things all rolled into one, but top of the list? Lucky. That was how she felt right now. Lucky he'd chosen her to be the person he wanted to spend this special day with, blessed such a man would be interested in her at all. She'd never imagined Matt could be the one who swept her off her feet, but now she realised, perhaps she hadn't dared to imagine it because she'd have been monumentally disappointed if he'd chosen someone else.

He'd taken his hand away now but Jo could still feel his touch on her skin.

'I'm afraid that as well as Steve – oh, and Anna and Poppy – Molly, Arthur and Tilly were all in on the plan.'

'Really?' She couldn't believe how much trouble he'd gone to. And all for her. 'But wait, Tilly's not coming because of the snow.' As he shook his head the truth dawned on her. 'There wasn't any snow! I should've known. When Tilly cancelled I checked weather reports to see if they were in for a snowstorm over Christmas up in Scotland but could only see rain symbols. I'd thought she was being overly cautious but after I got your postcard I didn't give it much more thought because I was too preoccupied with what was happening here.'

'That you might be meeting a crazy person, you mean?'

'The thought did cross my mind.'

'Tilly was in on it, and she hated having to lie to you, but Molly and Arthur were all for it.'

'Now why doesn't that surprise me? I might have guessed they were plotting with the way they were behaving in the café the day they left.'

'They were loving every minute, I expect. They gave me the keys – and Arthur had to tell your gran to stop prying when she wanted to know all the details. And I got a message from Tilly earlier to say she was safely tucked away at her parents' place, waiting for the all clear so she could walk the streets of Salthaven. I think she'd quite like to catch up with you later.'

'I'll bet she would.' She had so much to talk about with her best friend. It was time to admit she'd been hiding her feelings for this man from everyone including herself. 'It seems like a lot of effort to go to for a date. You could've just asked me out.'

'Now where's the fun in that.' His flirting made her nervous. This was a real date, a real promise of something special.

'Did you really make a full Christmas dinner in my tiny little kitchen?'

'I cheated a bit,' he admitted, 'and did pre-cooking at your grandparents' bungalow before smuggling it all down here. But it was all worth it.'

'Why didn't you say anything before?'

'And spoil this moment?' He moved closer and took both of her hands in his.

'Steve has been itching to tell me something for ages – I'll bet this was it.' Jo still couldn't believe the winter wonderland in here, her favourite place.

'Steve really does want to talk to you, but not about this.'

'Then what?'

'He's hopelessly and utterly in love with Jess.'

Jo's mouth fell open. 'Well, I never would've guessed. Then I need to do something about that in the new year.'

'Please do. He's driving me crazy, talking about her and trying to get the nerve to ask her out. He almost managed it at the pub when they were playing pool, then chickened out again.' He moved closer still. 'But now it's time to stop thinking about everyone else and do something for yourself, Jo. And I'm really hoping I was right to do all this.' He hesitated. 'Was I?'

She looked into the eyes of a man she'd known almost a year now, a man she'd spent more and more time with and whose company she couldn't imagine being without. Through her mind flashed all the times they'd shared together, mused about what she could dream up in the kitchen; she remembered the times she'd admired his strong forearms as he carried her produce into the kitchen each day, the attraction she could now admit she'd felt but had denied until she knew he felt the same way. Jess had once suggested Matt for Jo, but she'd dismissed the suggestion, thinking he'd probably have hundreds of women to choose between.

Standing in front of him now, Jo realised how fond she'd grown of this man. She'd been looking for someone to share her life with but somehow had missed what was right under her nose. 'Did you send the postcards and wait to do all this because you enjoy the thrill of the chase?' She hoped it was much more than that.

He shook his head. 'I knew you weren't ready, but I knew I was. And I've watched you give so much to other people, yet not take much in return. It's one of the reasons I fell for you.'

'You . . . you've fallen for me?'

'I'm afraid so. It was never a game to me. So what do you say, Jo? Are you willing to give us a chance?'

She moved closer to him, their faces inches apart now, and when he bent his head closer towards hers and their lips met, it was all the answer he needed.

*

They sat together on the window seat watching the snow fall outside, their hands entwined and Jo's head nestled against his shoulder.

'Do you remember dressing up for Halloween?' Matt asked. She murmured a yes. 'Do you remember me saying it was a shame about the stripy stockings?'

'I'm so glad your sister still had them, they made the outfit.' Jo watched his fingers pull away from hers and trace the palm of her hand.

'It wasn't exactly what I'd meant when I said it was a shame.'

She sat up to look at him properly.

'The words were out before I thought about it, because all I'd been imagining was how hot you'd be in those stockings. I thought you'd rumbled me when I said it. Had you really no idea about the way I felt?'

'I really didn't. I think my feet have hardly touched the floor since I came to town and I was too busy to notice much.'

'That's why I waited.'

'I'm glad you did.' She rested her head back against his shoulder and he pulled her in close.

'I wanted time to get to know you more,' he went on, 'without the pressure of asking you out. I watched you fall in love with the café, the town, and learn that this was the place you wanted to call home. I've wanted to settle down for a long while, but until you came along I couldn't really picture it. I heard you talking with your grandparents about how disappointed you were that Valentine's Day didn't work out, and after that I began to look forward to my early starts, knowing you were first on my rounds. I loved watching your eyes light up as you dreamed of new recipes for this place, what you could do with whatever I brought over from the farm. And when you started setting up nights of love in the café, I wanted to show you someone cared about you as much as you did everyone else, but I didn't want to frighten you off or make it awkward.'

'I did wonder about setting you up.'

'You did?'

'Yes, but I could never think of anyone I wanted to set you up with. Maybe it's because I never thought anyone would be good enough.'

'You know, sometimes I thought you might confide in me, speculate about who the postcards could be from.'

'I wanted to keep it to myself,' she admitted. 'It was my something special, for me to enjoy.'

He tilted her chin up towards him and kissed her again, this time more deeply. 'You've no idea how long I've wanted to do that.'

'Do it again,' she said with a smile.

And this time it lasted way longer, until Matt broke away first, his lips still hovering so close to hers she could feel them. 'Jo . . . I need to go . . .'

'Why?'

'I need to see to the lunch unless you want crucified sprouts and burnt gravy.'

She burst out laughing, and when they kissed one more time she knew the only person she ever wanted to go on a date with was him.

Cupid had scored the biggest bullseye of all with her nights of love at the café.

Epilogue

June

Dear Jo,

We're safely in our second home in beautiful Puerto Pollensa. Sasha helped us move in and we've settled nicely. We're enjoying the warm climate – even Gramps has been enjoying a daily swim at the beach, although he insists on going very early before the sun gets too hot – and we've been cooking our very own paella, using the freshest ingredients, although please tell Matt nothing will ever taste as good as anything he grew on the farm.

Retirement is like a dream, sharing our time between England and Spain, and we send much love your way.

Say hello to everyone in Salthaven!

Love Gran and Gramps xxx

July

Dear Jo,

Greetings from London!

We're taking a much-needed break at the end of our first year at university but instead of heading back to Salthaven to be together, I've just arrived in London from Exeter and

I'm meeting Dan at his halls of residence in Queen Mary University. We've booked a hotel in the city and we're heading out to a show tonight.

Thank you again for our night of love at the café. I know Dan doesn't say much, but he's so glad you picked the both of us.

Much love to you, Molly and Arthur,

Love Maddy and Dan xxx

August

Dear Jo,

We did it! Here we are in Italy. This has been a dream of mine for so long and when I used to see Geoff fishing at the end of the pier, I never would've imagined he'd come with me to set up our very own yoga retreat. He's doing yoga every day and hiking miles – he's like a new man! If he keeps this up I've promised we'll go fishing very soon.

We're enjoying the wine, the sunshine and the scenery, and out in the beautiful Tuscan countryside earlier on today, Geoff proposed!

Can you believe it?

He's made me the happiest woman alive and we thank you, Jo, from the bottom of our hearts.

Love Geoff and Valerie xxx

September

Dear Jo,

This place is crazy! Charlie has been on and on at me to make it to Florida one day and at last we've done it, as a family. We've been to Disney World, SeaWorld, Busch

Gardens, and today it's Universal Studios where I only hope there aren't too many scary rides. I swear I've turned grey over night at some of the roller coasters my son and wife have had me go on. It's like they've formed this evil team, determined to torture me to the max!

Say hello to Matt and I hope he's treating you right. Nobody deserves it more than you.

Love Ben, Lorna and Charlie xxx

October

Dear Jo,

So have you forgiven me yet for lying to you and breaking in to your café? Oh, and for the small fact that I've only known your good friend Jess for five minutes and I've already whisked her away surfing in Bali? Rumour has it she'll be getting her revenge next year and making me ski, but between you and me, I think I could be heading for some broken bones if she lets me down a slope. I'm much safer in the water.

Thanks for reading between the lines and setting me up on a date with this amazing woman who is trying to make me put down my beer right now and go for a run.

As if!

Catch you soon, Jo,

Love Steve & Jess xxx

December

To: Gran and Gramps

Greetings from Salthaven! I thought you'd like a postcard from here to remember your second home.

Thank you again for manning the café for a few days while

Matt and I took a break back in September – you've no idea how much we both needed it. With the farm and the café, the two businesses are keeping us crazy busy.

What are you doing in June? I know it's six months from now, but it never hurts to plan ahead. And seeing as you two are partly responsible for getting us together, we thought you could step up and give me some maternity leave.

Yes, you're going to be great-grandparents!

Sorry not to deliver this news in person, but Matt thought it would be fun to carry on the postcard tradition.

Merry Christmas – and may the new year bring as much happiness as the last one did.

Love always,

Jo, Matt and the bump xxx

P.S. Jess will not be happy! Matt won't let me do the Christmas Day swim this year on account of my condition and everything . . . shame!

Acknowledgments

A huge thank you to Clare Hey, publishing director at Orion, for taking a chance on me and my writing. We bonded over goat's cheese canapes at a party in London and the idea for the series, Café at the End of the Pier was born. Thank you, Clare for your insights into the story as we went through the editing process, it was a delight to work with you.

There are so many people in the Orion team who I would like to thank for getting this book through to publication. Firstly, Olivia Barber, Editorial Assistant, for juggling my emails and my many questions through the editing and proofreading process. I'd also like to thank Britt Sankey, Marketing Assistant, for her prowess with graphics and banners, and my gratitude also goes to the designers who made a beautiful and perfect cover for this book. And finally, a big thank you to Online Sales Manager Mark Stay who patiently worked with me – I think we were both banging our heads against the wall at one point – to resolve my author page issues. We got there in the end!

I started writing fiction back in 2011 and joined the Romantic Novelists' Association after successfully securing a place on the New Writers' Scheme. The feedback was invaluable and after sending two novels through the scheme, I published my first book. Since joining the RNA I have made many lifelong friends and their endless encouragement – not to mention their sense of fun at various events – has kept me going on my journey as a writer. Thank you everyone!

As always, thank you to my husband and my children. I dedicate a lot of my novels to them, because without their support I really couldn't do this job that I absolutely love.

And lastly, to my readers. Thank you for picking up this book and I hope you enjoy reading about the Café at the End of the Pier. I promise to bring you many more books in years to come!

Helen Rolfe x